Fatal Fade

Keith Morgan Chronicles #2

Brent Jeffries

Bluff Woods Publishing

ISBN-13 (eBook): 979-8-9876558-3-2
ISBN-13 (Paperback): 979-8-9876558-4-9
ISBN-13 (Hardcover): 979-8-9876558-5-6

For my beautiful wife and wonderful kids. This wouldn't happen without them. Thank you!

Chapter One

Nashville, TN. Wednesday

The situation that had unfolded in front of me over the last few hours was a bizarre clash of emotions.

It had started with a sense of joy. My frequent travel has granted me the opportunity to see, and play, a lot of golf courses. I enjoyed golf. The pleasant sights and landscapes mixed with camaraderie and competition were appealing to me.

The joy of golf, however, was far from my mind. The years I spent in Iraq and Afghanistan gave me the repulsive experience of seeing too many dead bodies. Way too many. I hated those memories and wished they weren't stuck in my head. But they were there forever.

Today, the horror of death had collided head-on with the joy of golf.

Before we had completed the first hole in today's golf outing, there was a dead body on an otherwise beautiful course.

"So, what's this fella's name?" A uniformed police

officer was standing back surveying the location, near and far, while asking questions. The patch over his right pocket said 'Keating' but he hasn't introduced himself. The patch on his shoulder showed he was from the Metro Police Nashville, so he was a local. He appeared to be around forty years old and fit, with a thick mustache, and looked like this wasn't his first rodeo. To his credit, he was taking in the complete picture before running right up to the body.

"His name is Bob Yates." I answered his question after realizing I was the one closest to the officer and the only person within earshot.

"Mmm hmm. And what's your name there, sir?" the officer asked me while writing something in the small notepad he took out of his pocket.

"Keith Morgan," I replied.

"I'm Officer Keating from the Metro Police Department, Mr. Morgan. Nice to meet you," he said before continuing and without looking up.

"And how do you know Mr. Yates, Mr. Morgan?" Officer Keating asked.

"I just met him at this event this week. I didn't know him before," I responded.

"And what event would that be?"

"The annual Big Data Summit at the Grand Marquis."

"So, y'all were at that event at the Grand Marquis but went golfing instead?" Officer Keating asked as he finally looked up with one eyebrow raised.

I concluded I'd have to start with the basics here.

"Yes, there is a conference here every year. During the conference, they offer a few activities on Wednesday afternoon, including golf. I chose the golf activity, as did, apparently, Bob." I wasn't completely sure I said it without a hint of sarcasm, but I tried.

"What time did this event start?"

"There was a 1 p.m. horn that started the event."

"Gotcha. And did you see what happened?" Officer Keating was writing and talking without looking up.

"No, I didn't," I replied.

"My notes say you called 911?"

"I did."

"Ok, so maybe you could lead me up to the time that you made that call?" With this question, Officer Keating stopped writing and looked at me.

I couldn't help but wonder how this Tennessee dialect developed with all the rolling words and drawn out vowel sounds that made 'time' sound like 'tam.' A very slow 'tam.' My wandering mind didn't distract me enough to delay my response. Thankfully. Sometimes it does.

"Ok, sure. Well, we were on the same four-person team for this event, and..."

Officer Keating stopped me before I could continue.

"Was it a scramble? Were you playing your own ball, or was everybody playing one?" He asked, as though he needed to explain to me what a golf scramble was.

"Yes, it was a scramble," I replied.

"And were the teams randomly chosen, or did you pick your own teams?"

So much for me telling my story.

"As far as I know, it was random. I simply signed up, didn't select any of the other team members. I know you could do that if you had a client here or something, but I didn't." That response wasn't completely true. But for now, it was my answer.

"So, you mentioned you met Mr. Yates yesterday. Did you know the other two players?" He was still rapid-firing questions at me.

"I met all three of them yesterday at the event reception. I didn't recall having met any of them before that."

I stopped short of telling him Bob was working for a company I was here to investigate. Bob didn't know that either, but it was my intention to start that research sometime today.

"And what were the other two gentlemen's names?" He continued.

"Darren Harper and Mo Subramanian."

I didn't know Darren and Mo as well, so I offered nothing more. I quietly awaited Officer Keating's next question, assuming he didn't want to hear the rest of my account.

Instead of another question, he just stood there, taking notes. Eventually, he rolled his hand like he was trying to get me to continue. So I did.

"Ok, so we drove out here to the eighth hole just before the start time of 1 p.m. After a quick discussion, we decided Bob should hit first, as he could hit the longest drives. After the starting horn sounded, Bob hit a big drive, but it faded badly and went over here toward the water. The rest of us hit shorter and further left. I was in the cart with Bob, so we rode down here to look for his ball."

I paused to take a breath, and it gave Officer Keating another chance to jump in. He was looking back at the tee box to judge the distance as he talked.

"Yeah, that is some drive! Probly 300 yards or more, especially to get over these mounds toward the water. MmmHmm."

He wrote a few more notes before continuing, appearing to be impressed by the distance of Bob's drive.

"Y'all rode in the cart together? Where'd the other cart go?"

"Yes, Bob and I rode together. The other two players

were in their cart and went much further left. Probably fifty yards back and fifty yards left of your location." I was motioning with my hand, but Officer Keating was too busy writing to see me.

Instead, he nodded and again rolled his hand. He was being nice about it, though; it didn't seem like a purposeful annoyance. But it was. I continued, determined to get this over with as fast as I could.

"So, Bob parked the cart on the top of this ridge where we're standing. I went back about twenty yards to look for my ball to the left of the ridge. We knew Bob's shot would probably be in the weeds if not the water, so he went toward the water on the right to look for it. That's when I lost sight of him," I said.

I was still pointing to the locations as I talked about them. Officer Keating took a second to look up from his notes this time as I made the motions. I could see him visually measuring where I was and where the other cart was.

"I guess they lost sight of him, too?" He was back at his notes while he restarted his questions.

"You'd have to ask them. I'm not really sure," I responded.

"Ok, sorry I keep interrupting, please continue."

I couldn't help but notice his 'I' sounded like 'ah.' But again, it wasn't enough of a distraction for me to pause.

"Sure. So, I found my ball and marked it. I knew we might have to use my ball if Bob's wasn't playable. Mine was farther than the other two. Then I came over here to look for Bob. That's when I saw him lying right there where he is." I offered only highlights at that point to see how much detail Officer Keating wanted from me.

"It looks like Mr. Yates was shot once. Did you see or

hear any other rounds landing in the area? Like off trees, rocks, water, anything like that?" he asked.

"No, not at all. I didn't hear evidence of a gunshot." I stopped short of telling Officer Keating I had extensive knowledge of gunshot and bullet sounds. It didn't seem pertinent, but I had made the same observation. Someone had taken one shot and had killed Bob with it.

"So, apparently Mr. Yates was in the wrong place at the wrong time?" he asked, with an eyebrow raised enough to make me uncomfortable.

"I guess." Even though I knew that was the wrong answer, I pretended to agree. In reality, I knew better. Why would one golfer get shot with a high caliber rifle with all the other golfers on the course today? It didn't feel random. And Officer Keating didn't need to know I knew that. Nor did he need to know I had already realized it was a rifle shot. And that it was a high caliber rifle, like a hunting or sniper version. And that the shooter had likely taken the shot from roughly three hundred yards away.

"Did you touch Mr. Yates or move him at all?"

"I touched his neck to see if he had a pulse, which I didn't expect after seeing the substantial hole in his chest. But no, I did not move him at all," I replied, making a face to appear shocked by the wound.

"What'd you do then?" Again with the questions while writing.

"I yelled at the other guys to stay put and I called 911."

"You didn't hear anything?"

"You already asked if I heard a shot. No. I heard nothing abnormal at all." I tried to remain calm at his tactic of repeating questions with slight variations.

"And you mentioned you started on this hole?"

"Yes."

"And Mr. Yates is the only one who hit his ball over here?"

"Yes."

"Huh," he said. It was more of an acknowledgement than a question.

Officer Keating looked around for a few seconds while I stood there.

"Don't go far, Mr. Morgan. I may have more questions later," he said as he nodded my way and turned to survey the area.

I surmised the nod was his goodbye.

So much for a pleasant week at the Big Data Summit, and so much for my plan for me to get some time with Bob Yates.

Chapter Two

Zapata, TX. Monday

Maria Sanchez had not expected her life to be like this when she crossed the Rio Grande into the United States two years ago. Yes, she wanted to escape the poverty and fear she had experienced in Mexico with her two children, but this was not exactly the escape she hoped for. Still, she was hopeful.

She heard stories of the opportunities in the US where she could have plenty to eat, shelter and safety for her kids, and the promise of a bright future. So far, all she had found was a job washing dishes at a local diner and a room in the manufactured home park just outside Zapata, Texas. The room in the home was large enough for her, her daughter Amelia, and her son Javier to sleep on their own beds. Mia and Javi, as everyone calls them, were ten and fifteen.

Even with the single room and the low-paying job, Maria was glad to be in the United States and out of Mexico. She dreamed of becoming legal, whatever that meant, or at least ensuring Mia and Javi had that opportunity. She wasn't sure how to make that happen just yet, but it was her dream.

Maria made enough to ensure the kids had food. No, they never went hungry in Texas. And they had a comfortable shelter. Yes, the space was crowded and loud sometimes, but it was comfortable. For all of that, she was grateful.

The kids were going to school here in Zapata, but Javi was restless and needed to find work. Without a job to keep him busy, Maria feared he would slip into the drug trade like so many other teens she had met. Her nephew was a mule for a cartel already, and he was only thirteen. Javi had somehow avoided that crowd up to now, but Maria knew he was on borrowed time.

That's why she had gotten him a job after school at the local warehouse for Atlantis Automotive. Now she just had to convince him to show up.

"Javi, it's a good job! And it will give you the opportunity to practice English. Speaking English will prepare you for a better job after you're done with school. This job is not even in the fields like most of your friends. If you can work your way up in that plant, you can avoid working on the farms," she said. Maria knew many of the other immigrants had taken jobs on farms, which required long hours outside in the searing heat. She had hoped to find something better for Javi.

They only spoke Spanish at home, but she had high hopes for Javi and Mia to grow up speaking English. Maria believed that would give them the opportunity to get a good job away from the Mexican border. To work with customers and Americans up north, you had to have enough command of the English language to speak to them.

"But ma, none of my friends work there! And I don't

know anything about aluminum or cars or anything," he said. Javi knew the warehouse was an assembly plant and distribution center for a large automotive parts company. He also knew they got their aluminum from huge trucks crossing the border from Mexico. In fact, that's all he knew about the place.

"It's not an option, Javi, you have to do it. I'm not taking no for an answer. It's for your future, and I've fought hard to get you this opportunity. You can't dishonor them by not showing up."

This time, the tone of Maria's voice stopped the discussion. The decision was final. Javi was going to work at the mysterious plant after school, starting tomorrow. Her friend had promised a good wage and fair treatment, which was more than she got at the diner. Plus, he told her Javi might get an opportunity to advance if he did well. She didn't have that option, either.

Javi wasn't about to tell her he didn't like her friend. He had no plans to tell anyone about that horrible guy. Maybe the guy felt sorry for Javi and that's why he was willing to help him. The emotional conflict started to get the best of him, but he couldn't tell mama why.

"Ok, ma. I'll go. But I'm telling you, they won't let me stay!" Javi slammed the door to their room and left. She knew he'd come back. He was a good boy.

Maria was right. During dinner of rice and beans with the other families in the house, Javi returned and ate his meal by himself in the corner. He didn't say much that evening, but Maria smiled through the evening, anyway. Javi was getting a chance most kids in his position never saw, and she knew this was his big break.

The next morning, Javi was back to his normal self as he

got ready for school. Even though Maria left before Javi had to leave, he always got himself to the bus stop, to school, and back home on his own. As Maria was preparing to leave for the diner, Javi paused with some questions.

"So, what kind of job did your friend get me at the ware house?" he asked.

"They need people like you to help unload the trucks from Mexico, then load parts onto trucks that go to the car builders. And the job is indoors! You won't have to stand out in the heat and dirt," she beamed, once again highlighting the fact that the job was not on a farm.

"And you're telling me a fifteen-year-old kid can do it while barely speaking English?" he asked again.

"Yes. That's what he told me," she replied.

"Hmmm," was his only response.

"So, don't be late getting home today. There's a bus that goes to the warehouse at 5 p.m. and you'll need to be on it. They pick up at the gate," she said.

The gate she was referring to was not really a gate. At least it isn't a gate anymore. Now it's just a couple of short poles next to the gravel driveway that led into their neighborhood. But the residents still called it the gate and Javi knew what she meant.

And with that, Maria was off for another day at the diner.

In another half hour, Javi was off to school. While he pretended not to like the idea when talking to his mother, he was secretly excited. It intrigued him to begin an experience in America that didn't involve school or people outside his family and his neighborhood. At least, that's what he thought the experience would be. He didn't trust his mama's friend, but he looked forward to the opportunity.

After school, Javi was at the gate at 4:45 p.m. and got on the bus when it arrived. It was his first day working at Atlantis Automotive Supply.

Chapter Three

Nashville, TN. Wednesday

I was on the phone with Paul Frazier when Officer Keating meandered back over to me. I had gotten back into my golf cart but hadn't yet left the area. Darren, Mo and I were still in shock about what had happened to Bob and had stuck around while we waited for... something.

"Hey Paul, just wanted to give you an update from here in Nashville. This assignment has gotten off track today. I had planned to get some time with Bob Yates today while we were golfing, but that won't be happening," I began.

Paul stayed silent. As the Gatekeeper for The Association, he was used to hearing surprising news. He had developed the patience to wait until the story came out before he responded. So, I continued.

"We had just teed off our first hole, and Bob hit his drive a mile long but way right. When he went to find the ball, someone shot him. He's dead." I stopped this time, with an intentional bluntness that would force Paul to respond.

Eventually, after a couple of deep sighs, he did.

"Wow. Well, I guess that means The Association may have been onto something there," he said.

"Or maybe it's just a coincidence," I said.

"Did anyone else get shot?" he asked.

"No. I was being facetious."

"Nice. I don't think it was a coincidence, either. You need to dig around there, Keith. The Association believes Atlantis was involved in something bad down in Texas," Paul said calmly.

"What do they think is going on there, anyway? It will be hard for me to find anything out now that Bob is gone," I said, having difficulty containing my frustration.

"All I know is their numbers don't look right. Something is going on with their supply chain that is making them way too profitable for their line of business. As you know from your previous assignments, The Association often has only high-level information to go on. At least that's how they start, anyway. You're the one who always gets us the details that start the ball rolling toward resolution. That's why we hired you," Paul responded, still as calm as usual.

It wasn't really an answer to my question, and this time Paul heard my sigh of frustration.

"Look, Keith, I know it's not ideal, but this may give you more opportunity than you think. With Bob's death, nobody will think twice if you talk about him with other people. You'll be able to bring up topics about Bob and his whole life, including Atlantis, that you wouldn't have been able to talk about before," he said.

I hadn't thought about it that way, and Paul had a point.

"Yeah, ok. Maybe you're right. But all I'm going to get from The Association is concern about some sort of anomaly that involves the supply chain?" I asked, trying again to get more direction.

"Hey, it's why you're Keith Morgan. You find the problems and you get them cleaned up. That's why The Association relies on you. Dig around. Find the anomaly. Then we'll decide how to get it to the authorities so you don't have to have another situation like you had at Willow Creek. We don't want any more shootouts with foreign criminals," Paul replied.

"That's good to hear. My kids still need their father, even if their father sucks," I smiled as I responded. I didn't really think I sucked as a father, even if I was making them stay home in Colorado with their grandparents while I was at this event in Nashville.

"Yeah, they do. Even if he sucks," Paul chuckled.

"But really, Keith, I think you can dig around now with no suspicion. We thought Bob was the right guy to talk to as the head of their supply chain, but I understand the CFO is there, too. Maybe you can get a minute with him." Paul wasn't going to let this go. This assignment was going to continue even without Bob Yates.

"Ok, Paul. I'll see what I can do." It was apparent I still have work to do for the next couple of days in Nashville.

And with that, we ended the call, and I got back to the chaotic scene still unfolding in front of me. I slowly walked over to Darren and Mo to test Paul's theory of open discussion about Bob.

"This is just unbelievable. I mean, who'd want to shoot Bob Yates?" I asked, somewhat rhetorically.

"Yeah, it sure is, Keith. Just horrible. Are they thinking he was the target? I mean, someone murdered him here at the golf course? How would they even know he'd be over there?" Mo asked.

"Good question. I guess they're just trying to figure it all out," I said.

"Well, if they only shot him when there were probably a dozen golfers in the area, I guess it almost makes sense that Bob was the target," Darren added.

We all stood there shaking our heads and staring at the ground when Mo started talking. It turned out Paul's idea about getting people to talk about Bob Yates was a good one.

"I guess he did seem to have something going on. I mean, he sat at the atrium bar yesterday with that poor woman for hours. Then he went to the club downtown and did the same thing. Most people would have passed out before leaving the hotel, the way he was drinking," Mo said, solemnly.

And with that, I had my first idea of where to go next.

"Wow. I guess I didn't know him that well. Bob was quite a drinker, huh?" I asked.

"HA! I'd say so! Yeah, I saw him with that woman last night at the atrium bar, too. I felt sorry for her. He just kept talking and she couldn't leave," Darren responded.

"He was with a woman?" I asked.

"Oh no. No, it was the bartender. Poor lady had to stand there and listen to Bob while slinging drinks for the bar. The place was full, but Bob was sitting at the end of the bar, where she sent drinks to the servers. She couldn't leave, so she had to just keep working. And listen to Bob." Mo said.

Mo shook his head as he recalled the situation.

"Then we all went to that club... what was it, the Fuzzy Mushroom or something? And Bob found a spot by the pizza oven and did the same thing to the cook. That ol' hippie guy had to listen to Bob while cooking and boxing up all those pizzas," Darren added.

"Wow. That's unfortunate for the cook, I guess. Although they're probably used to people like Bob chatting away while they work," I replied, ready to head back to the hotel and start digging into this further.

Lucky for me, Officer Keating stepped over again to interrupt our chat.

"Y'all are free to go. But we may need more info from you later. So if it's alright, I'd like to get your cell phone numbers before you go," he said. He was polite, but it wasn't a question.

After giving Officer Keating our numbers, we were all ready to head back to the hotel.

And I had a bartender to talk to.

Chapter Four

Nashville, TN. Wednesday

The Grand Marquis Resort in Nashville was an enormous place. There were four different wings, each with its own theme and design. The wings had four levels of rooms around three sides, with the rooms in the middle having sliding doors to small balconies overlooking the atrium. In the center of the four wings was a large glass-covered atrium with shops, restaurants, walking paths, multiple gardens, and streams. It also had the place I was planning to visit: a bar.

I dropped off my golf cart at the clubhouse and took the shuttle with Darren and Mo back to the hotel. The shuttle dropped us off next to the main entrance, with a short walk past all the valet workers hustling in and out with bags. The smell of exhaust fumes dominated the air, even though there were flowers everywhere that would no doubt smell much better when the vehicles were absent.

After we walked into the massive entrance lobby where all the guests were checking in, I said goodbye to Mo and

Darren. Bob's murder had obviously rattled both of them, and they said very little during the shuttle ride and during our walk into the hotel. They only nodded and mumbled as we shook hands and went our separate ways. Darren and Mo went toward their rooms and I watched them for a second.

While I watched my fellow golfers walk away, I paused and thought about how bizarre this afternoon had become. From a casual golf outing to a murder scene. While standing there shaking my head, I noticed a group of people off to the side huddled together. There was a uniformed police officer with two women I didn't recognize. One woman was crying hysterically, making me think it might be Mrs. Yates. I couldn't see the face of the other woman, but she was nodding soberly. She was also carrying a unique Gucci handbag. I could see the bag from a mile away, given its size and bright colors. As could everyone else, which was obviously her intention.

Assuming this must be a friend consoling the grieving widow, I felt a sense of despair for her. It was certainly a sad turn of events. After slowly shaking my head while I considered her grief, I began my trek.

The walk from the main lobby to the atrium bar takes about ten minutes. I went around the lobby restaurant, down a short hallway with a couple of shops on each side, then entered the smaller atrium of the next wing. This one had a dark green theme with a rainforest feel, complete with waterfalls and mist everywhere. There were people all around, taking pictures and admiring the foliage. I had to agree with the guests taking pictures. It was pretty spectacular.

This time, however, all the people who had stopped along the path were an annoyance. I focused on getting to the bar in the middle of the atrium. After navigating around all the tourists, stopping twice to avoid being in the background of family photos, I arrived at the center of the atrium.

This atrium had a similar theme to the atrium near the lobby, both with plenty of trees surrounding the streams below. Still, it seemed slightly different. It seemed a little more colorful and misty. There may have been more flowers or different colors in the trees, too. I didn't have time to contemplate it further, as I was on a mission.

I went up an open stairway and around the boat ride entrance toward the restaurants. Yes, there was a boat ride here that meandered down a small waterway full of fish through the entire facility. There were about twenty people in line for the boat ride when I went by. Continuing toward the bar, I went past more people, eating and standing around small tables sprinkled beside the walkway.

Finally, after passing even more shops and tourists, I arrived at the atrium bar. That wasn't really the name of the place, as the real name was "Nick's." But we all referred to it as the atrium bar. It was beside a noisy waterfall, and seated around fifty guests on two levels of casual four-seat round tables. Not every table still had four chairs, as guests had moved some chairs around to accommodate groups of various sizes. The bar area was closest to the waterfall, with twelve fixed stools in front and four large televisions behind.

As I walked up, I noticed there were already a fair number of guests seated around the tables. I already knew the bar opened for lunch around 11 a.m. so a crowd here at 3 p.m. wasn't really a surprise. There was a small stage area on the bottom level for music, but there was nobody playing right now. The most dominating sound in the area was the waterfall.

Mo and Darren mentioned a female bartender who was serving drinks but not waiting tables. I didn't see such a person in the area when I walked up. The bartender was a burly-looking gentleman who was big enough to be a bouncer. He was balding, had tattoos up and down his large arms, and moved around as though he was experienced with this type of setting.

I took a seat near the cash register and found my mind wandering.

Do they still call them cash registers? They're more like computer point-of-sale devices now, not really like the old-fashioned registers that I remember as a kid. I mean, the whole idea of saying 'cha-ching' was because of the sound those old machines made. I wonder what they'd say if that term was coined today? Tap? Click?

My mind had stepped away for a moment, as it is prone to do. I was ushered back into the moment by the bartender as he walked my direction. His gruff voice matched his appearance, but there wasn't the typical southern accent in his speech. He wasn't from here.

"What'll it be today, my friend?" His friendly demeanor betrayed his voice.

"I'll have an Old Fashioned with Maker's Mark, please," I replied with my usual request. It was my favorite.

"You got it." He replied.

As I waited, I tried to assemble the view as Mo and Darren had described it. Next to this register area was a small flip-up bar extension that lifted to the left to allow workers to come in and out. Next to that hinged section of the bar was a pair of gold rails that designated the server station. I assume this is where they said Bob was sitting.

There was, in fact, a small area at the end of the bar where you could sit directly next to the waitress station with the waterfall on the other side. I suppose you could sit there and talk, but the waterfall was noisy. You'd have to talk loud. Bob may have had a loud voice, but I was curious if the bartender heard everything he said.

"Here you go. Enjoy," the bartender said as he slid my drink to me on the bar with a cocktail napkin.

"Thanks," I said and held up the glass toward him. I decided to wait a minute to ask about the other bartender. I didn't want to be too obvious about my intentions.

"I hear this place really gets going in the evenings," I said after the bartender had handed out a few more drinks to other patrons.

"Yeah, you're telling me! Sometimes it's all we can do to keep up," he said.

There was my window.

"I don't know how you'd keep up with only one bartender!"

"Well, we don't, to be honest. We try to double up in the evenings during happy hour. In fact, here's my backup now," he said as he nodded toward the entrance from the atrium path.

There, carrying a backpack and a cup of coffee, was the person I suspect was on the other end of Bob's bar conversation last night. I watched as she walked around the tables and over to the bar next to me, flipped up the hinged bar section, and headed into the back.

"Hey Scott," she yelled at the current bartender as she walked by.

She was sort of the antithesis of Scott. She was small, but not really petite, with clear, fair skin and medium-length, curly orange hair. It wasn't a fake-looking orange, but looked natural. She had no visible tattoos, although she had a jacket on when she walked by. Her low-cut top looked more like a tip generator than a fashion statement.

She had on bright red glasses and smiled the whole time she walked by. I pegged her for very early twenties, probably barely old enough to tend the bar.

"Hey, Holly. How's the little guy?" Scott asked.

"He's great, thanks. Running me ragged!" Holly responded.

It's easy to see why Bob would have talked to her. She seemed very friendly. I decided I'd try to get her talking just like he did.

Chapter Five

Zapata, TX. Monday

The bus Javi got into felt like an old school bus, like the ones he had seen in town. Except it wasn't yellow. It was painted green and white with the Atlantis logo on the side. It also seemed even older than the school buses he rode, if that was possible.

There were several other riders on the bus when Javi got on. He assumed they must pick up Mexicans like him from all the manufactured home parks to take them to work at the warehouse. He often referred to the cluster of homes where he lived as a neighborhood, but he knew what it was. There wer still some old mobile homes mixed in with the newer manufactured ones, just like several other parks along this highway. The one thing that made him feel better about the bus was the number of teens mixed in with the other workers. Some looked even younger than him.

Nobody said anything to him on the way there. In fact, nobody really talked at all. He heard some whispering and laughing a few times, but that was it. In ten minutes, Javi and the Atlantis bus arrived at the warehouse compound. He got up with all the other riders and walked out, not sure where to go.

To Javi's relief, there was a Mexican-looking Atlantis worker waiting just outside the bus with a clipboard. When he saw Javi, he motioned for him to come over and asked him his name. Apparently, this guy knew everyone who rode that bus.

"You Javier Sanchez?" He asked in Spanish, again to Javi's relief.

"Yes, sir," Javi replied.

"Welcome to Atlantis. I'm Armando. Please stand over here," he said, and he motioned behind him.

Javi stood behind Armando and waited. Before the bus was empty, Armando had pulled two other people from the bus to stand near Javi. Both were at least as young as Javi, but he didn't recognize them from his neighborhood. He thought he may have seen them at school, but he wasn't really sure.

After everyone got off the bus, Javi and the two others were led to a smaller vehicle, like the ones Javi had seen at the golf course in Zapata. This one had six seats, though. One of the new guys sat in the front seat next to Armando and Javi got in the back with the other guy. Armando got in and paused before he took off.

"Welcome to Atlantis Automotive. I'll be taking you to your places in the warehouse where you'll be trained." He looked at his clipboard before he continued.

"So, you're Javi." Armando pointed to Javi with his pen without looking up.

"And you're Jorge, and you're Rojas." He pointed toward each of them as a way of introduction. Then he took off.

None of the passengers spoke to each other as they rode into the massive warehouse. They entered an open space in the side that looked like a huge garage door, and were exposed to a variety of scenes all at once. There were areas that looked like assembly lines, other areas where sparks were flying, and the vastness of the operation was impressive. At the end of the line, it seemed blocks of aluminum were being cut and shaped into parts that Javi didn't recognize. It was overwhelming.

Armando dropped off Jorge, then Rojas at two of the many spots in the warehouse where there were people packaging parts into boxes and loading them onto waiting trucks. It seemed to take forever to get from station to station. The place was huge.

Eventually, Armando stopped at what Javi assumed was his spot. Javi visualized they were on the right side of the warehouse and there were large trucks parked all along this side of the facility. He tried to see how many, but he could only see twenty before he lost sight. He couldn't see to the end.

Javi stepped out of his seat and stood there while Armando yelled from his cart, still in Spanish.

"Raul, where are you?" Armando sounded a bit irritated as he yelled.

"I'm here. I'm here." Javi saw someone, he assumed Raul, appear from the behind a large stack of boxes.

"This is Javier. He's your new loader. Show him the ropes. He's on the five to ten shift," Armando said.

"Got it, boss," Raul said. Then he nodded toward Javi.

"Welcome, Javier. Come on over, let's get some trucks loaded." Raul was smiling at Armando while he was talking to Javi.

After a brief fifteen-minute training exercise with Raul,

Javi began loading boxes onto pallets and onto the waiting trucks. It took no time for him to figure out what was going on. By the end of the shift, he knew how to read the orders from the screen of the tablet at their station, and he could find the boxes he needed to fill the orders. Raul didn't show him how to run the forklift to move the pallets, but he hoped that might come soon. That part looked like fun to Javi.

After his shift completed at 10 p.m., Javi heard a loud whistle. Raul motioned for him to head out the door beside their loading dock while he continued to load pallets onto a truck. Javi walked out and followed the other workers, heading toward the front gate of the facility.

It was 10:15 p.m. when Javi finally made his way to the place where he'd gotten off the bus earlier, just inside the enormous security gates at the front of the warehouse compound. He didn't realize how huge the place was until he came to work today. He also didn't realize how much they cared about security. All the fences, lights and security guards sort of gave him the creeps.

As he got back to the entrance, he saw the workers all waiting in a line before they got to the five buses waiting near the big gate. At first he didn't know why, but when he got closer, he saw each one getting handed cash as they walked by a small hut. Javi got in line with everyone else, and when he got to the end, a guy in an Atlantis polo shirt with crisp khaki pants was sitting in the hut. He wasn't Mexican.

"Name?" he asked gruffly.

"Javier Sanchez," Javi replied.

"High school rate," the man said.

Another man inside the little hut handed Javi a ten-dollar bill and motioned for him to move on. Javi didn't know what else to do, so he moved on. He wondered if ten dollars was the right amount for his five hours of work, but decided he'd ask mama later. For now, he was tired and wanted to go home.

There were several buses loading people at the entrance, and Javi had no idea which he should be on. After a brief moment of standing there looking lost, he noticed Armando was there to help the new guys find the right bus. When he saw Javi looking around, Armando pointed to the number twenty on his page, pointed to the second bus in the row, and waved for Javi to go. Javi got on bus twenty, feeling much better about working at Atlantis. Mama was right. He could do this.

The bus home had two of the same people from the ride there, but also a bunch more that he didn't know. As they did on the way there, the workers mostly rode in silence. There were a couple of guys near the back who were whispering and laughing under their breath, but everyone seemed afraid to talk too much. Or maybe they were too tired. Javi rode home without saying a word.

When the bus got to the gate in front of Javi's trailer court, three other people got off with Javi. Two were older men who walked away with their heads down, not speaking to anyone or even looking up. The third person looked a little older than Javi, and he didn't walk away. Instead, he stood there looking at Javi.

"Where'd they put you?" The other bus rider said when the bus drove away.

"I don't know what it's called, just one of the truck loading places," Javi said.

"I'm Gus. What's your name?"

"I'm Javier. Javi."

"Was this your first day?"

"Yeah."

"What did you think?" Gus asked.

"Well, I was glad they spoke Spanish. And they weren't mean."

"Yeah, they're not mean if you follow the rules and don't look around. Goodnight Javi. I'll talk to you later." Gus turned and walked away as he said it.

Javi smiled and took a deep breath. It was still over eighty degrees and there was still dust and diesel exhaust in the air, but he was happy. He made it through his first day of work at Atlantis. Javi was sure his mama would be proud.

Chapter Six

Nashville, TN. Wednesday

I sipped my drink and watched while Holly the bartender shed her backpack, donned a small apron, and came out to start her shift. Without the backpack and after a bit of preparation, she clearly looked like she was there to get some tips. Good for her and her little guy.

My plan was going to be tricky since I had opened a tab with Scott, the other bartender. But the location of this barstool was going to help me, just like it had helped Bob. During one of her trips over to the server station to put a margarita on the tray, I started talking.

"Whew, you guys are hoppin' in here!" I said, as she got within earshot.

"Yeah, it gets ridiculous during these big events," she said with a smile and a vivid Tennessee accent.

"I bet it does. And I guess I got a front-row seat for the action!" I said, trying to frame a path to a conversation about Bob.

"Yeah, you sure did. If it's too much, you can move over

yonder," she said, pointing to an open table further out. That wasn't the response I wanted, but her use of the word 'yonder' almost made me laugh. I hadn't heard that in a long time.

"Oh no, I didn't mean that. But thank you." I tried to brush it off while I reset my approach.

"Some people just like to be right here in the middle of it all," I said, turning things back toward the topic of the location at the bar.

"Yeah, I guess." She walked away before I had a chance to go any further.

I sat quietly, nursing my drink and watching while she went about her shift. Looking around, my mind ventured into one of its frequent and unnecessary analytical moments without warning. I counted seven kids in the bar area under twelve years old, and eight people over sixty-five. That means there were twenty people between twelve and sixty-five, with what I would guess to be a median age of thirty-eight.

Ok, that was embarrassing. Was I sitting there staring at people? I didn't think I was, but I had to be careful. My mind wanders, and sometimes it can be embarrassing.

"So, still taking in all the action of the atrium bar, huh?" Holly's jovial voice forced me out of my mental hiatus.

"Yeah, sure am. I suppose I'm the only one who likes this spot," I said, trying to see how difficult it might be to get her to talk about Bob.

"Oh, believe me, you're not the only one!" She walked away, looking at me out of the corner of her eye and shaking her head. That may have broken the ice.

Scott was also working the bar and the server station, and within a few seconds, he was back in my area to load several beers onto a tray.

"Hey Scott, I'll have another when you get a minute. I know they take a minute to make, so no rush," I said as he looked over.

"Gotcha, buddy. Just a sec," He said as he turned away. Within five minutes, he slid me another Old Fashioned and headed to the other end of the bar again. I smiled as I thought to myself. Sometimes a bit of kindness gets me my drinks faster.

I continued to sit patiently, watching the bar workers come and go, keeping an eye on Holly as she moved about the bar. The next time she headed over, I yelled over the ever-present waterfall noise.

"So, I'm not the only one who sits here? I don't see anyone fighting to get my spot." I chuckled and motioned toward the rest of the patrons at the bar as she looked my way.

"Well, there aren't many, I guess. But these events seem to bring out the crazies. Y'all always seem to drag at least one of 'em with you," she said.

I raised an eyebrow to see if she'd continue. Instead of continuing, she walked away to pour more beer. In a few minutes, she returned. I was beginning to get a grip on the cycle these conversations had to take. Bob must have sat here a long time to talk to her much at all.

"I'm not kiddin'! One of your crazies was here last night," she said the next time she came over to put drinks on a tray.

"He sat right where you are and literally talked my ear off. I betcha I know more about that man than his own wife!" She walked away again as she said it. By now, I understood she'd be back in a few minutes to continue.

And true to the rest of the conversation, Holly soon

returned to continue the conversation and load another tray.

"What do you mean, a crazy?" I asked when she walked over.

"Well, even if I didn't think he was crazy, two guys came up afterward and asked me all about what he was saying. They said he was under investigation for some sort of fraud, or something. They said he was prone to lying and making things up. Like I said, y'all bring the crazies out here with these events. That guy was proof!"

Once again, Holly walked away, and I sat there, hoping I didn't change my facial expression when Holly mentioned the two guys asking about Bob. According to her story, they were asking about him just one day before he was shot on the golf course.

The next time Holly came back, I couldn't help but ask questions as they were queueing up in my head.

"What would be so crazy that people would come investigate what a guy was saying?" I asked.

"Oh, believe me, I have no clue. He was just talking about a woman in Texas, or something. And something about having cancer. Then he spent about an hour complaining about having to lay people off while he sat here at the Grand Marquis in Nashville. He went on and on."

Then off she went again. It seems things were trickling in about Bob Yates, but this was a lot of work.

"Why would the poor guy lie about stuff like that? That seems innocent enough?" I asked when she returned.

"I got no idea. I'm not really sure he was," she responded.

"Then why would investigators care?" I asked as we got a brief slow moment to exchange more than one sentence.

"Well, you can ask 'em yourself, if you want. They're right over there." She nodded toward a table in the lower section of the bar as she walked away. I felt the hair on the back of my neck stand up as I watched Holly fill four shot glasses.

After a few minutes of trying to be casual, I shifted in my seat and turned so I could see the direction she had nodded.

There, sitting at a table by themselves and looking like fish out of water, were two conspicuous individuals. If I had to guess, they were low-cost hired guns for someone. They were ignoring their drinks and were intentionally avoiding my gaze as I looked their direction. I tried to remember if I had seen them around during the convention, but couldn't place their faces. Maybe I had, maybe I hadn't.

With the vague details Holly had just shared and the two gentlemen I had just seen at the atrium bar, my research into Bob Yates' death was starting to gain momentum.

Chapter Seven

Nashville, TN. Wednesday

I nursed my second Old Fashioned for an hour before deciding I had gotten all I was going to get out of Holly, the bartender. She was still chatting every time she came over, but clearly she had no more revealing details to share about Bob Yates. I had gotten it all in the first few minutes.

Apparently, Bob was having an affair with a Mexican woman. He may or may not have cancer, and may have had to lay people off at Atlantis. Upon initial review, none of those pointed to murder. They did, however, make me understand why he may have been drinking too much!

I was getting my wallet out of my pocket when a news bulletin caught my eye on the television behind the bar. It was Chris Valentine, the Atlantis CFO and Bob Yates' boss, standing there with his wife. They were clearly grief stricken and were talking about Bob. Chris was speaking in the soundbite, and his wife was crying with a handkerchief to her face while she held onto his arm.

"He was a great man. We had worked together for

years, and I considered him to be of the highest degree of integrity and honesty. It completely baffles me why anyone would want to hurt Bob Yates. Our family, our company and I are all devastated by this horrific news," he said.

The news carried on, but the message didn't change. Chris Valentine and Atlantis were grieving Bob Yates' death. I get it. It was indeed horrible. I paused for a few minutes with my drink while I considered the fact that Bob's life was lost today. Despite the many times I've been around death like this, it was never easy. This time was no different. I subtly held my drink in the air as a salute to Bob Yates. Then I drained my drink and sat solemnly for a few seconds before raising my head to check out.

After paying my tab and leaving a healthy tip for Scott, I waved to Holly and stood up from my chair. I hesitated long enough to make sure the two guys at the table down below saw me. They did and began shuffling like they were going to get up. There was no subtlety to their movements at all. These guys were rookies, and they planned to follow me.

I made my way out of the atrium bar and walked down the path through the rainforest at the far end of the walkway. It was early evening now, just past 6:15 p.m., and most of our event attendees were at a reception in one of the ballrooms. The fact that these two guys were here told me they were not typical Big Data event guys. I decided to find out who they really were.

As I neared one of the more remote areas of the walkway, I paused to look at one of the smaller fountains that were sprinkled throughout the atrium landscape. When I did, the two thugs nearly bumped into each other a few yards behind me. I turned and continued, heading one level lower to one of the maintenance areas I had noticed earlier in the week. It was next to the boat ride queueing area, which was now empty. I wasn't sure where the stairs led or what was down there, but I knew it would let me know the intentions of my followers.

The two guys followed me down into the maintenance area, which was a mistake. The stairs led into a concrete underground portion of the facility, with concrete walls on each side of the stairway. I peeled off behind one of the walls after I came down the stairs and waited. Within thirty seconds, I could hear them slowly descending the stairs while I stood still at the bottom, out of sight. If they followed me here, it was more than curiosity driving their actions. They could have stopped me earlier if they just wanted to talk.

Expert trackers would have sensed this was a good place for an ambush, but these two were too stupid to split up or change their tactics. They continued down the stairs in a slow and not-so-stealthy manner. I had to decide quickly if they had hostile intent, because they were certainly coming after me.

The first guy hit the last step, and I made my decision. These guys weren't following me just to say hello. With that decision made, I greeted the first guy with the palm of my right hand to his neck and ear. Before the second guy could evaluate what was happening, I shifted his direction with my left hand and caught his nose with the base of my palm. He dropped to his knees but wasn't out.

I was about to consider my sneak attack to be a mistake, as the first strikes were clearly a surprise to them. But before I could even process that thought, the first guy started to get into attack mode and jumped into a strange-looking fighting stance. He lunged at me with a right cross that I didn't expect, but I was able to dodge it. Mostly. It caught my head enough for me to see stars for a brief second, but also allowed me to grab his wrist and pull him forward with his momentum past my right side.

The second follower had a very bloody nose and watery eyes, but still tried to use his position on the stairs to initiate some sort of kicking motion. The timing and placement of the kick were off, and it grazed my thigh while sending him sliding across the concrete floor.

By the time I turned back to the first guy, he had regained his balance and was reaching inside the left side of his jacket with his right hand. If I was a betting man, I'd say he was going for a gun. He was still within reach, so I grabbed his right wrist with my right hand, then my left. Falling backwards to pull him toward me, I brought my knee up to his elbow and felt the disgusting sensation of cartilage and bone crunching as the force of my knee bent his elbow the wrong way.

Suspecting the other guy probably had a gun, too, I backed away and reached into the back of my own jacket and pulled out my trusty SIG P365. I had debated bringing it on this trip because of the pain of checking it at the airport, but at that moment I was certainly glad I went through the trouble!

When I turned and pointed the pistol at the second guy, he was still on the steps and was just beginning to stagger to his feet. Of course, shooting this little 9MM handgun in the concrete maintenance area in the middle of hundreds of hotel rooms never sounded like a good idea anyway, but it got their attention.

The whole scene took maybe five seconds, and I had left one guy with a dislocated elbow and another with a bloody, and likely broken nose. This wasn't really the way to meet people and make friends.

"Alright, what is going on here? What do you two want?" I ask after I back up far enough to clear their arms and legs. They were both looking shocked at the sight of the P365 and seemed to be in a situation that was well over their heads.

It was time to find out why these two clowns were following me and asking questions about Bob Yates.

Chapter Eight

Nashville, TN. Wednesday

The guy with the right arm difficulty answered first.

"What are you doing? We're with the hotel staff. We're just trying to see what you're up to down here," he said sheepishly.

That, of course, didn't make sense. And I knew better.

"Try again! You don't look like hotel maintenance men, and I saw you at the bar just a minute ago." I looked back up the stairs and around the area while I growled my response. Nobody was coming - yet.

They both looked at each other for what seemed like five minutes. The first was still nursing his injured elbow, the second had managed to wipe most of the blood from his face onto his dark jacket. As I saw them up close, I recognized their faces from the event this week. They'd been around. Finally, injured arm spoke up.

"You seemed to be spending an awful lot of time with that bartender, and she seems to have a tendency to tell stories," he said.

Now we were getting somewhere. It's where I anticipated they'd go, so I was ready with a surprised look and question.

"What? What kind of stories would a bartender at the atrium bar in the Grand Marquis Resort in Nashville tell that would get you two so riled up?" I asked.

Again, they looked at each other without answering for an eternity. I was afraid they'd just get up and walk away, so I took the opportunity to reach over and grab the good arm of the first guy and spin him around, locking it behind him. I had his left wrist in my left hand and my right hand around his chest, pointing the SIG at the second guy. With one bad arm dangling and the other pinned behind him, the first guy wasn't able to fight back.

"Ok, if that's how you want to play this. Let's see how you get around with no good arms to work with. How will you explain that to your boss?" I hissed while I pulled his wrist up toward his head. He winced and groaned and I could feel the ligaments and tendons stretching tight. I took a chance by mentioning a boss, but clearly these two weren't running the show.

"Look, man, we're just the messengers here. If you think you're going to get any details from us about this whole mess, you're crazy," the second guy blurted as he watched his buddy struggle.

So, there was a mess involved.

"Why were you questioning the bartender about Bob Yates?" I yelled it a little louder than I wanted while twisting further on the wrist of the first guy in my left hand and lining up the sights of my SIG on the second guy.

"We were afraid Bob got too drunk down there, that's all. When you know as much as he does, you need to be careful," the second guy was clearly trying to save his friend's other arm.

The first guy, with pain straining his voice, wasn't as patient as the second.

"He knows way too much about the project to be getting all chatty like that!" He was struggling with his voice as his arm was nearing its flexibility limit.

While I was absorbing that last statement, we all heard a rustling behind one of the doors along the concrete walls of the maintenance area. I quickly let go of the wrist in my left hand and inserted the SIG in my right hand back into the holster. It was a risk to let them go, but they seemed to be more interested in getting out of there than in causing me harm. My instincts told me they were not emotionally invested in hurting me so much as in getting out of there with no further physical damage.

Plus, they had given me enough information to work with.

The two followers began cautiously shuffling back up the stairs we came down moments ago. As they did, a maintenance worker opened the door and walked out carrying a bucket, and stopped when he saw us.

"Sorry, wrong turn. This place is enormous," I said with a wave as the three of us went up the stairs. The two followers were trying not to draw attention to themselves as we got closer to the crowded walking path. Still, one was wiping the blood from his nose and the other was gingerly cradling his injured arm.

"The project isn't worth this much risk." I muttered under my breath as we got back up to the atrium walkway. It was an attempt to get more info without telling them I had no idea what they were talking about.

They both turned around with a questioning look.

"I don't think Chris would agree with you on that," busted nose said.

"Either way, you need to leave me out of it. If Chris has any questions for me, tell him he can come ask them himself," I said.

By this time, I guessed they were talking about Chris Valentine, the CFO of Atlantis. Paul mentioned he was here, and I had seen him here at the event. Plus, the Atlantis headquarters office was nearby, so I knew he was around. I decided to take one more step into this topic as though I knew what the project was.

"Chris should have known the head of supply chain would be involved in projects like that. It's part of Bob's job," I said.

"Look, we don't even know what the project is, man. All we know is Chris didn't want Bob getting drunk and talking about what he had been doing down there. Now, I suggest you stay out of this or Chris won't be happy," busted nose replied.

"Or else he'll kill me like he killed Bob?" I blurted out without thinking about it long enough.

The response I got from the two wounded guys caught me off guard. They looked at each other and back at me, clearly surprised by what I was saying.

"What?" they replied in unison with a shocked look on their faces that they didn't try to conceal.

I sensed a way out of this whole mess because of their surprise.

"That's why I was talking to the bartender, gentlemen. Someone killed Bob Yates today. I suggest you talk to your boss about how it might look to have you two out asking questions about him," I said confidently.

Bob's death seemed to be a revelation to them, so I let

that sink in while I straightened my shirt and made sure my jacket was covering my SIG in the back of my belt. After a few seconds of questioning looks, they both dusted themselves off and turned around.

"I really doubt Chris would want Bob dead, man. That can't be right," said busted nose as he shook his head, deep in thought.

And with that, we went our separate ways. I assumed those two would be reassigned after they reported this meeting to their boss.

So, the story of Bob Yates was growing more complex. Apparently, he had cancer. He drank too much. He was involved with a woman in Texas. He had to lay off people from his team while at this event in Nashville. And he had traveled 'down there' to see some project for Atlantis that was so secret the CFO had to send spies to make sure he didn't discuss it.

Bob was a busy guy, but did one of those things get him killed?

Chapter Nine

Zapata, TX. Tuesday

Javi was getting dressed when he heard Maria talking to one of the neighbors in the hallway outside their room. Apparently, she was on her cell phone, leaving a message for someone.

"He started yesterday. This is so great. Thank you so much for taking care of Javi. You really didn't need to do that, but thank you. Bye."

Javier walked out just as she was putting the phone back in her purse.

"Who was that, mama?" he asked.

"It was just a friend, Javier. Just a friend," she said with a smile.

"I'm so proud of you. I knew you would do well!"

She hugged him and kissed him on the cheek and stood back with a beaming smile.

"Have a great time today. Remember, mama loves you," she said as she turned to head to the diner.

And Javi did, in fact, feel proud. He felt he caught on

pretty good and was now even a little excited to go back to the warehouse tonight. Plus, the small salary was a big help for his ego and gave him something to look forward to with every shift. He carried that smile all the way to the bus stop, and through his school day.

At 4:45 p.m., just like yesterday, Javi was waiting for the bus to Atlantis at the gate of his neighborhood. This time, Gus was also there. They were the first two to arrive.

"How was your first day?" Gus asked as they stood there waiting.

"Good. I thought it went good, anyway," Javi replied.

"Did they give you all the rules yet?" Gus asked.

"I'm not sure. What do you mean?" Javi replied. He didn't remember many rules during his first day, except to keep working, follow directions, and don't drop anything.

"Getting the work done is only part of it. You also have to follow the other rules. Nobody told me, either, and I got my friend sent away because of it." Gus dropped his head as he mentioned his friend.

"There is a section of the warehouse compound that we're not allowed to see. You can't help but notice it in the dark, because it's all lit up and has an extra layer of fence. Now that I'm telling you, you'll see it every time you go in or out, but you have to pretend you don't. The only people who go there are the shirt guys," Gus said.

Javi immediately assumed the 'shirt guys' were the workers at the warehouse who wore the Atlantis shirts, mostly with khaki pants. They were mostly older white and black guys, but not all. A few were Hispanic, possibly Mexican. They seemed to have the more important jobs.

"Why can't anyone else go back there?" Javi asked.

"None of us know for sure, but there are rumors."

"What are the rumors?"

"Well, for one thing, people say they are shipping drugs in Atlantis trucks, and they don't want nobody to see," Gus said.

"How did you get your friend sent away, and where did he go?" Javi asked.

"I didn't tell him that we can't walk around, and he walked back to look at the bright lights one night. They took him, and I haven't seen him since. I think they sent him back to Mexico. That's what happens to everyone who breaks the rules. They disappear," Gus replied.

Javi's excitement for his second day of work was beginning to turn much more anxious as he listened to Gus.

"I won't look at all!" Javi blurted out.

"That's a good plan," Gus said.

"Did your friend's parents come looking for him?" Javi asked.

"They tried, but nobody can get into this area. Those fences stop everyone, and his parents couldn't get the guards to answer any questions. Nobody makes waves with the police because the warehouse people are too powerful. I heard he wasn't the only one to be taken, but that it happens all the time. That's the other rumor about what they do back there. People say they ship drugs away, but they also say those trucks ship people away. All I know is, sometimes people show up for work here and never go home. So, Javier, you should never, never, go near that place. That's the biggest rule," Gus looked sternly at Javi.

"I won't," Javi nodded.

"Besides that, you just have to stay in your own area. Don't walk around and look like you're snooping. If you just do that and do good work, you'll be fine. That's what I do." Gus nodded to Javi with that last admonition and stopped talking as other bus riders gathered at the gate.

As they did the day before, the other workers stood quietly and waited while the bus pulled up. They all got on, rode silently to the warehouse, and got out again.

Armando was there again with his clipboard, but this time, Javi knew where to go and walked straight to his station. Armando grabbed a couple of other guys as they got off the bus, just like he had done with Javi yesterday. They must have been the new ones for today.

Javi navigated the same path he had ridden with Armando yesterday as quickly as he could. Even with Gus' warnings, he was excited to show that he could learn the job quickly. Along the way, he tried not to look to the back corner of the compound, but Javi couldn't help it. He kept his head down, but allowed his eyes to scan the horizon beyond the massive warehouse, and there it was. Just as Gus had said, there was another layer of fence way back there with lots of lights and another building. It was a similar shape to the vast warehouse he worked in, but not as big. He glanced only for a second and didn't look at it again.

Raul was already at the station when Javi got there. He nodded to Javi and stepped away from the pallet he had been loading.

"Let's work on getting you trained on the forklift," Raul said.

Javi was thrilled and became completely immersed in forklift training for the next thirty minutes. By the end of Raul's training, Javi was getting the hang of it and didn't need Raul's help.

Raul seemed to notice how well Javi was doing.

"Take over, Javi. I'll be back in a minute," he said as he stepped away from the forklift.

Javi remembered what he had learned the day before and quickly scanned the order on the tablet screen and loaded boxes onto the pallets. Then he used the forklift to load the pallets onto the truck.

He noticed Raul was stepping between large stacks of boxes that seemed to lead nowhere. Concerned about all the rules Gus had mentioned, Javi didn't watch Raul too closely and just kept working.

After the first half of his second shift, Javi was feeling like he was getting the hang of things here at Atlantis. It may have only been his second day, but already he had learned to fill orders with no help, had operated the forklift, and even fixed the computer when it locked up. He had totally forgotten all the warnings Gus had mentioned.

Then two of the shirt guys rode up on one of their little carts. They got out and yelled for Raul to come over. He stopped and looked up with a face full of fear. Javi looked on with his eyes wide open while Raul walked over to the shirt guys.

"Keep working over there, you," One of the shirt guys yelled toward Javi.

"Empty your pockets!" The other shirt guy was yelling at Raul while cornering him against the boxes.

Raul emptied his pockets in front of the two men.

"Now your shoes," one of them said to Raul.

Raul stalled and sheepishly rubbed his knuckles. He wasn't taking off his shoes.

"No, please. I'll stop, I promise," Raul began pleading.

"Shoes off, now!" they both said in unison.

The two shirt guys were closing in on Raul. He finally slipped his shoes off both his feet and stood with his head bowed, still pleading under his breath.

One of the shirt guys dumped Raul's shoes out and dropped several packets of white powder on the floor. Nobody needed to say what it was. Raul had been sneaking behind the boxes to take drugs from the stash he had hidden in his shoes.

"Hey you! Take over! We've been watching you, and we know you can do it!" One of the shirt guys was yelling at Javi while he tried to pretend like he was still working. He had no idea what to do except nod as they loaded Raul onto the golf cart and sped away. Javi had barely learned how to use the forklift and wasn't sure he could do everything Raul did, but he didn't really have a choice.

Remembering Raul had been taking little excursions behind stacks of boxes from time to time, Javi decided that must have been how he got caught. Taking that idea a step further, Javi glanced around the walls and ceilings as he loaded pallets for the next truck. It only took a few minutes to realize his every move was visible by a multitude of cameras scattered throughout the warehouse. Raul must not have known, or thought he was being smart by hiding behind boxes. Obviously, that didn't work.

Javi never saw Raul again, but he worked even harder until his shift was over at 10 p.m.

Chapter Ten

Nashville, TN. Wednesday

After returning to my hotel room from the scuffle near the atrium, I realized the knock I had received on my head was a little worse than I thought. I had a nasty lump forming and needed to ice it down a bit. I got some ice from the ice machine at the end of the hall, put it in the bag in the ice bucket and laid back on my bed with the bag between my pillow and my head.

The situation with Bob Yates was completely bizarre. With all the possible angles on this case, I decided now was a good time to talk to Paul again. Since The Association had sent me on this assignment, they clearly had some idea what I might find. While I didn't know the other members of The Association, I had learned they were well connected and well funded. They also seem to have the resources to find high-level information the average citizen wouldn't know. Paul had given me some general guidance for this assignment, but even he seemed surprised by what I had found so far.

"Hey Keith, what's up?" Paul said, as he answered my call.

"Well, things have gotten a little weird here," I began.

"Oh boy. Let me have it," Paul said, sounding like a concerned father to a crying child.

"First off, you were right about the freedom to ask questions after Bob's death. People don't think twice about discussing him. Which has, as it turns out, given me more than I bargained for." I stopped to catch my breath and frame my thoughts.

"Really. In what way?" Paul was trying to be patient.

"It started back at the golf course. During my conversation with the other two golfers on our scramble team, I learned Bob had been spending a great deal of time at one of the hotel bars. I also learned he had spent time downtown at a bar called the Fuzzy Mushroom or something like that. In both cases, he had found someone working there to listen to his problems. This afternoon, I went straight to the bar here at the hotel and found the bartender he was talking to. She gave me an earful."

"About Bob?" Paul asked, making me realize I hadn't clarified.

"Yes, about Bob. He had mentioned he had cancer. Then he talked about some woman in Texas, implying there was a relationship there. And apparently, he also had to lay off some people this week while he was at the event, which really upset him." I paused to let that sink in.

"Interesting. That all sounds bad, but not really deserving of getting yourself shot." Paul noted.

"Yeah, tell me about it. But as you might expect, there's more. She also told me two guys came up to her after Bob left and asked what he had been talking about. That took the evening in a different direction. As she mentioned it, she noted the two were sitting in the bar at that very moment," I said.

"Did you talk to them?" I could hear Paul getting a little anxious.

"Well, yes, I did. I left the bar and noticed they followed me. So, I led them to a secluded location, and we had a, uh, conversation.," I said, trying not to pause too long.

"Keith, are they still alive?" Paul asked with a little more urgency than I appreciated.

"Yes, Paul, I didn't kill people at the Grand Marquis!" I said.

"I did, however, give them reason not to follow me anymore. And I also learned Bob was aware of, if not involved in, some project at Atlantis that was under the nose of the CFO. And the CFO must have been worried that Bob was going to talk about it, because these two thugs were there to find out anything he said." I paused to see if Paul had a question. He did.

"Did they say what the project was?" he asked.

"Not exactly. But they said Bob had gone 'down there,' which I assumed to mean the location of the project." I stopped again.

"Ok, so we know he was involved with a confidential, or perhaps illegal, project. I wonder if 'down there' is the same location as his friend in Texas?" Paul asked.

"I wondered the same thing. I also think I need to go find this Fuzzy Mushroom place and see what he talked about there. This guy was into more than one mess, apparently!" I said.

"Great idea, Keith. And while you do that, let me dig into this with my contacts at The Association. They may be able to give me some more details to help narrow your search. Good luck!" Paul said as the call disconnected.

After a quick search on my phone of the local bars, I didn't find anything called the 'Fuzzy Mushroom.' I did, however, find a 'Mellow Mushroom' and quickly recognized it as a pizza restaurant chain. They had a location in Denver that I had been to before and had a location right downtown in Nashville as well. It was the closest name I could find to the 'Fuzzy Mushroom' that served pizza, so I put it into the Uber app and headed to the Grand Marquis rideshare pickup area.

The Uber driver, Samantha, drove a purple Nissan Juke. It probably wouldn't have been my first choice if I was the buyer, but as an Uber rider, it was fine. It took about twenty minutes to get from the Grand Marquis hotel to Broadway in downtown Nashville, where the Mellow Mushroom address took us.

Samantha stopped about a half block from the address as the crowds prevented us from getting all the way there. It was only Wednesday night, but it was Broadway in Nashville. This is the area that gets the nickname 'NashVegas' with people back in Colorado, and the crowd tonight certainly justified the name.

The Mellow Mushroom is one of the smaller locations on Broadway, but it is right in the middle of the hustle and bustle. Just across the street from Tootsies, with the distinctive purple sign, was a more subdued yellow sign for the Mellow Mushroom.

It was April, and was still getting cool in the evenings, but the Mellow Mushroom had their front windows open to the street. The drummer from the band playing on the stage was sitting right at the edge of the window. I wondered how that guy could concentrate with all these people passing just a few feet behind him on the sidewalk.

When I entered the door to the Mellow Mushroom, I

was immediately struck with two things. First, the smell of pizza hit me from the ovens in the back. Second, I realized this was a Nashville music bar that served pizza, not a restaurant and bar that had music. The priority was obvious.

The band playing to the right as I walked in was blasting some song by No Doubt that I recognized but couldn't name. The female singer was backed by a guitar, a bass, and the drums being pounded by the open window. They were good.

To my left was a stairway that led to another seating area upstairs, which appeared to have an open area to see the music below. Surveying the area based on what Darren and Mo had described, I decided Bob wasn't upstairs.

Just beyond the stage was a small dancing area, then four round tables, then a bar on the right side that extended to the back. At the back of the bar, there seemed to be a cooking area. There were four people seated on the metal stools around the bar, but surprisingly, that left five stools empty. The six tables to the left of the bar were full, but that wasn't where I wanted to sit.

I went to the bar and took a seat at the far end, just next to where a metal pizza rack held several pizzas. There were a couple of people working in the pizza area tonight. One was a blond female with a ponytail. The other was a middle-age guy, also with a long ponytail and a tie-dye shirt on.

This must be the 'hippie guy' Darren saw Bob talking to. I had some questions for him.

Chapter Eleven

Nashville, TN. Wednesday

I sat at the bar and ordered a beer. This was no place for my standard Old Fashioned order. I sat quietly for the first few minutes and watched the action. The band was playing a good mix of music I recognized, and the moderately large crowd was into it.

Behind the bar, drinks were flowing, and the pizzas were coming out about as fast as the crew could cook them. Some of them were going into boxes and out the back door via the delivery drivers, and some were going into the racks in front of me. Those would be carried to the hungry patrons sitting around me and upstairs. If I relaxed, I would have enjoyed a nice evening of music and pizza.

This, however, wasn't the time for relaxing.

After a few minutes, I yelled to the 'hippie guy' working diligently in front of me. I had noticed he had a name tag that said 'Mike.'

"I guess every night is a busy night down here, huh?" I said.

"Yeah, it's rare we get a slow moment," he replied.

He was quite busy, so I didn't talk again for some time. After another beer and six more songs, including an old country song I knew by Merle Haggard, I tried a new tactic.

"How often do you guys rotate bands?" I asked.

"Oh, I don't know. It varies. Some stay for weeks or months, some have shorter term gigs. I think it depends on the arrangement they get with the manager," he replied.

He clearly wasn't getting into the conversation.

"Sorry, man. I'm sure people sitting right in front of you while you work can be annoying," I said, taking yet another route.

"Oh no, it's no big deal at all. Don't take it personally. I'm just trying to get the pizzas out of the oven, man," he said with a slight smile.

I smiled and nodded while he continued to slice pizzas, box them, and stack them in the warmers. Then, he unexpectedly continued.

"Plus, there's no way you could talk more than the guy that was here last night!"

And there it was. The door was open. Sometimes these things just require a little patience.

"Uh-oh. I don't want to be the guy you talk about like that!" I laughed as I said it, trying to keep the conversation light.

"Oh, you won't be. This guy was one of a kind. By the end of the night, I knew the guy had a problem at work with budgets, had some sort of medical issue, and was dealing with an affair. You're already quieter than him!" For the first time, Mike looked at me when he spoke.

"Wow, sorry about that. I'll try not to talk about any affairs I'm having, for sure!" I joked.

"Thanks, man. Much appreciated!" He laughed before he continued.

"But it wasn't his own affair he was complaining about. The poor guy's wife was apparently having an affair with his boss. I mean, you can't make this stuff up!" Mike went back to work as he dropped that new bit of information.

"That's a sad batch of stories. I don't think I can match that. But let me know if there are others I should avoid!" I said. Again, trying to keep the conversation light. At the same time, I winced internally at the thought of Bob's wife having an affair he knew about. That must have been awful.

"Honestly, I think that's about it. But wow, that's enough for me, man!" Mike said.

Mike went back to cooking and cutting pizzas, and I went back to my beer and the sweet vibe of the Mellow Mushroom in Nashville. In the back of my mind, I had added another bullet to the growing list of craziness that was Bob Yates' life. On top of his apparent relationship with the woman in Texas, it seems his wife was also having an affair. And with his boss, no less!

I'm beginning to wonder if the two thugs from yesterday were telling the truth about why they were checking up on Bob. Since Chris, the CFO, was Bob's boss, they could just as well have been making sure Bob wasn't talking about his affair. I can't be sure, of course, but it's another possible reason they were snooping around. Or maybe it was just the mysterious project. Or maybe there's even more about Bob Yates that I need to dig up.

After finishing my beer, hearing another six songs, and spending a few more moments of idle chitchat with Mike, I decided I had learned all I could about Bob Yates at the Mellow Mushroom. It was nearly 10 p.m. and it was time to move on.

While I walked away from Broadway to find a good Uber pickup spot, I called home to talk to the kids. Oliver and Judy, their grandparents on their mother's side, were staying at the house this week. They had been a tremendous help to me and the kids since my wife's death five years ago.

Oliver's job allowed him to work anywhere, and Judy loved to stay with the kids and dote over them for a week. Kyle and Jamie were still young enough that they loved the attention, too. Kyle was eight and Jamie had just turned eleven, and they weren't yet into ignoring their grandparents — especially if they were being fed Judy's cooking!

"Hey, dad. Just getting ready to head to bed," Jamie answered quickly. It was almost 9 p.m. in Woodland Park, Colorado, where we lived, so she had to throw in something about getting ready for bed. Bedtime was coming soon, but I was pretty sure Judy and Oliver let that rule slip a bit when they were there.

"Oh, good, hon. How is everything there?" I asked.

"Great. We had some awesome fried chicken tonight!" She always led with the food. To be honest, I probably would, too, if I had been eating Judy's culinary creations.

"Nice! And how was hockey practice?" I asked, knowing Oliver had taken her to the rink earlier in the evening.

"Good. Same ol' stuff," she said.

We chatted a few more minutes before I spoke to Kyle, then to Oliver and Judy. It seemed things were going well at home, so I ended the call and let them get ready for bed. After ordering an Uber, I was in a gray Nissan Altima five minutes later with a very quiet driver about my age. He seemed content listening to his eighties rock music on the radio instead of chatting, and I didn't argue.

Given the variety of things I had learned about Bob

Yates, I decided to provide Paul with one more update during the ride from Broadway to the Grand Marquis.

"Hey Keith, what's up?" Paul said, as he answered.

"You're not going to believe this, but I've got even more dirt on our dearly departed Bob Yates," I said.

"There's more? What else was going on with him?" Paul sighed.

"Well, it seems he wasn't the only one in his marriage who was stepping out. He got chatty at a bar downtown this week and shared that his wife was dating his boss! I guess that means Mrs. Yates was having an affair with Chris Valentine," I said. The statement has me shaking my head as I talk.

"You've got to be kidding me!" Paul said. "That guy just can't win! And then he gets shot at an event like that. This whole thing is nuts. But, I guess the question remains: which one of these things would have been worth killing for?" Paul said, expressing the same question I had been pondering.

"Yeah, I guess that's the big question. Honestly, I don't know yet."

"Do you have a gut feeling yet?"

"Maybe, but let me dig around a bit. I'd like to find out more about this woman in Texas. Maybe he's shared more detail with some of the others here at the event. I'll keep my ear to the ground. I suspect you were right about people opening up about him after his death. It'll be easier to dig than it would have been," I said.

"Yeah, I think so. Let me know what you find!"

"Will do," I said as we ended the call.

It was time to go chat about Bob Yates with the other event attendees.

Chapter Twelve

Zapata, TX. Tuesday

After his shift, Javi was eager to find Gus and discuss the situation he had witnessed with Raul. He had been told on the first day that drug use was not tolerated, but the abrupt removal of Raul from the warehouse was overwhelming for Javi.

As everyone moved through the line to collect their day's pay, nobody spoke to each other. Javi followed that example and quietly waited. When he got to the front, the process started the same as yesterday.

"Name?" the shirt guy said.

"Javier Sanchez," he replied.

The shirt guy handing out the cash paused for a moment and looked at his notes. Then he whispered something to the other man in the booth, who handed Javi fifteen dollars.

"You get more because of your promotion. Good work," the guy said as Javi took the money.

"Gracias," Javi said without thinking. He was told to

only speak English to the shirts, but the extra money caught him off-guard. Luckily, nobody said anything, and he moved on.

When he got on the bus, Javi found Gus sitting in a seat alone and rushed to sit next to him. Nobody said much on the bus rides, but Javi had lots of questions. At the very least, he'd be next to Gus when they got off the bus at the gate.

"They took my boss away for using drugs," Javi said when the bus was moving, keeping his head down so the driver couldn't see him talking.

"Not here," Gus said, also keeping his head low.

Javi got the message and waited until they got off the bus to say another word. When they were alone at the gate and the bus was leaving, Javi unloaded.

"My boss was sneaking drugs behind the boxes and got caught. I think they caught him on those cameras that are all over the place. They must have been watching him. They came and shook him down and found drugs in his shoes. Then they took him away on a cart and I never saw him again. What do they do with people who use drugs at work? Is he in prison?"

"Wait a minute. Slow down," Gus said, holding his hands up to Javi.

"Look. It's like they told you on the first day. They don't allow drugs. Period. If he got caught, he's probably in prison. Or worse." Gus paused with his head down when he said those last two words.

"What do you mean by 'worse'?" Javi said, clearly sensing the hesitance in Gus' demeanor.

Javi had heard the rumors of people being sent back to Mexico for not following the rules in America. Was that what Gus was talking about? Is that really worse than an American prison?

"Javi, calm down. They're just rumors. But there are stories about people breaking the rules at the warehouse and disappearing. Not to Mexico, not to an American prison, and certainly not back to their homes." Gus kept his head down while he shared the rumors with Javi.

Javi stood still for several seconds while he absorbed what Gus had said.

"Just for breaking the rules? What do you think they're doing with these people?" He eventually asked.

"Nobody knows," Gus said.

"I don't think I want to go back," Javi said quickly.

"Mama can probably get me a job at the diner or something. I don't want to disappear," he continued.

"If you follow the rules, you'll be ok. Like I told you at the beginning, you just have to follow the rules." Gus tried to smile at Javi to calm him down.

"Plus, there's no place around that will give you a job like this. They give you cash and don't make you fill out any papers. It's not as bad as it feels right now." He tried to smile again as he encouraged Javi.

"Yeah, but I don't want them to take me away. Where do the rumors say people go, Gus?" Javi asked.

"I never ask," replied Gus.

Javi stood there another minute before he let out a deep sigh.

"Well, I guess I'll see you tomorrow, then," he finally said.

"Yep. See you," replied Gus.

Javi thought about the conversation with Gus all night. He wasn't sure how much he should tell mama. She seemed so proud of him getting the job at the warehouse and he had already made twenty-five dollars. He went to bed that night without saying anything, struggling with the thoughts of missing people instead of sleeping.

"How was work last night, Javi?" Mama asked after Javi woke up, dressed, and entered the kitchen. She was sitting with several other women at one of the tables in the cramped room.

"It was good. I can run the forklift now," Javi replied. With the other people in the room, he decided not to share his conversation with Gus.

"That's great, Javi! I'm so proud of you. I told you it would work out." She jumped up and gave Javi a hug.

"Thanks, mama," he said while she squeezed him awkwardly in front of the other residents.

"I knew my friend wouldn't let us down. He is an honest man, and he knows how we struggle. I'm so glad he helped us!" She was beaming, and it was beginning to make Javi uncomfortable.

"Yes, me too, mama. I've gotta get ready for school," Javi said as he pulled away.

Maria was too excited about Javi's success at the warehouse to notice his own subdued emotions. She chatted with her friends at the table while Javi got his breakfast and went back to their room.

Javi knew he didn't trust mama's friend, and he was beginning to wonder if the guy was setting him up for something bad. He tried to find peace in the situation. The experience Javi was getting at the warehouse was good. The money was good. But something scared him about that place.

He decided he would talk to mama the next day. Until then, he'd let her have her moment.

Chapter Thirteen

Nashville, TN. Wednesday

In order to get to my room at the Grand Marquis, I had to walk by a bar near the lobby area. It closed every night at 11 p.m. and I was passing through just before that time.

There were only a few people left in the area, including Darren and Mo. I decided to stop by and see how they were doing after our traumatic afternoon. The bar was just behind the lobby, past the restrooms, and was situated in the middle of a group of hotel rooms — not unlike the atrium bar in the middle of the whole hotel. This one, however, was much smaller.

There was a stream running beside the multi-level seating area with 8 round tables. The bar had ten old-fashioned barstools fixed to the floor. There were several varieties of plants around the edge of the seating area, giving it a bit of isolation from the hotel guests walking by. A small stage area was visible in the back, but nobody was playing this late.

"Hey guys, you shutting the bar down tonight?" I asked as I walked up.

There were two other groups still in the bar, but they seemed to be breaking up for the night. Mo was still sitting at the bar like he wasn't leaving soon, and Darren was sitting on a barstool with his back to the bar, facing me as I greeted them.

"Hey Keith. We're doing ok, I guess. I can't say I've had a day like this before. Not really sure how to process it. Beer doesn't seem to help, but it tastes good, so here we are." He laughed at his own joke. I could see Mo's shoulders shake with a chuckle, too. Their slurred speech and glassy eyes indicated they weren't on their first drink.

"Yeah, I'm with you on that. This was a sad day, for sure. Been thinking about Bob a lot this evening," I said. It wasn't a lie. Even though I had seen more death than I wanted to admit, the chaotic life of Bob Yates had made an unexpected impact on me. Maybe I just couldn't believe everything he was into.

"Yeah, so have we. Word's getting around, so lots of people have been chatting about it," Mo said as he spun his barstool around.

"I guess that's not surprising." I sat next to Mo at the bar. I waved at the bartender to decline a drink, which he seemed to appreciate. He was already washing glasses and shutting things down for the night.

"That was just an unbelievable situation out there. The more you think about what happened, the more it looks like Bob was somehow the target. I mean, a random shooter would probably want to hit more than one person. The cops were sniffing around that hotel across the lake from the golf course late tonight. I think the shooter must have been over there." Darren was talking, and Mo was nodding. Clearly, they'd been thinking and talking about this.

"That is indeed unbelievable. Did the cops find anybody or anything yet?" I asked, pretty sure these two wouldn't know but trying to make conversation.

"No clue. If they did, they aren't sharing," Darren said.

"It's wild, just absolutely wild," I said while shaking my head.

"They considered canceling the rest of the event this week. But I guess they decided that would send the wrong signal. For the moment, we're still on for tomorrow. I've got a speaking part in one of the sessions at 9 a.m., so I guess I'd better be going," Mo said as he stood up and motioned to the bartender to pay his tab.

"I'd better head in, too. I've got a meeting in the morning as well. It's sort of weird that everything's still moving on as normal, but I suppose I get it." I said as I got up.

"Yeah. I know I'll not be one hundred percent focused, but I'll be there too." Darren stood up and signed his bill as Mo signed his.

"See you guys in the morning then, I suppose," I said as I waved and headed to my room.

As I was walking around the bar area to the elevator, I remembered I was supposed to have breakfast with Jennifer Ellis in the morning. After our events at Willow Creek last fall, Jen had become a very close friend. Well, I guess even more than that. It still felt weird to admit that. She was the first woman I'd gotten this close to since my wife died.

Jen was here at the Big Data event representing her company, Diverse Data. She was from the same area of Colorado as me, and had been out with some of her customers this evening. We had planned to catch up in the morning. I grinned to myself as I thought about seeing Jen's smile in the morning.

I was still smiling when I got off the elevator on the third floor where my room was. My smile faded, however, when I saw two uniformed police officers standing at my door. From their posture, I could tell they had knocked on the door and were waiting for me to answer.

One officer appeared to be relatively new to the force, judging by his age. He was about my height but muscular, and obviously proud of it. The other officer was about my age, but a little shorter. He was looking at his phone when I approached them. When he saw me, I saw his right hand casually drop toward the Glock 19 in a holster on his hip.

"Can I help you, gentlemen?" I asked as I exited the elevator just two doors down from where they were standing.

"Are you Keith Morgan?" The older officer asked while showing the other officer his phone. I assumed the phone was showing my photo.

When the younger officer saw it, he went further than the older officer and put his hand on his pistol. They were clearly expecting me to run. Or to attack them. Their reaction to my presence confused me, but also told me something had gone wrong.

"Yes, I am." There was no point in denying my identity at this point.

"We'd like you to come down to the precinct with us, please," the older officer said.

"Am I under arrest?" I asked.

"No. We'd just like to ask you a few questions," he said. The younger officer just watched with his hand on his weapon.

"I talked to Officer Keating earlier today. Is this related

to that murder case from the golf course?" I asked, trying to get an idea of what was going on.

"It is, yes. We're still trying to fill in some gaps in the case, and you may have critical information," the officer said.

Something in the way he was talking and posturing didn't match his words. He was clearly anxious about my presence, but was asking me to come in voluntarily. They didn't try to arrest me, but it felt like they'd force me to come with them if I declined.

"Ok, sure. It's sort of late, but I'm glad to help," I said as I motioned for them to head to the elevator.

"After you," the officer said, motioning for me to lead the way instead. They still hadn't introduced themselves, which added to my concern. Of course, they did have name tags on, which told me I was heading to a Nashville police station with Officers Wilson and Newcomb.

As we rode down the elevator, I tried again to get some details.

"Do you know how long we'll be? I have an appointment in the morning," I asked.

"It shouldn't be long," Officer Wilson said, with Officer Newcomb still watching on silently.

After we exited the elevator and walked to their car parked just beyond the valet parking area, Officer Newcomb turned around and faced me.

"Do you have any weapons on you?" he asked.

"I do, sir," I responded. I suspected I knew what was coming next.

"What do you have and where?" Officer Newcomb asked.

"A SIG P365 in the back of my waistband," I answered.

"Do you mind if we check it out, then?" He held his hands out to let me know he was going to pat me down.

"Sure, go ahead," I said as I held up my hands. I looked around to see if anyone was observing this spectacle, but we were alone.

Officer Newcomb patted me down, taking special care around my belt in the back while he extracted my pistol from its holster. He held it up

"This isn't your run-of-the-mill P365." He looked at me when he said it, but it wasn't a question, so I didn't respond. The custom milling on the slide and the custom grip module make my pistol unique, but I didn't want to get into that topic with Officer Newcomb.

He shrugged at my silence and proceeded to remove the magazine and eject the round from the chamber in ceremonious fashion. Then he smiled at me and continued his pat down. I knew it was legal to carry the concealed pistol in Tennessee, but this exercise still felt uneasy.

After checking my pockets and my pants, he handed my disassembled weapon back to me and held the door open to their police car. He kept the single round and the magazine.

"If you don't mind, I'll hold on to these until you are ready to leave the station," he said as he motioned for me to get in.

If I had known what the night held, I would have canceled my breakfast with Jen.

Chapter Fourteen

Nashville, TN. Wednesday

The ride to the police station in the back of a squad car was an uncomfortable experience. Not only did the officers avoid any sort of communication with me, they had also arrested someone before me who couldn't control their bodily functions. There was a powerful stench of urine in the back seat I hoped wasn't seeping into my clothes. Or my skin.

I still had my phone in my pocket, which told me they weren't planning to charge me with anything immediately. Using that fact to my advantage, I texted Paul to let him know what was happening. There was no need to try to hide it, as the phone screen lit up the back of the car. Officer Wilson looked at me in the mirror but didn't say anything.

After what seemed like twenty minutes or more, we finally pulled into the parking lot of a police station in a somewhat suburban part of town next to a strip mall. It didn't look like the worst area of town, but not the best, either.

The posture of the officers stayed consistent, as Officer Newcomb opened the door while Officer Wilson stood several feet behind the door with his hand on his weapon. They were still very cautious with my presence. Which, in turn, made me cautious.

Officer Newcomb led me into the building, passing three officers on the way. They greeted each other, but didn't acknowledge me at all. After passing the booking area where four detainees were sitting next to officers at desks, Officer Newcomb opened the door of an interrogation room and motioned for me to enter.

"Have a seat, Mr. Morgan. We'll be with you in a minute," he said.

I suspected that might have been an optimistic expectation of their timing, and I was right. I sat alone in that room for nearly ninety minutes. At that point, the door burst open, and I was surprised to see Officer Keating enter the room with a plainclothes female officer following him.

"Mr. Morgan, thanks for coming in. I apologize for the delay," Officer Keating said as he reached out his hand.

I nodded and shook his hand.

"This is Detective Olivia Shaw. She has been assigned to this case and will be helping us out here." He nodded toward her when he said it. Detective Shaw nodded with a fake smile that only moved her lips. She didn't offer her hand and didn't speak.

Officer Keating sat at the table across from me and plopped down a folder in front of him. It was thin, telling me they didn't yet have much information on this case. Detective Shaw stood next to the door with her back leaning against the wall.

"Long day, huh?" I asked Officer Keating, trying to see if he'd engage.

"Yeah, it happens," he said with a forced, brief smile. He seemed too tired to engage. The fatigue also seemed to bring out more of his southern drawl.

He opened his folder and spread out a couple of the pages. After looking at them for a few seconds, he looked up.

"So, you indicated you were staying at the Grand Marquis for an event. ...the Big Data event?" He began with information he already had.

"I did," I said.

"And you stayed there the whole time?" He quickly went away from our previous conversation. I decided it wasn't time to play along nicely.

"I don't recall saying that," I replied.

"I didn't ask that question earlier, but I'm asking it now. Did you stay at the Grand Marquis the whole time you were in Nashville?" he asked firmly.

I took a breath as the next words out of my mouth would determine the nature of the rest of this evening. Should I demand a lawyer now and put this to an end? Was I really being considered as responsible for Bob Yates' death if I was on the golf course with him? Did they think I had somehow gotten someone else to kill him and that I set it up? Should I keep going and see where the conversation goes before I demand representation?

The thoughts were still circling when three loud bangs startled all three of us. Someone was knocking loudly at the door. After the third knock, the door cracked open a bit, and a head appeared in the gap. It was a head I didn't recognize, and on first glance, I assessed it as being the head of a lawyer.

Stepping back from the door, Detective Shaw opened it the rest of the way with a look of disgust on her face.

"Detective Shaw! Charming as ever," the lawyer said as he nodded her way and entered the room.

"I hope you aren't questioning my client without his lawyer present," the man said.

He had tanned skin, possibly Latino, and appeared as if he had just walked into the office in the morning. His suit was clearly expensive, I'd guess Armani, and was tailored to accent his athletic physique. He bubbled with energy that clearly annoyed the officers.

"We were just talking," Officer Keating responded. He was still sitting casually across the table from me, but his mood had soured substantially with our visitor's arrival.

"Oh, great. So, if we're just talking, I suppose you wouldn't mind me listening in? Perhaps we should start the talk with a good reason why you have detained my client at 12:30 a.m. on a Thursday morning when he is a guest of our fine Grand Marquis Resort and of our fine city?"

This guy was annoying, but I sort of liked him. I could see the police didn't share my opinion. While I was shocked at how quickly it happened, I had to assume this was the work of Paul Frazier and The Association.

"We are investigating a murder that Mr. Morgan is already aware of," Officer Keating began.

"And is my client a suspect?" The Lawyer hadn't even introduced himself yet but was clearly acting on my behalf.

"As we said, we're just talking. There are no suspects identified yet," Detective Shaw interjected.

The lawyer turned and looked at her.

"Fair enough. Then perhaps you'd like to share why we're here? Then we will decide if we stay to discuss it further or not." This guy was definitely earning points with me. I sat silently and watched him work.

"We'll be back in a minute." Detective Shaw opened

the door and motioned for Officer Keating to join her. They walked out and left me and the lawyer in the room alone.

I sat silent, knowing we were being watched and recorded. The lawyer did the same. He did hand me a business card. On the card were the following words.

* * *

William Renteria
Attorney at Law

* * *

There was a phone number below the name and title. That was it.

I looked at him and nodded, still hoping he had been called in by Paul and The Association. Out of nowhere, he started humming and tapping on the table. It only took a few notes before I recognized the song. It was one someone had asked me to memorize a few years back.

The song was Along Comes Mary, from the 1960s.

It was made famous by a group called The Association.

Chapter Fifteen

Nashville, TN. Thursday

We sat in silence for another fifteen minutes when William Renteria decided we had been waiting long enough. He stood up, walked casually to the door, and knocked once.

"My client and I would like to leave now. You have no right to detain us. Let us out now or I'll own this precinct." He was calm and collected, but clearly expected his words to change things.

They did.

The door opened and Officer Keating came in again with Detective Shaw in tow.

"Ok, we talked it over with the Lieutenant and we'll share what we can. Ok? So, just take a seat if you don't mind?" He was being more friendly now than before but also seemed tired and frustrated.

"You ok with this?" Mr. Renteria was looking my direction when he asked it.

I nodded my head. If nothing else, I was curious about what was going on.

"Good. Here's why we're talking to Mr. Morgan," he started, while looking at Mr. Renteria.

"You'll talk to me first, then we'll decide if you talk to Mr. Morgan," Mr. Renteria said. I almost laughed, but held it in.

"Come on, Will. We're just trying to get some answers, that's all." It was an exasperated Detective Shaw chiming in from her position next to the door.

Ok, so he's called Will. And Detective Shaw is comfortable enough with him to call him that in a casual fashion. That's interesting. She looks to be a little older than him, but I suppose there could have been a romantic history between them. More likely, she had been dealing with him at work for years and had developed a professional relationship. Either way, this was interesting to watch.

"Ok, ok, fair enough. Please continue, Officer Keating," Will said.

After a long sigh, he did.

"As I was saying, we're talking to Mr. Morgan because we are trying to solve the murder of Mr. Bob Yates. I discussed it earlier with Mr. Morgan when we met at the golf course where the crime occurred."

"Ok." Will said.

"During our initial investigation, we focused on a couple of possible locations where the shooter could have taken the shot." Before Officer Keating could get another word out, he was interrupted again.

"And I assume my client couldn't have taken the shot from his golf cart on the other side of the mounds near the lake," Will said. It impressed me how quickly he had gotten up to speed on the situation.

"May I please continue, Mr. Renteria?" Officer Keating asked while Detective Shaw sighed. She was rubbing her temples with one of her hands, while the other arm remained crossed over her chest. She was clearly losing patience.

"Sure. I'm just trying to understand what this has to do with my client."

"I'm about to get to that."

"Ok. Please continue."

This time, Will sat back in his chair and crossed his arms, looking back and forth at Officer Keating and Detective Shaw.

"One of the potential locations for the shooter is called the Nashville Inn. It's a large hotel across the street on the other side of the lake."

Officer Keating paused, but this time Will said nothing. Instead, he looked at his watch. I could see it too, and I saw it was now 1:15 a.m. And it was a very nice watch.

"There was a guest registered at that hotel with an interesting name." This time, Officer Keating seemed to pause for drama.

Will made a face.

"The name was Keith Morgan." Officer Keating closed his folder and sat back in his chair. He had made his point, and we now knew why we were called to the police station after midnight.

Will didn't skip a beat.

"So, you're implying my client was genius enough to book a hotel room in his own name, then magically position himself hundreds of yards away from the very golf course where you saw him to shoot Mr. Yates? Is that what you're saying?" Will was frustrated or was just acting like he was frustrated. And doing a good job of it.

"We're just looking for answers, Mr. Renteria. You have to admit it's a curious coincidence," Officer Keating replied, almost smugly.

I still hadn't said a word since Will arrived. Will looked over at me and whispered.

"You can tell them you didn't rent that room," he said.

"I didn't rent that room," I said obediently.

"Who did?" Detective Shaw piped in.

Will leaned over again, enjoying the drama.

"You can tell them you don't know," he whispered.

"I don't know who rented the room under the name of Keith Morgan at the Nashville Inn hotel," I said casually.

"How was the room paid for? I'm sure you were able to get a credit card number or something? And whoever checked in should have shown identification?" Will asked.

"Well, it seems it was paid in advance with a prepaid visa card," Officer Keating replied.

"I'm sure you reviewed all the video footage from the Nashville Inn. Did you find my client on any of that footage?" Will asked.

Officer Keating was getting agitated.

"No, we didn't," he replied.

"Then I still don't understand why we're here. You know my client wouldn't be stupid enough to do this, so what's your angle?" Will asked.

"If Mr. Morgan didn't reserve the room for someone to shoot Bob Yates, who would set it up to look like he did?" Detective Shaw said from her position at the door.

"That, Olivia, is why you're paid the big bucks." Will stood up when he said it.

"We're asking for Mr. Morgan's help," she said, while glaring at Will.

"My client said he doesn't know who did it. If he thinks

of anything that might help your case, we'll call you. I'm sure I have your number somewhere," Will said as he moved toward the door and motioned for me to follow.

"Hang on just a second. Can we talk in the hallway?" Detective Shaw grabbed Will's arm as he reached for the door.

"Sure, Olivia. Anything to help your case," Will said sarcastically. They left the room, leaving me sitting across from Officer Keating. Through the whole thing, he continued to sit calmly in his chair. This wasn't his first rodeo.

"I know you didn't do this, Mr. Morgan. But you see our problem, right?" He seemed to be playing the good cop part of the one-man routine now.

"Who checked into the room?" I asked in response.

"I can't tell you that. I suspect that's what they're talking about in the hallway. You'll find out soon if they are," he replied.

"Ok, then. Now, let's get to the actual evidence in the case. Someone wanted Bob Yates to hit the ball a long way to the right. They probably knew he golfed and could hit the ball a long way. I also understand he had a tendency to slice his drives. If it was me, though, I wouldn't trust that tendency. I'd want to make sure he hit a huge fade even if he nailed his swing. Has anyone checked to see if someone tampered with his driver?" I paused to assess his response.

He raised his eyebrows as if this was a new thought.

"Interesting idea. We have his gear, we can check that theory easy enough. But wouldn't he notice if someone tampered with his driver? I mean, I'd notice if someone drilled a hole in my driver and I only use it a few times a year," Officer Keating said.

"It's just a hunch. And you're right. It would have had

to be a professional modification. It wouldn't work if it was a hack job. Maybe just a shift of weight toward the toe, something like that. It wouldn't take a major adjustment to force the ball right like that, but it would have had to be invisible to Bob." I stopped and watched while Officer Keating wrote something down.

We only sat a few more minutes before the door opened again and Will motioned for me to leave with him.

"Let's go, Keith. I'll take you back to the hotel. We can come back if our friends here need more of our help," he said.

"They have a magazine and bullet of mine," I said as I stood up.

Officer Keating stood, reached into his pocket and pulled them out, handing them both to me reluctantly. I considered loading the P365 right there in front of them, but decided there was no need to provoke anyone. Instead, I just shoved them in my pocket and nodded. He nodded in return and stepped out of the way as we walked by.

It was 2 a.m. on Thursday morning when I left the police station.

Chapter Sixteen

Nashville, TN. Thursday

I followed Will out of the police station to the same parking lot where I had been escorted out of the police cruiser earlier. I found it strange that he could park back here, but I didn't mention it. He said nothing at all while we walked toward the back of the lot. I assumed we being recorded and also remained silent.

He didn't have to point to his car. I knew which one it was. There was a black Porsche 911 sitting by itself on the back row that might as well have had his name on it.

I walked to the passenger door and heard the door unlock as we got close to the car. He must have known how obvious the car was in this setting, because he still didn't say anything.

In fact, he didn't speak until we were out of the parking lot and halfway down the block.

"Paul sends his greetings," he finally said.

"Nice. Greetings to Paul," I said while nodding my head.

"And I'm Will Renteria. Nice to meet you," he said with a smile while sticking out his hand.

I shook his hand while we drove away from the station.

"I suppose you know who I am," I replied.

"Yeah, I suppose I do. Paul gave me a brain dump when he called. You're quite a name with The Association. I'm just glad to help you out in even a small way. I apologize for the attitude back there. It's part of the game," he said.

"I get it," I replied.

"Although I must say, it was a little weird that someone got a room with your name. Did you know about that?"

"No, did Paul?"

"No, he didn't mention it. We'll have to look into that one. But the really interesting part came out during my conversation with Olivia in the hallway," he began.

"Olivia? You two know each other?" I interject, trying to fulfill my curiosity.

"Yeah, but only from work. Nashville isn't that big, so we know most everyone. She's good, so she plays the game. For a bit, anyway."

"Ok, so what'd she share that was so interesting?" I asked.

"Well, it appears they do know who checked into the room that had been reserved under the name of Keith Morgan," he said with a bit of a dramatic pause.

"Oh yeah? Who was it?" I felt obliged to ask.

"Does the name Doris Yates ring a bell?" he asked.

"That wouldn't be Mrs. Bob Yates, would it?" I replied with my own question.

"It would, in fact, be Mrs. Bob Yates," he said.

"You're telling me Bob's wife was in the hotel where the police believe the shooter was? And that she was in a room that was reserved under my name?" I ask it as a question, but it's really just clarifying my own thoughts.

"Yeah. Weird, huh? It seems someone was trying to make a statement. Unless, of course, Doris Yates is a sharpshooter. Which I doubt," Will said.

"It seems they have talked to lots of the other event participants to see how Bob was behaving this week, but so far they haven't turned up as much as you have. I didn't volunteer what you've uncovered. They seem to know Bob Yates drank too much, but that's about it. Paul would like you to keep digging. The Association thinks one of the threads you're chasing may be a hot one." Will looked at me when he said it.

"Interesting," was all I could think to say.

"Yeah. Interesting is right," Will said.

"Did the cameras at the Nashville Inn see Doris coming and going? Is she really here?" I asked.

"They're still going through the footage. It wasn't well organized and there are hours and hours of it. I suspect we'll know by daylight who was in the room," he said.

We sat in silence for a few more minutes before a new thought crossed my mind.

"Do we know the caliber that was used to kill Bob Yates?" I asked.

"I didn't ask that question. Why?" Will replied.

"I'm just curious whether it was a common hunting rifle or something different. It made quite a sizable wound," I said.

Will shook his head for a moment. Then more silence.

"So, how did you get engaged with The Association? Are you on retainer or something? Paul got to you awfully quick," I finally said to break the silence.

"They're good people. This is the second time I've

worked with them in the last five years or so, and Paul was the gatekeeper then, too. It seems he still has that role. After the last gig, I know to drop what I'm doing when he calls." Will said in a suddenly solemn tone. I didn't ask what happened or why the change in demeanor.

He told me anyway.

"You're an associate, not just a fixer?" he asked.

"Yeah," I nodded.

"Then you know they get involved with some heavy situations. My last involvement with them was drug related. They found a cartel running right through Nashville. I was the conduit to get their findings to the police. It worked, but it wasn't easy. Those ruthless, spineless cartel thugs took out an exemplary officer. And a friend." He stopped there, clearly too emotional to continue.

"Sorry to hear that," was my unfulfilling response.

"But it was the right thing to do, and it cleared the streets of some terrible people." He recovered quickly and nodded as he drove.

"I don't always know what I'm after until I get into these things. At times, I think Paul keeps some details back to let me find out for myself. Other times, I'm convinced The Association has a lead but no actual intelligence. And I become the intelligence gatherer," I said.

"Is that what's going on here? Paul said he sent you here. Did he not tell you why?" Will asked. He seemed curious about how this whole thing worked.

"I guess it's complicated. They sent me here for a reason. The reason, however, was to get insight into some supply chain productivity and expense irregularities with Atlantis. Bob Yates would have been the best person to talk to about it. I maneuvered to get assigned to his foursome for the golf outing. Then this happened. I'd like to think they're not related, but I also don't believe in more than one coincidence at a time. Bob's murder was one. My name on the hotel room registration was two. I hope someone isn't sending The Association a message."

That thought had been in the back of my mind since I heard the story from the police back at the station. Will didn't have answers for that one. He said he'd look into it, but I'd have to ask Paul to get the real story.

Did someone know The Association had sent me to Nashville?

Chapter Seventeen

Zapata, TX. Wednesday

Javi got up the next morning intent on telling mama about his concerns with the warehouse. He hopped out of bed and got dressed just like every morning, and headed to the kitchen. Mama was already up and having breakfast with her friends.

"Hey mama, can I talk to you for a minute?" He tried to interrupt quietly, but Maria didn't make it easy.

"Here he is! My little warehouse genius," she said to anyone within a hundred yards.

Javi leaned in to ask again.

"Can we talk for a minute?" He was more insistent this time.

Maria understood and nodded. She excused herself and followed Javi to their room. After the door closed, Javi's smile faded.

"Mama, I think something is wrong at that warehouse," he started. He saw her demeanor shift when he said it.

"What do you mean?" She asked him with her eyes lowered to the floor. Why wasn't she looking at him?

"Gus says people disappear from there. I saw my boss get taken away on a cart for having drugs, and Gus says I won't see him again. Mama, they take people away for breaking the rules and nobody knows where they go. They don't go back to Mexico. They don't go home. Nobody knows. It scares me, mama." Javi stopped when he felt his cheeks burn and tears forming in his eyes. He didn't want mama to see him like this.

She paused for a second, looking at the floor, then raised her eyes to his. He saw concern and compassion, but he also saw resilience. At that moment, he knew she wouldn't let him quit.

"Listen, Javier. This is a huge company. They have lots of power. They give Mexicans good jobs and good opportunities. If you have to follow the rules to get them, that's just what you'll have to do. I want the best for you and Amelia here in America, but sometimes you've got to fight for it. Don't listen to Gus anymore. He doesn't know what he's talking about. Just work hard, do what they tell you, and things will work out," she said with a voice that became more stern the longer she talked.

He thought about telling her what he knew about her friend Bob, but he didn't. She had made her point and now he'd have to figure out how to survive the warehouse on his own.

"Ok, mama," he said.

She pulled him in for a hug.

"I'm proud of you, Javier. Your father would have been proud, too. You're a good boy growing into a good man." She squeezed him one more time. She always brought up Javi's father when she was trying to make her point. He didn't know his father, so the points weren't as impactful as she thought, but he knew it was intended as a compliment.

"Thanks, mama," he said.

The rest of the day went like normal. Javi went to school, took the bus home, grabbed a quick meal in the kitchen and got back out to the gate at 4:45.

He wanted to talk to Gus about his mama's friend, but he didn't know exactly how to do it.

At 4:55, just a few minutes before the bus was to arrive, Gus walked up to the gate where Javi was standing. They were the only two waiting for the bus today.

"Hey," Javi said as Gus walked up.

"Hey," Gus replied. He didn't look like he wanted to talk. Javi didn't care. He had to see what else Gus knew about the warehouse.

"I've been thinking about Raul and what you said," Javi began.

"Who's Raul," Gus replied. Javi realized he hadn't told Gus the name of his boss yesterday.

"That was my boss. The guy they took away yesterday," he replied.

"Oh." Gus dropped his eyes when Javi explained.

"Where do they take people who break the rules?" Javi asked, trying to get more information from Gus than he got yesterday.

"Nobody knows for sure." Gus kept his eyes down while he answered. Javi felt he knew more than he was saying.

"But where do you think they're taking them?" Javi was going to be persistent today.

"Look, Javi. I don't know. And even if I did, I probably wouldn't tell you. It's like I told you the first day. You just have to follow the rules and you'll be ok," he said, looking up to stare Javi in the eyes.

"Is it only people who break the rules who are taken?" Javi asked. He had been worried about that.

Before Gus could answer, the bus came over the horizon and another kid walked up to join them at the gate. Javi hadn't seen the kid around the neighborhood, but given his size, it appeared he was even younger than Javi.

"Hey," Javi said as the kid walked up. His eyes were wide, and he looked scared.

"Hi. Is this the bus to the warehouse?" The kid's voice was shaky as he asked. Javi guessed he was probably thirteen, but looked even younger with his slight build.

"This is the spot," Javi said. Gus just looked at the two of them without saying anything.

The kid said nothing else and Javi didn't push him. He decided he could give him the 'follow the rules' speech later if Gus didn't do it.

They rode the bus to the warehouse just like the last two days. Everyone was quiet and kept their eyes forward, except the new kid. His eyes were wide open as he watched the bus pull through the high double-fenced perimeter and into the facility.

Armando caught the new kid just as he had caught Javi on his first day. Javi assumed he'd be taken to his station and put to work. As he was walking to his station, though, Javi noticed the new kid being driven on a cart past the larger building and back to the private building with the extra fence. Javi decided the kid must have a special job to get to work back there.

Javi made a mental note to ask Gus about that later.

Chapter Eighteen

Nashville, TN. Thursday

By the time Will got me got back to the Grand Marquis, it was nearly 2:30 a.m. I knew I had to meet Jen at 7 a.m. for breakfast, so I went straight to bed hoping to get a few hours' sleep. It took my military sleeping techniques to get my thoughts clear and drift off.

I had to block out all the concerns about my name being on the hotel registration, about the insane life Bob Yates was living, and about his wife being in the hotel where Bob's shooter had been. Instead, I concentrated on stillness, darkness, blackness, weightlessness, and nothing else.

Then my alarm went off.

I showered, shaved, and got dressed after about three and a half hours of sleep. I should have gotten up earlier to hit the gym, but it wasn't happening.

When I got to the restaurant area next to the bar I was at with Darren and Mo the night before, Jen was already there with coffee. There was a huge buffet, but she had waited to get food until I arrived. As a pleasant surprise, she had coffee for me, too.

The unintentional smile came over me when I saw her, and my lack of sleep became an afterthought. For about one second.

"Whoa, Keith, what happened to you?" She didn't pull punches with me. I didn't even have time for a greeting.

"Sorry, I had a long night. The police had lots of questions about the Bob Yates shooting," I said as I sat down.

"No, I mean the bruise on your forehead." She pushed my hair out of the way to look at the bump I had gotten during my 'conversation' with the two thugs that were following Bob Yates. I had forgotten about it.

"Oh, that. Well, that's a longer story. Maybe we should get breakfast first," I said, trying not to get directly into the bizarre events that had transpired since yesterday afternoon.

"Ok, sure," she said reluctantly.

We made our way through the buffet and were back at our table in just a few minutes. I was hoping Jen would forget our topic from earlier. She didn't.

"So, tell me about the bruise on your forehead," she said the second we were settled.

I took a bite of my scrambled eggs, washed it down with a gulp of coffee, and filled Jen in on the last eighteen hours of my life. I left out the details related to The Association, as she, like most people, had no idea that organization existed. But I told her a lot.

Knowing Jen has a military background, I didn't leave out any of the details regarding Bob Yates' murder, the stories about his life, the two thugs who cornered me near the atrium bar, and the visit to the police station. I didn't tell her about the hotel room in my name. That could wait until I had verified some details.

Jen sat quietly and took it all in. Only when I was finished did she start with her questions.

"You saw Bob Yates on the golf course after he was shot? What did you think?" She started a generic question, but I knew what she was getting at.

"It was professional. He was hit center mass. I should say, dead center mass. It couldn't have been a much better shot. It was a high caliber round, looked bigger than a 5.56MM but not sure how much bigger. The police haven't shared any ballistics and I couldn't really look around too much," I replied.

"How'd they know he'd be over there? Was that the only spot they could get to him?" She was thinking the same way I had.

"That's a good question that I haven't quite gotten answered yet. The guys said he was known for his slice off the tee, but I wouldn't trust that. I told Officer Keating to check out his driver. To look for any tampering. We'll see what he comes up with. But if he was looking for his ball in the water, he would have been a sitting duck. A good sniper would have no problem making that shot from three hundred yards."

"Was that the distance?" She asked.

"More or less, yeah."

"Only one shot?"

"Apparently."

"Where do you think it came from?"

"I think the police have that right. If it was me, I'd hole up in the Nashville Inn and take the shot from inside the room. With a good can on the rifle, nobody would hear the shot. Then I'd pack up and get out before anyone knew any better," I replied.

"But you'd have to be sneaky. They have cameras everywhere these days," Jan said.

"Yeah, they do. I'm guessing some sort of cover, but haven't gotten to the hotel to investigate that yet. I'm planning to get there after breakfast, actually." I smiled and took another bite as Jen let all the details sink in.

"Why are you going there? Wouldn't the police get it checked out and let you know what they find?" I realized I made a bit of a tactical mistake by revealing that little part of my plan.

"I guess I'm just overly curious now, having seen what happened to Bob. You're right about the police checking it out. Darren and Mo said they were already there last night. But if I can find something that might help the police, I'm glad to do it." I stopped there and hoped it was enough of an explanation. It was, at least for the moment.

"So, the two thugs were just wondering why you were sniffing around about Bob Yates? They were just watching out for the CFO's 'project' in Texas?" She took a few seconds to formulate that one.

"Yeah, it seems they were just making sure no details got out. Sort of makes you wonder what's going on in Texas, doesn't it," I said, letting my internal thoughts bubble to the surface.

"Sure does. And are you able to live without knowing what that is?" Jen asked, as though she knew the answer.

"I'm not sure," I said, trying to make it sound truthful.

In reality, I was sure about the answer. I couldn't let it go.

We ate the rest of our breakfast talking about other things. After we were done, we walked out of the restaurant area and to the elevator. When the door opened for Jen's floor, she reached over and put her arms around my neck and put her face within about an inch of mine.

"I know you can't let this go. Just promise me you'll be careful," she said.

Her emotions startled me, but was able to nod in response. This was a new side of her I hadn't seen before.

Then she gave me a warm, long kiss before looking deep into my eyes and stepping out of the elevator. It wasn't the first time we had kissed. In fact, it was the twelfth, if anyone was counting. But this one had a deeper meaning behind it that I could see in her eyes. I don't know what she expected me to get into after our breakfast, but she was concerned.

Still, she was right about my intentions. I had to find out what project in Texas had been so important that the CFO was following Bob Yates around Nashville.

Chapter Nineteen

Nashville, TN. Thursday

When I got back to my room, it was almost 8:00 a.m., which meant it was about 7:00 a.m. in Woodland Park. I determined the kids should be up and getting ready for school, so I called Jamie for my morning chat.

They were indeed getting ready, and I heard lots of activity in the background during our five-minute call. After talking to Jamie, Kyle and Judy, I ended the call and headed to the rideshare area in front of the Grand Marquis.

I was heading to the Nashville Inn to see what my name was doing on one of their reservations.

During the ten-minute ride, I called Paul again to give him the latest update. These Uber calls were always risky for me, as I knew many drivers record their passengers. I also assumed none of them cared about the discussion so much as they cared about their safety. With that thought in the back of my mind, I put the phone to my ear.

"Hey Keith. How's life in Music City?" Paul answered immediately.

"Well, it's still interesting," I replied.

"Uh-oh. What's happening now? More Bob Yates stuff?" Paul asked.

"Well, sort of. But first, I need to thank you for sending Will Renteria to the police station. He got things moving in the right direction immediately. I'd probably still be there if he hadn't shown up, so thank you." I paused to get his response.

"Sure thing, Keith. Sorry you're having to deal with the locals down there. That was strange. Will also called me on his way back last night about your name being on a reservation at the Nashville Inn. He also mentioned Doris Yates was staying there? We're looking into that, but I don't see any way that could have happened. We'll keep digging, but that one has us stumped," Paul said.

"Wow. Well, I suppose that takes away the reason for my call, then. I was going to talk to you about that one. I'm headed to the Nashville Inn now to find out what's going on with that," I said.

"I suppose I'd do the same thing, but I feel obligated to ask you to be careful, Keith. We don't yet know what you're dealing with out there," Paul said.

"That's the second time I've heard that this morning," I said, immediately regretting it.

"What do you mean, it's the second time?"

"I had breakfast with Jennifer Ellis and let her know about Bob's story. She told me the same thing," I explained.

"She has good instincts. Did you tell her everything?" Paul asked cautiously.

"No, not everything. She knows about Bob Yates but not about the registration at the Nashville Inn."

He didn't ask if she knew about The Association. That topic wasn't even on the table, and Paul knew that.

"Ok. You seem to trust her. Is she doing ok after that Willow Creek fiasco?" Paul was asking about my last assignment, where Jennifer was brought into an unfortunate gunfight near where we live in Colorado.

"Yeah, she seems to be doing fine," I sighed. Apparently, the sigh was a little too obvious.

"You care about her. I hear it in your voice. Glad she's doing well." Paul stopped short of asking any more questions about Jen. I didn't know what he'd think if he knew we'd gotten close over the last few months.

"I'm at the hotel now, so I'll let you know what I find." I ended the call and got out of the black Tesla Model 3 at the entrance to the Nashville Inn.

Before I could take a step toward the door, my phone buzzed in my pocket. It was a local number I didn't recognize.

"This is Keith," I answered.

"Mr. Morgan, this is Detective Shaw. Do you have a minute?"

"Sure. What's up?" I stepped to the side of the front door of the hotel and took a seat on a bench in the landscaping.

"Officer Keating tells me you asked us to look at Mr. Yates' golf club last night. Which we did. And I wanted you to know you were right. Someone had shifted the weight inside the head of his driver to the toe. He had no chance of hitting a straight drive. That ball was going right no matter what he did."

"Wow. Even a blind dog finds a bone sometimes, I guess." I have no idea how that old saying popped into my head.

"HA! I haven't heard that one in a long time," she said.

"But I also wanted to let you know about how it was done. The job was very professional. You would never see it was tampered with by just looking. We had to take it apart to see it. Whoever did this took great care to set this hit up. I wanted to let you know in case you're digging into your name being on that room. Be careful." She paused after that.

And that was the third time today I had been warned to be careful.

"That's interesting. And thanks for calling. As luck would have it, I'm just heading into the Nashville Inn to see about 'my reservation' as we speak. You're right, I'm digging into that. I have to find out what that's about," I said.

"Yeah, I get it. Just don't do anything without us. We've been watching that place already, so our guys will probably see you if they haven't already. I get the sense we're not dealing with a group of kids here," she said with a sigh.

"Me neither, me neither," I said as we ended the call.

The Nashville Inn reminded me of a Residence Inn. It had a sprawling layout with multiple buildings scattered across several acres. It was sort of the opposite of the Grand Marquis, which had everything under one humongous roof.

I made my way to the front desk and tried the easiest way I knew to get into a room with my name on it.

"Hi. I'm Keith Morgan and I've just arrived to join my wife. Can I please get a key to my room?" I smiled and held out my driver's license.

"Sure, Mr. Morgan," the front desk receptionist said after looking at my license.

"Let's see, you're in room 262 across the street. Your, uh, wife has already checked in." She paused on the word 'wife' as she was clearly looking at the name on the guest list. While the registration had my name, Doris Yates would have needed to show an ID to get a key for herself. Apparently, she told them she was my wife. The receptionist had seen enough of these situations to conclude Doris wasn't likely my wife.

In thirty seconds, I had a key to room 262 and walked out of the hotel office. When I walked across the small parking area to the next building, I took a quick scan around to see if I could spot any police presence watching the building. It wasn't hard to find them.

There were two cars, one at each end of the building, facing the doors. They had parked in spaces intended for other buildings in the complex, but clearly they were watching the building where room 262 was. And they were watching me. I slowed down, wondering if my phone was going to start buzzing.

It did.

"This is Keith," I answered before I stepped into the building.

"What do you think you're doing? We've been watching this place all night!" It was Officer Keating.

"I'm going to my hotel room," I said casually.

"Oh brother. Well, at least let me come with you. I don't want you getting shot while we sit and watch," he said reluctantly. I was probably giving him a reason to get out of his car, so I'm guessing he didn't mind as much as he was letting on.

I paused at the door bnd saw Officer Keating step out of the car to the far left. He looked pretty chipper to me, having worked through most of the night and being back at it this morning. Then again, I was up most of the night, too, and I felt pretty spry.

"Good morning, Officer Keating," I said with a bit of sarcasm.

"Yeah." He clearly wasn't in the mood to chat.

"I guess this gives us a perfectly legitimate reason to go in, right?" I asked, knowing the answer.

"Sort of. It's not really breaking in if they gave you a key," he said.

"And they did," I responded.

"Ok, then. Let's go." Officer Keating put his hand on his weapon and motioned for me to unlock the front door.

The front door opened to a hallway with stairs on the left side. Room 262 was upstairs, so we casually ascended the stairs to the top and read the signs pointing right and left. Rooms 241 through 280 were to the right, so that's the direction we went.

"Did you see anyone coming or going?" I asked as we walked.

"No movement at all," Officer Keating replied.

That was interesting.

After navigating around to the back of the building by taking two lefts, we came to a room that I determined probably faced the Grand Marquis golf course. Which, of course, made sense.

Officer Keating stepped back and drew his weapon, keeping it pointed to the ground.

"Oh, come on. Do you really think Doris Yates is holed up in here waiting to ambush us?" I asked.

"Open the door, Mr. Morgan. I'm not taking any chances," he said.

I held the key card against the pad on the door and heard it unlock. Adrenaline was pumping as I turned the knob and opened the door. As I expected, Doris Yates was not in the room waiting to ambush us. In fact, she wasn't in the room at all.

The only people in the room were no longer alive, were laying spread-eagle on the beds completely naked, and were covered with blood.

The nose and arm injuries I had given them the day before were no longer a concern.

Chapter Twenty

Nashville, TN. Thursday

I stopped in my tracks when I saw the two bodies laying in the king size bed of room 262 at the Nashville Inn. My first thought was how lucky I was that Officer Keating was there with me, but that luck didn't last long.

"What is going on here?" Officer Keating asked rhetorically after we both spent several seconds gasping at the sight. At least I thought it was a rhetorical question. When I looked over at him, though, he seemed to be waiting for me to answer.

"Hey, I know as much as you do about this," I said, not being completely honest. Officer Keating didn't know I had met these two before.

"Ok, Mr. Morgan. Let's back out of here without touching a thing. We'll get the crime scene people in here right away. What in God's name have you gotten into?" That time, it was a rhetorical question.

"You said you guys were watching?" I asked as we backed out of the room.

"We were. Been here since about ten last night," he said. That meant they were dumped here soon after I had seen them at the Grand Marquis.

"There has to be some video footage of these two getting hauled in here. It's difficult to conceal a body, much less two. And I don't see any signs of the killings being done here. The rooms are otherwise clean, which means they didn't come in here alive." I was going over the crime scene in my head, but talking out loud. I stopped before I went any further. Officer Keating and the crime scene detective could figure this stuff out themselves.

While I didn't get to stay and investigate the room, I saw enough to get the message. The two thugs who had followed me last night had been executed cartel-style, with their bodies mutilated. The fact that they were laid out this way was intended to send a message to someone. Was it me?

The most vivid part of the message was the inscription of the letters 'CA' carved into the chest of both men. Well, that and their severed heads sitting on their pillows just above their bodies.

I wasn't sure who the message was for, but I couldn't imagine someone was trying to send me a message with this horrific display. It just didn't make sense. I'd read about this type of thing happening in Mexico, but I'd certainly never seen it here in the U.S..

"Hey, Officer Keating," I said as we stood in the hall-way. He had just ended a call for backup and crime scene support.

"When you guys were watching, you never saw Doris Yates go in and out of the hotel?" I asked.

"No, we did not. As I mentioned, we so no activity at this room. She was on the footage yesterday and the day before, but we haven't seen hide nor hair of her since we've been watching," he said.

"Hmmm. Makes you wonder if she's still alive, huh?" I said, again vocalizing my thoughts before I really thought about it.

"Yeah, I guess it does," he said. Then he switched topics.

"Did you recognize those two?"

"No, not that I could tell. I may have seen them at the event. It's hard to be sure, given their condition," I replied.

We both stood there quietly, pondering things for a few seconds.

"I'm going to step out for a minute. This is a lot to take in," I finally said.

"Yeah, ok. Just don't go far. We'll have to get reports on all this before you leave this morning. This doesn't happen every day in Nashville." Officer Keating was shaking his head as he made the statement.

After walking back outside to get some fresh air and give my version of the report to the officers, I stepped away to place a call to Paul. Someone had just dramatically increased the stakes of the Bob Yates murder and had wrapped me into it. I had told the cops I had seen the two men around the event this week, but stopped short of sharing my encounter. I was in enough hot water already with my name on the reservation to this room!

"Hey, Keith. What'd you find?" Paul asked when he accepted the call.

"You're probably not going to believe this," I started.

"Uh-oh. More unbelievable stories about the life of Bob Yates?"

"Not really. Things have taken a bit of a turn. First off, the local PD was watching the Nashville Inn when I got here, so the officer I had met on the golf course went in with me. I went to the desk to ask for a key to 'my room' and got it with no problem. It was, after all, my room."

"Mmmhmm." Paul was listening and typing in the background.

"We knocked on the door, but nobody answered. When I opened it with my key, we walked into a nightmare scene. There was no Doris Yates, but there were two bodies that had been brutally executed. They were shot through the head at close range with a small caliber, but the heads were then severed and placed on the pillows. Their naked bodies were spread on the beds with clear signs of abuse, and with the letters 'CA' carved into their chests. I mean, it looked like Mexican drug cartel stuff to me." I stopped to get Paul's take on the scene.

"Yeah, it sounds like something from a cartel. Or, at least from a cartel movie," Paul said.

"But that's not the worst part. The two guys were the same two who had followed me at the Grand Marquis last night. Nobody knows about that except you, but it was them," I said with a sigh.

"Hmmm. So, you think the message was to you? And done in the room where your name is on the registration. This doesn't sound good. We've still not found any reason for someone to be targeting you, Keith. But like I said earlier, you have got to be careful!" Paul said with more emotion than I'd ever heard from him.

"Yeah, I'm seeing that," I said with another deep sigh.

"I'll look for the relevance of 'CA' being carved in their chest. You're right about the Mexican cartels doing that kind of stuff, but why would they be there in Nashville?"

"I don't know. It definitely puts a new angle on this whole thing," I said.

"Yeah, it does. Help the locals where you can. We'll need them on this. But, as always, keep your eyes open for the killers and the motive. We're missing something on this. Something big. It doesn't seem like someone getting revenge for an affair anymore." Paul stated the obvious gap in our case so far.

There was a shuffling sound on the phone, and I could hear Paul moving around in the background.

"Hey, just a second," he said.

"Ok," I replied, a little confused.

"Oh, brother," he said a moment later, adding to my confusion.

"Are you near a television?" He asked.

"No. Why?"

"It seems Chris Valentine and his wife have taken to the airwaves to talk about how awful the death of Bob Yates was. They're even offering a reward," he said.

He got quiet again, clearly watching something on the news.

"Check it out when you get a minute. Chris is in rare form, with his wife standing right there with him. He's talking about Bob very kindly, while his wife cries. It's actually pretty good acting, if that's what it is."

"Yeah, I saw a brief clip at the bar. I'll have to pick the rest of it up online later," I said. I wasn't really in the mood to watch the news right now. It almost seemed suspicious that Chris was already in front of the media about Bob's death. Especially since he was one of the people I had on my suspect list.

And if it wasn't Chris, we had to find out who was doing the killing and why.

Chapter Twenty-One

Zapata, TX. Wednesday

After working his shift mostly alone, Javi was eager to get to the bus to talk to Gus. He wanted to tell him about the kid from the bus ride in who got to work at the private warehouse in the back.

He waited in line like the other two days, got his fifteen dollars and headed to the bus. While he waited, he looked for the new kid who was on the bus earlier. He wasn't on the bus and Javi didn't see him waiting in line for his pay. But that wasn't all that surprising, as Javi also knew some workers stayed later — or even got off earlier than he did.

Gus got on the bus a few minutes later and sat a few rows ahead of Javi. He'd have to talk to him when they got off. He sat quietly on the ride home, as did everyone else on the bus.

When they got to the gate of his neighborhood, Javi and Gus were the only two to get off. Gus was walking away as the bus took off, but Javi stopped him.

"Hey, Gus. Did you see that kid on the bus this afternoon?" Javi said.

Gus stopped, turned around, and nodded.

"I saw him on a cart out to that private warehouse in the back. I thought we weren't allowed to go out there?" Javi asked.

"Some people can, but you have to be chosen," Gus replied, holding his eyes to the ground. He didn't seem excited for the new kid.

"How do you get chosen?" Javi was getting excited, thinking he might have an opportunity to work at the private place.

"I don't know. But you don't want to be chosen, I know that," Gus said with a sad voice.

"How do you know that? If that place is so private, they would only take the good workers there?" Javi said, trying to justify his own thoughts about the private warehouse.

"It's not like that. I know you don't want to go there because that's where they took my friend. After they caught him looking around, a couple of shirt guys came and took him on a cart. I watched them take him to the bright, private building in the back, then I never saw him again," Gus said, still looking at the ground.

Javi's excitement about the new kid quickly turned to fear.

"So, they took the new kid away? He'll never be back?" Javi asked.

"I don't know, Javi. Just do your work and follow the rules."

"But the new kid never had a chance to follow the rules. They took him straight there on his first day." Javi's sense of fear was growing as he thought about the new kid.

"Yeah, sometimes that happens. But mostly with the

younger kids without parents. He probably came from Mexico alone. Maybe they're finding him a family, I don't know," Gus said. Javi could tell by his tone he didn't believe they found the new kid a family.

"What do you think they're doing with all these people?" Javi asked, getting concerned about his own safety once again.

"I don't know, Javi. Just follow the rules. I keep telling you, just follow the rules." Gus finally looked up to emphasize that last point. Then he turned and walked home, leaving Javi standing at the gate alone.

He stood there for a good minute before deciding to walk home. He also decided he was going to stay up late tonight until mama got home to tell her about the warehouse. It was time she learned it wasn't as great out there as she had told Javi on Monday.

When Javi got back to the house, he made sure Amelia was safe in bed and he laid down. Tonight, though, he didn't go to sleep.

Shortly after 11 p.m. mama quietly opened the door and came in without making much of a sound. Javi would usually sleep right through her arrival, but this time he was awake.

"Mama, I need to talk to you," he whispered as she settled into her bed. He was trying to stay quiet to keep from waking Amelia.

"You should be asleep, Javier. What's wrong?" She clearly sensed something wasn't right.

"I need to talk to you about the warehouse. It's not a good place," Javi said, keeping his voice low.

"Let's go in the kitchen, but you need to be quiet," she said.

They quietly made their way out of their room and

down the hall to the kitchen, where they could have a little privacy. When they got there, another mother from the house was putting away some groceries. She finished, said goodnight, and scurried off to her room.

"What do you mean when you say it's not a good place?" Maria asked Javi.

"Mama, people disappear from there. The guys wearing the Atlantis shirts take people away and nobody knows where they go. The people don't come home. They don't go to Mexico. They don't go to jail. Nobody knows where they go." Javi was having trouble controlling his emotions as he talked and kept getting louder.

"Shhhhhh! Be quiet, Javier. Nobody can hear you talk like this!" Maria scolded Javi while he stood there looking shocked.

"What? But people..." Javi didn't have a chance to get another word out.

"Stop! Just stop, Javier. Atlantis has been very good to our people and this community. They are the only reason most of us are here and not in jail or sent back to Mexico. This whole neighborhood exists because of Atlantis. You can't be talking bad about them anymore. If someone was taken away, they must have done something bad," she said sternly.

Javi didn't like the way mama was looking at him, but his fear of the warehouse outweighed his fear of mama. He had to try again.

"But mama, there was a new kid..."

She cut him off again.

"I said stop, Javier! No more. This conversation is over. You will go to the warehouse and do your job as they ask you to do it. If you do, you will get paid more and more, and you can have a good life here. If you don't..." Her voice trailed off as she stopped.

Maria looked at the floor and paused. Tears welled up in her eyes as she thought about the other mothers she'd seen crying for their lost children. She knew there were risks with Javi working at the warehouse, but the reward was even higher. Wasn't it?

"I'm sorry, mama," Javi said as he saw her change in demeanor.

"I didn't mean to make you cry. I just wanted you to know," he said.

"Javier, I'm proud of you. It is wise of you to watch out for yourself. Just follow the rules and I'm sure you will be ok. Do you understand?" She leaned in and hugged him as she said it.

"Yes, mama, I understand," Javi said.

But he didn't really understand how mama could send him to a place like that. Javi felt trapped.

Chapter Twenty-Two

Nashville, TN. Thursday

The paperwork from the Nashville Inn took less time than I thought. Maybe that was because Officer Keating was with me, or maybe it was because we simply walked in and walked out. But either way, the course of my day was now changed.

I walked across the street to the QuikTrip convenience store to grab some coffee and call an Uber. As I was pouring my cup full, my phone began buzzing in my pocket. I looked down and saw Paul's number, so I picked it up while trying to put the lid on my coffee with one hand.

"Hey Paul, I'm grabbing some coffee. What's up?" I said, as I answered.

"A couple things. Why don't you pay and call me back," Paul said.

"Sure. Two minutes," I said as I ended the call.

I paid for my coffee and walked outside and stood beside the building while I called Paul back. From my vantage point, I could see all the emergency vehicles at the Nashville Inn across the street. It was a chaotic scene.

"Hey Paul, sorry about that," I said as he answered.

"No worries. Listen, Keith. We have still found nothing at all that should link you to all this stuff, so we're still not sure how your name is looped into this. What I have gotten, however, is more detail on what The Association is concerned about with Atlantis," he said.

"Great. That will be a pleasant distraction," I replied.

"Yeah, I thought it might. So, this is what I know. Some of our associates have access to data that you and I do not, as you have seen before. This data, it seems, has shown that the Atlantis warehouse outside Zapata, Texas, has a strangely low volume of product being distributed outside the local area. They take in aluminum from Mexico, then fabricate parts for distribution. They have the expected number of trucks going in and out. They have a huge warehouse facility. And they have an abnormally large number of employees, apparently," he said.

"So, what's the problem, then? That all sounds normal," I reply as I sip my coffee.

"Well, the strange part is the lack of product shipping out. They do billions of dollars of business for the big three automotive companies in the U.S., along with a fair amount of international business. That Zapata plant, however, ships most of their product regionally. And some of it even ships to other corporations that have nothing to do with automotive," he said.

"They could supply other parts, couldn't they? Like maybe tractors, boats, other stuff?" I asked.

"Yeah, they could. But there is one more anomaly. The biggest buyers are other companies owned by relatives of Chris Valentine, the CFO. It sort of looks like he has his hand in both pockets, if you know what I mean. It just doesn't smell right." Paul paused as if he had shared what he knew about that topic.

"I wonder if this has anything to do with the 'project' those thugs were worried about. They sure didn't want Bob Yates talking about it. Maybe I should talk to Mr. Valentine about it," I said.

"Maybe. Or maybe you could just go down there and look for yourself?" Paul said. I sensed he was talking about a plan that was already in motion.

"You want me to go to Zapata, Texas? Won't that take lots of time away from my research here? It doesn't sound like an easy place to get to." I suspected there was no direct flight from Nashville to the Mexican border.

"Normally, you'd be correct. But given the circumstances, I think we can get you there in just a couple of hours," Paul said. I suppose it shouldn't have surprised me to find out he had access to private air travel.

"It would be nice to escape the chaos here for a while. Sure, I'll go. Set it up," I said.

"It's already set up," Paul said. He knew me well enough to know I'd accept the challenge.

"Of course it is," I chuckled.

"There's one more thing, Keith. After you told me about the 'friend' of Bob Yates in Texas, I was able to get some phone records. I'll text you the number of a woman Bob had been calling down there. There aren't a ton of calls, but it's the only number we see down there that wasn't tied to Atlantis. The phone is registered to Maria Sanchez, and that's all I know. There's an address, but it's a local diner. That's another lead you can track down while you're there."

This day was going to be much different from what I thought when I woke up this morning.

"Sure. Send me what you have. How long do I have to get to the flight?" I asked.

"They can take off when you get there. I told them you'd need an hour or so. It's about twenty minutes from the Grand Marquis so you can go freshen up first. I wouldn't plan to stay long. One night should be enough," Paul said.

"Got it. Thanks Paul," I said as we disconnected the call.

I pulled up the Uber app to get a ride back to the Grand Marquis and continued to watch the scene across the street at the Nashville Inn. The chaos was still visible, but they had removed two body bags from the hotel. The rest of the vehicles, flashing lights, and first responders remained.

A red Toyota Prius showed up in about two minutes with an Uber light in the window, and I got in to head back to my room. I had to pack for Texas. On the way, I got a list of information from Paul to guide the rest of my day.

The first text included an address for a local airport and the name of a car service that would pick me up. I didn't need an Uber for that trip.

The second text included a phone number for Maria Sanchez.

The third text included an address for the Atlantis Automotive warehouse and distribution center in Zapata, Texas.

The last one said I'd have transportation provided when I arrived, and that I'd need to drive about thirty miles to get to Zapata. The message ended by wishing me luck.

After a quick pack of my overnight bag at the Grand Marquis, I headed out to the valet area, where my car was already waiting. I handed my bag to the driver and got into the black Mercedes S-Class for a comfortable ride to the airfield, wherever it might be.

During the ride, I called Jen to let her know what was going on.

"Hey, you missed my session," she said as she answered my call.

"Yeah, sorry about that. I had some challenges at the Nashville Inn. I'll fill you in on that later. But I wanted you to know I'm taking a quick trip to Texas to research Bob Yates' friend down there. I'll be back tomorrow, but won't be there for dinner tonight," I said.

I had planned to take Jen out tonight for dinner and music at a club on Broadway.

There was a brief pause, then she recovered.

"Wow, that was quick! Are you able to get a flight?" She asked the obvious question for someone who didn't work with The Association.

"Yep, sure did," I said without getting into the details.

"Ok. You promised you'd be careful, so I'm going to hold you to that," she said as she regained her typical positive voice.

"Absolutely," I said.

We ended the call, and I sat back in the comfortable black leather.

In fifteen minutes, I was at a small airfield somewhere outside of Nashville. The driver carried my bag in from the parking area while I followed him. He led me through a simple checkpoint, where he mumbled something to a uniformed security agent and motioned for me to follow. I did, walking behind him into the hangar where there were several planes parked.

We walked past a couple of small prop planes and came to a black and gray Gulfstream G400 jet. I wasn't a jet expert, but I knew this would be a nice one. When I got inside, I wasn't disappointed. It had a common area, with four leather airline seats and a leather couch just behind them up against one side. There was a sink and kitchen area in the back with what looked like another room further to the back, behind an open sliding door.

I sat down in one of the seats and took a breath. The Mercedes driver put my bag in the closet near the front door and shook my hand before getting off the plane.

After he left, the pilot came back from the cockpit and pulled the stairs in. Apparently, nobody else was getting on the plane.

"Welcome aboard. You've got about two and a half hours if you'd like to get any rest," he said as he came back and shook my hand.

"Thanks," I said as I nodded in appreciation.

He didn't offer his name and didn't ask for mine and promptly headed into the cockpit.

In another five minutes, we were airborne and headed toward Texas.

Chapter Twenty-Three

Zapata, TX. Thursday

As is often the case when I fly, I fell asleep immediately after takeoff and didn't wake until our wheels hit the ground in Texas. I suppose it shouldn't have surprised me given my lack of sleep the night before and the luxury of the plane. I had already decided this is how travel was supposed to be!

I didn't know exactly where I was, so I grabbed my phone and looked up the location. As Paul had said, we were about twenty minutes northeast of Zapata. When I looked outside the plane, it appeared we were in the middle of nowhere. There were tumbleweeds, sage, and dust, but that's about it.

While we taxi'd to the hangar, I took the time to place a call to Maria Sanchez. I had decided earlier that I'd make her visit my first order of business in Zapata. Her phone went to voicemail, where I heard a pleasant voice offer a greeting in Spanish that I didn't quite understand. I hadn't studied Spanish since high school and hadn't considered how big of a handicap that might be this close to the border until this very moment. I hung up without leaving a message.

Paul had given me the address of the diner that Maria's cell phone was listed under, so I decided I'd go there first thing when I got off the plane.

I texted Paul to let him know I had landed and was going to drive into town. He responded with a thumbs-up.

When the plane stopped just outside the hangar, the pilot came back and opened the door to let me out.

"Thanks for flying with us. I hope it was a pleasant trip," he said as he handed me my bag and motioned for me to go down the stairs.

"It was great, thanks," I said in response as I descended to the concrete below. The heat, humidity and thick smell of dust was almost overwhelming. I'd been in hotter places, but this was surprising for April. It took a second to get my nose acclimated.

As I reached the ground, I noticed a man standing next to a blue Ford F-150 pickup truck off to the right near a gate that seemed to head outside the small airport. It was the only vehicle anywhere near our jet, so I took a chance and walked over.

"Are you Mr. Morgan?" The man asking the question was dressed in jeans and a t-shirt and was wearing a baseball cap and glasses. He looked like a normal guy from anywhere, USA.

"I am," I nodded.

"Here you go. You're filled up and ready for the trip. This should help you blend in around here. Just bring it back here when you're done and we'll take care of it," he said with a smile as he handed me the key fob.

"Thanks," I said. I had learned to never underestimate The Association. They always got me set up right.

After plugging my phone into the USB port with the cable that was already in the truck, I saw the alert for Apple CarPlay pop up on the screen. That was a nice surprise. I hit accept to start the app, entered the address into my phone and waited a second for the map to show up. Once it did, I set the XM dial to the Rock Nation station, shaking my head at the choice. I had to blame that selection on my dad. He played that stuff constantly while driving around Missouri when I was a kid, going to and from all my baseball games.

With the music turned up, I headed out into the vast nothingness of southern Texas toward a place I'd never been before. The map said I'd be there in twenty-seven minutes.

The first couple of miles were on a two-lane road with dust blowing over the sides. The passing of the truck churned up a dust cloud as I drove by, but there was nobody to drive through it in either direction. I was the only one on this road.

After two miles of lonesome driving, I came to a stop sign and a slightly larger two-lane road. They called it a highway down here. I made a left, which was my last turn before getting to Zapata fifteen minutes later.

The buildings in Zapata were mostly stucco and were older. There were a few modern ones mixed in, but the overall feel of the town was old. And a little run down. I passed four trailer parks between the airport and the town, and I suspect there were more in all directions to and from Zapata.

Did they still call them trailer parks? I knew many of the homes were now called manufactured homes, but a 'manufactured home park' didn't sound right. I even noticed one sign still referring to the place as a trailer community, although the sign could have been from the 1960s.

Viva La Fiesta was a small Mexican 'diner' near the middle of Zapata, and it was at the address Maria had given for her cell phone. I pulled into the gravel parking lot and parked next to one of the six pickup trucks already there. My vehicle definitely blended in.

It was 2 p.m. by the time I opened the door to the diner, and was once again struck by the path my day had taken. From breakfast at the Grand Marquis with Jen this morning to a late lunch at a Mexican diner near the edge of the country.

The Viva La Fiesta diner where Maria Sanchez worked was a clash of cultures. The tables and chairs could have been taken straight out of a fifties-style diner anywhere else in the country, with shiny silver legs and blue table tops and seat covers.

The smell and decorations, however, were clearly Mexican. There were colorful decorations on the walls, the tables, and hanging from the ceiling. I had to duck around a couple of hanging sombreros and pinatas to make my way inside.

There was no hostess, but there was a sign that said 'Please Seat Yourself,' so I did. I found a booth on the right side in the back where I could sit with my back to the wall and watch what was going on. I sat down and pulled the menu out of the colorfully decorated rack on the table. Then all at once I realized I was starving!

I watched as a waitress made her way over to my table. She smiled as she got there and asked if I wanted something to drink. Gratefully, she spoke English. I hoped I'd get lucky and Maria would be my waitress, but her name tag said

Carlita. I ordered a Diet Coke and opened the menu to the English section.

After looking through the menu and locking in on a couple of options, I watched the workers in the diner to see if I could find Maria. I noticed two waitresses, neither of which wore a name tag that said Maria. There were two men in the back cooking that I could see now and again through the window where the waitresses picked up their food. I assumed neither of them was named Maria.

I was beginning to think I had struck out when I saw another face pass by the window to the back. Her hair was up in a net and she had plastic gloves on. If Maria was really here, that had to be her.

Carlita returned and took my order for a chicken burrito and I once again was left to watch the diner. There were nine other patrons there with me, each engaged in their own conversations. Three tables of two and one table of three were already eating their food. It must have been the last of the lunch rush.

When Carlita brought out my burrito a few minutes later, I asked if Maria was working today. There was a brief look of fear in her eyes as she sized me up, and I realized I had made a mistake. I explained my question.

"A friend of mine from Atlantis sent me in here. He said the food was great, and he mentioned I should say hi to Maria." I made up the story but hoped it softened the impact of a stranger asking questions unexpectedly.

It worked. She smiled and loosened up.

"Oh, yes, she's here. I'll see if she can come out on her break," she said with a wink as she walked away.

I had no idea what I would say to Maria when she came out, but the first order of business was to devour the magnificent burrito sitting in front of me. It had more beans and rice than the ones I was used to back home at La Casita, my daughter's favorite Mexican restaurant back in Woodland Park. The flavor, however, was outstanding.

For the next few minutes, I lost track of time while the burrito took over my focus. In fact, I was so focused on my food, I didn't notice Maria standing next to my table until she spoke.

"Hallo," she said while I chewed away at my food.

Maria had taken off her gloves but still had her hair up in a net. She had a blue apron over a simple white dress that seemed too big for her thin frame. I'd guess she was in her early-to-mid thirties, and she looked tired but kind.

I stopped, swallowed hard, and stuck out my hand.

"Oh, hi. I'm sorry, I was enjoying your wonderful food," I said.

Her big brown eyes softened as she smiled and shook the tip of my fingers. Handshakes were not her thing.

"Bob Yates said I had to try the food here, and that I should stop and say hello," I said without thinking about what I'd say next.

Maria smiled brightly and sat down in the booth across the table from me. Bob's name was all the introduction I needed.

Chapter Twenty-Four

Zapata, TX. Thursday

I didn't know what to expect when Maria sat down. Did she speak English? What was her relationship with Bob Yates? Did she know about this death yesterday on the golf course?

All of those questions were answered in the first five minutes.

"How is Mr. Bob? I haven't seen him in two weeks. I want to thank him for getting Javier the job at the warehouse," she blurted out in broken English.

I decided it wasn't yet the time to talk about Bob's death, so I answered her questions as best I could.

"Well, Bob has been working hard. He's been helping make sure all the warehouses are running effectively." I tried to generalize my answers for now.

"And how is Javier enjoying his job at the warehouse?" I asked, trying to redirect the conversation.

"Oh, he's doing great. He loves to work there," she said,

but her eyes darted downward when she said it. Javier must not like his job. Now I had to find out who Javier was.

"What do they have him doing?" I asked.

"I don't know, but they let him work the fork machine already! That's very good for someone like my Javier, who is only fifteen!" She smiled as she talked about Javier. It was the smile of a proud parent. Javier was Maria's fifteen-year-old son.

"That's great. You should be proud. They must really like him if they let him operate the forklift," I said, assuming the 'fork machine' was really a forklift.

So, Bob Yates got Maria's son a job at Atlantis working in the warehouse. Her demeanor didn't seem to reveal a relationship beyond that. But Javier might have insight I could use to figure out what's going on at that facility.

"I'd love to get Javier's opinion on how we can make the job better. Would he be able to talk to me about it?" I asked.

She paused for a minute and took a cautious tone. Clearly she was apprehensive of letting Javier talk to someone she'd only just met, even if I knew Bob Yates.

"I can take you to him when I am done here?" Her statement was a question.

"Ok, that's great. Shall I pick you up when you're done? I don't want you to feel uncomfortable, but I'm glad to give you a ride," I offered.

Again, a cautious pause.

"Ok. I get done early tonight. Ten o'clock," she said. That didn't sound early to me.

"I'll be here. I drive that blue pickup truck out there," I said, pointing out the window toward my temporary wheels.

"Ok," she said meekly with a nod.

"And congratulations on Javier's great news," I said, trying to soften her feelings.

It worked a little, as she seemed to get a little more comfortable with the idea of riding home with a stranger.

We chatted a few more minutes while she was on break. During that time, I learned she was no longer married. Her husband was 'gone,' but I didn't ask her to clarify what that meant. She also had a daughter named Amelia, and she lived in a place she called Riverside, in a home with two other families. It was somewhere between the diner and the Atlantis warehouse where Javier was working.

The way she was talking, I still didn't get a sense there was anything romantic between her and Bob Yates. That was one motive I was starting to remove from the lengthy list of options.

After I finished my burrito and paid my bill, I did some scouting of the Zapata area. The Association had concerns about the product volume of the Atlantis plant, so I wanted to see what was going on there for myself. Plus, I had seven hours to kill before I had to pick up Maria to go talk to her son, Javier.

The drive out of town toward the trailer park and Atlantis plant took me past the exit where I came in from the airport. The drive was more north than northeast, but felt very similar. There was a two-lane highway heading north out of town, which ran along the Mexico border for several miles.

There was lots of dust, sagebrush and tumbleweeds, but not much else. The landscape looked flatter from the airplane, but down on the road there were mild hills every mile or two that kept you from seeing too far. After two of those hills outside Zapata, I came upon the Riverside manufactured home community where Maria lived with her kids. There was a bus dropping off kids as I drove by.

The area was clean and neat, as far as these communities go, but was still dusty and hot. There were no trees in the area that were big enough to provide shade, so the homes were all baking in the sun.

I slowed and looked around, but drove on.

After nine more low hills and mild valleys, my phone showed I was two miles away from the Atlantis warehouse and distribution center. I had noticed a fairly steady stream of trucks going the other way on the highway, so I knew I was getting close.

As the F-150 arrived at the top of the next hill, however, I was surprised by the magnitude of what I saw. There, in the distance, was a massive distribution facility. I'm not sure what I expected, but it certainly wasn't something this size. I slowed for a minute to take in the landscape that was unfolding before me.

The facility was completely surrounded by tall double fences with razor wire at the top. It reminded me of some of the military installations I had experienced in my past. I was too far to see, but I suspected there were cameras at regular intervals where guard stations incurred too much labor cost. Still, there were three guard stations visible around the perimeter.

The fence appeared to be at least a half-mile deep, and probably nearly that wide. Inside the fence was one massive warehouse and distribution center, and one less massive one in the back. The biggest one had trucks lined up all along the right side, which was the only side I could see. It was a busy place, with trucks moving in and out, and workers scurrying around all over the place. This place must employ most of Zapata and the surrounding area, from the size of it.

I drove past the facility and looked for a way around on the other side. I didn't see a road going behind the facility, but I was able to get a view from the left side of the large building. It looked very similar to the right side, with trucks and activity from each bay along the entire side of the building. From this side, I barely had sight of the other building to the back right of the huge fenced area.

After turning around a mile or so down the highway, I inched down the road from the far side, looking for any turnoff going behind the facility. I was about a half mile from the fence when I found one. It looked like a maintenance road, but with the four-wheel-drive capability of the F-150 I was driving, I didn't hesitate to turn in and see what I could find.

As I inched along the maintenance road around the facility, I turned off my running lights to be a little less conspicuous. With all the cameras along the fence, however, I was sure they'd find me if they wanted to. It was more likely, though, that they focused their security perimeter within the outer edge of the fence. It would be difficult to isolate potential threats this far beyond the fence. I used that likelihood to my advantage and drove on.

The volume of work at the plant struck me as interesting, given the inconsistencies The Association had found with the financial and volume records. I had never seen the other sites in the Atlantis network, but this one sure looked busy to me. If they weren't moving Atlantis products, they were certainly moving something else.

I found a slight ridge, pulled over next to some brush, and watched the site for an hour. The activity never ceased, especially with the smaller building near the back of the campus. That place had almost as many trucks as the rest of the facility, coming and going at a very high rate.

Sensing I had seen all I could see from the outside, I started the truck and got ready to leave. When I did, I noticed a large black SUV leaving the building in the back and heading toward the gate. It was out of place in the setting, so I took note and raced toward the road so I could follow the SUV.

I wasn't sure if it would lead anywhere, but my gut told me this was something. Plus, I still had a few more hours to kill.

Chapter Twenty-Five

Zapata, TX. Thursday

The SUV leaving the Atlantis distribution center turned right after coming out of the gate, putting them directly in my path as I exited the maintenance road to the highway. They were still a fair distance away, so I turned onto the highway well ahead of them and headed north.

Knowing there wasn't much to see between here and Laredo, I had to assume that's where they were headed. Going on that assumption, I pulled into a gas station fifteen minutes later in the small community of San Ygnacio to let the SUV get ahead of me.

As I sat in the truck pretending to search in the interior for something, I watched the vehicle pass by and got a better look at it. It was a late model black Lincoln Navigator, similar to one Oliver and Judy drive, with the back windows blacked out. The driver wore an Atlantis golf shirt and sunglasses, but I couldn't see anyone else in the car.

After the Navigator got a block or two past, I put the F-

150 back into gear and pulled in behind them. I stayed several cars behind and settled in for what I assumed would be another forty-five minute drive to Laredo.

I was almost correct.

Before we got to Laredo, we were going through a place called Rio Bravo. It seemed tiny, but there was one Exxon station on the route. The Navigator pulled into the Exxon station and parked next to another dark SUV. As I got closer, I saw the back door of the Navigator open and a well-dressed Hispanic man got out. He walked over to the other vehicle, which I now saw was a Mercedes G-class, and embraced another man who had stepped out of the Mercedes.

The two men seemed to be long-lost friends, and they continued to embrace and greet each other as the Navigator took off back toward Zapata. As I passed the station in the F-150, both gentlemen got into the back seat of the Mercedes and a driver quickly put the vehicle into gear and took off, heading toward Laredo.

I had a decision to make. It was now nearing 5:30 p.m. and I still had another point of interest to check out. Still, I was curious about what I had just witnessed. Given the time, I decided to turn around and head back to Zapata to get a better feel for the area.

Zapata is on the edge of a large reservoir created by the Falcon Dam. When I saw the name, I recalled seeing a bass fishing tournament on this body of water at some point. I didn't remember the details, but the name stuck with me. That also explained the high volume of bass boats behind pickup trucks everywhere around Zapata.

Where the Rio Grande river provides a natural boundary for miles and miles up to this point, the Falcon Reservoir is the boundary here at Zapata. The road across the dam, in fact, has a border checkpoint as you cross into or out of Mexico.

During the drive back to Zapata, I passed several Atlantis trucks coming toward the distribution center. Knowing the Mexican border was ahead, and remembering Paul had mentioned Atlantis received much of their aluminum from Mexico, I expected the trucks were crossing the border in this area.

After driving along the lake for some time, enjoying the evening view, I came to the checkpoint at the dam. There was a huge parking area outside the checkpoint, with limited traffic coming in and out at this time of the evening on a Thursday.

I pulled over in the parking area and stepped out of the car, pretending to take pictures of the sunset. As I did, I noticed several Atlantis trucks coming through the checkpoint from Mexico. Trying not to be obvious about what I was doing, I watched the border patrol agents look at each truck. They talked to the drivers, looked at paperwork the drivers provided, and opened the back for a physical inspection.

None of the inspections took very long, but every fourth one seemed to go much quicker. While I watched, I saw three different Atlantis trucks come through the checkpoint with absolutely no inspection whatsoever. The trucks looked very similar to the others, except for a cooling unit on top of the trailers. The agents would chat with the drivers and laugh while waving them through. Seeing this anomaly, I decided to follow one of those trucks to see if they went to the distribution center I had watched earlier.

It only took about twenty minutes to get my answer. All the trucks that I had seen come through the border checkpoint were headed to the Zapata distribution center. Each one came to the gate and was ushered through with minimal fanfare. I drove past the center and back to the maintenance road to see what happened to the trucks with the trailer coolers. The ones that didn't get the thorough border inspection.

The sun was setting on the horizon, so I shut off my headlights to be a little less visible. I didn't know if anyone was watching, but didn't want to take chances. Driving in the dark, it took a little longer to navigate the dirt road I had taken earlier in the day, but it was still only a few minutes before I was perched atop a small mound and could see the enormous facility lit up before me.

The first few trucks entered the facility and drove around to an empty bay and backed in. Then I noticed one bypass the huge building in the front and drive to the back, where the smaller, second warehouse facility was located. I hadn't been able to keep track of the truck counts, but I could see coolers on the trucks heading to the back building. I assumed those were the trucks that had avoided the inspection at the border.

What was so special about those trucks? Was this illegal merchandise? Was it drugs? Was there something else in them?

Rather than pull up to a bay, these trucks went all the way inside the building so they were no longer visible from my vantage point. If I was going to find out what was in those trucks, I had to get inside.

After watching the pattern for several more cycles, I determined these were indeed the same trucks that had avoided inspection. Something was up with those trucks.

The darkness also demonstrated another unusual aspect of the facility. The whole place was lit up like a top secret military facility. On top of the guards I had seen earlier, I now noticed K9 security guards roaming the area between the fences. Plus, the building in the back seemed to have even more security. The level of security seemed out of place for an aluminum parts manufacturer and distributor.

I wondered if this had anything to do with the 'project' Bob Yates was aware of that had gotten him tailed by the two thugs. But then why would the thugs have met their untimely demise? Was it even related at all?

After considering the whole scenario for a few more minutes, I realized it was about time to head back into town. I had to meet Maria Sanchez, and I was getting hungry.

Before taking off, I sat in the truck and made my evening call home. Jamie and Kyle were doing well and seemed to be getting along fine with their grandparents. Hockey practice and violin lessons were covered, and the kids were settled.

I turned the F-150 around and slowly drove back to the highway, where I turned my lights back on and headed into Zapata.

Chapter Twenty-Six

Zapata, TX. Thursday

I had a little over an hour before I had to meet Maria at the diner, and I was looking for somewhere to eat besides Mexican for my next meal. The only place I could find that wasn't fast food was called The Steak House, and was two blocks away from Maria's diner.

The Steak House was another stucco-looking building like most of the others in town, but was clean and had a nicely paved and lined parking lot. It had a newer sign out front and had tinted windows, so I couldn't see in, but I suspected the people inside could see out.

I pulled into the parking lot and noticed there was another parking area around the back. Surprisingly, that lot contained two rare vehicles for Zapata - or anywhere, for that matter. There was a black Bentley Continental GT parked next to a Mercedes G-class, like the one I had seen leaving the distribution center earlier. This G-class, however, was the AMG G63 version. Someone around here had an expensive taste in cars. And apparently black cars were a thing here.

I got out of the F-150 and headed in to spend the next hour.

Inside, the restaurant was much nicer than I had anticipated. The lights were dimmed to a dinner-appropriate level. The furniture was clean and up-to-date, with a well-dressed gentleman standing at a podium when I walked in. I could see a bar off to the left with a bartender washing glasses wearing a red vest over a white shirt with a bowtie. This was not at all what I expected. For a brief second, I even felt underdressed in my jeans and polo shirt.

Thursday night at 9 p.m. didn't seem to be a big dinner time in Zapata. I was able to get a table immediately, and when I was seated, I realized there were only a few other tables occupied. A server appeared quickly and asked for my drink order. She appeared to be Latina, probably Mexican, but spoke flawless English and didn't write down my order. It was for an Old Fashioned with Maker's Mark, which I'm sure was an easy one for her to remember, anyway.

When the server returned with my drink, I ordered a salad, a ribeye and a baked potato. That seemed simple enough and would give me time to get over to Maria's later. I was still most intrigued, however, to know who was driving the expensive cars parked out back. They might not stick out so much in big cities up north, but down here they really piqued my interest. And my suspicion.

While waiting for my salad to arrive, I took the chance to visit the restroom and to take a look around. It was in the back near the bar and allowed me to scan down the hallway to see if there were other dining areas not visible to my table. As I turned the corner next to the bar, I saw several doors leading to private rooms. One of them was occupied. Those must be the people with the expensive cars.

I couldn't see who was in the private room without making it obvious, so I pushed my suspicion aside and decided to watch for any movement in or out of the door-way. It seemed the only way in or out of that private room was via the front door I came in or the back door next to the bar. Both were visible from my table.

As I finished my salad, the people eating at the other tables began to file out of the restaurant. By the time I got my steak, I was the only person left in the dining room.

The steak and baked potato were quite good, and I was enjoying my meal — keeping an eye on the clock. I still had thirty minutes before I needed to pick up Maria, so I wasn't in a hurry.

Midway through my meal, I noticed movement at the back of the restaurant near the bar. A long-haired man in a slick suit emerged from the hallway with the private room and scanned the dining area. When he saw me, he looked me over and walked slowly toward the host who had seated me by the front door.

As the man walked by, I could see the outline of a substantial pistol on his right hip, and a look of malice in his eyes. He was surprisingly tall, probably six foot five or taller, and had a muscular build. If I was to guess, I'd say he looked like somebody's bodyguard. He stared at me so long as he walked by, I finally nodded his direction. He made no motion to me and leaned over to the host, where he whis-pered in quiet conversation while staring at me. The whole thing made me wonder if he was singling me out or if I was just an anomalous late diner at this restaurant and he was being cautious.

After a brief conversation, he headed back to the private

room. He continued to look me over the entire time, but didn't say anything or make any hostile movements. As I sat there, I wondered if he was simply sweeping the area before the private party broke up.

In another minute, I got my answer. The guy who had walked by earlier stood watching the dining room, which meant he watched me, while the other guests slipped out behind him.

I couldn't see the private party guests well, but I did see one male guest in a nice suit with dark skin and a crisp haircut. He was following a blond-haired woman who appeared to be in her mid-thirties. She was equally well-dressed and was accompanied by another bodyguard-looking type. They were out the door in seconds, but I saw the blond woman hug the guy in the suit before stepping away. It was not a romantic hug, but was a familiar one. Then I heard the door close behind them.

It would have been too obvious to run out and see who got into the Bentley or the G-Wagon, so I sat still and finished my meal. I could see the cars pass the side of the building and head out to the right, toward the Atlantis facility, but I couldn't see inside the tinted windows to see who had gotten into each vehicle.

The whole thing was odd, but I wasn't sure if it was anything more than that.

Looking at my watch, I noticed it was nearing time to pick up Maria. It was easy to get the server's attention since I was the only one there, and I was outside climbing back into the F-150 in five minutes.

Chapter Twenty-Seven

Zapata, TX. Thursday

The Viva La Fiesta diner was empty when I arrived to pick up Maria, except for a few workers in the back cleaning up. The lights in the dining area were off, as was the sign out front. A plastic sign hanging from a string on the door was flipped to 'closed.' It was 9:55 p.m.

Watching the workers finish their shift, I decided to call Jen to see how things were going in Nashville. I left in a hurry, and I was curious if she'd heard any new stories about Bob Yates since the news of his murder had to have circulated. Plus, I just wanted to hear her voice.

Jen and I had some long talks and some good times since we were thrown into a vicious gunfight in Willow Creek. She learned about my history in the military and my financial situation, and I learned about her military history, too. After that experience, we developed a bond that developed into a relationship and we were out together almost every weekend.

I was also aware of Jen's divorce, and she was aware of

my wife's death. She laughed at me when I told her it meant I was 'damaged goods' and said I didn't know the definition of that term. I still felt that way and she'd been very patient with me while we sorted out our relationship.

I realized I missed talking to her as I tapped her number on my phone.

She answered quickly and her voice boomed over the speakers in the F-150. I'd forgotten I had the sound system turned up so loud from the music I was listening to earlier.

"Hey, Keith. How are things down there?" I heard a noise in the background, evidence she was still out somewhere.

"All good here, thanks. Just looking around. How are things there?" I asked.

"It's good. Real good. The event went great, and my part is over. We're cutting loose a little tonight at the evening social event since none of us have to present tomorrow," she said.

"Good for you!" I said.

"Thanks. You should be here. There's lots of chatter about Bob Yates. People are loosening up, of course, as the open bar drags on," Jen said.

"Oh, really? Anything new?" I asked.

"Not really, no. It's more of an affirmation of what you said earlier. He had some bizarre things going on. People said he seemed stressed and maybe even depressed for the last several weeks. Everyone is still shocked at what happened, of course. But nothing really new on the potential leads. People talk about the wife's affair. Apparently, that was a big story across Atlantis. Plus, they said he had been stressed at work. Nobody I've talked to seems to know why," she said.

"Wow. This whole thing is just unbelievable. Listen,

Jen, I'll let you get back to it. I just wanted to check in. I should be back in Nashville tomorrow," I said.

"Thanks for calling, Keith. I appreciate it, and I'll talk to you tomorrow. Goodnight." Jen hung up the phone and went back to her reception. I decided I'd fill her in on the rest of my week when I got back the next day.

I sat in the truck and watched Maria Sanchez open the back door of the diner and step cautiously toward the F-150. Thinking about her situation, I could understand her hesitance. Even though we had broken the ice with the conversation over lunch about Bob Yates, I was still an unknown visitor to town and had asked to give her a ride home. I waved politely and smiled my most friendly smile.

"Hola, Mr. Keith," she said as she climbed into the truck. She looked smaller as she struggled to hoist herself into the rather tall truck.

"How was your day, Maria?" I asked.

"It was good. We were busy," she said.

Once she was settled, I took off and headed back out toward the Atlantis facility. She had told me earlier her home was that direction, and I didn't want to tell her I had driven by.

"This way, right?" I asked to make sure she felt she had control of our destination.

"Yes, sir. It's only about three miles," she said.

I had been debating whether to tell her about Bob's murder all day, but as we drove along in the dark, I decided now would be the right time. The task sucked, but it needed to be done.

"Maria, listen. I've got some bad news to share," I said.

She looked at me with fear, as though the bad news was meant for her.

"It's about Bob," I said quickly.

"Yes," she said in an appropriately eager tone.

"Bob was killed yesterday in Nashville. That's why I came down here. I didn't want to tell you while you were at work." I tried to be as soft with the message as I could while still being direct.

"Oh no," she said. Her tone was the sadness of a friend, but nothing more. And there were no tears. That made it a little easier, I guess.

"Yeah. I knew he had been in contact with you, so I wanted to let you know. He seemed fond of you," I said, searching for the right words.

"He did? That's nice. He was always very nice to me. He got Javier that job at Atlantis. And he came into the restaurant many times," she said with her head down, staring at her hands.

"I'm sorry," I said.

We sat in silence for the rest of the ride. After we were about a mile outside Zapata, Maria sat up in her seat.

"Up here on the right," she said, pointing.

I slowed as we neared the Riverside manufactured home community. When we pulled up, a bus had stopped and appeared to be dropping off riders. It looked like an old school bus painted with Atlantis colors.

"Javier should be getting off this bus," Maria said.

"Oh great. Should we pick him up, too?" I asked.

"Yes. He can ride to the house. It's just over there," Maria said, pointing to the row of homes to the far left.

"Javier! Javier!" Maria yelled out the window.

A thin teenage boy turned when he heard Maria and cautiously approached the truck.

"This is my friend, Mr. Keith. He is driving me home today. Get in!" She yelled at Javier as he approached the truck.

"Hi Javier. Nice to meet you," I said as he looked in.

After shaking my hand and looking around me, his mother, and the truck, Javier got in.

At Maria's direction, we navigated around several manufactured homes and a little playground to the stretch of homes where Maria and her two kids lived. She pointed to the third one on the left, and I pulled up in front. There were very few cars in the neighborhood, so it was easy to find space.

After we stopped, I paused to see what Maria would do. Without hesitation, she invited me in. I followed her into the home, with Javier following behind me. When we went inside the double-wide manufactured home, we were in an open living area with three couches, two chairs, a bean bag of some sort, and two end tables. There was a television standing hanging on the far wall, and a kitchen to the left.

There were three adult women in the kitchen sitting at the table, and five kids in the living room area. I guessed their ages to be from about three to twelve. Javier was older than all of them. There were no men visible in the home.

"This is a lovely home," I said with a smile.

Maria smiled, nodded, and motioned to the kitchen. When she did, the other women stood as if they were busy and shuffled away. That left me, Maria, and Javier as the only ones in the kitchen. Maria asked if I wanted a drink, which I declined, and said she'd be right back. She left down the hallway to drop off her things. Javier stayed in the kitchen but didn't sit. He rummaged through the cabinets and refrigerator while I sat quietly.

When Maria returned, she had a solemn look on her face as she sat down. Javier grabbed a glass of water and sat down with us.

"Tell me what happened to Mr. Bob," Maria said, again looking down at her hands.

Was that ever a loaded question! I paused, looking for the right words, and proceeded to tell Maria as little as possible about what I've learned of Bob Yates.

Chapter Twenty-Eight

Zapata, TX. Thursday

When Maria asked me to talk about Bob Yates, I could see Javier look down at the table. His reaction was subtle, but noticeable. I pretended to ignore it and gave Maria a superficial answer.

"It seems someone shot Bob while he was golfing in Nashville," was all I said.

Maria shook her head, looked down at her hands, but didn't show the emotion of someone who had lost a lover. Or of someone who had significant feelings for Bob Yates at all.

"I'm really sorry to hear that. He was a good man," she said with an appropriate level of concern in her voice.

I could see Javier visibly smirk when she said it. Maria was looking at her hands and didn't seem to notice. I didn't acknowledge the smirk and continued.

"Yeah, we were all shocked. As I said earlier, he spoke very fondly of you," I said, trying to draw out any reason Bob would have been talking about her in Nashville.

"He was very nice, yes," she said. That seemed to be all she was willing to offer. Then she took a breath and continued.

"I was surprised he helped get Javier a job at the big warehouse. I was surprised because I didn't go to dinner with him, but he did it anyway," she said. Then she stopped, still looking at her hands.

"You mentioned he helped get Javi a job a couple of times. How did he do that?" I asked, while looking at Javier. He didn't look up.

"Yes, he did. I'm not sure how he did it, but Javier started just this week," she said, looking at Javier while he stared down at the table.

"That's great! What are you doing for Atlantis, Javier?" I asked, trying to draw him into the conversation.

"I just load trucks. It's really not that hard," he said, finally looking up for a second.

"And you were surprised he did that? Why were you surprised?" I asked Maria.

"Mr. Bob was very friendly and kept asking me to go to dinner with him. I just don't have time to do that. Plus, he had a wife," she said.

I nodded, then she continued.

"Still, it is very sad someone killed him. Why would they do that?" She asked, as though she had no idea.

"Well, that's what I was going to ask you. Do you know any reason why anyone would be angry with Bob?" I asked.

"No, not at all. He came here many times to work at Atlantis, but everybody seemed to like him," she said. She seemed to be puzzled by Bob's murder.

Javier continued to stare at his hands, but I saw the smirk emerge from the corners of his mouth when I asked

Maria about Bob. It seemed the conversation was bugging him.

"Javier, do you know of any reasons someone would want to hurt Mr. Yates?" I asked.

"No. No, I don't," he said in an unconvincing fashion, finally looking me in the eye.

As we sat there, the kids from the living room began to cycle through the kitchen, grabbing glasses of water and various snacks. It was becoming more awkward to ask questions about a murdered man, and it seemed I wasn't learning anything new, anyway. I decided to let them resume their normal activities for the night.

"Well, I appreciate your help. I'll let you get to bed. I'm sure you have to be up early for school," I said, this time nodding to Javier.

"Yeah, the bus leaves at like 7:30," he said.

"Whew! And once again, I'm sorry to have to tell you about Bob like this," I said, nodding solemnly at Maria. Javier still didn't look up.

"Thank you, Mr. Keith," Maria said as she stood and nodded.

I waved goodbye and let myself out. The Association had gotten me a hotel room in Laredo, so I had a bit of a drive before I could settle down. After watching Javier, however, I decided my morning would involve getting a chance to talk to him alone at around 7:30 a.m.

After getting a few hours' sleep at the Courtyard Hotel in Laredo, I was back to Maria Sanchez' neighborhood at 7:20 a.m. the following morning. Javier was with a group of kids at the broken gate in front of the neighborhood.

"Hey, Javier. Maria thought you might like a ride?" I lied as he looked toward the truck.

"She did?" He looked conflicted.

"Yeah. Maybe we could stop by McDonald's on the way," I said, trying to bribe him to ride along with me. I wanted to find out why he didn't seem as concerned about Bob Yates' death as his mother was.

"Ok," he said. Then he walked over and got in the passenger side of the F-150.

"You like McDonald's?" I asked after he buckled in.

"Sure. But I'll tell you, just like I told Bob. I'm not one of those kids," he said sternly. It seems I had already gotten the reason for his lack of emotion about Bob.

"Oh, I'm sorry. I'm not sure what you mean. You didn't seem to be upset about his death?" I said, trying to start with the basics.

"Well, I guess I just knew him differently than mama did," he said, staring straight ahead as we drove toward Zapata.

"She seemed to like him," I said.

"Yeah, she seemed to like him. But she didn't know him like I did," he said again.

"What did you know about him that Maria didn't?" I asked.

He sat quietly, staring out the passenger window for several seconds. It seemed he was pondering what he wanted to say.

I waited quietly.

After what seemed like several minutes, he finally let out a long, deep sigh.

"That guy hung out with some kids who did bad things," he said, clearly trying to generalize an uncomfortable topic.

"I see. You mean like drug things?" I asked, not completely sure where he was going.

"That was part of it, but not all. They were kids who

needed money badly. And they'd do anything to get it. Even with older men." He stumbled across the words but eventually got it out.

"I'm sorry to hear that. I didn't know that about Bob. You mean he liked those kids? Did he take them places or buy them things?" I asked, still unsure of where Javier was headed.

"I think so. He took some of them away. I'm not sure what he did, but the rumors at school weren't good. People say he promised those kids lots of things if they went with him. Some went. I'm not sure what he did with them, but mama didn't know about that. If she did, I'm sure she wouldn't have liked him either." Javier turned and looked at me as he finished, a look of anger engulfing his eyes.

"Did other people know he did that?" I asked, realizing I may have stumbled on yet another potential motive for Bob's murder.

"I think so. But people here let the Atlantis guys do whatever they want. They give jobs to Mexicans, and they pay good money. People don't care about the other stuff," he said, again looking out the passenger window.

"So, nobody was angry with him besides you?" I asked.

"No, I don't think so. I just didn't like what he was doing. Some of those kids were my age and younger," he said.

"Does Maria know?" I asked.

"No."

By that time, we were pulling into McDonald's. We didn't say any more about Bob Yates. While we were waiting for our food, I got another idea.

"What is it like at Atlantis?" I asked.

"It's fine, as long as you follow the rules," he said without emotion.

"What rules?"

"Like, do your work. Don't do drugs at work. Don't look at the building in the back. Stuff like that," he said.

"What happens if you do something wrong?"

"You might disappear like the kids Bob talked to," he shrugged.

"What?"

"Yeah. They take people away who break the rules. Nobody knows where they go, but they don't go home and don't go to Mexico. If you break the rules, you can just disappear. The one other kid in my area broke the rules and disappeared on my second day," he said, still with no emotion.

"Wow. What did he do?" I asked.

"Drugs," Javi said. It was all he offered, so I didn't ask more about it.

"And why can't you look at the building in the back?" I asked, curious about what I had seen there last night.

"I don't know. The shirt guys just don't want you to," he said.

"Who are the shirt guys?"

"The guys with the Atlantis shirts. They run the place. The rest of us just do all the hard stuff." Javier was sharing more than he knew in this brief, emotionless conversation.

I asked no more about Atlantis. Javier enjoyed his McDonald's breakfast and waved goodbye when I dropped him off at school.

My trip to Zapata was done. It was time to head back to the airfield to get my flight back to Nashville. I had spent less than twenty-four hours here but had learned more than I expected about Bob Yates.

Chapter Twenty-Nine

Zapata, TX. Friday

After dropping Javier off at school, the trip back to the airfield took about thirty minutes. I used that time to brief Paul on the latest information about Bob Yates and Atlantis.

"Hey, Keith. How is Texas?" Paul asked when he answered the phone.

"Texas is hot. And dusty. And fortunately, I think, full of new information about Bob Yates," I replied.

"Oh, good. So it was an eventful trip?" He almost sounded surprised.

"Well, I think so. Or maybe it just made the whole thing messier."

That didn't seem to surprise him so much.

"Oh, great. How many skeletons can one man have in his closet?" I could almost hear Paul shaking his head.

"At least one more."

"Ok, let me have it," Paul said.

"I've not got all the details, but it seems Mr. Yates was a

little too friendly with some of the younger kids around here," I said.

"Oh, no," Paul sighed.

"Yeah. I heard it from Maria's son. And if the kids knew, I suspect some of the parents knew, too. And by the way, that Maria Sanchez relationship is a non-story. There's nothing going on there," I said.

"So, Bob was a pedophile?" Paul asked, bluntly.

"It seems he was at least a recruiter for a pedophile, if not involved himself. He was known to ask kids if they wanted to improve their lifestyle and then he'd take them away if they were interested. I couldn't gather if he was the instigator or the messenger," I said with my own sigh.

"Wow. You really can't make this stuff up," Paul replied.

"No, you can't. I also snooped around the Atlantis plant down here to see if I could recognize any obvious anomalies with the physical operation," I said, changing the topic.

"Good! What did you find out?"

"They have a steady stream of trucks coming over the border. Every fourth one, give or take, gets a free pass at the inspection station. It's like the border patrol agents are ignoring some of the trucks. After seeing that, I followed the trucks out to the warehouse and distribution center. It appeared the un-inspected trucks were sent to a separate warehouse facility in the back of the complex. I couldn't see what they had in them, but I'd guess a drug-sniffing dog could tell us." I paused to give Paul a chance to digest the comments.

It didn't take long.

"So, they're using their supply chain into Mexico to bring in truckloads of drugs?" This time, Paul sighed deeper than before.

"I didn't get a chance to check out where they went

after that, but if the LLCs you talked about earlier are taking delivery, they may be part of the distribution system," I said.

"That's a good idea. We need to check into those LLCs. Let me look into that," Paul said, back on his game.

"Ok. I'm headed back to Nashville now. I need to find out why my name was on that hotel room registration. That one has me concerned. It feels like I'm really missing something personal in this case," I said.

"I wish I could help with that, Keith. We're really looking hard, just not finding anything yet. We'll stay on it."

"Thanks Paul," I said as we ended the call.

The flight back to Nashville would give me some time to sort all this out. If the outlandish life of Bob Yates wasn't enough, the murders in the Nashville Inn had me further rattled. There had to be something there to help find out why they used my name.

When I got to the airfield I had flown into, I pulled up to the same gate I had driven out of the day before. The guard opened the gate and waved me in after a brief glance into the truck.

I pulled over near the hangar and parked the truck in the same spot I had found it. This entire trip was a strange experience. I had eaten two good meals, had driven along several dusty highways, and had met Maria Sanchez and her son.

And I had found out that Bob Yates may have been a pedophile, on top of everything else.

I walked into the gate area and saw the same pilot who had flown me in. He stood up, smiled, and shook my hand.

"Welcome back, Mr. Morgan. You ready to head back to Nashville?" He didn't introduce himself and I didn't ask his name.

"Yep. Ready to go," I said.

He motioned toward the jet sitting in the hangar.

"We're ready for you," he said.

I made my way up the narrow stairs and ducked into the plane, once again taken by the resourcefulness of The Association. And once again, deciding this is the way to travel!

After taking a seat along the left side of the plane, I looked out the window to say goodbye to Zapata and this Mexican border region. When I did, I noticed yet another black Bentley Continental GT pulling up to one of the jets outside the hangar. That makes two in two days, and that's more black Bentley Continental GTs than I've seen in a year!

The driver's door opened, and I was surprised to see the driver wearing an Atlantis polo shirt as he got out. I was equally surprised to see him open the passenger door for the blond woman I had seen leaving the private room at the restaurant last night. Maybe there weren't as many black Bentley Continental GTs here as I thought. It appears I'd seen this one twice.

The nicely-dressed blond woman stepped out of the car and went up the stairs and onto the plane by herself. The driver carried her bag up the stairs for her, then returned to the car and drove away. I thought back to the restaurant last night and remembered the blond woman had been with someone else then, too. I wasn't certain it was the same guy last night as the driver today, but it could have been.

Before the plane engines revved up, I made another quick call back home to check on the kids. As expected, nothing was new there and everyone was up and moving with their Friday morning activities. They barely had time for a chat and I didn't force it. Judy was the last person I spoke to before ending the call and settling into my seat.

Fifteen minutes after parking the F-150, I was in the air on the way back to Nashville.

Chapter Thirty

Nashville, TN. Friday

As the G400 descended into the Nashville area and my phone received service, I noticed a voicemail from Paul. I had continued to scour my memory for any reason I should be involved in this case during the flight, so I was hopeful he had some new insight. My name on that Nashville Inn reservation continued to nag at my brain.

"Hey Keith. I just wanted to pass along a quick update. It seems you can quit worrying about your name being on that reservation at the Nashville Inn. Our sources indicate the same name being used multiple times when Chris Valentine was traveling and Doris Yates was in the same area. It turns out Chris has a daughter named Morgan, and Doris has a son named Keith. They used that pseudonym to register at hotels they used for their, uh, meetings. I'm sure the local PD will come up with that link eventually, so you may have to play along for a while, but at least you can stop worrying about the personal link here. There isn't one. Later."

I felt myself breathe a deep sigh of relief even before Paul ended the message. The plane had landed and was taxiing to the hangar as I shook my head and looked out the window.

So, the reason my brain couldn't link my past with this case was because the link didn't exist. Now I had to hope the Nashville police and Officer Keating found those details soon enough to leave me alone!

The thought barely entered my brain when my phone vibrated with a call. I looked at the number and thought to myself. Speak of the devil.

"Officer Keating, how are things going?" I asked as I took the call.

"Mr. Morgan, you're not answerin' the door at your hotel room. Where are you? We need to talk." He sounded agitated.

"We've been meeting with several customers before they head out, trying to get as much face time as we can," I answered, lying about my location.

I had remembered him telling me not to go anywhere when we were at the Nashville Inn, but I had frankly ignored that directive when I went to Zapata. It was a quick trip, and I suspected I would be back before he needed to talk to me again. It seems I was correct. Barely.

"Good 'nuff. How far away are you? I think it's best we talk face-to-face," he said.

This didn't sound good.

"I can meet you in the lobby in, say, thirty minutes," I said, once again avoiding his specific question.

"Sounds good. I'll meet you there," Officer Keating said after a frustrated sigh.

He ended the call before I could say anything, leaving me a bit concerned. I would expect him to be in a better mood with me if he had found out about the reservation name, so that must not be the topic.

As I exited the plane, I noticed the same driver who had brought me here yesterday standing next to the building. This airport, if you call it that, was a little more formal than the one in Zapata, so we had to walk through a tiny seating area to get to the parking lot door. His Mercedes was next to the curb when we walked out the door, and he opened the back door and let me inside.

On the way back to the Grand Marquis, I continued to wonder what Officer Keating wanted to talk about. Had he learned there were some details I had omitted about Bob Yates? *Did he find out about my trip? Maybe he found out I had been asking questions at the atrium bar and the Mellow Mushroom downtown?*

Wanting to avoid having to explain my overnight bag to Officer Keating, I asked the driver to drop it at the concierge after I had gone in. I also asked him to leave me at the rideshare area rather than the lobby drop-off where Officer Keating would likely be waiting.

The walk to the lobby door was less than five minutes from the rideshare circle drive, and I saw Officer Keating standing just inside the door when I walked over.

"Mr. Morgan, welcome back," he said as I walked into the Grand Marquis lobby.

I nodded and reached out to shake his hand. He obliged, but seemed more interested in getting to the conversation topic. Whatever it was.

"Do you mind if we sit down?" He motioned toward a corner of the lobby where there were two plush chairs with no occupants. On Friday morning at the Grand Marquis, that was a rare occurrence.

I walked to the chairs and sat in the one on the right

with the best view of the lobby. It was a habit to put my back to the wall and my eyes everywhere else.

He sat in the chair next to me and turned it to face my chair, struggling with the weight and size of it. Eventually, he settled and folded his hands in front of his mouth. He didn't say anything for several seconds, appearing to collect his thoughts. I doubted that's what he was doing and viewed this as a bit of showmanship.

As I watched him sit silently, I determined Officer Keating was trying to make me uncomfortable, so I'd be defensive when I answered his questions.

"You mentioned you had seen the two victims in the hotel room around the event this week," he finally started.

"Can you tell me where, exactly, you saw them?" He leaned forward and stared at me intensely.

My mind struggled with how to answer his question. Clearly, he must have known I had seen them and must have known they were at the bar. Otherwise, he'd avoid this drama. I had noticed cameras around the hotel but not everywhere, and I was pretty sure there were none where I had 'met' the two victims in the maintenance area.

I sat back and looked up as if I was trying to remember.

"I believe they were at the reception Monday night," I said slowly, still thinking.

"It also seems I remember seeing them at the golf registration." I tried to evaluate what Officer Keating might know already, as he seemed to be waiting for a big revelation here.

"And I may have seen them at the bar one night," I said as I returned my gaze to Officer Keating.

He didn't seem to hear what he wanted, but it was enough that he got to his point, anyway.

"So, it seems they were indeed at the bar Wednesday night after Mr. Yates' murder. The hotel cameras have pretty good coverage here, so we saw them there. We also saw you at the bar talking to the bartender. What was that about?" Officer Keating asked.

I realized he probably saw me glance at them if he watched carefully, and he may have also seen them leave shortly after I did. While I was pretty sure my scuffle with the two wasn't on a camera, I couldn't be completely certain.

"Well, I was a little shaken up by the incident on the golf course, that's all. Why do you ask?" I decided to see if I could get anything out of him.

He took a deep breath, as though he was deciding what to tell me.

"For one thing, they left just after you did. Then, some-time later, those same two were seen heading to their rooms in visible physical discomfort. They were very much alive, but had clearly run into some sort of trouble. If you know anything about it, I'd suggest you fill us in. It would be better if you volunteer the information than if we have to take the time and manpower to find out ourselves. In the meantime, the killer or killers are still out there."

He paused and looked at me, and waited for an answer. When he didn't get one, he continued.

"Right now I don't have you down as a suspect for the Bob Yates murder because it was physically impossible for you to be there. But your name on the room registration and these two fellas following you and turning up dead? I'd say I have more evidence against you than anyone else!"

This time, he was going to stare at me until I said some-thing. If he knew it wasn't my name on the registration, he wasn't going to share it. And I couldn't tell him what I had learned from Paul.

It was time for a limited confession to Officer Keating.

Chapter Thirty-One

Nashville, TN. Friday

"I noticed those two guys paying a strange amount of attention to me while I was sitting at the bar. When I got up, they got up and followed me." I paused while I evaluated what to say next. Officer Keating didn't indicate he knew anything more, so I decided to stop there.

"How did you know they followed you?" He asked.

"Because I stopped in a private area and caught them tailing me." I said.

"Is that it?" Officer Keating asked.

"We had a conversation and came to an understanding," I said.

"How did you come to an understanding?"

"It was just a brief conversation. That's all," I said. If he knew more, he wouldn't be asking so many open questions.

"They seemed to get the worst of your conversation," he said.

It wasn't a question, so I didn't respond. Instead, I decided to reverse the discussion.

"Have you been able to talk to Doris Yates?" I asked.

"We have," he said. That was it.

It sure would be easier to talk to him if he knew about the name on the registration.

"Did you get any insight into the two dead 'fellas' in the hotel room?" I asked, using his description of the two thugs.

"Yeah, we did. They were a couple of Chris Valentine's staff here for the convention. Mrs. Yates is saying she didn't know them. We're looking at more of the surveillance footage to determine if we see them interacting. So far, we haven't seen Mrs. Yates in the Grand Marquis at all. She says she wasn't here for the event." He raised his eyebrows as he said the last sentence.

I decided to throw him a bone, and to see if he was hiding something.

"There were rumors around about Chris Valentine and Mrs. Yates," I said. Then I watched Officer Keating closely.

I could see a brief sigh before he responded.

"Yeah, that seems to have been one of the worst-kept secrets in Nashville," he said.

"Did you get any footage of Chris Valentine at the Nashville Inn? Is that why she was there?" I was pushing it, but I wanted to see how much information Officer Keating had gathered.

"Well, yes. In fact, we do have footage of Mr. Valentine on the premises. I can't give you more than that, but you get the point. We do not, however, have reason to believe it was Mr. Valentine that killed the two individuals in your hotel room."

I couldn't tell if it was a slip-up by Officer Keating or if he was trying to get under my skin. I decided to give him the benefit of an angry look and a deep sigh, then I continued to see what he knew.

"There were also rumors about his health," I said.

"Yes. We are aware of Mr. Yates' health concerns," Officer Keating said, now smirking at the fact that he annoyed me. So Bob Yates was indeed sick. Interesting.

Before I could ask anything else, Officer Keating shot back.

"Did you get any of this information from the two fellas you beat up at the Grand Marquis Wednesday night?" He was acting as if he had cornered me, so I carefully considered how much to tell him before I continued.

"Look, Officer Keating. Those 'fellas,' as you call them, were not at the top of the food chain. They were asking me about some project that Bob was working on. It seems someone put them on watch to make sure Bob didn't say anything about that project. When they saw me talking to the bartender, they feared I may have been asking about it. Which I wasn't."

I stopped and sat back, rubbing my temples and trying to look like Officer Keating had won this little battle, but also watching to see if this was new information for him. He didn't even try to hide the fact that it was indeed new information.

"A new project, huh? Did they say what it was?" He asked as he frantically grabbed his notepad and scribbled something.

"No, they didn't say a thing about it," I said, somewhat truthfully. I tried to make it look like I was dismissing the idea, despite where I had spent the last twenty-four hours.

"Ok. We'll look into it," he said, closing his notebook.

"I guess Chris Valentine is pretty upset about his two associates being viciously killed and strung up in the same room he was apparently using for his tryst with Mrs. Yates?"

I asked, driving right into one of my theories on this whole thing.

"Yeah, he was pretty upset. He even left the event early to head back home," Officer Keating said casually, clearly finished with this conversation.

"Oh, he has a home here?" I asked.

"Yeah, it's quite a place. He's holed up in there now and has asked for some time to process all this," he said.

"So, you don't think he had any part in it?" I asked.

"I didn't say that. But you just leave the investigation with us. Ok, Mr. Morgan?" Officer Keating stood up and put his notebook in his pocket when he said it.

That was a message I get frequently on these assignments for The Association. It seems their work always puts me next to police work of some kind, and often overlaps with it significantly. I decided to call Paul Frazier after speaking with Officer Keating to see how they'd like me to play this. Officer Keating clearly didn't want my help, but I've already had to drop him one breadcrumb to get him moving toward Zapata. I suspected it wouldn't be the last time I'd have to do that.

"Oh, I have no interest in being a policeman, Offer Keating," I said. That one was completely honest, but didn't commit to shying away from my assignment.

"Good," he said as he donned the mirrored aviator sunglasses he'd had hanging on his pocket.

I decided to solicit a little more information from Officer Keating using a different tactic.

"I'm still curious about the two guys in the room with my name on it. Do we have any idea how they got in there? Did they walk in? Did someone kill them elsewhere and somehow haul them in? With the cameras in that hotel, I'd hope we saw something!" I was unable to hide my exasperation as I asked the questions.

"Look, Mr. Morgan. I already told you to leave the investigation with us," he responded tersely.

That response didn't sit well with me, so I decided to push it one more time.

"Look, Officer Keating. Someone used my name to rent a hotel room that may have been used to murder Bob Yates and was definitely used to send a message with two dismembered corpses. I think I have a right to know about my adversary here." As long as he doesn't mention the name on the room wasn't mine, I'm going to use that to my advantage.

Officer Keating sat for a moment in the lobby of the Grand Marquis, looking at the passing guests and workers. After a minute or so, he leaned in.

"The people who did this knew what they were doing. They used a delivery van. They took it to the cargo area and loaded the corpses into the freight elevator in the loading dock. They knew where the cameras were and they avoided them. We know there were two guys, but we know little more than that. And you're right, you should stay on your toes while we sort this out. But honestly, Mr. Morgan, if they wanted you dead, you'd be dead." He sat back after making that point.

"Yeah, I suppose you're right," I said as I stood up.

"You sure you don't know what this is about?" He asked with a hint of skepticism.

"I wish I did," I said, shaking my head.

"Ok. If you think of anything, please let me know. In the meantime, I'll keep you informed of any new developments that may pertain to your safety," he said, also standing.

With that, Officer Keating nodded and stepped out of the hotel. I watched him leave, then sat back down in my chair and called Paul Frazier.

Chapter Thirty-Two

Zapata, TX. Friday

Javi walked to the neighborhood gate at 4:45 p.m. just like the last few days. He was just getting there when he heard Gus yelling at him from behind.

"Hey Javi, wait up!" Javi turned around to see Gus running up to him.

"Hey. What's going on?" Javi asked. It was unusual to see Gus running like that. He usually seemed pretty calm and, well, slow.

"Nothing's going on with me. I just wanted to see what was going on with you," he said.

"What do you mean?" Javi asked.

"That guy who picked you up yesterday. Who was it?" Gus asked. The direct tone of the question caught Javi off guard.

"He was just a friend of my mom's. Why?" Javi asked.

"A good friend? I mean, was he nice and all?"

"Yeah. Why are you asking these questions?" Javi was getting suspicious.

"Look, Javi. I can't tell you everything that goes on here, but there are some guys around who aren't really nice people. I warned you about watching yourself at work, but we also have to pay attention outside of that place. There are bad guys all over and you need to be careful," he said.

"Oh, no. He wasn't one of those bad guys. In fact, he was talking to us about one of those bad guys," Javi responded.

"He was? You know about them? And he knew about them? What did he say?" Now it was Gus who seemed suspicious.

"The guy was just telling my mom that one of her friends died. Apparently, he had her number on his phone, so they were just letting her know about it. That's all." Javi was trying to smooth out Gus' concern, as he really seemed riled up about this.

"Oh, ok. Which one of the bad guys was it?" Gus asked, calming a bit.

"A guy named Bob. My mom called him Mr. Bob. I don't remember his other name," Javi replied.

Javi was shocked to see the look on Gus' face. He looked like he had seen a ghost.

"Was it Bob Yates?" Javi thought he now saw fear in Gus' eyes. He wasn't sure.

"Yeah, I think it was. Why?"

"I have to make a phone call," Gus replied with a look of panic on his face.

He got his phone out of his pocket, stepped a few feet away, and put the phone to his ear. He was so close and was talking so loud Javi could hear every word he was saying. Gus seemed to be panicking as he talked.

Javi could only hear one side of the conversation, so the whole thing made no sense to him.

"I need to talk to you. What do you mean, we can't talk?" Gus yelled into the phone.

After a few seconds, he yelled again.

"He's dead, and he was the only one I talked to. What am I supposed to do now? I have people depending on me!" Gus finally looked up and noticed Javi staring at him.

He started talking quieter, but still urgently. He was only on the phone a few more minutes, then he put the phone back in his pocket and stood there for a minute. He was staring into space like he was thinking about something.

"What's going on, Gus? Who was that on the phone?" Javi asked.

"I can't tell you, Javi. Just an important guy," Gus said.

"Was my mom's friend important, too?" Javi asked.

He was beginning to get a bad feeling about Gus. He knew his mom's friend had been talking to kids at school and in town, and that those kids had disappeared. It only happened a few times, but enough for Javi to think it wasn't a coincidence. Now Gus was talking to someone on the phone about that same guy, and Gus was sounding like he was involved.

"I can't talk about it, Javi. You shouldn't either," Gus said.

Now Javi was getting really suspicious.

They didn't mention it again while they waited for the bus.

When the bus came, Javi let Gus get on first and then took a seat by himself. Gus didn't seem to care, as he appeared to be swallowed up in his own thoughts. He looked out the window and didn't even acknowledge Javi when he walked by.

The bus took its normal route to the Atlantis facility, entered the gate, and stopped to let the passengers out. Javi watched Gus as he got off the bus. He didn't look up, didn't look around, and didn't speak to anyone as he headed to his station.

It was almost like Gus was scared of something. As Javi walked to his station at the loading dock, he wondered what Gus was involved with that would put him on edge like this.

Javi had thought Gus was one of the good guys, but he may have been wrong.

Chapter Thirty-Three

Nashville, TN. Friday

"Hey Keith, what's up?" Paul answered in his usual chipper voice.

"I just had a conversation with our friendly neighborhood police officer," I said, getting straight to the point.

"Is that Keating?" He asked.

"Yep, the one and only. It seems he still doesn't know why Keith Morgan was on the registration at the hotel, but he did share some other information," I started.

"Good! Do tell," he said.

"It seems Chris Valentine was pretty shaken up and has holed himself up in his local residence. I may want to pay him a visit. While I know the message of the two dead guys in the hotel room wasn't for me, I'd like to know what it was about. I'm not sure if it's related to what's going on in Zapata or not," I said.

"Sure. I can get you the address. If he murdered those two guys, though, you need to be careful, Keith. You may walk into an ambush."

"Maybe, but I don't think so. And there's more. Perhaps not surprisingly, whoever dropped off the two bodies at the Nashville Inn knew what they were doing. There's no evidence and no camera footage that will be helpful. Keating even went as far as to tell me to stay on my toes, but that I'd be dead if they wanted me dead. It seems he thinks they're sending me some sort of message."

"Yeah, I'd probably think the same thing if I didn't have the link to the name on the hotel registration. Play that as long as you can. You can probably use it to your advantage," Paul said.

"Believe me, I am," I smiled.

"Great minds, I guess," Paul said.

"If you can get me the address of their house, I'll see what Chris knows. He may not talk to me, but I'll present my visit more as a friendly gesture and see how that goes. He didn't know we were researching the company, did he?" I asked.

"No, only the board and the CEO knew. They didn't want Chris or the other executives to know they were for sale."

"Ok. That makes it a little harder, but I'll just try to work my way in there with kindness." I was figuring out how to get to Chris Valentine as I was talking.

"Good idea. And we're looking into all the details you got from Zapata. It seems likely it's a drug running plant, but it's hard to know without some evidence or witnesses. Both are hard to come by in that sort of environment," he said.

"Yeah, no kidding. That place is locked down like Fort Knox," I replied.

"Let me know what you find out about Valentine. If that guy knew what was going on down in Zapata, he may be the one behind the whole operation. Plus, we need to get this to the authorities if there really is a drug trafficking operation through that facility," Paul said.

"Got it. I'll keep you updated," I said as I ended the call.

I was pondering how to get inside Chris Valentine's office when I saw Jennifer walking through the lobby. She was alone, and dressed casually for the last day of the event. Her jeans and running shoes made it look like she was on a casual stroll, as did her long-sleeved athletic top. Her straight sandy-blond hair was pulled back on the sides and she was carrying sunglasses. As usual, the sight of her made me smile.

I flagged her down as an idea came to me.

"Hey Jen," I called out as she saw me and headed my way.

"So, how was Texas?" She asked as we hugged briefly and she sat down in the chair recently vacated by Officer Keating.

"It was interesting," I said, as I tried to determine how to frame the situation.

"Oh yeah? Interesting how?" She asked.

"Well, do you have a few minutes?" I asked as I realized this wasn't a two-minute conversation.

"I was heading out for a walk, but it's about lunchtime. We can get something to eat while you fill me in, if you want?" She offered.

That sounded great, as I realized I hadn't had a full meal since my steak last night in Zapata.

"Sure, let's do it," I said.

We stood up and started walking back inside the Grand Marquis toward the atrium area where the restaurants were located. I was internally evaluating which one would allow for a private conversation when Jennifer beat me to the punch.

"I think the Mexican place has the most private tables. What do you think?" She was getting on the escalator up to the walkway when she turned to ask the question.

"Yeah, you're probably right. That sounds good to me," I answered.

"Has there been any more discussion about Bob Yates since yesterday?" I asked, almost afraid of what other stories might emerge from his life story.

"No, not really. Nothing new since we last talked. Most people are leaving Nashville today, though, so there's not as many people chatting around the hallways," she said.

"Hmmm." I guess I made it sound more questioning than I meant to.

"Why, what were you hoping I'd hear? What did you find down there?" She was pretty insightful.

"Well, it's a pretty long story, so I suppose I can start now," I smiled as we walked down the same path I had walked Wednesday night when the two thugs were alive and following me.

"Please do, you've got me very intrigued," she said

"Remember, I told you about the challenges I had at the Nashville Inn?" I started with the gruesome details about the two thugs.

"Yep," she responded as we continued to navigate the other hotel guests along the pathway through the atrium.

"Well, the challenges weren't exactly my personal challenges, but had to do with what I found in the room," I said, then paused to determine how I should explain what I had found.

She looked at me and waited while we walked toward the hostess of the restaurant.

"You remember the two guys who followed me Wednesday night?"

"Yeah."

"They were in the room when I got there." I said, waiting to share the more critical details until we sat down.

Jennifer looked at me questioningly but said nothing as we arrived at the hostess podium and asked about a table for two. She grabbed a couple of menus and asked us to follow her to our table.

The restaurant was on the edge of the atrium in the back, but still held onto the rainforest theme. There was a black railing that separated the walkway from the restaurant, with tables sprinkled around various plants and fountains. It was a pretty neat place, and a good place for a private conversation. As an added bonus, they had good burritos here.

The hostess led us to a table near the back of the seating area, far from the walkway and the hostess station. There were large brick planters on either side of the table and no occupied tables within earshot. It was the perfect place to brainstorm with Jen.

"Your waitress will be with you shortly," the hostess said as she dropped the menus on the small, round table and walked away.

It didn't take long for Jen to force me back on topic.

"The guys who were following you were in the room when you got there? What did you say to them?" Jennifer asked.

"Well, that's the more disturbing part. I didn't say anything, because they were dead," I said, again waiting for that part to sink in before I described the scene.

"Whoa, Keith. What have you gotten yourself into this time?" She asked rhetorically while shaking her head.

"Were they shot or something?" Jen continued when I didn't answer.

"Well, yes, but even that's not the most disturbing part." I tried to keep from sounding too concerned while also divulging the critical details.

"Sorry to have to fill you in on this just before lunch, but it's sort of important to the story. They had been decapitated, laid out on the bed, and their heads were sitting there on their pillows. They had the letters CA carved into their chests. Clearly, they were put there to send a message." I stopped there to let all this sink in. After our experience at Willow Creek, I knew she could handle the grotesque description, but it was still a lot to process.

Before Jen could respond, the waitress appeared, and we paused to order. As soon as the waitress turned her back, Jen was back on topic.

"This sounds like cartel-type stuff, Keith," she said matter-of-factly.

"Yeah, it does," I replied, nodding.

"Is there more you need to tell me about this?" She sat back in her chair, clearly expecting there was more to the story.

Of course there was.

"Yeah. Let me tell you about my trip to Texas," I said as I leaned in for a summary of my trip.

Chapter Thirty-Four

Nashville, TN. Friday

Our drinks arrived, as did chips and salsa. Neither of those things took away Jennifer's focus on the topics we were discussing.

"Ok, so what about Texas?" She was back on point when the waitress turned around.

"First off, the location was way down at the bottom of Texas near the eastern side of the border with Mexico," I started.

"Near Laredo?" Jennifer asked as she picked up a chip. I don't know why, but the fact that she knew Laredo sort of surprised me.

"Well, yeah. The place was called Zapata. You know it?" I asked.

"Not really, I just remember Laredo from geography class, I guess. Not really sure. Sorry, I'll stop interrupting," she said as she dipped the chip into salsa and put it in her mouth.

"No problem with the interruptions. I'm sure I'll leave

things out if you don't ask me. Anyway, I got down to Zapata where Bob had been visiting," I realized I was not explaining about my flight, nor how I got some of the knowledge I was about to share, but I wasn't about to say anything about The Association. Luckily, she let it go.

"When I got there, I looked up the woman Bob had been talking to down there. She was a very pleasant woman, and I could see how he would like her. But she didn't put off the vibe of a romantic acquaintance. When I told her of his death, she was sad, but not in a personal relationship sort of way. It was strange," I said, nodding to myself as I talked.

"Ok, so that's weird," she said, putting a finger to her mouth as she said it.

"Oh, sorry. I said I'd be quiet," she said.

I just smiled before I continued.

"Yeah, I thought so, too. But it seems he just befriended her at the diner where she worked, and nothing more. He even got her son a job at the Atlantis plant down there. Which is, by the way, one bizarre facility," I said.

I could see the wheels turning in her head as she listened. She started to say something, but stopped and just nodded.

"The Atlantis facility down there is a huge place. It's clearly the central distribution center for all their shipments from Monterrey and probably has some manufacturing or assembly capability. It also had the security of Fort Knox, which stuck out like a sore thumb in that landscape. Everyone knew what it was, they knew it was secure, and they knew it brought jobs to the area. It was almost like Atlantis could do no wrong in the eyes of the locals," I said.

Again, Jennifer just nodded as I continued.

"It really is ok for you to ask questions," I said as I could see she was holding back.

She let out an enormous sigh, as though she was about to burst.

"Thank goodness!" She dropped her chips and let out her questions.

"I don't mean to challenge your reading of people, because you're good at it. But you said the woman didn't seem to have an emotional response to Bob's death. Are you sure she didn't already know about it? Or that she was just a good actor?"

"I don't think so. I watched her pretty closely. There was definite sadness there, but not like the gut-wrenching type you'd expect from a lost love," I replied.

"And she had nothing to do with the Atlantis plant down there?"

"Nope."

"And you mentioned the two guys who followed you were asking about some project? Did you find out anything about that?"

Now she was getting ahead of me.

"I'm not sure, but let me add a few more things," I said.

"Sure, sorry." She smiled again and picked up another chip.

"No worries. So, back to the plant. I watched their trucks coming in and out of the facility for a while to see if anything was odd beyond the security setup. I noticed a pattern where some would go to the large building that seemed to cover most of the activity, but some would go to a smaller, even more secure facility in the back corner of the property. There was a consistent stream of traffic going there, maybe about a fourth of the trucks in total."

I stopped and got a drink, waiting for a question. She didn't ask and simply nodded instead.

"There's a border station at Zapata, so I also watched

the trucks coming across the border for a while. After just a short time, it became clear some of the trucks were not getting as much scrutiny as others were. I suspect the border patrol, at least some of the guys there, had been convinced to let some of the trucks pass without inspection," I said.

This time, she spoke up.

"So, they're running drugs through their Atlantis trucks into that facility in the back? Or even worse, people?" She got right to the point.

"Maybe. It surprises me they could be that obvious and not get caught, but maybe. There were enough fancy cars around there to make you think someone had cartel money."

"Hmmm," she said, clearly pondering the evidence I was sharing.

I paused with the Atlantis information to share what else I had found out about Bob Yates.

"There was also a bit more insight into Bob Yates. The woman, Maria, had a son who was maybe fourteen years old. When we discussed Bob in his presence, I could see a different expression from his mom. He was stoic about it, but didn't show any emotion at all. If anything, he almost seemed glad to hear it. I gave him a ride to school and got some insight into the reason."

I considered how to articulate the next thought.

"It seems Bob was getting noticeably friendly with some of the down-and-out kids in the area. Kids who would disappear soon after talking to Bob," I said, carefully.

Jennifer's eyebrows went up at that comment.

"Whoa. That's not where I expected this to go," she said, clearly surprised.

"Me neither, but the kid seemed pretty genuine about it. He definitely believes Bob Yates was causing some of his peers to disappear."

Jennifer was shaking her head and looking down as our food arrived. We sat quietly and thanked the waitress as she set our burritos on the table.

After she left, Jen continued to express her disbelief about Bob Yates.

"I guess anything is possible these days, but that just doesn't seem to fit with the rest of Bob's story. Although, it also puts the events up here in Nashville in a different light, huh?"

It wasn't a question so much as an observation.

"Yeah, it does. Which brings me to the reason I called you over," I said.

"Ah, ok. Here we go," she smiled between bites.

"I'd like to talk to Chris Valentine. We know Mrs. Yates was around the hotel, but we also know Chris was there, too. Knowing he had me tailed for something going on down in Texas, I'd like to talk to him about it," I offered.

"And why aren't we just letting the police deal with this?"

It was a good question, and one for which I didn't have a suitable answer. I hadn't told her what I know about the name on the registration, but that would expose the fact that I have details the police do not. I also couldn't pretend I was working with the police on this one, because that would be easy for her to uncover if something goes wrong and we have nobody to back us up.

I hadn't thought this through when I called her over, so I had to improvise.

"With Bob's death, we have the unique opportunity to offer our condolences in a personal way. It's Friday, we'll all be leaving the event tonight or tomorrow, so we can make it look like a personal visit about Bob. ...which it really is, if you think about it," I said with as sincere of a smile as I could muster.

"So, you're wanting me to go with you to the home of the CFO of Atlantis to offer our condolences for the death of one of his employees? Knowing he had you tailed in the hotel just two nights ago? Don't you think we'll be walking right into a death trap?"

"Maybe, but I don't think so. He'd have to expect we were working with the police. If anything, he'd be more afraid that I was coming after him," I responded.

"Plus, I think they are a Diverse Data customer, aren't they?" I added.

"Oh, come on, Keith. He'll see right through that one!" She actually laughed at that part of my idea.

"But I suppose it's as good an idea as any. Besides, you need someone to keep you alive," she said as her smile faded a bit.

"Whatever it takes to get you over there. I think it'll be safer with both of us there and maybe we'll find out what's going on," I said.

"Ok, I'm in. We'd better get there quickly. It may take some talking to get to him, if we can at all," she said.

With that conversation out of the way, our afternoon visit with Chris Valentine was set.

Chapter Thirty-Five

Nashville, TN. Friday

After finishing our lunch, Jen and I agreed to meet back in the lobby in thirty minutes to catch an Uber to Chris Valentine's house. I had stopped by one of the shops and picked up a sympathy card, trying to make our visit look legitimate.

Still wearing the jeans and polo shirt I had on when I left Zapata several hours ago, I also decided to change clothes. I selected a business casual outfit that would have been appropriate for the final day of the software event.

I arrived in the lobby ahead of schedule and took a seat near where Jen and I had met earlier. I could see most of the lobby from that spot, but the volume of guests was picking up. Weekends at the Grand Marquis were a big deal for vacationers.

As soon as I sat down, my phone vibrated with a call from Paul.

"Hey," I said as the call connected.

"Ok, we've got a way in to talk to Chris," Paul said.

"Then I don't have to rely on my substantial charm and effervescent charisma?" I said with a smile.

That one actually made Paul laugh.

"Effervescent, huh? HA! That sure sounds like you. But while that may have worked, no, you do not," he replied.

"Good. Then how are we going to play it?" I asked.

"I contacted one of the Atlantis board members we have been communicating with. I told him we were sad to hear about Bob's death. I also told him we were concerned he had all the insight into the supply chain operations at Atlantis. I said we had a guy there at the event and we wanted to talk to Chris to see where he might recommend who we contact now that Bob's gone," Paul replied.

"Ok. Good to have friends in high places, I guess," I responded.

"I guess. That means you have to ask about the supply chain a little, but there's no need to press it. They're going to tell Chris that Rocky Mountain Equity is looking to make an investment in Atlantis, that's all."

I decided I'd better tell Paul that Jennifer was also going.

"Ok, that should be easy enough. Listen, Paul, I also have Jen going with me. We should be able to cover that with her employment at Diverse Data, but wanted you to know." I listened closely to see if Paul had any concern.

"That should be fine. This is only a social visit and high-level discussion. We're not really sure how much information Chris got back from his thugs after they met you in the Grand Marquis, so he may or may not even recognize you. If he does, you'll have to be careful," he said.

"Yeah, we thought of that," I replied.

"And one more thing. He's not at the office, he's at home today. I'll text the address, but I'm told he'll be expecting you. Let me know how it goes," Paul said, implying the call was over.

"Yeah, we heard that, too. Ok, we'll let you know," I said as I disconnected the call.

After another five minutes, Jennifer appeared around the huge guitar statue that adorned the far end of the lobby. She had changed into a pair of dark dress pants with a white blouse. Her outfit was nicer than mine, but I had gotten used to that. She was also carrying a card.

"What?" she asked as she arrived at my seat. It was only then that I realized I was smiling at her as she walked over. It happens all the time when I see her, and it's embarrassing. I need to learn to control that a little better.

"Oh, nothing. Just chuckling at a message from the kids," I lied as I stood up and located the Uber app on my phone.

She gave me a nod, probably seeing right through my lie, and we headed to the rideshare area outside the hotel entrance. Within five minutes, we were in a gray Toyota Camry headed for Chris Valentine's house. Jennifer didn't ask how I knew the address, but probably assumed I just looked it up. I didn't. Paul had sent it to me after we talked.

"We're just going to say we are here to offer our condolences and support?" Jennifer asked as we drove toward Chris' house.

"Yeah, I think so. I will pass along the card and will talk to him briefly about Rocky Mountain Equity's concern with their supply chain. I can also tell him I had gotten close to Bob, because he won't know if that's true or not. You can offer your condolences as a software partner who had worked with him. That should get us enough credibility to chat for a few minutes," I said, mixing Paul's plan into our plans.

"I'm not really sure you need to say anything. If he sent the two guys after you, I'd expect him to know exactly who you are. In fact, I'd expect he won't let us in the door," she replied.

"Yeah, maybe. But I'm not really sure how much he was directly involved with his thugs' activities. Nor am I sure he knows what I look like. This entire trip is a bit of a long shot anyway," I agreed.

"But if he had those two killed like that, we'd better be extremely careful here." Jennifer was stating an obvious point that I had considered earlier.

"Yeah, I agree. Plus, we know he's working from home today. That means we're heading to his house, which will give him the advantage if anything goes upside-down. If we see any cartel-looking individuals there, we need to retreat immediately," I said.

The potential danger was something I had assessed, but it really didn't seem like Chris would allow that sort of activity in his home. It would be too obvious to his neighbors. He might have a discrete bodyguard or something, but only if he's got something to hide from. A typical CFO of a company the size of Atlantis wouldn't need security like that.

As we left the tall buildings of Nashville behind, the driver took the ramp onto the highway heading south. I realized I didn't even know where the address was taking us, so I took a second to look it up. Chris lived in a village called Leiper's Fork, with the address showing the city of Franklin. It didn't take long to realize Mr. Valentine had done well for himself. Zillow placed his property value at over eight million dollars. That number seemed high to me and made me pause for a second.

Jennifer was looking out the other window, so after

reflecting quietly, I texted Paul to find out Chris' CFO salary. Atlantis was a private company, but the board had shared lots of detail with Rocky Mountain Equity. Paul would probably have the executive compensation in the package somewhere.

With the message sent, I sat back to enjoy the drive to Leiper's Fork, Tennessee. It turned out it was quite a beautiful drive, indeed. We passed one massive property after another, each covering multiple acres of well-manicured landscape. Many also had horse barns and wooden fences, with some even having large gated entrances. It was quite a contrast with downtown Nashville and the area near the Grand Marquis.

It took about ten more minutes to get to the Valentine property, which was one of the larger properties we had seen. The driveway seemed to be a mile long and looked like brand new concrete. There was immaculate landscaping along both sides of the driveway, and around the massive, two-story, modern house in the distance. My search revealed the house was built in 2009, but it looked brand new.

There was a large horse stable off to the right behind the house, and I could see the front of a barn in the distance. By habit, I counted six visible security cameras on the way in. That meant there were probably at least twice that many I hadn't seen.

When we got to the circle drive in front of the four white columns in front of the house, the Uber driver couldn't help but gawk at the property.

"Wow! Nice place," he said, almost involuntarily. Even the locals were impressed with Chris Valentine's accommodations.

"Yeah, our friend is a lucky man," I said in response, doubting it was luck that put Chris here.

"He's really lucky," Jen said as she gave me a questioning glance. She was probably thinking the same thing I was. This house was far bigger than Chris Valentine should be able to afford.

"Would you mind sticking around for just a second to see if he's home? If we don't get anyone, we'll just leave our cards and head back. If they let us in, we'll get another car," I said.

"Sure," he responded.

Jennifer and I got out and tried not to look around like we were as impressed as we really were. I'd seen expensive places all over the world, but this one had some sort of unique grandeur. Chris didn't put off the vibe that the house did, that's for sure.

We walked to the door and hit the doorbell, noticing the seventh visible camera just above the button. It was a similar unit to the one I had at home, with a camera and speaker for communicating with visitors. After a couple of seconds, a pleasant female voice came over the doorbell speaker.

"Can I help you?" the voice asked.

"Yes, thank you. We are friends of Mr. Valentine and business partners with Atlantis. We were in Nashville for an event and had planned to meet at the office. I understand Chris is working from home today?" I tried to make it sound like we had this all setup ahead of time.

To my surprise, the response was quick and cordial.

"Absolutely. Mr. Valentine is expecting you. Just a moment," the pleasant voice said.

A few seconds later, the large wooden door opened to reveal the splendor of Chris Valentine's home.

Chapter Thirty-Six

Leiper's Fork, TN. Friday

The front door opened to a two-story foyer that was bigger than our entire main level back in Colorado. There was a huge chandelier hanging from the ceiling, with stairways leading up to the left and right. Beyond the stairway on the left was an apparent office or library, and to the right was a living area with couches, a television, and a huge saltwater aquarium. The place was impressive.

"Mr. Valentine will be right with you. Please have a seat in the living room," the pleasant voiced woman said as she motioned for us to the living area to the right. She was dressed casually, but from her actions and tone, I suspected she was a nanny or housekeeper of some sort.

We took two steps down into the room and moved toward two of the tan leather chairs next to the big sofa. Only when we got down the stairs did we see the stone fireplace that dominated the wall on our left. A large photo of Chris, a woman, and a teenage girl caught my eye. The woman, in particular, looked familiar.

The room was open all the way to the ceiling two stories above us, with exposed beams and woodwork all around. Where the outside looked modern and opulent, this room looked like it belonged in a log cabin in Montana. If the log cabin was a city-block wide.

The furniture in this room matched the hunting lodge feel, with lots of brown leather and wood, but I noticed an absence of any deer antlers or hunting trophies. I would have expected that in Colorado. There were a pair of skis, some snowshoes, and a fly rod on the back wall, though. Apparently, the vibe was supposed to be outdoors but not hunting.

"Can I get you something to drink?" The woman with the pleasant voice had returned. Or maybe she never left. I wouldn't have noticed.

"No, thank you," was all I could mutter.

"Not even water?" She seemed rather persistent.

"Sure, I'll take some water," I finally replied, trying to stop gazing at the house.

"Me, too," echoed Jennifer, also pausing from her own open-mouth gazing around the room.

We sat down and continued to look around, at one point catching each other's eye. She nodded, obviously as impressed as I was. Yes, Chris Valentine was living well.

Our drinks were delivered in fine china tumblers, served on a silver tray that I could only assume was real. There were perfect ice cubes in the glasses as well. I wondered if this tray and tumblers were worth more than my entire kitchen. I enjoy nice things as much as the next guy, but I certainly didn't spend my money in the kitchen.

We were sipping our water for just a moment before Chris came down the left stairs in the foyer. He looked like he always did, except for jeans instead of dress slacks. He still had his Italian loafers, an expensive shirt and a sport jacket that was Armani or something similar.

Chris was in his early fifties but still had a full head of hair and an athletic build. If I had to pick his profession from his appearance, I'd say it was more likely he worked in sales versus finance. He just had that sort of look about him.

"Welcome! I'm sorry you had to drive all the way out here. I work here on Fridays sometimes. And, of course, we're all pretty shaken up about Bob Yates," he said while reaching out his hand.

If there was any fear or recognition when he saw me, he covered it well. His smile appeared genuine, and he didn't shy away from the handshake when I stood up. He nodded his head politely when I handed him the card. He presented himself as an excellent actor, if that's what he was doing.

"It's no problem at all. I'm Keith Morgan from Rocky Mountain Equity, by the way. And please accept my most sincere condolences about Bob. He was a good guy," I said as Chris shook Jennifer's hand, giving her much more of a smile than he gave me. I wondered how he would react hearing my name, as that's the name he and Mrs. Yates had used on their hotel reservations. I saw a brief wince, but he was so focused on Jennifer it was hardly recognizable.

"I'm Jennifer Ellis from Diverse Data. On behalf of our company, I'm so sorry. We worked closely with Bob and we're all just heartbroken," she said as he continued to shake her hand and smile. She was trying to hand him her card with the other hand, but he had locked in on her eyes.

"I suppose you already know who I am, from what I hear. And yes, he was indeed a good man. Such an incredible tragedy, and for what reason? I just can't imagine why anyone would want to do harm to that guy. Everyone loved him," Chris said as he finally broke the handshake with Jennifer, took her card and turned to sit on the couch between our two chairs.

"It's a shame, indeed. So sad. This is a fantastic house, by the way," I said, motioning to our surroundings.

"It's good to marry into money, I guess," Chris said, without elaborating.

"Well, we don't want to take much of your time, but I know Bob was responsible for your supply chain operations at Atlantis. As a potential investor, and with apologies if this sounds insensitive, we just wanted to see if you had a contingency plan to ensure operations continue on the same trajectory," I said, taking cues from my earlier conversation with Paul.

"Oh, believe me, I understand the need for due diligence in a situation like this. There's no need to apologize. In short, yes, we have contingencies in place. Bob was an excellent leader and had established an industry-leading distribution system during his time with Atlantis. His legacy will live on with the network and system architecture that he built. I expect to name one of his direct reports to his position on an interim basis while we settle on a permanent solution with an outside hire," he said, smiling politely as he spoke.

I needed to see if I could get some information on the project and Zapata, but wasn't sure it would work.

"That's great to hear. Thank you for that. And any projects he had been involved with will continue?" I asked.

If he recognized my attempt to get more details, he didn't show it.

"Oh, absolutely. There's nothing really out there in its early stages, so the projects that are running have a pretty good foothold. We'll struggle to replace Bob's leadership and knowledge, but we have his substantial track record to work from," he said, again sounding polite and confident.

"Excellent. That's great news. And again, I apologize for asking this type of question at such a hard time," he said.

"No problem at all," Chris said.

"So, you don't really see a financial impact to the business after Bob's departure?" I asked, just trying to close out the discussion on a final note.

"No. No, I do not. It will be tough for our tight-knit crew to get over his passing, but the company will forge ahead," he said, solemnly.

"Great. Thanks for your time, Chris. We'll get out of your hair," I said as I stood up.

"Sure. And I hope the drive wasn't too much of a chore," he said as he also stood.

"Oh, not at all. This area is beautiful," I said.

"I'm really taken by this room, Mr. Valentine," Jennifer started.

"Oh, please call me Chris," he interrupted.

"Oh, ok. Well, Chris, I'm really enamored with the decorating here. If this was a Colorado lodge, there would be elk and moose heads blended in with trout all over the walls," she said.

"Believe me, I'd like to have some of my trophies up there. But I'll have to admit, I don't do much of the decorating here. That would be my wife's forte," he said, holding his hands up in a surrender pose.

"I'll grab an Uber, real quick, if you don't mind," I said while I began swiping on my phone.

"Oh, that's probably not a good idea. It will take forever out here," Chris said.

I hadn't thought of that.

"Let me have one of our staff take you back. It won't be a big deal at all," he said casually.

"Oh, ok. I honestly hadn't considered how far out we were. I'll check and see what's available," I said.

The app showed a driver within three minutes, but I decided it might be helpful to be alone with one of the Valentine staff members for a half hour.

"Well, looks like you're right," I said.

"No issue at all. Hang out here for a second and I'll get someone to help," he said as he stepped around to the office or library, whatever it was.

In about thirty seconds, he was back.

"We can go out this way and we'll get you back to the Grand Marquis. That's quite a place, isn't it?" Chris asked, clearly trying his best to have a casual conversation.

"It really is. It seems to go on for miles," Jennifer said.

Chris led us past the room we were in, through a dining area that looked like it could seat a small army, and out onto the back deck of the property. From there, we could see the barn and vast acreage even better.

"You should come back when you have time to ride," Chris said to Jennifer, motioning toward the back of the property.

"Oh, do you and Mrs. Valentine have horses?" Jennifer asked. I almost laughed out loud as she was toying with Chris. It was obvious they had horses, and that she wasn't impressed with his tactic.

He caught it and simmered down.

"Yes, we do. There's your ride coming around, now," he said as he motioned toward the far left of the house. Only then did I see a large garage that was only visible from the back of the house. It had three two-car doors on it, but was clearly big enough to hold a dozen cars or more.

"You're a car guy?" I asked.

"Oh, not really. If anything, Mrs. Valentine is more of a car enthusiast than me," he said.

While we were talking, a BMW 5-series pulled around in front of us.

"This is Mark. He'll get you back to the hotel. Thanks so much for coming out," Chris said, shaking our hands one more time before we climbed into the back seat of the car.

And with the slam of the BMW doors, Jennifer and I were headed back to Nashville.

Chapter Thirty-Seven

Leiper's Fork, TN. Friday

"Where are you guys staying?" Mark, the driver, asked as he started the car. Either he was a conversationalist or Chris hadn't told him where we were going.

"We're at the Grand Marquis. And thanks for doing this! We could have taken an Uber, but it seems there aren't many of them around here," I said.

"Nah, it's fine," Mark said with a strong Tennessee accent.

"You have to do this often?" Jennifer asked.

"Not really, nah. I mean, we all have to drive Mrs. Valentine around whenever she wants, but that's it. Mr. Valentine usually drives himself," he said.

"That's quite a garage they have back there. They have some nice cars?" I asked, partly trying to get Mark to talk and partly because I was interested.

"They have a few, yeah. He likes his German vehicles, like this one, but she likes the more flashy cars," he said.

"Oh yeah. What's your favorite to drive?" I asked.

"Probably her Bentleys. She has a couple, and the smaller one, if there is such a thing as a small Bentley, is really fast. Plus, it's a convertible, which is nice in the summer. Only problem is, it's not big enough to sit in the back, so she has to sit next to me. That's just weird," he said.

"Oh, nice," I said, swiping and typing on my phone. The thought of Mrs. Valentine driving around in a Bentley reminded me of my trip to Zapata.

I was already on my phone trying to find recent photos of Mary Perez-Valentine. Her name was hyphenated everywhere I saw it online, which sort of fit with the message we were getting from Chris and Mark. The photographs in the house caught my eye as they resembled the woman I had seen in Zapata, but her hair wasn't blond in any of the photos.

There were photos of her all over the internet. It seems Mrs. Perez-Valentine was quite a businesswoman and socialite. And after swiping through a few pictures of her, I was certain that's who I had seen in Zapata.

"We weren't introduced to Mrs. Valentine at the house, but it looks like she's on the road quite a bit?" I asked, using the unhyphenated name like Mark did.

"Yep. She travels a lot. Just got back from Texas yesterday, in fact," he said.

Jennifer caught that one and glanced my direction. She could sense I had discovered something.

"Chris mentioned Mary was the one with the money. I knew he did well as the CFO, but their property is amazing," I said, trying to make Mark believe I knew Chris and Mary better than I really did.

"Yeah, no kidding. Y'all didn't even see the whole thing. That place is huge. It's one of the biggest ranches in the area, which is sayin' something out here. I don't know if she came from money, but she sure has it now. Although she hates the ranch part of it. She just likes the lifestyle," he said.

"What do you mean by that?" I asked.

I could see a mild smirk come across Mark's face, which he quickly covered.

"Oh, I don't know. It just seems she's more into spending money than he is, that's all." I could see Mark shut down with that last sentence, like I had gone a little too far.

I glanced over at Jennifer and could see her acknowledge the thought. We couldn't look at each other or talk about it in the car because Mark could easily see and hear us both.

We sat in silence for a few minutes, looking out the BMW windows at the green and manicured properties. When we got closer to the highway and the landscape changed, I decided to try a different tactic with Mark. I had learned a fair amount already, but I was still curious about a few things.

"Does the staff at each of those properties rotate around? I mean, do you guys know who are the best and worst owners to work for?" I asked.

"Oh yeah, it's a merry-go-round. There's always one or two who have been there forever, but the rest of us move around to the best pay and best treatment," Mark responded.

"Really. So, where does the Valentine ranch rank on that scale? Are people trying to get in or trying to get out?" I asked.

I could see Mark thinking about his response just a bit.

"They're sort of in-between, I guess. There ain't many places where I get to drive people around like this, but their knowledge of managing a horse ranch is pretty low. That makes them sort of unrealistic sometimes. But they spend money once we convince them it's needed. We've all learned we can get Mrs. Valentine to spend money as long as we say it will make her look good against her neighbors." Mark smiled at that thought.

Jennifer and I laughed and nodded to keep Mark engaged.

"That's pretty smart," I commented. That got a smile out of Mark. Then I continued.

"Do they keep the labor staffed up pretty well, even with the turnover you mentioned?" I asked.

Again, I could see the wheels turning in Mark's head.

"Yeah, I'd say so. Although we lost a couple of guys this week who just quit showing up. They were more of the driver types, but they helped out on the ranch some. We didn't even know they were leaving," Mark said.

Bingo. So, the two thugs were employed at the ranch, not at Atlantis. At least that's how Mark had perceived them.

"Oh, wow. That's weird to me. I guess that probably happens with ranches? I mean, people just decide to move on?" I asked.

"Naw, not really. People down here are pretty loyal and have a sense of appreciation for their jobs. It's rare for guys to just disappear like that. If word gets out, they won't be able to get jobs down here again," he said.

We were on the highway and within a few minutes of the Grand Marquis, so I thought I'd make one last attempt to get information from Mark.

"Word around the event this week is that Chris was rather friendly with one of the women there. Do you guys ever get stuck trying to hide that type of stuff from Mrs. Valentine?" I asked.

That one made Mark laugh out loud.

"Y'all have no idea! And I'd guess it's more than one if I know Mr. Valentine. That's one of the worst-kept secrets in Leiper's Fork. Thankfully, I don't think she even cares. We all think that's why she gets to spend money like she does. He gets his fun, and she gets hers," Mark said matter-of-factly.

This was one of the more informative car rides I'd had in a while.

In another few minutes, we were pulling into the parking area of the Grand Marquis and headed around to the circle drive that led to the lobby. Mark drove around as though he knew the place well and stopped right at the door.

"There ya go. Hope y'all have a nice visit to Nashville," he said, staying in the driver's seat. I surmised he didn't feel he needed to open the door for people who came to the house via an Uber ride.

Jennifer could hardly hold her comments until we got into the lobby. Then she burst.

"Wow, was that a bizarre trip!" She blurted out as soon as we got into the lobby.

We headed to the area where we were sitting earlier and took a couple of empty chairs.

"Yeah," was all I could respond before she took off.

"I mean, that property was fantastic!" She started with the first thing I had noticed.

"It was," I agreed.

"But that screwed-up relationship. And that guy reminded me of a bad salesman that ran into a boatload of money, not of a CFO. But it seems like his wife doesn't care as long as she gets her money to spend," she said, shaking her head.

"Yeah, that was nuts," I agreed again.

"But he really liked you," I couldn't help but add with an evil smirk.

"Yeah, I could probably have gotten myself a nice car to drive around in," she said with a smile.

"But for some reason, I don't feel his affection would put me in a very exclusive group," she added with another shake of her head.

We chatted about the trip some more before heading to our rooms. Jennifer had a closing event to attend, and I wanted to make a call or two. I didn't tell her about seeing Mrs. Perez-Valentine in Zapata yet. I needed to talk to Paul about that one.

There was clearly more to this story than we had gathered so far, and this trip had bolstered my hunch that Chris Valentine was involved in the Bob Yates murder.

Chapter Thirty-Eight

"Hey, Keith. How is Chris Valentine doing?" Paul asked when he answered the phone.

"It appears he is doing quite well, actually," I replied.

"Oh, really?" Paul sounded surprised.

"I didn't see any grieving at all, but didn't see any remorse, either. But honestly, that guy is so shady I'm not sure he would show it. He's a piece of work," I said.

"In what way?" Paul asked.

"It's weird, really. He comes across as very superficial and almost flaky. He was smitten with Jennifer, and his staff says he's rather liberal with his affection for women."

"You talked to his staff?" Paul interrupted.

"Yeah. He had one of his drivers take us back to the hotel," I said.

"He has drivers?" Paul sounded surprised again.

"Yeah, I'm getting to that," I said.

"Ok, sorry," Paul replied.

"They aren't solely drivers, but they are staff at the

ranch who drive the two of them around from time to time," I said.

I could hear Paul start to ask another question, but he stopped. I continued.

"The property out there is worth millions, which is why I asked for his salary. He says he married into money, which may be, but he's definitely living way beyond his CFO compensation. They have acres and acres of land, some number of horses and luxury cars, and it seems Mrs. Valentine is quite the traveler and shopper herself."

I let Paul get his questions in.

"Seven hundred thousand," Paul said.

"What?"

"Chris Valentine's salary and bonus total seven hundred thousand dollars. It was in the package the board sent us," he said.

"Ah, interesting. Then Mrs. Valentine must be raking it in somehow, because she seems to have some lavish spending habits. The driver indicated that's what she gets for looking the other way when Chris steps out on the marriage," I said.

"Let me dig into that a bit. She may own one or more of those companies we found doing business with Atlantis. That would make sense, in fact, if they're laundering money through the Atlantis supply chain. I get the feeling the board doesn't know, so Chris must be doing a good job hiding it," Paul said.

"Not too good. It seems the entire area around Zapata knows about it," I replied.

"Yeah, I guess that's true. He must be confident nobody down there will talk," Paul said.

"Let me find out. I'll give Maria a call and see if she'll

talk to her son. He may be willing to give her some names, at least," I said.

"Good idea."

"The driver also mentioned two of their staff disappeared this week. They weren't shaken about it because they have a regular turnover of workers, but he said these two just didn't show up, which was rare. I think we know what happened to them. It all just points to Chris Valentine being involved with Bob's death, in addition to whatever's happening in Zapata," I said.

"It sure does. This may mean another trip to Texas before you head home, if you can do it. Are the kids expecting you back tomorrow?" Paul asked.

"They are, but Oliver and Judy can cover, I'm sure. I can stay another day if I need to." I didn't love the idea, but if it will get us to the bottom of this, I decided I'd make it work.

"Ok, I'll let you know shortly. Let me know what you find out from Maria," Paul said.

"Sure. I'll catch you later," I said, ending the call.

I immediately dialed Maria's number in Zapata, suspecting she was probably working at the diner and couldn't talk.

I was right. The call went to voicemail, and I left her a message.

"Hi Maria, this is Keith Morgan. I hope you and the kids are well. We're digging into some of Bob's travel details and wanted to see if you could help. We believe he was working with some locals on behalf of Atlantis, and I know he got your son a job there. Would you mind asking if he would talk to us about what he's found at the plant? We're specifically wondering if he's met other people who know Bob, especially if they had worked with him or got their jobs through him. Thanks for your time, feel free to call me back as late as you wish. I know your shifts can be long, so don't worry about the time. Have a great day."

After disconnecting the call, I leaned back in the hotel desk chair and rubbed my eyes. There was so much going on with Bob Yates and Atlantis, it was hard to keep everything together. With all these moving parts, I was sure I was missing something obvious. Or maybe I'm over-complicating the whole thing. Maybe Bob found out about the drug activity, or whatever it was, in the plant in Zapata and Chris had him taken out.

I didn't have much time to think about it before my phone buzzed on the desk. Surprisingly, it was Maria's number. I didn't expect her to call back until she got home, but she must have taken a break.

"This is Keith," I answered, just to be sure it was Maria on the other end.

"Hi Mr. Keith, this is Maria. You called about people who may know Bob?" She sounded like she was outside.

"Yes, thank you for calling back so soon. I didn't expect to hear from you until after your shift," I said.

"It's ok, I'm outside," she said, stating the obvious as I could hear cars passing in the background.

"Great. So, as I mentioned in my message, we're trying to see what type of contacts Bob had made there in Zapata. We're just trying to make sure we get all his business covered by other people now that he's gone," I lied, trying to make it sound as official as I could.

"Oh, sure. Well, my son Javier may know people, but he hasn't told me. I can give you his number," she offered.

That wasn't expected, but I was glad she did it.

"That would be outstanding, Maria," I responded, sounding overly excited.

After she gave me Javier's number, she added.

"Javi's working until 10 p.m. tonight, so he may not be able to talk until then," she said.

"That's fine. This is very helpful, Maria. Thank you for helping us out," I said.

It seemed Maria really trusted Bob if she was willing to give out her son's phone number to Bob's friend she had only known for a couple of days. Interesting.

I dialed Javier's number and left a similar message. Hopefully Javier Sanchez could help me find out more details about Bob's interaction with his friends in Zapata.

Chapter Thirty-Nine

Nashville, TN. Friday

After leaving the message for Javi, it was almost 7:30 p.m. and it was time for dinner. I remembered there was a closing event for the Big Data conference and decided I needed a social break for a while. I freshened up a bit and headed for the ballroom where the festivities were being held.

The walk to the ballroom took several minutes, as I had to go past the atrium and through another set of hotel rooms before entering an entirely different atrium area. This one was smaller than the main atrium and was between hotel rooms on one side and a massive conference center on the other side. I had to get to the back of the atrium where the conference center entrance was.

After walking through the atrium, I went past the first several doors and down an escalator. As I got near the Grand Ballroom, I could hear the music from the band, the chatter from guests, and the clinking of plates and silverware. Apparently, this was quite an event.

I didn't recognize the band, but it soon became clear it was a cover band of dance hits from the last several years. I could handle that.

The Ballroom was wide open tonight, with all the partitions and dividers pushed back. With those dividers gone, I could see a stage all along the back side to my left, and a full dance floor in front of the stage. There were drink stations with bartenders sprinkled throughout the rest of the ballroom, and at least four visible buffet stations.

"Hey Keith, get yourself a drink, man. This band's awesome!" The voice came from behind me. It was a sales associate from a software company I'd worked with before. I think his name was Mike, or Mark, or Mick. I didn't remember, so I had to improvise.

"Oh, don't worry, I will," I said with a smile and a wave.

I headed toward the bar and got in line as other people I knew from the event shook my hand and greeted me along the way. It seemed more people had stayed than I expected, because this place was hopping!

There were no mixed drinks here, only wine and beer, so I grabbed a Blue Moon and headed to the nearest buffet. I didn't get to the line before I was headed off by Darren Harper from the golf event. He had clearly had a few drinks already and was abnormally chatty.

"What a week, huh, Keith?" He said as he put his arm around me.

"You're not kidding, Darren. How're things?" I asked, smiling politely.

"Awesome, man. I mean, except for that whole Bob Yates incident, of course." He obviously realized his mistake as soon as he said it.

"Yeah, that was sad. To Bob," I said, holding up my bottle.

Darren tapped my bottle with his and nodded, taking a sip.

"Hey man, you should come hang with us over by the dance floor. We've got a table right up front where we can take in the action," Darren invited.

With no better option, I agreed.

"Sure. Let me get some food and I'll head right over," I said.

I hadn't seen Jennifer, but suspected she was already in full party mode with her friends from Diverse Data who had come to the event. I'd catch up with her later.

I spent the next couple of hours sitting with a bunch of drunk software guys, on and off the dance floor, back and forth from the bar. The band was good. The food was great. And the drinks kept coming.

The band was playing a Lady Gaga number when I felt a hand on my shoulder and someone was leaning into my ear. The voice was familiar and made me smile.

"Looks like you got in with the party crowd up here," Jennifer said.

I turned and smiled when I saw her. She had changed back into her jeans, but still had the blouse and jacket on from earlier. Her hair was down to her shoulders and wasn't pulled back this evening. Apparently, I took too long to take in the sight of her.

"What? You offended that I think you're at the party table? You're allowed to party, Keith," she said.

"Oh yeah, that's what I do. I party," I said.

"Looks like you need another beer," she said. It was true.

I got up and followed Jennifer to the bar station a few tables behind us. She got a white wine of some kind and I grabbed another Blue Moon. That was my fourth one in the last two hours, which I count diligently at events like this to avoid any public mishaps. Two per hour was my maximum, so I was doing ok.

We chatted and watched a couple more songs while we finished our drinks. I didn't think I could enjoy it more, except for the noise. I decided to see if Jennifer felt the same way.

"You want to head over to the atrium bar where it's quieter?" I asked.

"YES! Great idea," she said excitedly and instantly stood up.

Again, I smiled.

We headed to the atrium bar and ordered drinks. I could get an Old Fashioned there, which I did, three times over the next couple of hours. I wasn't sure what time it was, but the guy playing the guitar and singing all the old country music songs was packing up his gear. I didn't remember if they stopped at ten or eleven, but it was one of those.

I don't know if it was the alcohol or the constant smiling, but I decided my relationship with Jennifer was at the point I could get a little more forward. I caught her eye, leaned in, and kissed her softly. She was clearly a bit surprised and blushed. But mostly smiled.

"I'm having more fun here than at the gala," I said.

"Yeah. Me, too," she nodded.

"I think it would save you some steps to spend the night in my room tonight. It's about 200 steps closer," I said, continuing to look into her eyes.

She leaned in this time with another long, soft kiss.

"With that sort of concern for my wellbeing, how could I turn down that offer?"

She finished her drink and stood up. I was already done with mine.

We navigated out of the atrium bar, down the hallway past the many, many hotel rooms. Past the lobby. It seemed to be taking forever, but eventually we got to my hotel room.

I pulled the card out of my pocket and held it to the door, standing back to let Jennifer in.

She stopped inside the door and threw her arms around my neck. I squeezed her around the waist and we made out like teenagers.

I felt like a kid, having not done this since my wife was alive. Surprisingly, the thought of her didn't ruin the situation or make it feel wrong this time. I was ready.

"I'll be right back," Jennifer said as she stepped into the bathroom.

I stepped over to the desk and pulled my phone out of my pocket, and put my key down. When I looked at my phone, I saw there was a missed call from a number I didn't recognize.

Now I had a decision to make. I had called the kids earlier, so I was pretty sure it wasn't about them. Plus, it wasn't a Colorado number; it was a.... Oh no! Suddenly, the realization hit me that I had left the voicemail with Javier Sanchez earlier and hadn't been watching for his return call.

As the urgency of getting to the voicemail overrode the alcohol, I tapped the message to see who it was.

It wasn't Javier's number, but was the same area code.

Chapter Forty

Zapata, TX. Friday

Javi went through his Friday evening workload at Atlantis in a robotic fashion, trying to keep his conversation with Gus from stealing his focus. Gus had been so nice to him, it made Javi feel awful to know even Gus could be corrupted by mama's friend Bob.

He was loading a pallet onto the truck when he felt his phone vibrate in his pocket with a call. Knowing he was on camera, he didn't want to even look at his phone while he was on the clock, so he let it go.

The shift eventually ended, and Javi made his way back to the bus from his station. He was putting his earnings in his pocket on the bus when Gus came in. He didn't look up when Gus came by, but to his surprise, Gus plopped into the seat next to Javi. His heart stopped, but he did his best to smile as he looked up.

"Hey," Gus said as he sat down.

Javi nodded but didn't speak.

"I wanted to say I'm sorry for how I reacted earlier. Mr. Bob was a friend of mine, and I didn't know he died. The news made me pretty sad," Gus said as he looked down at his feet.

"But who were you talking to on the phone? It sounded like he was more than just a friend," Javi replied.

"Yeah, I guess he was. But I can't talk about that. You'll just have to trust me I guess. Anyway, I'm sorry," Gus said as he looked up at Javi.

Javi didn't know what to say, so he just nodded. After spending his entire shift worried about it, he had to think about this whole situation for a minute. To buy some time, he pulled his phone out of his pocket and remembered the call he'd received earlier. Sure enough, there was a voice-mail from a phone number he didn't recognize.

Javi listened to the message from Keith Morgan, and his chin dropped as Keith asked if Javi knew anyone who had worked with Bob. Gus saw his expression change.

"Are you ok?" Gus asked.

"Yeah, yeah. Sorry," Javi didn't know what to do, so he just put the phone down and looked out the bus window.

The bus took off and headed toward their stop. Javi watched Gus for the next few minutes, looking for any sign that he was faking his grief for Mr. Bob. When he was convinced Gus wasn't acting, he shared the message he'd gotten.

"That message on my phone was from the guy that was here earlier this week. He was asking about anyone who may have 'worked with' Bob Yates," Javi said, accenting the words 'worked with,' so Gus would notice.

Javi watched closely as Gus' countenance changed from excitement to fear to confusion.

"Really? Exactly what did he say?" Gus asked.

Javi pulled the message up and handed his phone to Gus. Gus listened and gave the phone back without saying anything. He looked like he was in deep thought.

"You were working with him?" Javi finally asked.

Gus didn't say anything, but after a few seconds, he nodded.

"Where were you sending the kids?" Javi asked.

"It's not what you think, Javi," Gus replied.

Javi didn't know what to think.

They were silent for the next few minutes until they arrived at the gate of their neighborhood. They both got off silently, but Gus grabbed Javi's arm as they were getting ready to walk away.

"Hey, can I have that number? I think I'm going to call that guy," he said.

Javi nodded and pulled the number up, then held it up for Gus to type into his phone. He could see Gus was still struggling with the idea.

"He seemed like a nice guy," Javi said.

Gus nodded, paused a few more seconds, then hit the button to call Keith Morgan. Javi watched closely as Gus held the phone to his ear, eventually shaking his head. Javi assumed Mr. Keith wasn't answering.

"Hi. My name is Gustavo. My friend Javier says you want to talk to someone who worked with Bob Yates. I used to work with him. Please call me." Gus put the phone down and still looked to be deep in thought.

"He didn't answer?" Javier asked.

"No," Gus replied.

"It's pretty late. Maybe he'll call tomorrow," Javi replied.

Again, Gus just nodded. After standing there looking

like he was deep in thought for several more seconds, Gus sighed and turned for home. Javi watched him for a second, then headed toward his own home.

He would spend the next few hours wondering what Gus was working on with Bob Yates.

Chapter Forty-One

Nashville, TN. Friday

I was standing in the middle of the room listening to the voicemail with my mouth open and barely noticed Jennifer peek out and start walking out of the bathroom. She could tell from the look on my face something was up.

The voice on the phone sounded like a young man, maybe Javier's age. He said he worked with Bob Yates and I should call him back. I looked at the time of the call and realized it was only about thirty minutes ago. Knowing the shift Javier worked, I determined it wasn't too late to call back. I had to find out what type of work Bob Yates was doing in Zapata.

I turned to see Jennifer leaning against the wall with her arms crossed. She wasn't angry, but looked concerned.

"I'm so sorry, it's from Zapata. Apparently Maria's son found someone who worked with Bob Yates," I said.

"It's ok, Keith. Maybe this just wasn't meant to be," she said with a sorry smile.

"No, I mean, I'm really sorry. Really, really sorry. You have no idea how sorry," I pleaded.

"Really, it's ok, Keith. Call the kid back," she said.

I nodded and tapped the phone to call back the kid named Gustavo, who said he worked with Bob Yates.

"This is Gus," he answered. It took me a second to realize Gus was short for Gustavo.

"Hi Gustavo, this is Keith Morgan returning your call," I said.

I could hear some shuffling on the other end.

"Just a second," Gus said. I assumed he was getting to a private place to talk.

"Take your time," I said.

"It's ok now. You can call me Gus," he said.

"Ok, Gus. You said you worked with Bob Yates?" I got right to the point.

"Before I tell you about that. Why do you want to know?" Gus asked. He sounded scared.

"We're researching Bob's death up here in Nashville," I said.

"Are you the police?" Gus asked.

"No, I'm trying to help them," I said.

That seemed to give him some concern. He was silent for several seconds.

"I'm just trying to get to the truth, Gus. I realize there was some illegal activity down there that Bob was involved with. You don't have to be scared about that. We're not looking to turn you in," I said.

"You don't get it at all! Bob wasn't doing illegal things!" Gus sounded irritated and was almost screaming.

"But Javier mentioned Bob talking to some kids who would end up disappearing," I said.

"Javi doesn't know what he's talking about!" Gus was yelling again.

"What do you mean, Gus? What was Bob doing?" I asked.

I could see Jennifer looking at me curiously. We had both switched into problem-solving mode now. The mood we were in when we came to the room was long gone. I shrugged at Jennifer, not understanding where this was going.

"Bob talked to some kids, yeah. But he wasn't hurting them. He wasn't doing illegal things. He was helping them. They were in trouble and Bob helped them get out before the shirt guys got them," Gus said.

"When you say shirt guys, you mean the Atlantis employees?" I asked, making sure he was using the same definition as Javier.

"Yeah. The guys at Atlantis who all wear the same shirts," he said. I remembered seeing several of them when I was there, including the drivers of the Lincoln, the G-Wagon, and the Bentley.

"Ah, ok. So Bob was helping? What did he help the kids do?" I asked.

"Bob sent them out of here. He got them to places where they help kids like us. Not places where they send you to do bad things. That's what the shirt guys did. They took kids and sent them to bad places. We heard stories," Gus said, getting quiet.

"How many kids, Gus? How many went with the shirt guys?" I asked, getting angry as I listened.

"I don't know, probably hundreds. Or more. They find them coming across the border and put them in trucks. Or they pay the cartels to bring them over. Then they split them up at the warehouse and send them away in different trucks. We never see them again," Gus said, sounding sad about what he was telling me.

"Who all knows about this, Gus?" I asked.

"I don't know. People seem to ignore it. Atlantis is huge and powerful. If you say something wrong or you don't follow their rules, they just take you to the back warehouse and you disappear. So nobody says anything. We just keep quiet," he said.

"So, if Bob was helping kids, did he ever say who was responsible for the kids going to bad places?" I asked.

"No. He just said we have to be careful. He said they'd kill us if they knew we were taking their kids. He knew who they were going to take, somehow, and then sent them away. He said we had to watch our backs. I couldn't talk to anyone except him about it. Now he's gone. I don't know what to do," Gus said, fear entering his voice.

"It's ok, Gus. You're doing the right thing. You have no idea who you might have been hiding from? Was it the shirt guys? Someone else?" I asked.

"Well, we definitely didn't want the shirt guys to know. But there was someone else. Sometimes he'd call me and tell me to be especially careful because people were coming to visit from Nashville," he said.

That thought sent a chill down my spine. Was Chris Valentine going to Zapata himself? And did he have his wife helping him? Is that why I saw her down there? She sure didn't seem like someone to be afraid of.

"Is that the only thing going on at the Zapata plant?" I asked, trying to figure out why I had seen all the trucks bypass the border inspection.

"Well, no. But that's what Bob was helping with," Gus said.

"How were you helping Bob?" I asked.

"I would tell him when new kids came across. If new kids showed up in town or at Atlantis, I told Bob about them. Then he'd make sure they didn't get into the Atlantis trucks. He didn't get all of them, but he got many. I helped him get some kids out. He paid me when I did and made sure I had a job at Atlantis." Gus sounded a little more positive now.

"What else is going on out there? Are they transporting drugs in those trucks?" I asked, bluntly.

Gus got quiet.

"Yeah, I think so. I haven't seen it, but I've heard about it. And I hear some of the workers get paid with drugs. But if they take them at work, they disappear. Like the kids," Gus said.

I remembered the G-Wagon leaving when I was watching the plant two days ago.

"Do they sometimes transfer important people in the trucks from Mexico, too?" I asked.

"Yeah. We all think they're cartel leaders or something, but we don't really know. They just drive away in nice cars with the shirt guys. We're not allowed to look at them, but we see them," Gus said.

Then he switched gears with an aggressive tone.

"How did Bob die? Did the cancer kill him? He always talked about that, saying the cancer was going to kill him," Gus said.

"Well, Gus, no. The cancer didn't kill him. Someone shot him," I said, knowing this would not sit well with my new friend Gustavo.

There was a long pause as he almost seemed to hold his breath.

"Oh no. Who shot him?" Gus asked.

"I'm afraid we don't know for sure," I replied cautiously.

"Oh no, oh no," Gus kept repeating it, sounding more fearful every time.

"Take a breath, Gus. It's going to be ok," I said.

"If they know I was working with him, they'll kill me. I know it. They'll kill me. I'm dead," he said, panic seeping into his voice.

"But Gus, you've been going to work this week, right?" I asked, trying to settle him down.

"Well, yeah," he replied.

"And nobody is bothering you there, right? And nobody is following you?" I asked, hoping I knew the answer.

"No, I don't think so," I said.

"Then I doubt they know about you. Just keep going to work and everything will be ok," I said, calmly.

"Good. Plus, I did call Mr. Valentine and let him know I was worried," Gus said.

I nearly dropped my phone.

"You called who?"

"Mr. Valentine. Bob always said that was his boss. I had the number but never talked to him until earlier today," he said.

"Ah, I see," I said, trying to keep from screaming into the phone.

"Gus, are you scheduled to work tomorrow?" I asked.

"Yes. Just like every day except Sunday," he replied.

"Good. Just go to work like any other day. Everything is going to be fine," I said.

"Ok. Thanks Mr. Morgan," he said.

After telling him it was going to be ok, I sat there shaking my head. It sure didn't feel like everything was going to be ok.

Chapter Forty-Two

Nashville, TN. Friday

I ended the call with Gus and stood there for a minute, staring at the floor, trying to rationalize what I had just heard.

"What, Keith? What's going on?" Jennifer asked, jolting me back into reality.

She had turned the lights on, had gotten a bottle of water, and was sitting in the chair in the corner since I had been on the phone.

I didn't know exactly how to start.

"Well, it seems we had Bob Yates wrong. Again," I started.

"Wrong, how?" She asked the obvious question.

"Well, according to this Gus kid, it seems Bob Yates was helping kids escape from a potential human trafficking situation," I said.

"Hold on. Human trafficking? So the trucks with the cooling units DID have people in them?" Jennifer was almost yelling. I realized there were some missing pieces of the story I need to share.

I also needed to call Paul. The Association was onto more than I previously thought. But first, to Jennifer's question.

"Well, yeah, apparently. And drugs, as we previously thought," I said, shaking my head.

"You have got to get this to the authorities, Keith. This is huge. And horrible," Jennifer said.

"Yeah, I do. Listen, I'm going to make some calls. What time do you fly out tomorrow?" I asked.

"Sometime around noon," she replied.

"Great. Let's plan to have breakfast and I'll fill you in on what I learn," I said.

"Sure. You know, you really get yourself into some crazy situations, Keith," Jennifer said, giving me a curious look.

"Yeah. Seems like I do, doesn't it?" I said, shaking my head.

After a brief goodbye hug and kiss, Jennifer left the room, and I was able to call Paul. It was 10 p.m. in Colorado, but I knew he'd take my call.

He did, after only two rings. And he sounded like he wasn't yet in bed.

"Hey Keith, what's up?" Paul said, as he answered.

"Well, I just spoke to a friend of Maria Sanchez's son," I said.

"Oh, really. And what did you learn?" Paul asked, fully focused.

"Well, it seems I had the wrong impression about Bob Yates' interaction with the community in Zapata. Or better said, Maria's son Javier had the wrong impression," I started.

"You mean he's not in the business of pedophilia and human trafficking?" Paul asked bluntly.

"Well, no. It doesn't appear that he is. This kid, Gus, says he had been working with Bob to get kids out of the human trafficking system, not into it. Gus believes the Atlantis operation in Zapata is using their trucks to transfer drugs and humans into the United States and to various distribution centers around the country. And given the layout of the facility that I described earlier, I suspect they have a dedicated building in the back where they handle all that traffic. That explains the over-the-top security, too," I said, letting it sink in.

I heard Paul sigh on the other side, with a delay that was rare for him. This must have been a revelation for him, as he was taking some time to digest it.

"Wow," was all he said when he eventually spoke.

"Yeah, I know. And I think they may be also transporting some higher-ups in the cartel, too. I stumbled upon an apparent VIP coming out of that facility and being handed off to someone in a nearby town. Both were in high-end cars and appeared, at least on the surface, to be from outside the country. The challenge, of course, is proving any of this right now. This kid, Gus, is our only real witness, and there's a problem," I said.

"Oh boy," was all Paul could say as I continued.

"Apparently the kid knew that Bob worked for Chris Valentine," I began.

Before I could say anything else, Paul seemed to offer an involuntary response.

"Oh no," he sighed as I kept going.

"And when he heard about Bob's passing, he put a call in to Chris. He didn't know what we know, of course, and he may have just set himself up to 'disappear' like the other kids he talks about," I said.

"We need to get down there and make sure that kid stays safe," Paul said.

"Yeah, we do. I told him to go to work tomorrow like normal, trying not to scare him, but we really need to get him some coverage before his workday even starts. He can't go back out to that plant alone," I said.

"Nope, he can't," Paul said. I could hear Paul thinking while I added my last thought.

"I think I should go back down there, Paul. We can get the locals involved, but that's going to take a bit of time and justification. I can be there by morning if I need to," I said.

"Yeah, I'm thinking that same thing. But we probably need to supplement you on this one, Keith. Let me check my calendar, too. This is where The Association's limited coverage comes into play. We have people scattered across the country, but I don't think we have anyone down there near the border. I'll check and get back to you in a minute," he said.

"Ok. Can you guys get me another charter?" I asked.

"Probably, but I'll need to call right now," Paul said.

Before I said anything else, he went into a new thought.

"Is Jennifer there with you?"

I didn't know if he meant at the conference or in my room, so I covered both ideas.

"She's here at the conference and I've seen her around, but I'm in my room now. Why do you ask?" I said.

"Well, we've had some discussion after Willow Creek. Her data analysis and tactical skills were pretty impressive. There are some thoughts within The Association that she might be valuable to our cause from time to time," Paul said.

"Now, wait a minute, Paul," I said before he could finish.

"She was exceptional in Willow Creek, that's for sure,

but I'm not sure we should throw her into something like this. I mean, she's a data analyst from Colorado who's out here for a software event," I said, more forcefully than I intended.

"Yeah, and you're a business consultant out there to evaluate acquisition targets," Paul responded.

"Yeah, but," I started, but Paul interrupted.

"And don't you think it would be fair for her to get paid for taking these risks just like you do? We don't 'throw you' into these situations either, Keith. We send you to investigate and you jump right in without asking. That's part of your value to the organization, of course, but it's not our ask. It's your character. From the way she responded with you when you were forced into action, I'd say it's her character, too," he said.

I sat for a minute, trying not to tell Paul he made some good points. The thought of Jennifer being in the same risk profile as me somehow didn't feel right. I had certainly done so willingly, but that was different. At least that's what I kept telling myself. But now, faced with the possibility of Jennifer joining The Association, I had to realize it wasn't really different at all.

"I suppose I shouldn't make a decision like this for Jennifer. She should get the opportunity to decide for herself," I finally said.

"Do you know where she is?" Paul asked.

"You mean you're going to do it now? On a Friday night at 11:30 p.m.? After a closing ball with an open bar?" I added, again sounding more exasperated than I meant to.

"Do you have a better idea? I mean, there's never a good time for this, Keith," Paul said calmly.

Again, I thought for a few seconds before I replied.

"I guess that's fine. Should I call her?" I asked.

"Yeah, please do. If you can be with her when we talk, that would be best," Paul said.

"Ok, I'll call you back when I get her," I said as we ended the call.

I sat there shaking my head for a few minutes before dialing Jennifer's number. She picked up immediately.

"Hey Keith, is everything ok?" she asked.

"Yeah, sure is. I was just wondering if you could come back and talk," I said.

"Keith, I think the moment has passed," she started.

"No, no, it's about the Bob Yates case," I interrupted.

"Oh, yeah. Sure. I'll be there in a couple of minutes. Sorry about that," she said, sounding a little embarrassed.

"Ok, thanks Jen, see you in a bit," I said as I ended the call.

I sighed heavily at the thought of my relationship with Jennifer becoming a professional and dangerous one in the next few minutes.

Chapter Forty-Three

Nashville, TN. Friday

Jennifer knocked on my door in less than ten minutes, and I let her in. She could see on my face that I was in deep internal conflict.

"What's wrong, Keith? Did something happen?" she asked.

"No, no. Not really. I was just talking to someone who thought it might be good to get your perspective on something," I said, trying to stay as neutral as possible. And trying to smile.

"Ok, sure," she said.

I got out my phone and walked to the table by the window, and sat down in one of the two chairs. Jennifer followed me and took the other chair.

I dialed Paul's number.

"Hey Keith," Paul answered.

"Hey Paul, I'm here with Jennifer. You're on speaker," I said.

I sat the phone down on the table and sat back in my chair.

"Oh, hey, Jennifer. Thanks for taking my call at this late hour. I truly apologize for the inconvenience, but I think you'll realize the urgency shortly," Paul started.

"Ok," Jennifer said with a questioning tone while looking at me.

"First, let me introduce myself. My name is Paul Frazier. Keith and I have known each other for, well, over ten years now. We met during our time in the military and worked together with some security contract agencies as well. I think a great deal of Keith and consider him to be one of my closest and most trusted friends," he said.

"Ok," Jennifer said again, still looking at me with questions in her eyes.

"About five years ago, Keith and I became partners in our business, Rocky Mountain Equity. As you probably know, Keith is a brilliant business consultant and is especially knowledgeable in the high-tech industry. He's been invaluable to our company in our evaluation process for acquisition targets. But that's not why I've asked Keith to bring you here tonight," Paul said.

"Ok." It was the same response from Jennifer as before.

"Keith and I are also part of a unique group of people with similar, but very diverse, backgrounds. I mentioned Keith's background in technology, but my background is different. I come from a finance background. But both of us share an interest in making sure our country, which we love and have risked our lives for, is moving in the right direction. Our group, which we formally refer to as The Association, includes people with skills like us and others who may not have the tactical skills but provide financial backing," Paul said.

This time, Jennifer sat back in her chair and looked to be deep in thought while Paul continued. She struggled to keep her mouth from falling open in shock. I sat still and watched, forcing myself to avoid showing any emotion.

"The Association includes only a few hundred people, all with significant positions in their areas and with substantial financial resources. When they see, or perhaps even sense, something is going wrong that is outside the normal resources of the police or government jurisdiction, they call me to put together assignments to investigate," he said.

"Was Diverse Data just an assignment for you, Keith?" Jennifer suddenly interjected, staring at me with pain in her eyes.

I didn't know exactly how to respond. If I knew this day would come, I would never have gotten Jennifer involved with the investigation that led to Willow Creek.

"The assignment with BradComm and Diverse Data was an assignment, yes. You'll never know how sorry I am that the assignment bled over to our, uh, relationship," I said with a struggle.

She sat silently for several seconds and Paul remained quiet to let everything sink in. Eventually, he continued.

"To be fair to Keith, our assignments are usually not that dangerous. Typically, we gather data and other types of evidence and hand the situation over to the authorities. When we found out how far the criminal activity had gone, however, it was too late. You know everything that happened after that," he said.

"So, Keith works for a secret organization that sends him on missions to save the United States. Is that what I'm hearing?" Jennifer asked, suddenly sounding sarcastic and angry.

"He's not like a superhero, if that's what you're asking.

And again, we don't put Keith or any of our associates in harm's way intentionally or without their consent. We are simply trying to help where help has not yet arrived. That's what happened when we asked Keith to work with Diverse Data last fall and, well, that's what's happening now," Paul said, finally getting to the point.

"Ok, so why are you telling me all this? Why not just keep it a secret and keep lying to me about it?" Once again, Jennifer sounded sharp and angry, and I could see tears beginning to form in her eyes.

I looked down, feeling guilty for her justified wrath.

"We want your help, Jennifer. We'd like you to become an associate with The Association. And we'd like to do it as fast as you're ready. You have, of course, the option to decline. Some do. But we wouldn't be talking to you if we didn't think you were a fit. You have skills with data and analytics that we can always use, plus you demonstrated you also have the tactical skills that can be valuable in an emergency," Paul said, stopping to let Jennifer absorb the thought.

She put her head in her hands, then rubbed her temples.

"You called me in here late Friday night, with an obvious challenge that needs urgent intervention, and hit me with this whole black ops-sounding thing? This is completely surreal," she said, shaking her head.

"I understand your hesitation, Jennifer. Let me offer a bit more regarding our group. We have heads of major corporations, state and federal legislators, and influencers of all major financial markets. We have people with knowledge and expertise of virtually every major technology and business line in the country. We don't break the law, we just use it to our advantage. Lastly, if you agree, we'll supplement your income with Diverse Data to cover your assignments with The Association," Paul said.

Jennifer didn't seem to notice the thought of money so much as the involvement of Diverse Data.

"How would you do that? How would you..." Her voice slowly faded as she realized how it might work.

"Rocky Mountain Equity owns Diverse Data now, so you'd just send money through their payroll? Isn't that laundering?" She asked, figuring out the model quickly.

"Oh no, not at all. You would absolutely be going on assignments for Diverse Data, and the payments would simply be payment for those assignments. The company will report them, you will report the taxes, and everything is above board. It's just that the assignments will contain elements that may not be publicly available," Paul said.

Jennifer thought for a minute, then looked at me.

"So, why were you here this week, Keith? Was it an assignment? What was the secret job you had for The Association?" Jennifer asked, still a little sharp with her tone but softening.

I looked at the table before I started. I considered asking Paul for permission to share, but decided against it. I wasn't interested in seeing more wrath from Jennifer.

"I was asked to come here to investigate Atlantis as a potential acquisition target for Rocky Mountain Equity. The Association had become aware, in ways I don't have visibility to, of some supply chain irregularities with the company. I was using the cover of Rocky Mountain Equity to snoop around. I had gotten the golf event planning guys a few beers the night before and had gotten myself assigned to a foursome with Bob Yates. That was it. From there, you know the rest of the story," I said, trying to sound sincere.

"This assignment is not atypical. It just went upside down when Bob was murdered," Paul added.

Jennifer looked down and again appeared to be deep in thought. After several seconds, she looked up with resolve.

"Suppose I go on one of these 'assignments' and realize it's not what I want to do. Do I disappear?" She asked.

"Oh, no, not at all. As I said, everything is above board with The Association. You can leave at any time. You may even decide to only take assignments when you're ready, which is also fine. Of course, we may ask you to be flexible if urgent needs arise, but it's always your choice. I can tell you from experience, this isn't the military," Paul said.

After looking around in thought for a few more seconds, Jennifer seemed to come to a decision.

"Alright, I'll do it. It may be the wine talking, though, so maybe we should reconnect in the morning when I don't feel so agreeable," she smiled a half-smile.

"You can wait. You don't have to decide now," I blurted out before thinking about what I was saying.

"I said I'll do it," Jennifer said with grit and determination eating into the smile.

It was great to see even half of her smile return, but I knew there were now fractures in our relationship. She had learned I was keeping a gigantic secret from her ever since we met. I'd have to work on that later.

"Ok, agreed. In fact, if you're available, you can meet Keith in the lobby around 7:30 a.m. to catch a ride to the airport. Keith is headed to Texas, and we'd love for you to go with him if you can," Paul said.

Jennifer's face took on a look of even more resolve, almost gritting her teeth.

"I'll be there," she said firmly.

"Ok, it's a date," Paul joked, not realizing the sting of his words.

"But wait, I have a flight tomorrow." Jennifer said, already thinking about the logistics.

"Send me the details, and I'll take care of that. I'm sure I can get you on the flight with Keith on Sunday morning," Paul replied.

"Ok," Jennifer said, tilting her head and raising her eyebrows as though she was impressed.

"Thanks guys, we'll talk in the morning," Paul said as the call disconnected.

I expected Jennifer to ask questions about the process, about the pay, about the number of assignments or how they work, but she asked nothing. Instead, she stood up, took a breath, and walked out the door.

I didn't hear from her until the next morning.

Chapter Forty-Four

Nashville, TN. Saturday

I didn't sleep much Friday night between the alcohol and the situation with Jennifer. Even my military sleep training failed to help for the first time I could remember.

Jennifer didn't call about breakfast, so I was forced to get something on my own for the first time here at the Grand Marquis. Instead of going to a restaurant, I went to the coffee shop next to the lobby and got coffee and a sausage croissant. I still felt bad about putting Jennifer through Paul's conversation last night, but the delicious croissant added a bright spot to my morning.

At 7:20 a.m. I made my way to the lobby to meet with our driver. As I walked, I got a text message saying our car would be a black Mercedes S-class. Again.

When I got to the lobby, Jennifer was already down there, standing near the front doors with a styrofoam cup looking out the window. I knew she could see my reflection in the window, so I walked up as confidently as my brain would allow.

"Good morning," I said as I got next to her.

"Hey," she said. There wasn't the usual sparkle in her eyes, but I couldn't be sure if it was the conversation or the wine.

"Are you sure you want to do this?" I asked.

She continued staring forward out the window, watching the cars come and go in the pickup area outside the hotel lobby.

"I don't know. There's a lot to think about here," she said.

"You don't have to go. Paul was right. Nobody will say a word if you decide not to take his offer," I said.

She looked over at me for several seconds, looked like she was about to say something, then returned her gaze out the window.

"I believe you. But I have to think about this. Despite my anger at your dishonesty about the whole situation up to now, I guess I do still trust your judgment. Do you think these guys are on the right track?" She asked earnestly, so I gave her an earnest answer.

"I do. I've been on twenty-one assignments over the last five years. Some last for a day or two, some last weeks or months. There's always a reasonable cover. There's always a valid reason to go, and there's rarely an incident like we ran into at Willow Creek. And so far, they've been able to provide me with more than adequate support when I needed it," I said, not breaking eye contact.

"What do you mean 'so far' you've had adequate support?" She caught the nuance in what I said.

This time, I turned and stared out the window.

"This place in Texas is pretty remote, and we don't really know the lay of the land. It's different when I'm in a place I know, with a situation I'm able to dictate. That's not the case here. Atlantis is an unknown, the evidence of a drug cartel is an unknown, and frankly, Zapata is an unknown. I would be lying if I told you I was completely comfortable about this," I said.

We both stood there looking forward for another few seconds when my phone buzzed with a text message. I looked at the message.

"Our car is here. It's that black one over there," I said, pointing to the same car I had ridden in a day earlier.

"Nice. Looks like The Association travels in style," Jennifer said.

"Just wait," I said with a meek smile as we walked out the door.

We walked to the car and got inside, and I could see Jennifer nodding as she looked around. We had water, snacks, and a rather pleasant environment to spend the next few minutes in.

Fortunately, the reality of The Association's resources began settling in and Jennifer started asking questions.

"Paul said they'd pay me for this. And this is a nice car. Clearly, they have substantial financial resources. How does all this work?" She started with the basics.

"I can't pretend I know all of it, but I'll tell you what I know. We call Paul the gatekeeper, because he's the one who schedules everyone for these assignments. He is sort of the gateway into The Association overall, as far as my involvement goes. He has access to the financial resources, which are managed by someone else, through the investment arm of Rocky Mountain Equity. They can manage the transfer of funds through their venture capital funding entities, ultimately arriving at the company that's paying you and me. And, of course, all the others like us. Then, when Paul lets them know a payment is required, they issue the bitcoin payments to your wallet," I said, hesitating to see if Jennifer would ask about that part.

"I suppose I'll need to set up one of those," she said.

"Yeah, that's pretty important. It doesn't make the money invisible, of course, but it puts it in a more flexible currency for some. I've had no issues with the whole process so far, and have been quite pleased with how it works," I said.

"And these assignments? Who comes up with them? Is there a vetting process or do they just get sent to Paul and he reacts? That part seems sketchy to me, since that's where all the control seems to be," she said.

"That was probably one of the two biggest hurdles when I started, along with not knowing where the funding was coming from. I don't really see all the details behind the assignments, but Paul has told me there's a small group authorized to select them. He says there's an informal vetting process that occurs between the senior associates. Again, I don't know who they are, which is by design, but they send the assignments to Paul. Then Paul decides whether to assign someone, and who that might be," I said.

"How many people take assignments?"

"I don't really know, but I've met others. There are at least twenty, I'd guess. If not more," I said.

She thought for a moment, then continued.

"Can you give me an idea of the assignments? Like, what did they tell you about Atlantis?"

"It was relayed to me exactly as I described it last night. The Association had noticed irregularities in their supply chain, and wanted to check it out. I assumed that was purely financial, like embezzlement or something, as that's pretty common. I never know how much The Association knows about the assignment ahead of time. Sometimes, it feels like they're leading me to the evidence to help get the authorities what they need," I said.

"So, that's the relationship I've seen you have with the locals. You're trying to help lead them to whatever The Association finds." It was a statement, not a question.

"That's the delicate part of this. We have to find the actual issue, whatever it is, then make sure the evidence is legitimate, then get the authorities to that same conclusion. That, of course, assumes The Association is right. I never assume they are. The last two cases have also led to a far broader criminal enterprise than anyone expected. That includes this assignment," I said.

We sat in silence for the next few minutes, but it felt like Jennifer was loosening up about the whole situation. I decided to press my luck.

"Hey Jen, I'm really sorry. I never meant to mislead you or ..." I didn't get another word out before she raised her hands in front of her as a sort of surrender.

"I know. I know, Keith. I see that now. But you're going to have to give me some time with this. Let's get to the bottom of whatever's going on in Zapata and go from there," she said, turning to look at me.

"Ok, fair enough," I said.

We arrived at the same airfield I had returned from yesterday, and Jennifer realized how we were traveling to Texas.

"Well, ok then. I could probably get used to this," she said as we pulled into the private hangar.

She smiled at me, and I nodded. Maybe our relationship would be ok, but it certainly would never be the same.

Chapter Forty-Five

Zapata, TX. Saturday

The flight from the airfield outside Nashville to the one near Zapata gave Jennifer some time to think about what was really happening. It also gave me an opportunity to consider how we might get substantive evidence from the Atlantis plant. Or from their trucks. Or from Gus and Javier. Ok, I didn't really have it all well-formulated just yet.

We sat facing each other in the plush leather seats and said very little for the first few minutes after takeoff. I could see the wheels turning in Jennifer's head and I felt I needed her to sort out the situation on her own. It seemed to take about half an hour for that to happen. Which was good. There were some more details I needed to share before we landed.

"Ok. I'm still a little uncomfortable with this whole 'Association' thing, so I apologize in advance for asking more questions," she finally said.

"That's fine. I don't know everything, but I'll tell you what I know," I replied.

"Whose plane is this?" Her first question was already off on the wrong track.

"I have no idea," I replied.

"You just got on a plane going to God-knows-where because Paul told you to?" She asked, as though it was absurd.

"Well, yeah," I replied, deciding not to tell her I had done much worse just because Paul said so. But that started when we were working in Afghanistan, not with The Association.

"Wow. You really, really trust that guy," she said.

"Yeah, I do," I acknowledged.

She sat for another minute and seemed to cross some threshold.

"What is your plan for Zapata?" She asked, suddenly.

"I want to talk to that kid who called me. Gus. We probably need to keep him with us until we find out if he's in any danger. We know he called Chris, but we don't know if Chris did anything about it. I have to assume he will, knowing what happened to Bob Yates," I said.

"Ok, so we get Gus. Then what?" She was kicking into gear now.

"I want to meet with Maria again, then focus on Atlantis. We have to get actual evidence of their operation there. If not an eyewitness, at least a video or something. I found a maintenance road just beyond the facility where you can see the whole place, and I've asked Paul to get us some video equipment out here," I said.

"We're going on surveillance, then?" It was more of a statement than a question.

"Yeah, I guess we are. And investigation. I'd also like to find out how to tie Chris Valentine to this whole thing.

Maybe Gus or someone else has seen him around Zapata," I said.

"Got it," Jennifer said, apparently satisfied with the high-level plan.

We sat in silence for several minutes before I tried an apology once more.

"Look, Jen, I'm really sorry about last night..." And once again, she cut me off.

"There's no need to apologize. With everything I've learned in the last twelve hours, that seems like a long time ago. Like I said, I need some time to process this," she said firmly.

"Ok, ok. I'll stop pressing it," I said with a sigh. This was a weird sensation for me. I was usually the one trying to slow down my relationships. This one seemed to be going very well until that talk with Paul. But, of course, I certainly realized the significance of that conversation.

We discussed a few more logistical items over the next several minutes until we could feel the plane descending into the Zapata region. As we got close enough to see the landscape, we both looked out the window to take a more strategic view of the area.

"It's pretty flat out here. How were you able to get a view of the facility without them seeing us?" Jennifer asked.

"The overall area is flat, yes, but there are some ridges and ravines that are subtly strewn across the flatness," I said.

"Yeah, I guess I see that. I wouldn't call it sniper-friendly, though," she replied. She was already into contingency planning in case our investigation goes poorly.

"No, it's not. Plus, the facility has guard towers that are high enough to see pretty far if they need to. They'll definitely have the upper hand on sniper locations. Let's hope it never gets to that," I said.

She nodded.

The G400 landed with a bump, and a few minutes later, we stepped off the plane near the same hangar I had been at just a day before. It didn't feel nearly as uncomfortable as the first time.

And like before, there was the trusty Ford F-150 sitting near the gate, just like I had left it. I wondered if anyone had even moved it. When we got to the truck and opened the doors, however, I realized someone had definitely been there since I left it.

Inside the truck were two tactical bags. There was also a rifle case laid across the floor in the back and a camera bag sitting in the back seat. Clearly, someone had loaded the truck before they returned it to the airfield. I considered digging into the bags while we were sitting there, but given the cameras around the facility and the wide open view of the truck, I decided against it.

Instead, I gave Paul a call.

"Hey, Keith. You guys make it in ok?" Paul said when he answered.

"Yeah, no issues at all," I replied.

"How's Jennifer?" Paul asked before I could add anything else.

"I think she's coming around," I said.

"Good. You need her to come around quickly, so make sure you give her the support she needs. I know you guys are down there to look around and gather evidence, but you've seen firsthand how vicious these cartels can be. You two need to be careful," Paul said.

"Believe me, I know. Although I will say it helps to have the support packs you left us here in the truck," I said.

"Yeah, I thought it might. Hopefully, you won't need the tactical gear, but I didn't want to risk leaving you down there unarmed. You'll also find the camera equipment you asked for," he said.

"I saw the bag. Thank you," I said.

"Sure. If anything goes wrong, let me know ASAP. As you might expect, you're a long way from help, so you two are pretty much on your own," Paul said as a final warning.

"Got it. I'll keep you updated," I said as we ended the call.

"All good?" Jennifer asked as I put down my phone.

"Yep, all good. Let's go see Gus. I'll check in on the kids on the way," I said as we pulled away. The casual calls home from various locations around the world had become common in recent years. I'd learned to keep a calm voice regardless of my surroundings. I suppose that was some-thing I learned in the Middle East years ago. It's a skill I sometimes wished I didn't have to use.

I spoke with Judy and the kids for a few minutes, making sure they were on schedule for their typical spring Saturday. As I expected, they were. We said our goodbyes, and I promised I'd be back home in Woodland Park tomorrow.

Then, just like two days earlier, I pulled up to the gate, and the guard opened it without a question. And just like before, I pulled out onto the dusty two-lane highway headed south toward Zapata.

This time, however, the stakes were a little higher because Jennifer was traveling with me. We also now had knowledge of actual crimes being committed. I was still manufacturing a plan to get some type of evidence as we drove along, keeping in mind there were people here capable of committing some heinous murders like I had seen in Nashville this week.

Chapter Forty-Six

Gus was playing video games with the other kids who lived in his house when his phone buzzed in his pocket. He kept playing, but made a mental note to check the phone at the next break. It was another thirty minutes before he looked at it.

The message was from a Nashville number he didn't recognize. When he finally listened to it, it was also a voice he didn't recognize. The voice told him he was in danger, and that someone would pick him up at the gate in an hour. That meant he needed to be at the gate less than thirty minutes from now. While the message didn't give details, the realization that Bob's murderers may come after him took his breath away. That had to be the reason behind the vague message.

Gus packed a duffle bag with a change of clothes and grabbed a bottle of water before he nonchalantly walked out the door and toward the gate. He looked at the time and realized he was actually getting out there a little early. He slowed down, took a breath, and cautiously made his way past the other manufactured homes and kids playing. Gus wondered if this would be the last time he saw this place.

While he was navigating around a group of kids playing soccer in the street, Gus received a call from a number he did recognize. It was Mr. Keith from yesterday. He accepted the call as he neared the gate.

"This is Gus," he said.

"Hey, Gus. We decided to come down and pick you up just to be safe. I'm sure everything is going to be fine, but just in case, we'll be arriving at your neighborhood soon," Mr. Keith said.

"I know. I got your message. I'm already here at the gate," Gus said.

"What message?" Mr. Keith asked. The question confused Gus.

"The one you sent a few minutes ago. In fact, I think I see you now," Gus said as he watched a black G-Wagon pull up to the gate.

"Gus, that's not us! You need to run away! Do not get in that vehicle, Gus!" Mr. Keith was yelling as the G-Wagon pulled up next to Gus.

Gus didn't hear the warnings, and waved at the shirt guy who rolled down his window on the passenger side. He thought he recognized the shirt guy from the Atlantis plant, but he wasn't sure.

"Hey, Gus," he said in a friendly tone.

"Hop in. You may have heard Bob Yates was murdered in Nashville. I'm sorry if this is news to you, but we want to make sure you're safe since you were working with him. Your work is very important, but also dangerous," the shirt guy said.

Gus nodded as he pulled the door open and climbed

into the back of the G-Wagon. He had never been inside a vehicle like this before, and was taking in the feel and smell of new leather as the driver took off. It took him a minute to notice Mr. Keith wasn't there.

"I thought Mr. Keith was coming?" Gus asked, as he realized neither of the two shirt guys looked like Mr. Keith.

"Who?" The shirt guy in the passenger seat turned and asked after they looked at each other with puzzled expressions.

The question gave Gus an uneasy feeling. He didn't know what to say or what to think. He sat still while the shirt guy looked at him.

"Who were you just on the phone with, Gus?" the shirt guy finally said.

"And who is Mr. Keith?" The shirt guy now seemed agitated as he reached back and grabbed Gus' phone.

"Look at me," he said as he held the phone to Gus' face to unlock it.

"Who is Mr. Keith," he asked again.

Gus was getting more and more uneasy as they rode along. He considered jumping out of the vehicle, but at highway speeds, it would have been suicide. He concluded he'd have to play along until he could escape safely.

"I met Mr. Keith with Bob. He came down from Nashville after Bob was killed. He said he wanted to keep me safe, and he was coming to get me. I thought the message came from him," Gus replied.

The two shirt guys looked at each other again.

"What is Mr. Keith's last name?" they asked.

"I don't remember. I think it started with an 'M'," Gus said, trying to remember.

The shirt guy in the passenger seat looked annoyed.

"Try to think, Gus. It's important. These guys may try to hurt you," he said.

That made little sense to Gus, but he no longer knew who was good and who was bad.

"Can I please have my phone back?" Gus asked.

"We need to keep it, Gus. You know they can track you with your phone, right? So, we'll get rid of it when we stop," the shirt guy said. Once again, the answer made Gus more uncomfortable.

He thought of a new tactic.

"Uh-oh, I think I forgot my wallet back at the house," Gus said while frantically pretending to check his pockets.

The shirt guys gave an evil sneer and looked back at him.

"You won't be needing your wallet," the shirt guy in the driver's seat said.

It was at that moment Gus realized he had gotten into the wrong vehicle. Again, he thought about jumping out of the moving vehicle. Would that be better than what was coming for him? He decided it would and tried to unlock the door.

It didn't unlock.

The shirt guy in the driver's seat saw him struggling with the door.

"The doors have child-proof locks, Gus. You can't get out. There's no need to try to bust the windows, either," he said calmly.

"Where are you taking me?" Gus asked when he finally gave up trying to escape the vehicle.

From that point on, the shirt guys were silent.

Gus asked repeatedly where they were going, right up to the point they pulled into the Atlantis facility.

When they went through the gate, Gus looked for

anyone who might be able to see him trapped in the back of the G-Wagon. He didn't see anyone watching, but the driver saw him looking around.

"Don't even try to get help, Gus. These windows are tinted so dark nobody can see in. Just relax," the driver said.

A feeling of doom settled on Gus as the G-Wagon drove past the main facility to the small, secret facility in the back. He heard the passenger talking on the phone.

"We seem to have found someone who was trying to get to him before us. His name is Keith something. Gus thinks it starts with M," he was saying.

"Yeah, that could be it. But if it is, he's down here right now," he said after listening for a second.

"Got it," he said as he ended the call and put his phone down.

He began thinking about ways he might escape from the building in the back if they left him there. He had no intention of dying out here or being taken away by one of the human trafficking trucks he had heard about.

If Gus was going to die two weeks before his seventeenth birthday, he was going to die fighting.

Chapter Forty-Seven

Zapata, TX. Saturday

Jennifer heard me yelling into the phone, trying to keep Gus from getting into the vehicle he thought was us.

"What was that about? Did someone else pick him up?" she asked.

"I think so. He said he saw me and hung up, so I suspect someone else pulled up just then," I replied.

"Chris Valentine's guys?"

"Probably. I don't know who else it would have been."

"Where would they take him?" Jennifer asked.

"I'm not sure, but I suspect I know," I replied.

Then, as we were racing down the road toward Gus and Javi's neighborhood, the black G-Wagon going the other way caught my eye. I got a sick feeling in my stomach when I saw it.

As we pulled up to the gate of Gus' neighborhood, I saw no sign of him and I suspected I knew what had happened. Chris Valentine had gotten to Gus just before we did. Now we had to figure out how to get him back.

I turned around and floored the F-150 in the direction the G-Wagon had been going. That direction, as I suspected, was toward the Atlantis facility outside town. We had planned to head out there at some point, anyway.

"What's the plan?" Jennifer asked.

"It's still in the early stages," I replied honestly.

"Is there a way in besides the road?"

"I don't think so."

"Can we get onto one of those trucks, or maybe the buses?" Jennifer asked, noticing the Atlantis vehicles that were mixed randomly into the traffic. As she said it, she began digging into the tactical bags that were left in the truck.

"Ok, we've got a couple of pistols here, some ammo, some body armor, and some water," she said as she rummaged through.

"Good. I think you're right, by the way. I think the trucks might be our best shot to get in. There were specific trucks that went to the back of the facility. I'm guessing that's where they'll take Gus. If we can get there before they move him, we may have a shot to get him out," I said, beginning to formulate a plan to make that happen.

I pulled over at the next dirt road and turned the F-150 toward the highway. Then I waited. Since it was Saturday, there was less traffic than normal, and much of it appeared to be vacation traffic. Still, there were the Atlantis trucks cruising by every once in a while. Knowing the ones that avoided the security check at the border also went to the back of the Atlantis facility, I looked for the telltale cooling units on top of the trailers to identify them.

While we waited, I rummaged through the second tactical bag. I pulled out one of the handguns and noticed it was a SIG P365, not a Glock 19 or Beretta M9, like the other three pistols in the two bags. By now, Paul knew my preference. It was a little smaller and was my personal favorite for general concealed carry. Of course, Paul probably didn't realize I already had one with me, but the thought made me smile a bit. Getting my personal pistol checked onto the flight from Colorado was a pain, but I've gotten used to that red tape. That meant we had two P365s, a Beretta M9 and two Glocks between the two of us. Unless something went horribly wrong, the handguns and the four boxes of ammunition provided plenty of short range firepower.

Jennifer pulled out the Beretta, dropped the magazine, checked the ammunition, checked for a round in the chamber, then slammed the magazine back into the pistol before stuffing it into her purse. Clearly, she knew how to handle that weapon, and somehow she had enough room in her purse for it.

There were various other items in the two tactical bags, including the vests Jennifer had mentioned, some zip ties, medical kits, and to my surprise, even a Taser.

Looking at the rifle box that was on the back floor, I started assembling the details of my plan.

"Can you shoot that thing?" I asked Jennifer.

"Well, I see it's a Remington case, so does that mean it's a 700?"

"Honestly, I'm not sure. But since they know we're military, it probably is," I said.

Jennifer unbuckled her seatbelt and reached between the two front seats into the back. It took some stretching, but eventually she unlocked the case and accessed the contents.

"Yeah, I can work with this. It's a 700 with a tripod and a nice Leupold scope. A really nice scope," she said.

"That's good, because we may need some long distance coverage in this terrain," I replied.

"Do they always set you up like this on your assignments?" Jennifer asked, clearly still curious about The Association and their resources. I was the same way early on, so I understood.

"Yeah, they do. If, of course, I need it. Paul was telling the truth about the danger. It's rare we need this kind of support from them," I said.

She nodded and continued digging in the case.

"There are two boxes of twenty rounds, so forty overall. If we need more than that, we're in trouble," she said matter-of-factly.

"True. Let's hope we need none," I replied.

"Always. Now, what are we doing here on the side of the road?" Jennifer asked.

"The trucks that got through the border crossing without inspection all had cooling units on top of their trailers. Something in that cargo couldn't get too hot. I want to get in there and see why that is, then hijack one of them to get into that facility and get Gus," I said to Jennifer as I watched.

"Ok. So, you can identify them, but how are you doing to get into one of them?" Jennifer asked.

Before I could answer, I saw one coming down the two-lane highway that led to Atlantis, and I pulled out in front of it. I knew there was one stop sign before the facility, which was my one chance to make a move.

"What are you doing, Keith? Please tell me you have a plan," Jennifer said.

"I'm going to block them and try to get into the driver's seat before he can radio back to Atlantis. I'll have to make it look like an accident," I replied.

She took a deep breath before responding. I felt her shaking her head beside me, but I didn't look over.

"Well, ok then. So, what do you want me to do?" She asked.

"There's a maintenance road about a half mile past the facility. It's hard to see, but it's there. It's just an old dirt road, nothing paved or gravel. Take that road and head into the field until you can see the smaller building at the back of the property. You'll know what I mean when you see the place. It's heavily guarded and has lights and cameras everywhere. Honestly, the whole place looks like a prison, but that piece looks like maximum security," I said.

"What do you want me to do when I can see it? Watching won't help much," she replied.

"Yeah, I'm pretty much on my own at that point. I would, however, love sniper cover if you can provide it. I think you can get the truck into one of the lower areas to the point that it's barely visible, if at all. Then, I'm hoping you can find a vantage point where you can see the truck and the building. I'll try to stay visible if I can, but at some point I'll have to see what is really going on in there. I'm hoping I can swap for one of those Atlantis shirts or something so I can blend in," I said with as much optimism as I could muster.

"You know, hope isn't a strategy, Keith. And you said hope twice just now," Jennifer replied, looking concerned.

"Oh, sorry. I'm 'strategizing' that I can get an Atlantis shirt," I said with a smile.

She didn't laugh, but raised an eyebrow and shook her head instead.

"Look, I won't do anything stupid in there. But it's Saturday, and I expect a much lower volume of workers than they'd have during the week. Plus, if something goes wrong, I'll punt quickly. I'd also suggest getting Paul up to speed on our location and the situation, in case we need support," I said.

Jennifer nodded and looked at her phone.

I waited until we got to the stop sign, then slowed the F-150 to a complete stop. Then I put the truck in park and raised my hands like something was wrong. I popped the hood and got out. I walked around shaking my head and waving my arms like the truck had broken down, watching the truck driver behind me while I did it.

He looked more annoyed than helpful, which threw a wrench into my plan. Jennifer seemed to notice and improvised a plan of her own as she jumped out of the car and started yelling.

"I told you this wouldn't work! You never fix anything right, you moron! I ain't ever going anywhere with you again! How am I going to get home, you loser!" She was laying it on thick.

It worked. The driver saw Jennifer yelling with an instant southern accent and got out of his truck. I sauntered his way as he opened the door, arms still waving.

"I'm sorry, man, I thought I had this thing fixed," I said to him as he slowly stepped out.

He was completely focused on Jennifer, which allowed me to move in behind him and zap him with the Taser I had slid into my pocket. Kudos to Paul and The Association for providing the perfect tool for this unanticipated situation.

The driver went stiff then lost control and fell out of the truck cab toward the ground, when I caught him and pushed him inside. There were no cars close enough to see, and the small strip mall just up the road was closed or deserted.

With Jennifer's help, I used the zip ties to secure his

feet, removed his shirt, zip tied his hands, and added some duct tape across his mouth. He wasn't going anywhere, even when he regained use of his limbs again in a few minutes. I put on his Atlantis shirt, took his badge and lanyard, and put it around my neck, then laid him behind the seat in the cargo area of the cab. While Jennifer got into the F-150, I got into the driver's seat of the Atlantis truck.

Jennifer took off from the stop sign in the F-150, and I took a quick glance around the cab of the truck. Fortunately for me, it was a modern version with one of the new automatic transmissions. I knew how to drive a manual, but driving one this size was a chore and might draw attention if I fumbled through the shifts of a manual transmission. I put the truck in gear and took off while the Atlantis driver began grunting behind me.

We'd know in a few minutes if my plan to get inside the Atlantis facility was going to work.

Chapter Forty-Eight

Zapata, TX. Saturday

The first test of my plan was getting in the front gate of the Atlantis facility with the truck and my simple disguise. The disguise was only slightly more sophisticated than the shirt I had stolen from the driver. I also found his sunglasses and an Atlantis hat in the cab of the truck.

That was the extent of my disguise and my less-than-elaborate plan to enter the Atlantis facility.

It thrilled me to see the gate begin to open as I got close, even without me opening the window of the truck. It seems they were comfortable enough during their weekend shifts to avoid having to stop every truck that came in.

Step one of my entry into the Atlantis facility was complete.

From my vantage point two days ago, I had seen the trucks all take the same route around the right of the large building in the front. I did the same, trying to act as confident as I could while I navigated the route with a truck larger than anything I had driven in my life.

As I drove along, I wondered if Jennifer was having any luck getting into position with the F-150 out in the field to my left. Once I passed the large building, I thought I could see a dust trail from a vehicle, but it was too far to see if it was her. I kept going. We needed to get Gus out of here before he met the same fate as Bob Yates.

There were people milling around the back facility as I neared the huge doors, but not nearly as many as there were during the week. That's good, because if anyone knew all the drivers, they would recognize an outsider when they saw me.

The doors to the smaller facility were open, and I drove right in as though I knew what I was doing. While it was smaller than the other building, this was a large building compared to most. I estimated it was half the size of a football field as I pulled in.

From here on, everything was new. I hadn't been able to see inside the facility before and had to take it in all at once while looking as casual as I could.

The area I entered as I pulled the truck into the facility was open through the middle, which certainly helped with my ability to maneuver. There was a straight shot through to a similarly large door on the other side that was currently closed. I had seen that door from my vantage point in the field, but it never opened while I was watching before.

There was one truck already queued by the closed door, which appeared to have been there for a while. I decided that must be where I should stop and I slowly inched forward across the facility.

To my left were offices just inside the door I entered, with pallets and stacks of boxes in neat rows beyond the offices. I couldn't see all the way to the left side of the building, but it appeared there were more offices along the far left.

The boxes looked relatively normal and could have contained any number of aluminum automotive parts. There was nothing strange there, as far as I could tell.

To my right, there were maybe twenty stations of apparent fabrication equipment. Most appeared idle for the weekend, but a few were active with noisy machines and sparks in the distance. Again, that all seemed normal to me and didn't explain the cooling units or the special treatment of the facility.

As I inched the truck along toward the far side, I passed the pallets and boxes on the left and the fabrication stations on the right, and seemed to enter a more secure area. There was a floor-to-ceiling chain-link fence separating the areas, with an open area for trucks to pass through.

Beyond the normal-looking warehouse area on the left, I came to a smaller area where a handful of workers were packaging various drugs into car part boxes. There were powders, liquids, and pills in all types of colors and sizes. They were going into the same boxes I had been passing on the left, which made me wonder how many of those boxes were really car parts versus drugs.

After taking video of the drug stations while trying not to ogle, I turned to the right. That's where the need for cooling units became clear.

Lined up for what seemed like thirty yards were chain-link cages that appeared to be the size of large jail cells. Each was around ten feet square, with benches around the inside edges of each unit. It was difficult to see how many sections were there, but I saw at least ten at first glance.

The fenced-lined cells contained people of all ages. Most looked to be Mexican, but I couldn't be sure. I had to stop myself from staring at the scene and hitting the truck in front of me. After the initial shock, I realized what I was seeing.

Atlantis had a drug and human trafficking business right here in their distribution center outside Zapata, Texas. There were probably fifty or more in the various fenced areas right now, most sitting and drinking water or eating. There were some children laying on the floor or on benches, but most of them were just hanging out casually chatting. They could see each other through the chain-link, and there seemed to be no urgency at all with the group. They looked comfortable.

As I slowed to a stop behind the other truck at the far side of the facility, I heard the Atlantis driver behind the seat start yelling for his coworkers. Apparently, he had recognized where we were. I didn't have time to create a clever strategy to keep him quiet. Instead, I turned and slugged him. Twice. He moved just when I swung the first time and caught my fist in his ear, but I got him square in the chin the second time. He crumbled into a silent, unconscious heap in the back.

Nobody came to greet me or to check on my truck inventory, which I assumed was due to the lower staff on duty for the weekend. So, I scanned the area and developed a quick plan to gather evidence.

Along the back right of the wall, behind the human cages, was a restroom. I got out of the truck, put my phone in my right hand and walked along the front of the cages and around to the far wall, subtly taking video as I went.

When I rounded the corner to the back right of the facility near the restroom door, I stopped breathing for a brief second. I saw Gus sitting on a bench along the back side of the last cage. He was alone in his cage, which didn't seem good to me. There was a lock on his cell gate, so Gus was stuck.

I quickly scanned the ceiling and walls, looking for security cameras and recording devices. It didn't surprise me to see several, so I walked casually to the restroom door. I didn't see another Atlantis person along the way, and I quickly decided on my next step.

I entered the bathroom, locked the door, and pulled out my phone to send the video to Paul.

I learned in that instant that the facility I was in had shielded telecommunications signals, and I wouldn't be getting in touch with anyone. It was time to adjust my plan.

Chapter Forty-Nine

Zapata, TX. Saturday

After considering other options to communicate with the outside world, I decided I wouldn't be able to get the video out right now. I'd have to deal with that later. My primary task was to get Gus out of this place.

I walked out of the restroom and immediately came face to face with an Atlantis employee who was headed to the same restroom I was leaving. I nodded, trying to be casual, but he looked puzzled, like he didn't recognize who I was. Before he had a chance to act on that confusion, I lunged at him and landed a punch to the throat.

While he gasped for air, I grabbed him by the shirt and dragged him into the bathroom and closed the door. This gave him the opportunity to recover just enough to start flailing at me with a barrage of wild punches. Most were ineffective, but before I could respond, he had caught me in the ribs with a good one. After a struggle that took way too long for my comfort, I pulled the Taser out of my pocket. I jabbed it into his stomach just as he lunged for a wild right cross, and he went down.

After I locked the door, I took a look at the guy's clothes and tried to decide what to do with him. I didn't have any zip tics with me, and the P365 would make enough noise to completely blow my cover. I couldn't have him yelling, though, so I quickly decided he needed to be silent, just like the guy in the truck.

Once he stopped shaking from the electricity surging through his body, I made sure he would remain quiet for at least a little while with a quick blow to the temple. He was a bigger guy than me, but didn't need a second punch before he was lights-out on the floor. I drug him into the corner, looking around for somewhere to hide him. Seeing no good options in the tiny restroom, I decided I needed to get out of here now and just leave him. It was risky, but I didn't have a choice. I rubbed my sore ribs and walked out as casually as my adrenaline would allow.

Back in the warehouse, I looked a little closer at the locks on each of the gates holding all the cages shut. They seemed to have a card reader versus a key or combination, which gave me an idea. I had the truck driver's badge on the lanyard around my neck. Could I be so lucky that this badge would open the locks?

I scanned the area to see if anyone was looking. Seeing nobody else at all, I walked over to the lock holding Gus' cage, and he finally looked up. It took him a second to recognize who I was, so I subtly nodded and held out my hand to tell him to stay seated. The people in the other cages barely even looked up as I pressed my badge against the lock on his gate, which instantly opened the lock.

My next step would dictate how the rest of the day went.

I glanced around the cages at the truck ahead of the one I drove in. It appeared its trailer was locked, and it seemed ready to move. Someone had also opened the door in front of the truck, so it had a clear exit path. I wasn't sure if it was fully loaded, unloaded, or partially loaded, but I had to take a chance. I motioned for Gus to get up.

When Gus stood, I grabbed him sternly and jerked him toward the truck. It was a bit of a guess regarding how he was treated on the way in, but it seemed to be the right one. Nobody said a word or even seemed to notice. I pulled him toward the first truck, which was all closed up and facing the huge open door on the side of the building.

Taking the chance that I had just knocked out the driver of this truck, and that he had left the keys in the ignition, I pushed Gus up and into the passenger side and closed the door. Then I headed around to get into the driver's seat. If anyone was watching closely, they would have noticed that Gus didn't get into the cargo trailer but got into the cab. Apparently, nobody was watching at that moment.

I climbed in and was delighted to see a key fob sitting right there on the console tray. With several good luck steps in a row, I knew my streak couldn't last forever. Still, I started the truck and put it in gear, pulling out of the facility with Gus in the truck with me.

As soon as the truck exited the far side of the building, I was once again in unfamiliar territory. I had seen trucks entering and exiting the facility while I watched from the ridge just a couple days before, but I hadn't paid specific attention to their route or their stops on the way. That lack of knowledge proved costly.

While I frantically tried to call Jennifer on my mobile phone, I made every attempt to look casual while I guessed at the exit route. There were towers, trucks and a couple of small buildings to avoid, but it looked like a relatively straight shot. I went as slow as my nerves would allow.

When we were several hundred feet from the building, my phone service came back on and I got to Jennifer.

"What's going on? Are you ok?" Jennifer said when she picked up.

"Yes, but listen. I'm going to need some help. I saw a couple of G-Wagons parked near the front of the facility when I came in. Are they still there?" I asked frantically.

After a second, she responded.

"Yeah, I see two of them. Why?"

"I think I need you to disable them. I'm about to bust out the front in one of their trucks," I responded.

"Oh, brother. That's you in that speeding truck? Ok, I can give it my best shot. It's going to disclose my position, though. Even with the suppressor on this rifle, they'll figure it out once they start looking," she said.

"I think that's a risk we'll have to take. Right now, they're on a casual weekend shift and nobody is expecting anything. I realize that's going to change real soon, but it's an advantage for the moment," I said.

"Ok, here goes nothing," Jennifer said.

"Thanks Jen. Do it quick, then get in the truck and meet me at the next intersection on the highway. It's about three miles down and there's a stop sign. That's it. We need to swap vehicles, get to the plane, and get in the air before they figure out what happened," I said, not completely sure how to execute that next phase of the plan.

"Wow. That's some plan, Keith," Jennifer said sarcastically. I could hear her trying to concentrate on her aim while she talked.

"I'll leave you to it. Gus and I appreciate the help," I added.

"Wait, you have Gus?" Jennifer said with a bit of surprise in her voice.

"Yeah, I do. And I'm sure they'll realize that pretty quickly. We can discuss the details when we're safely on our way back to Nashville," I said.

"Fair enough," she said, sounding even more focused on her aim.

"See you in a bit," I said as I ended the call and focused on the gate we were approaching.

As I got closer, I could see the two G-Wagons sitting outside the front door of the large facility. I watched for a second and thought I saw a tuft of dirt fly up around the rear wheel of the nearest one. Nobody moved nor sounded any sort of alarm, but the tire also didn't deflate. After another second and another apparent shot, the result was different.

When Jennifer's second shot hit the right rear tire of the first G-Wagon, it caught the attention of two Atlantis workers at the front gate a few yards away. They turned and looked back, not really sure what to do. A few seconds later, when another shot took out the left rear tire of the other G-Wagon, they jogged over to see what had happened.

I assumed that was Jennifer's cue to vacate her hiding spot. It was also my cue to get out of that facility!

It took another twenty seconds for me to get to the closed front gate, at which point the guard flagged me down.

"You're early!" The guard yelled from his window as I pulled up.

"Yeah, just got word they need me on the road a little sooner," I replied, completely making it up.

"Badge?" The guard reached out his hand as he asked the one-word question, but then the short-wave radio in his little hut screeched.

I could hear a frantic voice exclaiming on the radio.

"STOP THAT TRUCK! I just found the driver in the bathroom! That's not the right driver! Stop that truck! There's a VIP in there," the voice on the other end clearly didn't know I could hear. I wondered what a VIP might be, remembering the individual I had seen escorted away earlier in the week.

It made no sense to worry about it now, and I steered the truck directly through the closed chain-link gate at the front of the facility. It was surprisingly easy to get through with the huge truck, and I was on my way down the highway in seconds.

Without the G-Wagons to chase me, the guards scrambled around for a few seconds before taking out their handguns and firing at the truck. I guessed they couldn't think of anything else to do.

With bullets streaking by the cab of the truck, I pushed as hard as I could to get to Jennifer and the F-150. We were no longer undercover, but were instead blatantly visible to the few observers on the road.

After watching the whole escape unfold, Gus finally spoke.

"Where are we going?" he asked sheepishly.

"Have you ever been to Nashville?" I asked while we raced down the highway.

"No," Gus replied.

"Well, you're in for a treat," I said, trying to smile at Gus. He was clearly scared to death.

"You're safe now," I said, trying to reassure him.

Gus nodded and gripped the door handle as we hurtled down the highway toward his unknown future.

Chapter Fifty

Zapata, TX. Saturday

It took about four minutes to get to the intersection where Jennifer was waiting for us. When we passed the maintenance road she was on, I could still see the trail of dust settling, but I didn't see anyone following. Yet.

"Are we going to get out here?" Gus asked as we approached the intersection and slowed down. Jennifer had the F-150 off to the side, headed toward the airfield.

"Yeah, but give me a second to maneuver this truck into position. Just a second," I replied.

After turning the truck toward Jennifer, I stopped and reversed, blocking the intersection in either direction. There were two pickup trucks watching as I pretended to get stuck in the sand beside the road. After going back and forth a couple of times, I surmised the road was adequately blocked. If anyone came behind me from Atlantis, they'd have to navigate around the trucks and through the sand to follow us. Hopefully, this would add to their delay.

I got out of the truck, waved my hands to the other

drivers like I was very distressed by my predicament, and motioned Gus over to the F-150. He hustled over, and I followed. The other drivers were getting out of their pickup trucks and looking around as we sped away toward the airfield.

I called Paul as soon as Jennifer got going.

"Hey Keith, what's up?" Paul answered.

"Well, Paul, I'm afraid we've run into some logistical risk that we didn't anticipate," I said, generalizing the situation.

"Ok. Well, that probably means you don't have time to generalize much more, so get to it," he responded.

"We witnessed Gus being picked up by the Atlantis guys before we got to him," I started.

"Oh no," Paul sighed.

"That's not all. I followed them to the Atlantis facility," I said.

"Is he still there?" Paul blurted out before I could continue.

"Well, no. He's not. He's sitting next to me in the F-150," I added with a bit of caution.

"Uh-oh, Keith. You certainly have increased the risk there! Do they know you have him?" Paul asked.

"Judging from the gunshots aimed at us on the way out, I'd say they do. We've disabled their vehicles at the plant, but I'm sure they've recovered by now and are likely somewhere behind us. I guess the point is we need the plane ready to get out quickly and evasively," I said, finally getting to the critical point.

"Ok, I'm sending that message as we speak," Paul said, sounding distracted.

"Plus, I got a quick glimpse of what goes on in that special building at the rear of the Atlantis facility," I added.

"Mmm hmm," Paul still sounded like he was doing something else, so I continued.

"It's a drug and human trafficking operation," I said, to bring Paul back to the conversation. It worked.

"What?" Paul asked, clearly focused again.

"I saw firsthand. In one part of the facility, they were packaging drugs into boxes that appeared to mimic their standard products. In another part, back where Gus was being held, there were probably fifty people being held in makeshift chain link cages. I found Gus...," I was interrupted by Gus at that point.

"They weren't being held," Gus said, shaking his head.

"What do you mean?" I asked, now focused on Gus as Jennifer kept us speeding along toward the airport.

"Those people weren't being held. They were there on purpose. They want to get to America, and the Atlantis guys get them here. I bet they paid lots of money to get over the border. Their locks were open. I saw them," Gus said calmly, staring forward.

"Gus says those people weren't held against their will. It seems they actually paid for the service, somehow," I said.

"I've read about this. The cartels control many of those services from Mexico. They offer these high-priced packages to people from Mexico, or anywhere else, to cross the border. I guess Atlantis has somehow gotten into that racket," Paul said.

"You know, I think pieces of this are linking together. During one of my snooping sessions the other day, I saw a single individual get taken from the Atlantis facility to a drop-off point down the road. He seemed to get some sort of VIP treatment compared to the people I saw today. Maybe they have multiple levels of 'service' they provide," I said, putting a sarcastic tone on the word 'service.'

"Well, I guess it's good to be diversified," Paul added, matching my sarcasm.

"So, they just run a transport service for people from Mexico who can pay their fee?" I asked, now talking to Gus.

"Yeah. But not just Mexico. Those people were from other places, too. I heard some talking about Colombia, and some didn't even speak Spanish," Gus said.

I took a second to pass the additional information to Paul, then stopped being the intermediary.

"Let me put you on speaker, Paul," I said, tapping my phone.

"Ok, so they're running a diverse trafficking service out of their Zapata plant," Paul summarized.

"Not everyone pays," Gus interjected.

"What do you mean by that?" Paul asked.

"They also take people who don't want to go. I've seen them. It's mostly kids. I don't know where they take them, but they never come back. And they don't go to Mexico. Those are the ones I was trying to help Mr. Bob save. I thought that's where I was going before you got me," Gus said, giving me a somber look.

"And you don't know where they go?" I asked.

"There are rumors, but I don't really know," Gus said.

"What are the rumors?" Paul asked over the speaker.

"People think they take kids to be slaves. We all knew to never get into those trucks alone. They also take kids who don't have parents here, or kids who don't follow the rules," Gus said, again speaking in a solemn tone and staring straight ahead.

"You said you've seen them take kids?" Paul asked.

"Yeah. So has Javi," Gus said.

"But you don't know where they take them?" I asked.

"No. We just know they go to the building in the back, where I was, and then we don't know," Gus replied.

"Alright, Keith. I just got confirmation the plan will be ready when you get there. Do you see anyone tailing you yet?" Paul asked.

I looked behind, and saw nothing out of the ordinary, yet.

"No, but I'd expect that to change soon. Jennifer has us flying down the road to the airport. We're just pulling in now," I said as Jennifer slowed at the gate to the small airport. I could see the guards hustling to open the gate as they saw us.

"Got it. Just get out quickly and safely. We'll have to figure out what to do with Gus when you get to Nashville," Paul said.

"It doesn't matter. I'm dead, anyway," Gus said grimly as he continued to stare forward.

"Why do you say that?" I asked.

"The cartel will kill me. They know I was helping Mr. Bob. And by now, they know I escaped. They will find me," he replied.

"Gus, we can help you stay safe. You don't have to be afraid of them," I said, trying to calm him a bit as Jennifer steered the F-150 through the gate and toward the parking area.

"You don't know them. They won't let it go. I'm dead," he said, clearly ignoring my attempts to console him.

"We'll work on that when we fly. We're getting into that airplane over there and heading north to Nashville, Tennessee. You'll be far away from here in just a few minutes," I said, again doing my best to turn around Gus' emotional state.

"We're here. We'd better get moving," Jennifer chimed in as the truck pulled to a stop.

We all got out of the F-150 and ran over to the Gulfstream just a few yards away. The pilot helped us up the stairs and into the plane and quickly jumped in behind us, locking the door in place.

"Are you still there?" I heard Paul talking on my phone when we sat down. I had forgotten he was still on the open line.

"Yeah," I answered, holding the phone up.

"Call me when you get airborne. I've got some news on the LLC trail with Atlantis and Chris Valentine," he said.

"Can I get service in the air?" I asked.

"Wow, you don't fly private jets much, do you?" Paul said rhetorically.

I still felt compelled to answer. "No."

"They have Wi-Fi now, and it's good. You'll be able to talk like you're on your internet at home," Paul said.

I felt instantly naïve with my lack of knowledge about flying in private jets. I thought first-class commercial was great, but this was proving to be some level beyond that.

"Wow. Ok, I'm not sure why I didn't think of that, but I'll call you shortly," I said, ending the call.

I buckled my seatbelt and watched as Gus sat staring at the inside of the jet. It was probably his first time on any plane, much less a private version like this.

"It's ok, Gus. Just buckle your belt and relax. You're going to be out of danger soon," I said.

In the back of my mind, however, I wondered if Nashville was even less safe for Gus. It certainly wasn't safe for Bob Yates.

Chapter Fifty-One

Between Zapata and Nashville, Saturday

As the pilot frantically started the engines and maneuvered the plane toward the runway, I poked my head in to ask about getting to the internet on the plane. It turns out Paul was right. He pointed to a card on the back of the exit door with the connection details and continued to get us out of Zapata.

We watched closely out the windows, waiting for someone from Atlantis to come flying down the road with guns blazing, but it didn't happen. It seemed our ploy with the truck stretched across the intersection had bought us the time we needed.

Only when we were safely in the air did I take a moment to take a breath and realize how lucky we had just been.

"I'm gathering you don't fly these private jets much," Jennifer said as we continued to ascend.

"No. Is it that obvious?" I asked.

"Well, not really. But if you didn't know they had Wi-Fi," she said, tilting her head questioningly.

"Yeah, I guess it's that obvious," I said, nodding.

"That's really not your style, anyway. It doesn't surprise me," she said, looking out the window.

Gus was glued to the window and was gripping the seat tightly. I felt bad having to rush him onto the plane like this, extracting him from the life he knew. He seemed to know it was necessary, however, and was being as brave as we could expect.

"You alright, Gus?" I asked.

"Yeah," he said without looking away from the window.

After connecting my phone using the details from the pilot, I called Paul again, keeping it on speaker so Jennifer could hear. Gus was sitting behind us and could probably hear everything too, but he'd already been exposed to most of this.

"Thanks for calling back, Keith. You guys safely away?" Paul asked when he answered.

"Yeah, I think so. It looks like we got out before they realized where we were. I have Jennifer's NASCAR skills to thank for that," I said, smiling at her.

She just smiled politely and nodded.

"Good. Glad to hear it. I wanted to give you an update on the different companies who are buying products from Atlantis, especially the ones tied to Chris Valentine," Paul began.

"Ok. I've got you on speaker so Jen can hear," I replied.

"Great. First off, you were dead on with your suspicions about the businesses. But it wasn't Chris' family that owns all the LLCs. It's his wife's family," Paul said.

Jennifer and I looked at each other with our eyebrows raised.

"You know, he mentioned he married into money. It was an off-the-cuff comment when we were at his house. Maybe that was part of his cover. So, he put the LLCs in her name and her family's name?" I asked.

"Not hers, just her family. There are four primary LLCs that are owned by her siblings. On the surface, they look like reasonable companies. They have normal addresses and are set up with the state and with the IRS. They've filed taxes like normal for over five years, all of them. But I suspect they have very few real customers except the dirty money from Chris' side hustles you've uncovered there. I checked the satellite views of the plants, and all four of the locations were very small. They may supply a few auto parts to the local communities, but there's nowhere near enough of a facility to handle the volume of product they claim to be buying from Atlantis. I think they're laundering money through those four businesses," Paul said as he paused.

I took a deep breath to take in what I was hearing.

"Why would Chris Valentine do something like that?" I said, pondering the recent evidence out loud.

"I have no idea. Greed? Power? Who knows why these people do what they do," Paul said.

I looked at Jennifer, who was shaking her head at what we had just heard.

"There's one more thing about this whole situation that smells funny," Paul continued.

"Oh yeah, what's that?" I replied.

"Mrs. Valentine is from Mexico. She only became a naturalized citizen after she married Chris. I don't know if that has anything to do with all this, but it could," Paul said.

Once again, Jennifer and I looked at each other with eyebrows raised.

"I can't believe that's just a coincidence," I said.

"Me neither," Jennifer chimed in.

"It seems Chris Valentine may be smarter than we think. He marries a Mexican woman, brings her siblings into the country to run businesses as a front for his trafficking business?" I summarized out loud.

"It seems that way. Now, we have to prove it. The Association has limited resources down in that part of Texas, but we've notified the police of the situation. They, of course, will want evidence. Our word isn't good enough. Right now, I think Gus is the only evidence we have," Paul said.

At that point, I remembered the videos I had taken inside the Atlantis facility. With all the commotion since then, I'd forgotten I still had them on my phone.

"I may be able to help with that. When I took the Atlantis truck to the facility..." I didn't get any further when Paul jumped in.

"When you took what? And took it where?" He couldn't contain his shock.

"It wasn't really that big of a deal. Jennifer and I had to get inside that plant to get Gus. I temporarily commandeered an Atlantis delivery truck to get in there. Then I took Gus and jumped into another one to get out. Did I forget to tell you that?" I said, smiling at Jennifer.

"Yes. Yes, you did. Is there anything we need to clean up down there?" Paul asked.

"I don't think so. It went pretty smooth. We were helped out by a light weekend staff at the Atlantis facility, but that's not the point. While I was in there, I was able to shoot some quick video of some detainees in the facility. They were in a chain-link fence and were..."

Gus interrupted from the seat behind me.

"I told you, they weren't detained!" he yelled.

"I'm sorry, you're right," I said to Gus.

"Gus corrected me. They weren't really detainees so much as human cargo. But, in any case, I'll send you the video. I also got some drugs being packaged into Atlantis shipping boxes. I don't know how good the video is, but it's better than nothing," I said.

"Send it over. I'll take a look. In the meantime, you guys need to watch yourselves out there. Someone thinks this is important enough to kill. More than once. So, don't think they won't be willing to do it again. They clearly want this whole thing hidden. Now that Chris Valentine knows you are onto his operation, I suspect you're in his crosshairs," Paul said.

"Yeah, I've thought about that," I said, happy I was the only one they'd seen. Jennifer was still an unknown to the Atlantis people, which gave me some level of comfort. Of course, they certainly knew about Gus now.

"I may fly out there to help get Gus settled in," Paul said as we got ready to end the call.

"Ok," I said with a bit of question.

"You know, in case you guys need a little help," Paul said, sounding oddly generic.

I decided he must be trying to say we were in a dangerous situation that he thought was bad enough to merit his direct involvement. That thought gave me pause, as this had never happened on any of my previous assignments with The Association. If he felt that way, I was in no position to argue.

"Sure," I said as the call ended.

We sat in silence for a few minutes when my phone, still in my hand, buzzed with an incoming call. I looked down and couldn't keep my jaw from dropping.

The call was from Chris Valentine.

Chapter Fifty-Two

Between Zapata and Nashville, Saturday

I held the phone up for Jennifer to see, receiving the same dropped-jaw expression I had just made. I gathered myself, cleared my throat, and accepted the call.

"This is Keith," I said as the call connected.

"Mr. Morgan, you have no idea what you're getting into." It was indeed Chris Valentine, and he sounded angry.

"Is that right?" I said.

"Where are you hiding? Are you still in Zapata? Or are those plane engines I hear in the background?" Chris said.

"I don't know what you're talking about," I said, aware Chris probably knew exactly where I was by now.

"You know there is video surveillance all around that Atlantis facility. Your face is on the video as clear as day. Plus, you didn't think to take out the two truck drivers you beat up. They're already talking to the police, who will be on your tail in a few minutes," he said.

I decided I'd better change tactics, or this conversation was going nowhere.

"Did Bob Yates uncover your operation down here at the Zapata plant? Is that why you had him killed?" I asked.

Chris Valentine didn't skip a beat.

"I didn't have Bob Yates killed, Mr. Valentine. You have this all wrong," he said.

"I'll be back there in a couple of hours. Maybe we can talk about it then?" I asked.

"Unfortunately, you will never see me again, Mr. Morgan. You see, this whole mess has put me in a very precarious position. I'm afraid I need to stay out of sight for a while. But, as you might expect, I have the resources and the contacts to make that happen," he said.

He was about to continue when I decided to up the ante a bit.

"What do the letters CA mean, anyway?" I asked.

"What? Why do you ask that?" Chris responded.

"You know, the letters you carved into the chests of your lackeys who didn't take me out. They followed me but didn't silence me, so you unceremoniously removed their heads and carved CA into their chests. Remember now? Anyway, what does CA stand for?" I asked again.

It seemed my question had startled Chris, as he paused a minute before answering. His voice had a new sense of tension when he spoke.

"You have this all wrong, Mr. Morgan. Now, if you'll excuse me, I bid you a good life," Chris said as he ended the call.

I looked at the phone with a bit of confidence that I had shaken Chris Valentine with my knowledge of the victims at the Nashville Inn. I was still staring when Jennifer spoke up.

"What was that about?" She asked.

"He says I'm wrong, so I told him what I knew about the

murder victims at the Nashville Inn. Then, it seems, he decided he was done talking. He said I'll never see him again, so I guess he's using his contacts to flee the country. It wouldn't surprise me if he'd head right back here to use the network he has already established to get out. He probably knows more ways to cross the border into Mexico than I could even count," I said.

"Yeah, probably," Jennifer responded.

We sat quietly for a few more minutes while our flight continued toward Nashville. After a few minutes, I decided I was going to see what I could learn from Officer Keating as soon as we were back in Nashville. I was hopeful there was some evidence from Bob's murder and the Nashville Inn by now.

It turned out I didn't need to wait that long. My phone buzzed with a call from the Nashville Metro PD a minute later.

"This is Keith," I answered as usual.

"Hi Mr. Morgan. This is Officer Keating. You have a few minutes?" His voice was calm and casual.

"Sure. What can I help you with, Officer Keating?" I asked.

"Well, I suppose it's more of what I can help you with," he began.

"Really? How so?" I asked.

"We've found a bit more information about the situation at the Nashville Inn. Some if it has to do with you. Well, I guess it would be more accurate to say it actually confirms that the situation does NOT have anything to do with you," he said.

"Ok," I said, waiting for him to get to the punch line.

"It seems the name 'Keith Morgan' was a name Mrs. Yates used to reserve rooms with an acquaintance. They used the names of their children, Keith and Morgan, to maintain a level of anonymity with their, uh, excursions," he said.

"You mean the rumor is true? Mrs. Yates was having an affair?" I asked, forcing him to the point he was having difficulty making.

"It appears that is the case, yes," he said.

"Does that mean her lover may have had something to do with her husband's murder?" I asked, again trying to push Officer Keating along.

"I cannot confirm nor deny that, Mr. Morgan. That would be revealing details of an ongoing investigation," he said.

"Wow. That's good news, then, Officer Keating. I'm relieved to hear I'm not the target of whoever executed those two men. It seems I am more the victim of having two first names," I said, trying to sound like this was the first time I was hearing the news.

"Yeah, I thought you'd enjoy hearing that," he said.

"Any word on who shot Mr. Yates? As you might expect, seeing him like that has left me deeply concerned," I said, trying to pull out more details.

"Well, yes, but I can't get into that. All I can say is we located a suspect using surveillance from the days leading up to Wednesday. It seems they had been planning this for some time. We received an anonymous tip that led us to the suspect. He was packed up and, we believe, ready to head south. You're lucky you weren't mixed up with these guys, Mr. Morgan. They're bad news. This points to a drug cartel hit from Mexico," he said. It was clear Officer Keating was trying to showboat a bit with the grandiose nature of his findings.

"No way! You mean Chris Valentine was mixed up

with the cartel?" I asked, again leading the conversation. Officer Keating was so proud of his work he didn't hesitate to share what he knew, despite saying he couldn't.

"I can't go quite that far just yet, Mr. Morgan, but you can rest assured we'll find out if that's the case. We don't need no cartel activity up here in Nashville," he said with a bit of pride.

"That's hard to believe. Nashville is a long way from the border. What makes you think it was a cartel hit?" I asked.

"Well, there are some details that I can't share about the suspect and his choice of tattoos, but the primary evidence was his weapon of choice. When we pulled him over near the hotel, he had the murder weapon in his trunk. I don't know if you know weapons, Mr. Morgan, but the cartels have recently acquired a substantial number of large caliber sniper-style rifles from the US. It's been in the news. This appears to have been one of those rifles," he said. His tone was grating on my nerves a bit, but I was getting more information the longer I let him play 'expert.'

"Oh wow. Yeah, I think I have seen that on the news. Something about 50 calibers, if I recall," I said, trying to sound like I was not sure.

"Exactly right, Mr. Morgan. It was a 50 caliber rifle called the Barrett M82. You can google it when you get a minute. Someone had removed the serial number, so we're not completely certain where it came from, but it's a 'weapon of choice' for the cartel." Officer Keating seemed happy with his conclusions.

I decided I had learned enough for now and was ready to end the call. Officer Keating, on the other hand, was still ready to sling out more details.

"It helped that we found calls on Mr. Yates' phone to a number in Texas. The number seems to be to a Mexican lady who is in the country illegally. If I was a betting man, I'd say she probably knows why the cartel was after Mr. Yates. We're gettin' boots on the ground down there to check it out," he said, again more proud than he should have been.

This side of Officer Keating was in stark contrast to the professional version I had seen up to now. I suppose he just got a little too much pleasure out of solving a case.

As long as he ended up with the correct evidence, he could be as proud as he wanted to be.

Chapter Fifty-Three

Nashville, TN. Saturday

"What was that about?" Jennifer asked as I ended the call with Officer Keating.

"Well, it seems Officer Keating is putting some pieces of this case together from Nashville," I replied.

"Which pieces?" She asked.

"He says they found the shooter through an anonymous tip, and that the shooter had a cartel tattoo and was carrying an M82 that matched the ballistics for Bob Yates' murder," I said.

"Whoa, a 50 caliber? You didn't tell me he had that big of a hole in his chest," she said.

"Yeah, it was quite a mess," I said.

"And they received an anonymous tip? How convenient. So, Chris calls in an anonymous tip to have the shooter picked up and now he disappears. So he's clear?" Jennifer was shaking her head as she said it. It wasn't really a question.

"Yeah, I guess. If they were careful, the shooter probably has no ties to Chris, anyway. Officer Keating wouldn't confirm they were targeting Chris, but it sure looks like he's the one they're after," I said.

"Wow. Let's hope they get him," she said as she got quiet and stared out her window.

The rest of the flight was more about what to do next than about what had happened in Zapata. Jennifer and I decided we should get Gus into the Grand Marquis, where we knew we could watch him. At some point we'd have to turn him over to someone who could really help him, but not until we were sure Chris Valentine was not able to get to him.

We landed smoothly and braked to a stop, with Gus again gripping his seat firmly while staring out the window. I suspected this was his first time this far north, so I was ok to let him soak it all in. The terrain up here was a little different from down in Zapata, with far more green and thicker forests around the rivers. It also wasn't nearly as hot.

After the plane stopped and we were let out, I realized the Mercedes that had picked us up before wasn't here this time. Instead, it was a black Cadillac Escalade. It seems The Association had made adjustments when they knew Gus was with us.

At least that was my first thought. When we arrived at the Escalade, the driver told us we had to wait another fifteen minutes for another passenger.

I assumed I knew who the other passenger was. In fifteen minutes, I knew I was right.

Paul Frazier emerged from the next plane carrying a tactical pack and walked over to the Escalade.

"May I introduce to you, Mr. Paul Frazier," I said to Jennifer as he walked our direction.

"Really? You knew he was coming?" She asked.

"He said he was joining us, but I guess I didn't really believe it," I said.

"I thought you said The Association doesn't usually need to send other people to help," she said as she watched Paul walk toward us.

"They usually don't. The cartel involvement may have increased the risk here, I'm not sure. Or maybe he just likes Nashville. Or maybe he was telling the truth when he said he wants to help with Gus. I really have no idea," I said as the driver opened the back of the Escalade so Paul could drop off his pack.

Paul then came around and opened the back door where me and Jennifer were sitting. Gus had taken the third row seat for himself.

"Jennifer Ellis, I presume? It's a pleasure to meet you," he said as he reached across me to shake Jennifer's hand.

"The pleasure is all mine," she said with a courteous smile.

"I would have thought a woman like you would have better taste than this," Paul said as he let go of her hand and nudged me with his elbow.

"And I thought you'd be taller," she shot right back with a smile.

We all laughed at her quick wit as Paul reached back to Gus with his hand extended.

"Gustavo, como esta usted?" Paul spoke to Gus in Spanish.

"I'm good," Gus replied in English, shaking Paul's hand.

"Glad you responded in English. That's all the Spanish I remember," Paul said. Gus smiled.

Next, Paul stepped back and gripped my hand in a firm handshake.

"Good to see you, brother," Paul said more seriously than I expected.

"I suppose you're going to tell us why you're here?" I asked as Paul went around to the front passenger seat and climbed in.

"Yeah, I suppose I will," he said as the driver put the SUV into gear and took off. Paul said nothing more.

"When do you suppose you'll be doing that?" I finally asked.

"Oh, you mean now?" Paul said. He seemed to be more engaging than he usually was on the phone. This was the Paul I remembered from our time in Afghanistan and Iraq.

"Well, besides my love for country music, it's really just to help with all the moving parts out here. The Association knew of the supply chain inconsistencies, as we had discussed, but your discoveries have turned this whole thing up a notch or two. Or a hundred. Now, we want to make sure the whole operation is shut down right from the top, and we also want to make sure Bob's work gets the visibility it deserves. And most importantly, we want to make sure this young man is taken care of," Paul said as he turned and nodded toward Gus.

"You sure it's not because we stumbled on cartel involvement? And that the hit on Bob Yates was apparently made using a cartel asset? And that Chris Valentine may be using his wife and her family to run their trafficking business in collaboration with the cartel in Mexico? And that you think three associates on the ground are better than two, especially when you just recruited one of them with the expectation of low-risk assignments," I asked, expecting Paul knew more than he was saying.

"No, I'm not sure," Paul said after several uncomfortable seconds, staring straight ahead.

After a few more seconds, he turned and offered a forced smile to me and Jennifer. Gus was once again staring out the window and seemed unaware of the discussion going on in the seats in front of him.

"You seem to have gathered some more evidence since we last talked," Paul said, trying to get us back on track.

"Yeah, I've been on the phone with a couple of people," I said.

"Good. Who would that be?" Paul was back in his gatekeeper mode.

"First, I spoke with Chris Valentine," I said.

"Oh, really? And what did Mr. Valentine have to say?" Paul said as he jerked his head around.

"Well, he says I've bitten off more than I can chew. He says the surveillance footage from Atlantis shows my face clearly and that I'm on their list. They also know I have Gus," I said.

"That didn't take long," he said.

"No, it didn't. Oh, and he also said he's leaving and I'll never see him again. I took it to mean he's leaving the country," I said.

"Yeah, we may be too late with him. Although he may be bluffing to throw you off," Paul said.

"Maybe. Because when I pressed him on why he killed Bob and those two thugs, he said I have the wrong idea. Then when I asked what CA stood for, he hung up," I said.

"CA? Oh, you mean from the dead guys?" Paul asked.

"Yeah," I responded with a sigh.

"Well, that's meaningful. Hopefully, he really is gone and will leave us all alone," Paul said.

"That would be nice, but I doubt it," I said honestly.

"I agree. That'd be giving up, and it doesn't sound like that's his way," Paul said.

After we absorbed the details of my conversation with Chris, I continued.

"Next, I got a call from Officer Keating. He finally found out it wasn't my name on the hotel registration," I started.

"Well, it's about time! I hope you were still able to act surprised," Paul said.

"Yeah, I tried. He also told me they had a suspect in custody from an anonymous tip. That's where I got the details of his cartel tattoo. Keating says they found the guy with an M82 in his possession. He seemed proud to tell me it was a cartel hit, and he was cleaning the cartel out of Nashville," I said.

"Hmmm," Paul said, appearing to be deep in thought.

"What?" I asked.

"Do you think we have it wrong?" He asked after taking a deep breath.

I thought about it for a minute.

"I don't know," I said.

"It would seem too tidy for the whole thing to end with a global manhunt for Chris Valentine, don't you think?" Jennifer chimed in, having been listening quietly.

We all sat there for a few minutes as we neared the entrance to the Grand Marquis.

"Yeah, it sort of does. What are we missing?" I finally said.

Nobody had that answer. At least not yet.

Chapter Fifty-Four

Nashville, TN. Saturday

The Grand Marquis was a crowded place this Saturday. The weekend crowd had far more kids than the weekday version, with this weekend having an especially large number because of the dance competition going on at the conference center. I had seen the signs all week, and now I was seeing all the dancers. Everywhere.

The line of cars waiting to get into the lobby area was longer than I had seen before. We were not yet at the door when Paul was apparently tired of waiting.

"We'll get out here," he said while opening his door.

"Oh, ok, sir," the driver said, abruptly putting the Escalade into park and hustling out his door to the back of the SUV where Paul's bag was.

Jennifer and I had no bags, so we got out and helped Gus out of the third row. We all went inside, with Paul offering his thoughts for our next steps as he looked at his watch.

"It's well past lunchtime and I'm assuming we're all

hungry. Why don't we meet at the Old Stagecoach in about ten minutes to decompress and strategize on bringing this whole thing to a conclusion," he said.

The Old Stagecoach was the nicest restaurant at the Grand Marquis. They specialized in fantastic steaks, but my favorite item on the menu was their Maple Old Fashioned.

"Great," I said, perhaps a little too quickly.

"Sounds good," Jennifer added.

"Gus, you come with me. We'll get settled in my room and I'll show you around. Don't worry about anything. We'll make sure you have what you need while you're here," I said to Gus with a nod and a smile.

Gus smiled back meekly, but was clearly awestruck by the spectacle of the Grand Marquis lobby. The huge guitar with all the guests gathered around taking selfies had his interest for a moment. Then he drifted his gaze to the waterfalls and streams that meandered through the tropical forest vegetation.

It was easy for me to forget how big and impressive this place was, having been here several times before. I paused before we left to let Gus take it all in. Eventually, he saw me waiting and nodded for me to lead the way.

With that, we all separated and headed to our rooms. Gus followed me up the escalator toward our suite, with Paul just a few steps ahead. Jennifer went to the right toward the section with her room, closer to the atrium.

After the lengthy trip to my hotel room, Gus finally spoke up.

"This place is huge," he said with a sense of awe.

"Yeah, it is. And this is only one section. Just wait until you see the rest," I said, nodding and smiling.

I opened the door and showed Gus the room, allowing

him time to use the restroom and look around at all the amenities. He stood on the patio overlooking the atrium waterfall for several minutes when I finally had to urge him along.

"You ready for lunch?" I asked as I joined him on the balcony.

"Oh, yeah. Sorry, I've just never seen anything like this," he said.

"I understand. These big hotels are quite entertaining," I said as we moved across the room and out the door.

I didn't push Gus too fast along the route to the Old Stagecoach, letting him absorb all the shops and scenery along the way. His eyes stayed big and his mouth stayed open for most of the trip. By the time we got to the restaurant, Paul and Jennifer were already there.

They both smiled at Gus when we walked up, obviously recognizing his awestruck expression.

"They're cleaning a table for us," Paul said as we walked up.

I nodded at Paul.

"This is a pretty wild place, isn't it?" Jennifer asked Gus.

It was at that point that I realized I had never really introduced Gus to her.

"By the way, Jennifer, this is Gustavo. He's the brave young man from Zapata who was helping Bob Yates. I should have introduced you sooner, but I got too involved with our predicament. Gus, this is my friend Jennifer," I said, nodding to each of them.

"It's nice to meet you. Thanks for helping to get me," Gus said.

"It's my pleasure to meet you and to help get you out of

there. I really didn't do much," Jennifer said as she looked at me.

While they chatted, the hostess let us know our table was ready.

Once again, Gus was totally entranced with his surroundings as we made our way to the table. The restaurant was embedded in one of the rainforest sections of the hotel atrium, with water flowing under the floor and trees hanging overhead. Our table was near a small waterfall at the back of the seating area, which was perfect for our discussion. It also gave Gus a good view of the surrounding area, which he seemed to enjoy.

After we were seated and ordered our drinks, Paul got down to business.

"Alright, so we seem to be getting to the bottom of this whole thing. From all you and the police have uncovered, we know Bob was murdered by a Mexican cartel sniper. We know he was working to extradite young people from a potential human trafficking situation. We know Gus was helping him." Paul smiled and nodded at Gus while he paused.

Then he continued.

"We know Atlantis was involved with a rather substantial drug and human smuggling operation using their facility in Zapata. We know Chris Valentine had set up several LLCs with his wife's family to wash their cash," Paul said, but was interrupted by Gus.

"Who is Chris Valentine?" Gus asked.

We all stared at him for a minute, then I responded.

"Chris was Bob Yates' boss," I said.

Gus nodded, but I decided to take it a step further. I pulled out my phone and started looking for recent news reports about Chris. I found an article with a photo of

Chris and his wife at a Bob Yates memorial event just yesterday.

I enlarged the photo and showed it to Gus.

"This is Chris Valentine," I said as Gus looked closely at the photo.

"Hmmm," Gus said.

"You don't recognize him?" I asked.

"No," Gus said, "but I recognize that woman."

"You do? From where?" I asked, while we all leaned in.

"She goes to the plant all the time. The shirt guys bring her in. She always talks to the guys in the fancy trucks and drives away in her fancy car," he said.

I remembered seeing her at dinner in her Bentley, along with her dinner guests in their G-Wagon. It seems Gus had seen her in similar situations.

"Yeah, we believe Chris sent her down there to handle some of his business. He also set up multiple businesses with her family members to help hide his illegal smuggling," I said, trying to simplify the situation for Gus.

Gus didn't seem convinced.

"I've seen her talking to the border guys and the cops, too. She knows everyone," Gus said.

"Why would she talk to the border guys and the cops?" I asked, thinking I already knew part of that answer.

"I think the border guys let the trucks come in from Mexico. The cops probably ignore all the missing people. I don't know," Gus said.

His response filled in one more piece of the puzzle.

"You're probably right," I said, looking at Paul and Jennifer.

Gus sat still for a moment, then he added an additional point.

"She scares me."

Chapter Fifty-Five

Nashville, TN. Saturday

We all sat for a moment to absorb what Gus had just said.

"Why does she scare you," Jennifer finally asked.

"I don't know. She just seems mean. And everyone else seems scared of her," he said.

"Do you think that's because she's the wife of the CFO?" Paul asked.

"Maybe. But I don't know what a CFO is. She just scares me, that's all," he said as he focused his attention on the menu.

We all followed his lead and spent a few quiet minutes observing the long list of menu options at the Old Stagecoach restaurant.

Our drinks arrived, and we gave the server our food orders. After a few idle comments about the steak versus pasta options and how our meal timing was screwed up with a 2 p.m. lunch, we set out to discuss our plan of action.

"Ok, so where do we go from here?" Jennifer asked to kick things off.

"I think we should try to get back into Chris' house," Paul said.

"That's a bold move. We already know he's not there. At least that's what he said," I responded.

"Yeah, but she may not know that," Paul said, referring to Mrs. Valentine.

"I guess that's true. What would we be looking for if he's not there?" I asked.

"Pretty much anything we can find. Where is he? What does she know about his activities and behavior? How did her siblings become owners of companies who buy Atlantis products? And after listening to Gus, why does she spend so much time in Zapata?" Paul said, stopping to take a sip of his drink.

We all followed along and sipped our own drinks.

"That makes sense. Maybe we can have her turn Chris in to the police. I'm sure they're trying to do the same thing, but it feels like we're a couple of steps ahead of them," Jennifer said.

"Plus, that's a sweet place to visit," she added.

"That's a bonus," Paul said.

"I also want to drill into a couple of things," I said.

Everyone looked at me and waited for me to continue.

"We know Chris was having an affair with Bob's wife, Doris. I wonder if Mrs. Valentine knew about it. Chris really tried to impress to me I was on the wrong track by identifying him as the one responsible for all this. I wonder..." I stopped mid sentence.

"You wonder if she may be setting him up?" Jennifer asked to fill in my thought.

"Yeah, I guess that's it," I said.

"You're getting soft, Keith," Jennifer said with a smile.

"Yeah, I agree. This all seems to point directly to the good CFO," Paul said as he drained his drink.

When he noticed us looking at him, he added.

"I mean, it's five o'clock somewhere, right?"

We all smiled and took another drink of our own beverages. We were starting to get into more light-hearted conversation when Gus tuned in from his constant amusement of the facility to offer a question.

"If you go to the Valentine house, do I have to go?" He had fear in his eyes when he asked the question.

"I don't think so, no. You can stay here in my room," I said, looking at Paul for approval.

"Absolutely, Gus. You can stay here and watch TV in Keith's room while we visit the Valentine residence. There's no need for you to have to go through that," Paul added.

We nodded at each other and sat back as our meals arrived. I had been trying to limit my red meat intake on this trip, but the filet at the Old Stagecoach is just too good to pass up. I smiled my approval as the lovely steak and asparagus was set in front of me. Looking around the table, I could see everyone else was equally pleased with their meals. Even Gus, who had ordered a traditional cheeseburger, seemed pleased with the presentation.

"This is awesome," Gus said on cue, with the enthusiasm in his voice matching the look on his face.

"Yeah, this place does a good job," Paul said, smiling at Gus.

We were about midway through our meals, having a nice conversation that let us all escape the chaos surrounding Gus and Bob Yates, when my phone buzzed in my pocket. I knew it was bad manners to accept a call during dinner, but knowing our overall situation, I pulled the phone from my pocket and glanced at the number.

It was an unknown number with a Kentucky area code. I must have looked puzzled, because Jennifer felt compelled to investigate.

"What's going on, Keith?" she asked.

"Well, it seems I'm getting a call from Kentucky," I said as I put the phone back in my pocket.

"You sure you shouldn't answer that?" she said.

"I don't think I know anyone from Kentucky who would need to interrupt this filet," I said with a smile.

Everyone smiled and nodded, and we continued our chatter through the rest of the meal. Somewhere during the conversation, I felt the vibration in my pocket to indicate the caller from Kentucky had left a message. I made a mental note to check it later.

We were just declining dessert when Gus took the discussion in a new direction.

"So, what happens to me? Do I go to the police?" Gus asked, looking intently at each of us while we considered his question.

"Well, the first thing, and the most important thing, is to make sure you stay safe," Paul said, trying to squelch Gus' concerns.

"What would you like to happen? Would you like to go back to Zapata? Or would you like to start a new life somewhere else?" I asked, realizing I was heaping a huge amount of responsibility on his young mind.

Gus paused for a minute before he responded.

"If it's safe, I'd like to go back. I have friends there. They do good things for people from my home," he said, obviously referring to Mexico.

"But if it's not safe, I'd like to stay here," he said, sitting back and looking around at his lavish hotel surroundings.

We all chuckled politely at his simple response.

"I think we'd all like to live here if we could," Jennifer responded with a smile.

"We'll make sure we find a good place for you," Paul finally said, smiling at Gus when he said it.

I wondered what that really meant for Gus. There was a lot to sort out before we came to that point, I guessed.

Sitting back and refocusing on the immediate future, Paul rubbed his hands together and leaned in.

"Let's make the call to the Valentine residence and let them know we'd like to stop by. We can tell them we want to discuss more details about how they plan to address their supply chain leadership gap with Bob's passing. We can suggest we need more details than we got with your visit earlier this week," he said, looking at me.

"Yeah, we were more focused on Bob's passing. We mentioned it briefly, but didn't really spend much time on the supply chain vacancy Bob left," I said.

"Great. Sounds like we have a plan," Paul said.

We acquiesced to a delicious selection of desserts before we ended the meal and headed back to the lobby. My tiramisu was sitting heavy in my stomach as we made the long walk back to the door. I stopped by my room with Gus to leave him with the TV and some strict instructions.

"Please don't leave the room, Gus. Until we know where Chris Valentine is, we can't be sure you're not in danger. It's safest if you stay here," I said.

"Sure, Mr. Morgan. I won't go anywhere," Gus said as he scrambled to turn on the television.

"We'll be back in about two hours, I'd guess," I said, having already lost his attention.

"Ok, sure," he said, while scrolling through the channels.

"Wow, there are so many," Gus was saying as I left him to meet Jennifer and Paul in the lobby.

On my way there, I pulled out my phone to see what the caller from Kentucky had to say. The message was long, and the voice surprised me.

"Hey Keith, this is Chris Valentine. I've come to know you are sniffing around this whole Bob Yates thing, and I want to tell you something before I go completely off the grid. I mentioned earlier you have this whole thing wrong. Let me explain what I mean. I didn't kill Bob Yates. He was a friend and a close confidant. Yes, I had succumbed to temptation with Doris, but Bob was a good man. He and I were helping kids, along with Gus. I now realize you rescued Gus, and I appreciate that. Gus was helping Bob and me get kids out of Zapata. There is a group of Atlantis people who have created a human trafficking ring that sends these kids into unfathomable circumstances. It's very lucrative for the people involved with the trafficking, but it often ends in death for these poor kids. Bob and I had recruited Gus to help identify at-risk kids to send them far from Zapata before they get ensnared by that ring. Now, here's the reason I'm leaving: the ringleader for this entire operation is not me, it's my wife. Mary has a long relationship with cartel leaders in Mexico and has built that into a very, very large business. I had no idea she was into this type of stuff when I met her. She used her contacts, along with my tendency to fall to temptation, to lure me into a night of forbidden pleasure with a young lady. A young lady, I found out later, who was only seventeen years old. Mary has been using a video of that horrible mistake to keep me quiet for the last ten years. But now I'm coming clean. I'm not a murderer. I'm not a sex trafficking mogul. I don't have relationships with drug cartels. My wife does all of those things. You need to convince the police of that. It's not me. It's her. And she found out Bob and I were helping kids get away. That's why she killed him. Then she sent the message to me about the Nashville Inn murders. CA stands for Christopher Anthony. That's my name, and that's what she calls me when she's joking around. Or when she's really mad. This message is too long, and I'm leaving now. And I meant what I said: you won't hear from me again."

I stood at the door of my room with my mouth open. Was this a game Chris was playing? Was I really wrong?

Maybe this trip to Leiper's Fork would help me find the truth.

Chapter Fifty-Six

Nashville, TN. Saturday

I recycled the voicemail from Chris Valentine in my head while I walked to the lobby of the Grand Marquis. Gus was thrilled with the television channels the hotel provided, so he barely noticed when I left. I was confident he'd still be there on the couch watching something when I returned. The voicemail message, however, had my mind spinning.

Apparently, I still looked stunned when I walked up to Jennifer and Paul near the front door.

"What's going on with you?" Jennifer asked.

I snapped back to my best smile and swiped my phone to the voicemail that had sent my mind adrift.

"Remember that phone call I got during lunch?" I asked as I put my phone on speaker.

"Yeah," Paul said.

"The reason I didn't recognize the number is that it was a burner phone purchased in Kentucky. Purchased in Kentucky by none other than Chris Valentine," I said, using a more dramatic tone than I probably needed.

"Really? What did he want?" Jennifer asked.

"I'll let you hear it for yourself. Let's walk over to this corner for a minute," I said as I motioned toward a quiet area away from the traffic of the front doors.

When we got to a quieter space, I played the voicemail from Chris Valentine. Both of them stood quietly, Paul with his typically stoic look and Jennifer with her mouth slowly opening in shock as she listened.

"Whoa," Jennifer said as the voicemail ended.

"Do you believe him?" Paul asked.

"That's the battle you saw going on in my head when I walked up. I'm not really sure," I replied.

"Does that change our plans for the day?" Jennifer asked.

"I'd say it just gives the trip to Leiper's Fork more urgency," Paul said.

"I agree. We need to see if we can figure out what the truth is. I mean, we met Chris and saw him in his home setting. To me, he seemed like he was selling something every time he talked. That makes me suspicious of anything he says, especially something like this," I said, motioning to the voicemail on my phone.

"Yeah," Paul said, clearly in deep thought.

"What are you thinking?" Jennifer asked Paul.

"We need to get her talking. I'm sure she doesn't know Chris has left that message. Especially if he's telling the truth, and she thinks she has him blackmailed into silence," Paul said, looking for confirmation from the two of us.

We both nodded.

"Ok, then let's get to it. I called ahead and told Mary we needed to have a discussion with Chris about the acquisition, given our concerns about Bob's death. She didn't mention Chris at all, but told me to come on out. Our car should be waiting by now. Let's see what we can find out," Paul said as he motioned to the front door of the lobby.

We left in the same Escalade that had dropped us off, in the same seats we were in before. Paul turned in his front passenger seat so he could talk to Jennifer and me.

"Ok, so if Chris is telling the truth, Mary is in charge of this whole operation. If I take a step back and think about all this, there's really no way to know whether she is or isn't the one calling the shots. It really could be either of them," Paul said.

"That's what I've been trying to figure out. It sure seems like there would be something that pointed to one or the other of them. All we have right now is Chris' word that goes against everything we were thinking so far," I said.

"But did we even consider the possibility that she was the leader of all this? I know I didn't. So, it's not that she was ruled out, she just wasn't ever 'ruled in.' I can't come up with one shred of evidence I'm aware of that would clear either of them," Jennifer added.

We all stood there shaking our heads as we tried to remember all the details of the last few days.

"Well, it sounds like we're all on the same page, then. Let's see what we can find out when we get there. I'll lead the discussion on the acquisition. Keith, you can chime in on anything you've learned about their supply chain. We just need to get her talking as much as we can. Jennifer, you can supplement wherever you hear anomalies," Paul said as he turned around and faced forward again.

The rest of the trip was filled with casual conversation about Nashville, the surrounding landscape, and the beautiful farms we passed along the way. In less than thirty minutes, we were pulling into the driveway of the massive Valentine estate.

"Wow, you were right, Keith. This is quite a place," Paul said.

This time, as we pulled in, a ranch worker directed us to pull around to the back of the house. This put us in the same area where we were picked up to leave after the last visit. As we pulled around, Paul saw the garage that was hidden from the front, as well as the barn and stables further back on the property. I could see him checking it all out, but he said nothing.

We got out of the Escalade, and Paul told the driver to head into town and wait for our call. I wasn't certain which town he meant or how far away it might be, but we were about to be on our own out here at the Valentine ranch.

Mary Perez-Valentine met us on the massive deck that covered the entire back side of the house. She was dressed far more elegantly than I had seen her in Zapata, with a white pantsuit and red scarf. Now that I was aware of her Mexican heritage, it seemed obvious as I saw her now. Her blond hair was pulled back, and she had on a huge white hat with red flowers. It almost looked like she was ready for the Kentucky Derby.

My mind wandered for a few moments while I tried to remember when The Derby would have been run this year, but I quickly gathered my thoughts for the task at hand. I needed to stay focused on the challenge of identifying the true criminal in charge of the Atlantis trafficking empire.

Paul was the first to speak as we walked up the stairs to greet Mary.

"Hi Mary, I'm Paul. We spoke on the phone," Paul said as he reached out his hand.

Jennifer was next in line, coming up the stairs.

"This is Jennifer Ellis, one of our associates at Rocky

Mountain Equity," he said, motioning toward Jennifer and stepping back.

"Mary Perez-Valentine. It's a pleasure to meet you," Mary said. She even used her hyphenated name in her introductions, which seemed weird.

"And this is Keith Morgan. He's another one of our associates and an expert in global supply chains," Paul said, exaggerating my expertise to suit the moment.

I watched to see if Mary recognized me from our brief encounter at the restaurant in Zapata, but I saw nothing in her eyes. Either she was really good at hiding it, or she didn't know I had seen her in Texas. As I looked at her, I wondered why she had dyed her hair blond. The picture above the fireplace showed her with her darker, more natural color, which was stunning. The blond color she wore now looked fake in comparison.

"Hi Keith, it's a pleasure to meet you," she said. At least I didn't have to wait for her to spit out her full name.

"Let's head inside. Sophia, my darling, could you please bring us four glasses of sweet tea? Thank you, dear," Mary said toward the girl who opened the door for us as we entered. If Chris was a salesman with his behavior, Mary had taken it up a notch. It was almost as if she was acting in an old southern movie.

We followed her into the same room where we had met Chris. I found myself looking for clues, this time, versus admiring the home like I had done the first time. Jennifer and Paul seemed to be doing the same thing as we all entered the room and took a seat.

Paul and Mary sat on the couch, with me and Jennifer in the chairs on either side. The fireplace was on, which seemed weird for a warm day like this, but the room was still comfortable. I guessed it was just for ambiance.

After a few pleasantries and compliments on the house and property, it was time to get to business. Paul was the one who brought us into business mode.

"Will Mr. Valentine be joining us today?" He asked, knowing what Chris had said on my voicemail.

"He should be home any minute. He had to make a quick run into town," Mary said without skipping a beat.

This was the first of many lies we'd hear from Mary that Saturday afternoon.

Chapter Fifty-Seven

"Should we wait for him?" I said to Mary, wondering how she would navigate Chris' absence.

"Oh, no. I'm a consultant with Atlantis, so I'm familiar with Bob's work at the company, too. I'd be glad to answer any questions you may have. I am, after all, certainly interested in making this equity play a success," she said.

Paul looked at me with a smile and started. It clearly wasn't the response he expected, and was unconventional, but gave him the opportunity to keep digging.

"Well, as you are obviously aware, at the request of your board of directors, Rocky Mountain Equity is in the process of evaluating Atlantis for a potential equity position," Paul started.

Mary didn't bat an eye at that comment, and simply nodded as Paul continued.

"And it saddened us to hear of Bob Yates' death this week. It was quite a shock. We were here earlier in the week passing along our condolences to Chris, but wanted to get a more logistical view of Atlantis' plans as well," Paul said.

"Oh, sure. That's understandable," Mary said. She was sitting upright on the couch with her hands crossed in her lap as though she was posing for a photo.

Paul was about to continue when our iced tea arrived. It was in a similarly nice set of tumblers as the other day, and on a similarly nice tray, and was carried by Sophia. She was the woman who had held the door earlier. She wasn't the same person who had given us drinks when Chris was here, but that could've simply been the difference between weekday and weekend staff.

While the drinks were served, I looked around the house for any anomaly that might point to the positioning of Chris and Mary with Atlantis. There were no obviously incriminating photos or signs, but there were enough to get us into some polite conversation.

"I see you have lots of photos of your beautiful family. Do they live near here?" I asked, noticing several photos of what appeared to be quinceaneras or similar events with teenage girls in glamorous outfits and festive settings. As I looked around, I realized virtually all the photos were of Hispanic families. None appeared to include Chris except one huge photo of the two of them, with their daughter above the fireplace mantle.

"You are too kind. No, unfortunately, most of my family lives further south, but we try to get everyone together when it's possible. As you can see from the photos, we use birthdays and special events to get together as often as we can," she said with a smile.

"It's nice to be able to do that, I agree," I said, returning her smile.

I was beginning to understand why Gus was afraid of

this woman. She smiled and said the right things, but there was a cutting feeling to everything she said. If Chris Valentine made you feel like you were being sold to, Mary Perez-Valentine made you feel like you were about to be eaten.

"Thank you for the tea. This is wonderful," Jennifer said, matching Mary's smile.

"You're welcome, dear," Mary said, which sounded weird since she was probably only a few years older than Jennifer. It sort of matched the rest of her vibe, though.

"Is that your daughter?" she asked, nodding above the mantle.

"Yes, it sure is. Our daughter Morgan is right there. She's out on her horse right now," she said.

"Oh, you have horses?" Paul asked, playing the same game I had played with Chris just a day earlier.

The question earned him a somewhat pleasant smile from Mary, almost like she was taking pity on him for not knowing something so obvious.

"We sure do, yes. Many of the properties around here are horse properties. It's one of my passions, I suppose," she said, which I knew to be another lie based on the driver's comments about her yesterday.

"How do you find time to ride with all the family trips and the business with Atlantis?" Jennifer asked. She was keying in on two of the areas Mary seemed most comfortable talking about.

"Oh, it's not that bad. Chris and I don't travel all that much with Atlantis, but it's great to get out and see our team when we can. I still try to ride at least once a week. It really helps me stay even," Mary said with a condescending nod. Jennifer matched the nod with an equally condescending nod of understanding. It was strange watching her mirror Mary like this.

"You are so brave. That would scare me to death!" Jennifer said with a leg slap and a giggle that sounded like it came from an entirely different person.

"You said you were a consultant at Atlantis?" Paul asked, getting back to the corporate discussion.

"Yes. They bring me in to help evaluate distribution center locations and performance. My family visits have introduced me to a variety of lower cost areas in the south. Those areas have turned out to be excellent locations for Atlantis expansion," she said, walking right into our target discussion area.

"I understand Chris has been involved with quite an overhaul of the Atlantis supply chain efficiency in recent years. Were you part of that work, too?" I asked.

"Oh, absolutely. We're really proud of what we've been able to do with that optimization. While we know there were some temporary cost impacts while we upgraded equipment and facilities, we know it will pay off in the end with a much more cost effective supply chain operation," Mary responded as though she was an expert and was intimately involved.

"It sounds like you may be as involved with this as Chris?" I asked with a chuckle, as though it was a joke.

"Well, Chris is the CFO and a good one. But he's not a supply chain guy," she said. There was a bit more of an edge in her tone when she talked about Chris.

"Then perhaps you understand our concern about the ongoing execution of these initiatives without the expertise of a person like Bob Yates," I asked, ignoring her self-promoting supply chain comments a moment before.

"Oh, it won't be easy. Bob Yates was a good man and a fine employee. He also had years of experience with Atlantis and their supply chain. He will be sorely missed.

But I think we're past the point of any one person blocking the success of the project, really. It's well under way, with a well-defined execution schedule. You'll see a much more efficient operation in the next six months," she said, with a confident nod.

"Do you know who will fill Bob's position?" I asked, repeating a question I'd asked Chris the day before.

"We have a couple of very bright up-and-comers in the organization. Chris is evaluating them for the position. One of them will be named in the next day or two," she said, again with more confidence than I'd expect from a 'consultant.'

"Oh, really? That's great. So, no need to go through the trouble of an outside hire," Paul said, sounding pleased to hear that news.

"Oh, no, not at all. We'll have it all covered in-house," she beamed.

Once again, Chris or Mary wasn't being truthful, even on something as simple as backfilling Bob's role.

"You seem to know the operation fairly well yourself. Have you visited any of the Atlantis facilities to see first-hand how they operate? Or are you more involved in the strategic side of the business?" Paul asked.

"Oh, I don't get into the nuts and bolts of aluminum parts, no. I'm more involved with strategy and planning. Bob was the one who would visit the plants and manage the day-to-day execution of our program. That's why we're promoting an insider to stay on top of it. I'd not be able to help them with that," she said.

"We noticed some abnormal expenses recently in one of the facilities in Texas, near Zapata," Paul blurted out. I thought I noticed a blip of reaction from Mary, but she recovered quickly while Paul continued.

"Would that be part of this investment you were mentioning earlier? Upgrading equipment or something?" Paul asked with an investor's voice.

Mary sat there for a moment and slowly morphed into a different emotional state. Her tone completely changed and her eyes went dark. It was almost like she just remembered she wasn't really supposed to be nice to us.

"I'm sorry, would you please excuse me for a moment? I need to check on my daughter," she said as she abruptly stood and walked out the back door.

We sat there for a minute, feeling awkward. Then Paul made a statement I hadn't really considered.

"If Chris was telling the truth, I may have just taken our visit a little too far," he said solemnly.

When Mary stepped back into the house a few moments later, we all watched and listened closely to see if Paul was right.

Chapter Fifty-Eight

Leiper's Fork, TN. Saturday

Mary came back into the house, flanked by two of her ranch workers. Two others followed them and stayed by the door.

All four of the ranch workers were carrying rifles, and Mary seemed distressed. My first inclination was that Paul had definitely tripped something with Mary Perez-Valentine. I leaned back to feel my SIG inside the back of my waistband.

"It seems my daughter may have had an issue with her horse out in the field. Would you mind joining me while we take a quick drive to make sure she's ok?" Mary asked with what seemed to be a forced smile.

Was it really a forced smile, or was I just thinking it was forced? Maybe it was a genuine smile, and I had misread her reaction to Paul. I would have certainly been distressed if my daughter Jamie was out in a field somewhere with no way back. I shook myself away from my internal musing and back to the request in front of us.

We looked at each other, sure we were all thinking the same thing: was this trip a ploy to get us out in the field where Mary and her staff could eliminate us? Or was her daughter really in distress out there on her horse?

She seemed to sense our hesitation.

"We can continue our discussion along the way," she said with a much broader smile.

"Should we not wait for Chris to return?" I asked, trying to avoid a trip to the field.

"Oh, I don't think that's necessary. The team just informed me he's running a bit late and won't be here for some time," she said. While she replied, one of the ranch workers at the door opened it and held it, luring us to the exit.

Mary's answer about Chris was, of course, another lie.

We reluctantly followed one of the ranch workers out the back door and onto the vast deck. From there, we could see a black Bentley Bentayga sitting in the rear driveway. The sight of it reminded me of Mary's love of luxury rides. Including her Continental GT down in Zapata. I wondered how many Bentleys she had, and how much money she must have spent on them. But the current situation prevented me from doing too much internal analysis on the topic.

"You can ride with me and Nick. We can have the others meet us with the trailer," Mary said, nodding at Jennifer, Paul and me.

I looked at Paul for any guidance, only seeing a subtle nod of confidence in his gaze. He clearly felt he was prepared to head into the unknown in the back of a Bentley Bentayga. Seeing that attitude, I answered firmly.

"Sounds great. I hope your daughter is ok," I said to Mary with a smile as genuine as I could muster.

"She sounds fine. A little rattled, maybe, but she's concerned about the horse. With the trailer, we'll be able to get the horse, too, so it'll all be taken care of," Mary said with a motion toward a Ford F-350 sitting next to the barn. I noticed it wasn't yet moving in the same direction as us and didn't appear to be attached to a horse trailer.

I also saw Mark, the driver Chris had summoned to take us back to the hotel yesterday. He was watching curiously while he tinkered with one of the many ATVs in the parking area. It had to appear an odd sight, all of us to be standing there preparing to load into the Bentley.

We climbed into the luxury SUV, all three of us across the back seat. I thought I remembered these vehicles having a third row, but this one didn't. Instead, we snugly belted ourselves in for whatever was about to happen. Mary hadn't made any comments that led us to believe she was on to our investigation, but if she was, a trip to the pasture would be a good way to settle things.

Watching Mary interact with her staff, it was clear she was the one in charge. The camaraderie we had seen between Chris and the team didn't exist with Mary. She was all business, and she was the boss. The more I watched, the more I began to wonder about Chris' voicemail message.

Within a few moments, we were on a gravel, then dirt road that led directly away from the house and the barn. Looking out the front windshield, I could see no other houses or structures of any kind. All I could see were green rolling pastures for miles. It sure felt like we were headed into the wilderness, albeit a very pleasant-looking one.

Mary, true to her word, started the drive with a continuance of our previous conversation at the house. She turned toward us in the front passenger seat while one of the staff drove the car to the supposed location of her daughter.

"You were asking about one of the facilities in Texas before I was interrupted? Can you remind me what that was about?" Mary asked, even though she wasn't interrupted at all and had stopped the conversation herself.

Paul took the question.

"Yes. We had noticed during our due diligence that the location in Zapata, specifically, had a rather high expense ratio compared to the throughput. It wasn't astronomical, as there was a fair amount of order volume listed, but the expense to order volume ratio seemed higher," he said.

"Hmmm. That's interesting. I wouldn't say I'm familiar with that location myself, but I know the team had been upgrading trucks and loading dock automation in recent years. There may have been some increased operational expense tied to those upgrades," she said.

Her casual conversation and tone were confusing. Either she still didn't know why we were here, or she was as cold as ice and wasn't going to show us any sign of her intentions. Either way, we kept going down the dirt road.

"Chris did seem to spend a lot of time down there, that's for sure," she said matter-of-factly.

"Oh, is that right? Was he working on the upgrades or on something else?" Paul seemed to be pushing it a bit.

Mary paused rather dramatically and looked down. She eventually shook her head a minute and spoke solemnly without looking up.

"I really wish there was a better way to say this, but I think Chris had some other reasons for visiting Zapata. Reasons that may not be legal. Or moral. Or acceptable on any level," she said, still looking down.

We shared quick glances between us, but Paul kept going. While he was talking, I inched my phone out of my pocket as subtly as I could and started the audio recorder. If

Mary was going to start talking, I wanted to get every detail. I didn't know where her conversation was going, but I sensed I might want to document everything as best I could.

"What do you mean by that?" Paul asked innocently.

"I happened to find some photos and videos on Chris' phone that make me believe he may have been engaging in inappropriate activity with young girls. Most of them appeared to be Mexican, and I recognized some of the locations. He was going to Zapata on a regular basis to meet up with these girls," she said, finally looking up with tears forming in her eyes.

This was beginning to feel like an acting exhibition, but it was still hard to know if it was Chris or Mary telling the truth.

"So, you had evidence of Chris with underage girls and you didn't share it with the police?" Paul asked pointedly, leaning forward as the Bentley tried to smooth our ride over the more and more rugged road.

"How could I?" Mary yelled. She gave an exasperated sigh before continuing.

"Chris held everything for me. If I turned him in, my family would go broke. They depend on him and his business for their families. I couldn't let them down!" Mary was now emitting little sobs between her sentences.

Paul had evidently had enough.

"Chris seems to tell a very different story, Mary," he said, sitting back in his seat.

Mary seemed to change her facade instantly. The sorrow was gone, replaced with a hard, seething anger.

"Is that right? What did Chris have to say?" She almost hissed the question.

At the same time, I seemed to notice her catch the eye of

the driver. In a move that seemed to be on her cue, he picked up his radio to talk.

"It's right up here," he said and put the radio down. He looked in the mirror at the F-350 that was now just behind us. There was no horse trailer behind it.

"Chris indicated you had more influence over this whole program than you're saying. In fact, he said you framed him with the young girls some time ago to buy his cooperation," Paul said, going for the jugular.

I was curious about Paul's tactics at that point, knowing we were out here in an unknown landscape and were outnumbered by Mary and her four armed employees. He must have thought we could turn Mary before we got ourselves into trouble.

In the next few moments, we would find out that potential strategy was flawed.

Chapter Fifty-Nine

Leiper's Fork, TN. Saturday

"Well, of course he says that. He's trying to frame me to buy his own innocence. But, the photos and videos aren't that old. Some are from as recently as two years ago. And it wasn't just one time. There are many girls over a period of years. Did Chris tell you that?" Mary asked, still hissing and now staring straight ahead.

"No, I guess he didn't," Paul admitted, catching Jennifer and my gaze for a brief second. He seemed to be getting concerned.

"Yes, I hid his problem. But I did it for my family. Each of them leads a humble life here in the United States and they do it because Chris' job has provided us with the opportunity. He may have a horrible vice, but he's been good to my family. I couldn't just deny my family by sending Chris away," she said, now shifting to a voice of resolve.

"Your family members still lead humble lives? Where

are they?" I asked, building my own story about what was going on here.

"They live in small towns around Texas. Chris got them jobs with some of the plants there, and they have thrived," she said, turning around and looking at me again. This time, with a bleak smile.

"I'm glad they're doing well," I said.

She nodded to the driver toward the left, and he veered off the barely visible dirt tracks. Once he turned, we could see a deep ravine coming into view just ahead of us. Fearing we may be headed toward an unfortunate encounter, I decided to dive in just like Paul had.

"When's the last time you saw your family?" I asked.

"It's been a few months. Why do you ask?" Mary said, continuing with the sober smile.

"So, that wasn't your brother you were meeting in Zapata at the Atlantis plant? The one who drove away in the G-Wagon? The one you had dinner with? I saw his picture on your mantle, and I can certainly only hope to get to his humble level of existence!" I said, watching her tense up as I spoke.

She opened her mouth to speak, but reconsidered. After several seconds, she went in a new direction.

"I looked you up, Paul. I know you're on the board of Rocky Mountain Equity. I also know you hire Keith for consulting work from time to time. It looks like you've only recently added Jennifer for more of that consulting work. Now, however, I'm beginning to think you do much more than that. Who do you really work for?" Mary asked, now in more of a take-charge tone.

"Your research was correct. That's what we do," Paul said.

"Well, it seems Rocky Mountain Equity may have

gotten you three into a bit of trouble here," Mary said, again nodding to the driver. He pulled near the edge of the ravine and slowed down the Bentley.

Now, it seemed it was time for Jennifer to step in.

"Your daughter isn't out here, is she?" Jennifer asked.

Mary let a sinister laugh slip out. "No, she's nowhere near here. She's at boarding school," she replied.

"How can you let this stuff go on with Chris without reporting it? You have a daughter! How could you do that to those innocent daughters from your homeland?" Jennifer asked angrily.

Mary held onto her stoney gaze as she looked at Jennifer.

"You can't begin to know what you're talking about. I have helped thousands of families escape more difficult times than that to get to the United States. People trust me and my brothers to get them to a safe place, and I deliver," Mary said, beginning to shed her innocence with every sentence.

"And yes, I was in Zapata with my brother. He was returning from a trip to Mexico to expand our business. And I guess that means, Mr. Morgan, that you were there twice this week? You were the one who stole a truck to get an up-close and personal look at the facility and kidnap one of our employees?" Mary said, turning her attention toward me.

So, she knew someone had taken Gus, but didn't see the video to know it was me. Either that, or she was once again demonstrating her acting skills. Or maybe my hat and sunglasses disguise in Zapata was better than I thought.

"If you were only bringing in paying clientele, as illegal as that is, you probably wouldn't have been so worried about me seeing it. We found evidence that you were taking kids off the street, lots more than just for Chris, and taking them away. I'm sure they didn't pay you. In fact, I'm quite sure your paying clientele were on the receiving end of those victims." I used the word 'victims' for emphasis, pausing on it a second before I continued.

"Then I came to know you would take adults, too. When you or your team decided they were no longer of value to Atlantis, you took them away. I'm curious if you were sending them into the trafficking ring or just killing them, but either way, it's not the good, clean family business you describe. Then, to top that off, you took Gus! Why would you do that? He was a loyal worker who had done nothing wrong!" I said, intentionally pushing my anger and trying to see what she knew about him.

She threw her head back and laughed when I mentioned Gus.

"Oh yes, Gus, Gus, Gus," she said, almost gleefully.

"No, I'm afraid we came to know he was not quite as loyal as you say. You see, I had gotten word that Bob Yates was trying to put a dent in my business. That idiot thought he could save the world, especially after he found out he was sick. We just didn't know how he was doing it. But then, when I realized it was actually Chris who was orchestrating the whole thing through a fit of guilt, it was easy to track down his little ring. Yes, Gus was loyal, but not to Atlantis or to me. He thought Bob Yates and Chris could save him. I guess he needed you for that, didn't he?" she said, shaking her head and looking at me with cold eyes.

For some reason, I felt a sense of relief at her admission that Gus had escaped. But that relief was only temporary.

"And you didn't bring him with you, so I suppose Gus is at the hotel? Did you really think leaving him at the hotel was a good idea?" Mary said as she got out of the car. She leaned in and looked at each of us for a moment before continuing.

"I'm done answering questions. Get out of my car," Mary said as the three guys from the other car approached. I could see one of them at each back door, and I glanced behind to see the third guy standing a few feet back to cover them.

The doors on both sides of the Bentley opened on cue.

"Step out, please," the guy on the right said, stepping back and raising his rifle to his waist. I couldn't tell what kind of gun he held, but it was clearly a hunting rifle and he was not planning to use it on an animal out here.

I was beginning to see how amateur this whole operation was. It almost amazed me she had been running this illegal activity with an apparent lack of skilled security. Nobody checked for our guns, never took our phones. It's almost as if she thought she was invincible. That thought gave me a brief pause while I hoped my phone was still recording. If it was, it now had enough to sink Mary Perez-Valentine. If I could get it out of here intact.

Knowing we needed to formulate a strategy quickly, I tried another tactic before we had to take action. I could see Paul and Jennifer's eyes surveying our situation while I did the same.

"Let me see if I have this right," I began as we all stood. Mary was in front of us with her driver, now holding his rifle at his waist. The other three men stood semi-circle beside and behind us.

"I'm guessing your family isn't quite as humble as you indicate. In fact, I'd say you came here with a purpose. You latched onto Chris knowing you had a plan. You locked him into it with his horrible vice with those girls and kept him involved all this time by stringing along that unfathomable behavior. The thought of your lack of human empathy for those girls just disgusts me," I said.

Mary's teeth clenched, but she just stood there while her men watched and waited. Before she could respond, I continued.

"Then you built an empire here. You have your vast home here in Nashville, you fly on private jets, you put your family in positions where they can and will keep some of your secrets, and you control it all. You import drugs, you provide 'immigration' services for some paying customers, and you 'import' innocent people to other paying customers. This is quite a racket. Then, along comes Bob Yates and starts working with Chris and Gus to disrupt things. He probably knew he couldn't do as much about the drugs and innocent Mexicans just trying to get a better life, but he wanted to stop the sex trafficking. Since that's probably your most lucrative business, you couldn't have that. So, you had your team find someone to work on Bob's golf club and then had one of your brother's snipers do the rest," I said as I looked back and forth at Mary and the three men I could see.

"Do I have that right?" I asked, without waiting for an answer.

"And I think you saw me on the video feed getting Gus out of the Zapata facility. Maybe you didn't know it was me, but I think you did. Even if you didn't know before, you figured it out soon after we got here. Then, you thought you could swing the story against Chris to save yourself and bury him. Once you realized your story wasn't working, you decided to bring us out here and get us out of your way, just like you did to Bob Yates. Is that about it?" I asked, more dramatic than is my nature.

As I ended the review of what I suspected was going on,

I spread out my arms to loosen my shirt in the back. If I had to get to my SIG in a hurry, I needed my shirt out of the way.

Mary smiled.

"That's pretty close, I guess," she said.

Remembering my phone was still recording, I moved to close all the gaps in the case while I had her talking.

"Why set up that ridiculous showcase at the Nashville Inn? What was that message supposed to say?" I asked.

"Oh, that," she smiled. "That was just for Chris. Those were two of his trusted morons. I hoped he'd realize he needed to get in line when he saw that. Clearly, his 'bad boy turned good' quest over the last couple of years was more important to him. But he'll get his, don't worry," Mary said, keeping the evil smile on her face.

"And I guess the team here is carrying weapons that might match the ones used to kill those 'morons'?" I asked, nodding toward the gun her driver was holding. If we were getting the details, I decided we may as well get them all.

"Meet Nick. Nick is not only a loyal driver, but he's so much more." She slowly walked over to the driver while she talked, planting a dramatic kiss on his cheek. Then she continued.

"Including, as luck would have it, an excellent hunter. Good enough, in fact, to track down those two, take them out without a witness, then help with the handiwork you saw at the Nashville Inn. And while I'm getting everything off my chest, my brother did indeed have a brilliant sniper. One who could, for the right price, hit a human on a golf course from a hotel room on the other side of a lake. All made possible, of course, by the expert golf club tweaks we were able to convince the pro shop to make to Bob's golf driver. We told them it was a joke, so they agreed. This whole thing wasn't easy, Mr. Morgan. It took some work. The golf club, the hotel room in the same hotel as Chris and Bob's wife, the beheaded goons setup in their room. It really did take some work. We set it all up to frame Chris and Doris, and we executed it so well! Now you show up to tear it all down? No, you're not going to ruin this for me!" Her voice raised as she came to the end of her little speech.

"Ma'am, we need to get moving," Nick the driver said as he raised his rifle to his shoulder.

Mary nodded and stepped back toward the car, turning to watch what would happen next.

"Move over here," Mary's driver said as he moved out of our way and motioned us toward the edge of the ravine. I was getting the idea they planned to shoot us and send our bodies down there for easy disposal.

I was about to go for my SIG when the driver crumbled to his knees on my left, using his left hand to grab his throat, which was now spraying blood. Realizing what had just happened, I pulled the SIG out of its holster and dove to the ground in one motion, just as the sound of the gunshot finally reached our ears. The driver held onto his rifle in his right hand, firing aimlessly as his consciousness faded away. Someone had shot him from a substantial distance. The bullet arrived before the sound, but now all hell was breaking loose.

Rolling into a prone position, I faced the closest of the other three men, none of whom were quick enough to realize what was happening. They paid for their delay.

Four shots rang out in three seconds.

Chapter Sixty

Leiper's Fork, TN. Saturday

After the initial volley of shots, there was a brief pause, then two more shots were fired. One came from my SIG to prevent the guy on the right from getting his rifle on target, like he was trying to do. The other came from Jennifer. Her Beretta M9 was still smoking.

Mary's driver, having stumbled sideways during the skirmish, was now inching closer and closer to the edge of the ravine while now clinching his neck with both hands. It was clear he was fading quickly, and as he stumbled to the ground, he found his way over the edge. There was a sickening thud seconds later as his body landed somewhere in the chasm below.

While that was happening, Jennifer and I were slowly getting to our feet to make sure the other three team members were out of commission. They were. The guy on the left was the only one still moving, so we went to him first and kicked away his rifle. I found a Glock 19 in a holster on his hip, which I also threw to the side. Just to be sure, we also discarded the pistols from the other two, even though they appeared to be no longer with us.

After a quick search for any other weapons, we put pressure on the gunshot wound in the survivor's upper right chest. Paul had missed his vital organs by a small margin, but this might give us a chance to get a witness to Mary's illegal antics. That would be critical if this case went to trial in the future. My audio recording would be compelling, but a witness would also be helpful.

The thought of Mary made me turn and look for her. She had scrambled toward the car just as the first shot was fired, and was now getting into the driver's seat of the Bentley. I looked at Jennifer, who was responding with the same instincts as me. We were turning and positioning ourselves to fire at Mary and the SUV, but I quickly decided against it. I held up my hand so Jennifer could see my thought.

Mary had nowhere to go. Let her try to run. I wanted to make sure she was captured alive.

"Ler her go. We'll get her," I said to Jennifer.

And I had the recording from my phone. At least I hoped I did.

Turning to see where Paul was, I reached into my pocket to see if my phone was still recording from when I turned it on in the car about twenty minutes ago. It was.

I stopped the recording just as I saw Paul struggling to get up, with blood staining his shirt from an apparent gunshot wound to his left side. He looked down and put his hand over the wound before looking up at us.

"I guess I'm not as quick as I used to be," Paul said as he looked back up.

"Let me take a look at that. Are you ok?" Jennifer asked, walking over to Paul.

"Yeah, I think so. He shot right through me, but it sure hurts!" Paul said, shaking his head.

Jennifer pulled up his shirt and looked him over.

"Yeah, the wound is far enough away from anything important, I think. But you'll need to be cleaned up," she said.

While they were talking, I kept my hand on the chest of the injured assailant and began scanning the horizon to see where the long distance shot came from. Someone had saved our lives by taking the first shot at the driver just moments ago. Jennifer and Paul noticed my gaze and began looking the same direction, far out to our left.

"Who do you think that was?" Jennifer asked.

"I have a hunch, but let's see if I'm right," I said as a dust cloud emerged a couple hundred yards away.

We watched that dust cloud on our left get closer while the cloud of dust from Mary's Bentley Bentayga faded into the distance behind us. She probably thought she was really getting away.

I checked my phone for service, seeing none, and put it back in my pocket. I would need to use that recording to put Mary away, but first we had to get out of here. One of Mary's comments had me extremely concerned, and we needed to get back to Nashville as quickly as we could.

After a few seconds of listening to the grunts and groans of the guy with a hole in his chest, the sound of the approaching vehicle emerged. Once I saw it, I knew who was coming toward us. I didn't say anything just yet.

The car emerging from the dust was a BMW 5-series, struggling to navigate the rough dirt roads out here near the ravine. In fact, the car appeared to be the same one that took Jennifer and me from the Valentine ranch back to the

Grand Marquis just yesterday. When it got closer, we could see the person behind the wheel was the same driver, too.

I waited until the car was even closer before I said anything.

"It looks like Mark, doesn't it?" I said to Jennifer.

"Yeah, it does. And I assume that's Chris in the passenger seat," she said, obviously thinking the same thing I was thinking.

We were right.

"You two know who that is?" Paul said, still straining with the wound in his side while he looked on.

"Yeah. It's Chris Valentine and a guy named Mark. Mark was the driver who took us back to the hotel yesterday. We had taken an Uber out there and needed a ride. During the conversation with Mark on that trip, he told us that Chris preferred the German vehicles like this BMW. Plus, he mentioned he enjoyed driving them. The way he talked about Chris, there seemed to be some sort of bond between the two of them," I replied.

"You knew they were coming?" Paul asked in a somewhat strained tone.

"Oh no, I didn't know that at all. I was ready to go to town with my SIG before that first shot. I didn't know Chris and Mark were anywhere near here. It wasn't until they fired the first shot that I realized who it might be," I said.

The car stopped in a cloud of dust, and both front doors opened. Chris Valentine was dressed much more casually than I had seen, with jeans and cowboy boots. His driver, Mark, stepped out cautiously and grabbed his rifle out of the back seat.

"You guys ok?" Chris asked as he walked over, surveying the situation.

"Thanks to you, yeah," Paul said, struggling a bit with his breath.

"So, you're not in Kentucky, then?" I asked, referencing the phone number from Chris' burner.

"No, I guess not," he said.

"How did you know we'd be here?" I asked.

"I had a hunch. Then, when you said Gus was here, I knew they'd never let you go. Even if she tried to spin a tale and pin the whole thing on me, or on her brother, or whoever she could pin it on, you'd figure things out. Like I told you on the voicemail, she's the master here. We're all her puppets. I've been her puppet from the beginning, and I'm done," Chris said with a sad voice of resolve.

"What do you mean by that?" Jennifer asked.

Chris ignored the question and stared at the injured man I had been watching, who was struggling to sit up.

"Looks like our friend Jaime here may have pulled through. We should get him some help," Chris said, changing the conversation.

"By the way, where's Gus?" Chris asked, looking around.

"Please tell me he's not in that Bentayga with Mary!" Chris was starting to get agitated as he looked in the direction the Bentley had gone.

"No, he's still at the Grand Marquis in my room," I said, starting to feel a sense of dread as I recognized the risk of that fact.

Chris, with more emotion than I had seen from him through this whole thing, screamed at us.

"He's where? You can't leave him there alone! They'll find him! Call the cops and tell them where he is. Does Mary know?" Chris had latched onto the one thing that had been bugging me.

"Yes, she mentioned it before she took off. She knows I left him there," I said, realizing we needed to leave. Now.

Chris shook his head anxiously.

"You guys have to go. Mark can get you there in a hurry with the F-350. I'll stay here to watch this guy. You guys head on out. Now." Chris wasn't just making a suggestion. He was resolved to get us out of that field to save Gus. He motioned toward the F-350 and nodded toward Mark.

"Fair enough. We'll send help as soon as we get phone service," I said, rummaging through the pockets of the F-350 driver to get the key fob.

Chris nodded, but seemed to be far away with his thoughts. He looked down at the man on the ground, who was beginning to get pale and fade into unconsciousness.

"I don't think he's going anywhere, but I want to be sure," he said, as he rolled the man over and picked up one of the Glocks that was still lying on the ground.

Chris held the weapon with more confidence than I had expected, clearly having some level of experience with pistols. He looked up and yelled again.

"Go! Just go! You have to save Gus! He trusted Bob and me. We can't just leave him to Mary and her army. They'll do horrible things to that kid! Get Gus, and get Mary! I know I can never make up for what I've done, but she has to pay!" Chris stopped just short of pointing the gun at us to demonstrate the urgency.

We were already on the move. I threw the fob to Mark, and he jumped into the driver's seat, while Jennifer and I helped Paul into the front passenger seat. After closing his door, we jumped in the back as Mark sped away.

We were only a few feet away when I heard a gunshot over the sound of the revving F-350.

I put my head down before I turned around, knowing

what I would see. I sensed from his demeanor that Chris wasn't able to carry his demons any further. The sight of him crumpled on the ground behind us confirmed my fear.

Paul saw me turn back around and gave me a nod. He, too, understood what had happened.

Chris had taken his own life.

Chapter Sixty-One

Leiper's Fork, TN. Saturday

Mark blasted down the dirt road toward the Valentine house like we were in a baja vehicle. Which, of course, we were not. The F-350 was doing its best to smooth out the road as we sped along, but it could only do so much. Even after struggling to get our seatbelts on, the three of us were bouncing around in the cabin like pinballs.

Despite the bouncing and constant swerving left and right, I had to get in touch with Officer Keating. I had to let him know about the danger Gus was in, and I needed to get him the recording from my phone in case something happened to me. When the Valentine house came into view over the last ridge, the first bar of reception appeared on my phone.

"Should we stop at the house and send someone to help Chris?" Jennifer asked as the dirt turned to gravel and we raced toward the house even faster.

"I don't think that will be necessary," I said, looking at

her with a solemn nod. Apparently, she hadn't heard the gunshot before, but she understood immediately and nodded in return.

"Got it. Ok, then let's go," she said, getting a node from Mark in the rearview mirror.

As we sped past the house, I noticed no sign of the other Bentley Bentayga Mary had taken from the edge of the ravine. She was gone.

The next few minutes of driving were as chaotic as I had experienced in a long time. Mark expertly navigated the winding roads from Leiper's Fork, somehow avoided downtown Franklin, and had us on the highway in what seemed less than three minutes.

I had fought through the bouncing ride to get the recording of Mary's confession to Officer Keating. Once it was sent, I dialed his number.

"I suppose you're going to explain what you just sent me?" Officer Keating didn't seem to be in the mood for a greeting.

"Yes, and I'm going to ask for an urgent favor," I said quickly.

"Ok. Let's hear it," he said.

"The audio recording I sent you will reveal that Mary Perez-Valentine was behind the murders of Bob Yates, and the two individuals you found in the Nashville Inn," I started.

"Oh it does, huh? Ok," Officer Keating said, sounding amused.

"Yeah, it's quite a lot. She'll talk about the pro shop tampering with Bob Yates' driver. She identifies the killer in alignment with your findings and even takes responsibility for calling the hits on the two guys at the hotel. There's more on there, but for the moment, I'll need you to let that go," I said before taking a deep breath.

"How can I possibly let this go?" Officer Keating sounded exasperated after what he'd just learned.

"There's a kid at the Grand Marquis who is in danger. I brought him back from Zapata, Texas. He was working with Bob Yates to disrupt, among other things, a human trafficking ring being operated through the Atlantis supply chain. He's in my hotel room. At least I hope he's still in my room. Mary said she knew he was there, which means he's not safe. She has people all over the place, including Nashville, who do her bidding. We need to get this kid, Gus, some protection immediately. I'm also on my way, but we're about ten minutes from there," I said, finally stopping to let Officer Keating react.

After a couple of seconds, he responded.

"Ok, I'm not real close, but I'll head over now. I'll get another car over there for backup. Please don't do anything stupid when you get there, Mr. Morgan. This is a police matter and you've probably already gone too far, based on what you just said," Officer Keating said in an accusatory tone.

"Yeah, maybe, but I'm going to do what I can to save that kid. He trusted me to bring him here and keep him safe, and I plan to honor that trust," I said, trying to keep my voice calm.

Officer Keating let out a deep sigh, then responded.

"If this thing is really happening, as you say, Mr. Morgan, you need to stay out of the way. We'll need to run this the right way," he said with slightly less conviction than before.

"Ok," is all I could get out in response.

"I'm on my way," Officer Keating said as he ended the call.

When I put my phone down, I realized I had the attention of the other three people in the car. Strangely, it was Mark who spoke first.

"Gus is at the hotel, then?" Mark asked, looking at us for confirmation.

"Yeah. You know about Gus?" I asked.

"I suppose I know about all of them," Mark said, now gazing straight ahead as we sped along, now on the highway.

"All of them?" I asked, clarifying what he was saying.

Mark glanced in the mirror to look into my eyes, then back to the road.

"I've known Chris for a long time. Mary had her loyal men, and Chris had me. I know he was trying to make up for his past. I know he has saved hundreds of people from Mary's grasp, and I know Gus was helping him. Let's leave it at that," he said, again catching my eye in the mirror.

"Fair enough. And yes, Gus is at the hotel. Mary realized it when he wasn't with us, and I'm guessing she and possibly her team are already there. Now you know why we have to hurry," I said, as though Mark could possibly go faster.

"Two minutes," he said, weaving in and out of traffic on the highway in the massive pickup truck.

Paul shifted in his front seat, looking down at the growing bloodstain on his shirt.

"You guys may need to deal with this one on your own. I'll need to get this taken care of," he said.

"Understood. Hey Mark, how long have you worked for Chris?" I asked, trying to assess how to proceed with him.

"About two years. I had been working several security

jobs after getting out of the Army, and he gave me the best offer I had gotten yet," he replied.

The timing matched when Mary said Chris had decided to go 'good.'

"So, did you ever see him engaging in any illicit acts? Or any illegal activity of any kind?" I asked.

Mark looked in the rearview mirror again to catch my eye.

"No, I did not. But he talked a lot about his 'sins of the past.' It really seemed to haunt him, right up to the end," Mark said somberly.

"Ok. I know this is a tough time for you, but we may need your testimony later, if you're ok with that," I said, trying to gauge Mark's involvement with Chris.

"Absolutely. I've seen nothing but good from that man, despite what he may have done before I met him," Mark said after a solemn nod.

"Great. I'm sorry about Chris, by the way. And thank you for your service. The three of us share a similar history," I added, nodding at Paul and Jennifer. Mark nodded his acknowledgement.

We sat quietly for a few minutes while Mark raced toward the Grand Marquis. When we pulled into the long entryway, I was disappointed to see no police lights with sirens blaring at the entrance. Sadly, I saw no police presence at all. Without police support to fall back on, I crafted an impromptu plan. It was just past 6 p.m., and the hotel traffic was picking up for the evening. Mark had to balance the need to get to the door quickly with the need to avoid calling too much attention to our speed.

"There are two paths to my room. One is straight in through the lobby and up the escalator, then an immediate left. The other path is to the left before the lobby, then around the back side to an elevator bank just around the corner. That elevator comes out just at the other end of the hallway where my room is. Jennifer, you take the elevator and I'll head straight up the escalator," I said as Mark slammed on the brakes at the curb outside the lobby.

"I'll go with Jennifer," he yelled as he got out. He didn't ask for permission. Knowing his devotion to Chris and his recent mission, I didn't care.

"The guy in the front seat may need an ambulance," I said to the nearest valet while the three of us barged our way into and through the hotel lobby.

We ran as quickly as we could, trying not to make a commotion despite our pace. Jennifer and Mark found the hallway to the left and hustled that direction, while I made my way to the escalator as quickly as I could. It was only about thirty seconds before I rounded the corner of the hallway where my room was located.

Nothing looked abnormal. I refrained from pulling out my SIG and walked quickly and cautiously toward my room, pulling the room key card out of my pocket as I got to the door. I held the card to the lock pad, which seemed to take forever to unlock.

When I cracked open the door, I noticed Jennifer and Mark cautiously approaching from the other end of the hallway. When they saw me, they ran down the hall in my direction.

I pushed the door the rest of the way open, this time giving in to the urge to draw my pistol. Within a few seconds, it was clear I wouldn't need it. The room was empty. No Gus, no Mary, and no sign of any struggle. Since Gus had no possessions when he got here, it was impossible to tell if he had left on his own or was taken. We had to assume the worst.

Turning to see Jennifer and Mark standing in the doorway behind me, I yelled out a couple of brief instructions.

"He's not here. We know they can't be far, and we know they didn't go out the front. There are entrances at each atrium, but only two are open. I'll take the one on the other side of the center atrium, and you two take the maintenance area to the right of the lobby we just came in. There may be more routes, but those are the closest," I said, running past them and retracing my steps back down the hallway.

I heard the door slam behind me as we all ran in search of Gus.

Chapter Sixty-Two

Nashville, TN. Saturday

Saturday evening was a big deal at the Grand Marquis. The events being held at the venue for the weekend were reaching their climax, and the many restaurants and bars around the hotel were full of people. So, too, were all the hallways and walkways between my room and the other exits. Any attempt to hurry without drawing attention to myself was futile.

So I just ran.

"Pardon me! Emergency! Sorry, sorry, I've got an emergency, sorry!" I just did my best to disguise the danger with the appearance of an unknown need to run.

It worked ok.

As I got to the main atrium, I stopped to scan the whole pathway from the entrance just beyond the hotel rooms. From there, I could see most of the trail, including the exit on the other side. Sure, someone could hide inside the plant coverings if they wanted to, but I didn't think Mary or her people would be stopping here. They'd be on the move.

And it was that need to keep moving that made them obvious when I finally saw them. Everyone else was sauntering along at a casual pace, some even slower than that. There were conversations going on, plant and stream-gazing, and lots of oohs and awes as people slowly walked along the trail.

Except for one man, one woman, and one teenager just now heading past the halfway point of the path. Mary, Gus, and another man were racing toward the other side of the atrium path where I knew there was an exit. They were obviously moving faster than everyone else, and were not worried about who saw them.

Even from across the atrium, I could see Gus looking around with fear in his eyes, seeking out anyone who could and would help him. Mary and the other man were focused straight ahead and holding tight to each of Gus' arms.

I had to cut them off before they got to the exit.

The walkway across the atrium was filled with guests taking photos and lingering, but there was another walkway on the floor of the atrium that weaved through the plants and stream. A quick scan let me know it had less traffic than the pathway above, so I bolted down the stairs to my right rather than walking across. It was a longer but faster option.

I passed the maintenance area where I had met up with the two goons just two days ago and continued running on the narrow path through the atrium. There were two small bridges to navigate that cross the stream, then a sharp right, then two turns to the left before I had a view ahead. There was another set of stairs on the other end that they'd have to bring Gus down, so I kept my eyes peeled for that stairway while I ran.

As I crossed the last bridge, I caught a glimpse of Mary looking behind her as she descended the stairs toward the back of the atrium and nearing the exit. I was too far away to say anything or to catch them, but we locked eyes from across the beautiful flowers and greenery. When she saw me, she paused just long enough to sneer, then said something to the other person holding onto Gus and continued ahead.

Gus turned around after Mary spoke, and saw me continuing my chase before being jerked ahead by his two captors. The other captor also turned around. He, too, caught my eyes just long enough for me to recognize it was Mary's brother. The same person I had seen in Zapata and in the photographs at Mary's house. He had a look of anger and determination as he sped into the hotel area, around the corner to the left and toward the exit.

I arrived at the other side of the atrium just a few seconds later, although it seemed like hours. Running toward the corner, I realized I was exposing myself if I continued around the corner blindly. Accepting the risk, I raced around the last corner toward the exit.

As I came around the corner, I saw Mary and her brother wrestling Gus into the back seat of a car that took off quickly. So quickly, in fact, that their tires squealed loudly as they tried to navigate the tight circle drive. This area wasn't being used by guests, so there were only a few people walking on the sidewalk. They all turned and stared as the car, which I now recognized as a silver Kia Optima, sped by.

The sight of them zooming away gave me a quick idea. I found Officer Keating's number on my phone and hit the call button, hoping he had not yet entered the hotel lobby.

"We're just pulling in. Got delayed on the freeway," Officer Keating said as he answered.

"That's good, actually. I just chased Mary and her

brother. They dragged Gus into a silver Kia Optima and headed around toward the rideshare area. If you head there now, you should be able to cut them off. I'll have to circle back through the facility to get there," I said frantically, yelling into my phone as I ran back toward the lobby.

"Got it. We'll go there now," Officer Keating said as he immediately began yelling orders over his radio.

I ended the call and made a similarly quick call to Jennifer as I ran, so she and Mark could head that same direction. We were both several minutes from that area, so we had to rely on Officer Keating until we got there.

Running back down the same path I had just come, I nearly knocked over a family of four taking photos next to a lovely waterfall. After catching their toddler and yelling my apologies, I resumed my run and got back to the front of the atrium in just a few seconds. Now I had to navigate the hotel hallways toward the next exit the Kia would pass, hoping Officer Keating would have stopped them.

As I rounded the last corner toward the door, I saw Jennifer and Mark just ahead of me rushing out the door. They were scanning the vast parking area when I joined them seconds later.

"Do you see them?" I asked as I caught up.

"Look! Over there!" Jennifer was pointing out to the far left, where we could see flashing lights moving rapidly between the rows of cars.

Simultaneously, we all ran in that direction, realizing we were completely at the mercy of the police to stop Gus' captors. Our running couldn't match the speed of the chase unfolding in front of us.

More lights appeared as we ran, some of them stopping at various points in the parking lot, while others continued to race through the rows of parked cars.

We kept running until we heard a loud crash, which I expected to mean the chase had ended. After a brief pause to assess what had happened, we shifted our direction toward the crash and each drew our pistols. With a quick glimpse at each other and a nod in each direction, Jennifer took off to the right of the crash, Mark to the left, and I headed straight toward it.

I passed through two rows of parked cars before I caught sight of what was happening in front of me. There were two police cars parked at angles behind the Kia, which was now smashed into a light pole near the center of the parking area. It seems the driver had tried to round the corner toward the open center lane of the lot but had not been able to maintain enough traction to navigate the turn before contacting the pole.

There was steam rising from the front of the Kia and both doors on the side nearest me were open. The other side was smashed against another car, so any escapees would have had to come out in my direction. The airbag from the Kia had deployed, and I couldn't see anyone still inside the vehicle.

Policemen were cautiously watching from behind the two marked cars that had pinned in the Kia. Their guns were drawn. Out of the corner of my eye, I could see other police cruisers cautiously bearing down on the scene. There were still guests around, so nobody wanted to shoot or to drive more erratically than was absolutely necessary. Still, it was starting to get chaotic out here.

Finally getting close enough to see inside the car, I realized the back seat was now empty. Mary, her brother, and Gus were all somewhere in this parking lot. Shifting into search mode, I caught the eye of Jennifer and Mark, who were approaching from each side. With a quick motion to each side, we stopped running and started to instead carefully scan the parking lot for the Kia's previous backseat occupants.

Before I could see them, I heard Gus scream.

"Over here! We're over here!" Gus' voice was only one row to my left and the sound of it apparently caused Mary's brother to abandon the idea of capturing Gus and to fend for himself.

He stood above the cars and began firing a handgun in all directions.

Chapter Sixty-Three

Nashville, TN. Saturday

It was still light enough outside to see Mary's brother clearly as he frantically aimed his pistol to the right, to the left, then ducked down. Then raised up a car or two away from his last position, fired again, ducked down again, and repeated the process. After one or two of these episodes, I could see he was trying to work his way toward a creek crossing to the far end of the parking area.

I decided to let the police chase him while I went toward the sound of Gus' voice. Jennifer and Mark had made the same decision, and we all closed in on the area where we had last heard Gus scream.

As we quickly but carefully surrounded the area, I wondered how Mary was keeping Gus from escaping without her brother to help. As I was rounding a small SUV at the end of the last row where I thought Gus would be, I got my answer.

Gus came racing away, kicking and squirming away from four grasping arms, which were more than the two arms I expected to see. Then I realized the driver must have tried to assist in Gus' capture and getaway.

Waving at Gus, I lowered my weapon and frantically motioned for him to get down and come my direction. I knew Mary's brother was still out there somewhere, and he was armed.

Gus saw me and turned my direction, ducking down as he did. It seemed to take an eternity for him to get close, but eventually he got near enough for me to run out and grab him, ducking even lower as we slid between the two nearest cars and started moving toward the hotel.

Fearing we may get ambushed at any moment, I kept peeking over and under the cars as we went by, looking for feet on one end and heads on the other. I was on the ground looking for approaching feet when I heard Jennifer scream.

"Get down!" She was just ahead of me and to my left. The sound caused me to cover Gus and look up, trying to see the direction of the potential risk.

Finding Jennifer over one row from where we were, I could see her pointing her pistol behind me. Ducking and turning away from her apparent target, I heard a gunshot behind me from some distance away, then felt a crash of glass falling on the back of my head. Someone had shot the car window just beside where Gus and I were hiding. Several other shots thumped into the metal of cars nearby. I didn't know if the shots were targeting us or were stray, but there was no time to evaluate.

I yanked Gus around behind the next car and paused. Before we had stopped, I heard a volley of gunshots from across the lot and hoped they had gotten whoever was behind me. Given the direction he was running earlier, I suspected it was Mary's brother.

We sat still for a few moments, leaning against a Toyota

4Runner, similar to the one I had at home. In a gentler moment, I might have gotten homesick at that thought, but the adrenaline of the current situation prevented any random reflections.

"You guys ok?" It was Jennifer, sliding to the ground next to us.

"I'm good. You ok, Gus?" I looked at Gus, realizing I hadn't heard him speak.

He still didn't speak, just nodded his head with a look of terror on his face.

All the focus on getting Gus to safety had kept me from realizing the absurdity of what was happening here. There were marked and unmarked cop cars throughout the hotel parking lot, flashing lights all around, guests being ushered inside the hotel to safety, and shots being fired from a variety of directions. And we were at the Grand Marquis hotel in Nashville. The spectacle of it all was surreal.

"I think they got Mary's brother. He was at the far end of the parking lot behind you when those windows got shot out. You two were behind the target. Mary and the driver are still holed up near their car over there," Jennifer said, pointing to her left.

"Stay here with Gus. I'm going to see if I can talk to Mary," I said, not really sure why adrenaline causes me to do such things.

"You sure? I think the cops can handle it," she said.

I was already moving.

I poked my head up above the cars to assess the situation, seeing an ever-growing line of officers sealing off the area just two rows to my left. I was behind two officers who had taken shelter behind a couple of SUVs near the 4Runner I had used for cover. Jogging toward them, I yelled to make sure they heard me coming.

"We've got the kid! He's safe!" I was standing when I walked over, quickly wondering if Mary and the Kia driver had firearms. That thought caused me to duck back down as I reached the nearest officers engaged in the standoff.

I could now clearly see the Kia smashed and smoking, now only one car to my left and three cars ahead of me. With the position of the officers, I assumed they had Mary pinned down.

"Does she have any weapons?" I asked the officer.

"We've seen no fire from her or the driver," he said, "but we can't be sure."

"Have you run the plates on that Kia?" I knew that was a long shot, and I suspected I already knew who owned it.

"We're running them now. Let me see if we have the owner yet," he replied, just before talking into the mic on his shoulder.

"Not yet," he replied within a few seconds.

"Let me know when you find out whether it belongs to Doris Yates. For now, I'm going to assume it does," I said as I mapped out my next move.

I decided Mary would have fired by now if she was armed, which may have been a risky decision, but I stood and raised my hands, getting the attention of the officers.

"What are you doing?" The nearest officer was frantically motioning for me to get down as he screamed the question.

"Tell everyone to hold their fire. I'm going to talk to her," I yelled back at him.

The officer paused, shook his head in frustration, then reluctantly grabbed the mic on his shoulder and said something I couldn't hear. After another second, he nodded for me to proceed.

I walked toward the Mary's location cautiously, still not

completely sure she and her driver were together and were unarmed. Surveying the surrounding scene caused me to take a deep breath. There were policemen and vehicles circled all around the wrecked Kia, all at a safe distance and mixed among the parked cars. There were no longer any hotel guests to be seen, although I envisioned plenty of eyeballs and camera lenses in the hotel windows behind me.

I walked ahead, slowly.

"Mary, this is Keith Morgan! Let's just talk for a minute. I'm not going to hurt you," I yelled as I got close to the wrecked Kia.

"Go away, Keith! It's over!" Mary was closer than I thought. I stepped ahead one more car and found her sitting on the ground behind a Chrysler minivan. She was sweating and out of breath, leaning over with her head rested on her knees. Her white pantsuit was dirty and disheveled, and the red scarf was gone. She looked nothing like the crisp, in-charge person who had been out at the ranch earlier.

"You don't want this to go badly, and it can," I said.

"I don't care anymore. They killed my brother. I've lost everything. Even if I get out of this, I'm better off dead," she said without looking up.

"Where's Doris?" I asked, causing her to look up, surprised.

"What do you mean?" My question clearly shocked her.

"I know you needed help to get Bob's golf club. I know you had to have access to his schedule this week. I also know you've had insight into his movement for some time in order to set this up. Doris had to have helped you," I said as I sat down next to Mary.

"But what I don't know is why," I sighed as I awaited her response.

Chapter Sixty-Four

Nashville, TN. Saturday

The concrete in the parking lot was hot as I sat next to Mary, leaning against a random minivan. Luckily, the perimeter of police officers had stayed back and had remained silent, leaving an eerie silence in the air.

Mary thought for several seconds before shifting her tone, almost like a switch went off in her head. In a moment, she went from angry and defeated to a more hurt and sheepish demeanor. She even started to cry.

At least that's what she wanted me to think.

"Doris made me do it! It was all her idea. She and Bob were having trouble, and she wanted us to help. I knew she was going behind my back with Chris, but she forced me to..." she was beginning to muster up some actual tears and was forcibly sobbing when she was interrupted by a scream to our left.

"HOW DARE YOU!" It was Doris Yates, who had been sitting quietly around the corner from us near the front of the van. As I had suspected, she had been the driver of the Kia.

Now she was standing and glaring at Mary. And she had a Glock 19 in her hand, aimed loosely in Mary's direction. Seeing that, and knowing there were hoards of police officers watching and not understanding what was going on, I stood up and raised my hands. It was my attempt to keep the police from shooting Doris from all angles.

"Wait a minute, Doris. Don't do anything you'll regret," I said.

"HOW DARE YOU," she repeated to Mary, "you forced me into this just like you did everyone else. I never, ever wanted you to kill Bob," Doris screamed through clenched teeth and tears.

Then she faced me.

"I didn't want to do this. Any of it. She showed me pictures of Bob talking to kids in Texas and told me he was doing horrible things with those kids. She said she was going to the press if I didn't help her. I didn't want to believe her, but she had pictures. SHE HAD PICTURES!"

Doris was sobbing now, and the gun was pointing in random directions as she talked. It was clear she wasn't comfortable with it in her hand.

"Doris, relax. We know what Mary was doing," I said.

"She was trying to frame Chris for it, too. I was never involved in any of this. Now, Bob is dead because of me," Doris was fading into a defeated state while she mumbled.

"Just hand me the gun and let us deal with her. We know she set this whole thing up," I said, slowly moving toward Doris while she sobbed.

She continued to sob while her face shifted to one of hostility. Then, all at once, she pointed the gun directly at Mary with anger and determination in her eyes.

"You have to die for what you've done," she said through clenched teeth.

Seeing what she was about to do, I jumped in front of Mary and knocked the gun sideways just as it went off. In an instant, we were covered by a dozen or more police officers as they joined me in wrestling Doris to the ground and prying the Glock out of her hand.

Officer Keating ran to the middle of the fray and pulled me back, then grabbed my shirt collar and pulled me close to him. I resisted the urge to show him my hand to hand combat skills, and let him get to his point.

"Mr. Morgan, that was one of the stupidest things I've ever seen. You could have ruined this whole thing for us! Not to mention, you could have gotten yourself killed," he yelled and pushed me against the van, staring angrily into my eyes from about six inches away.

For a moment, I couldn't help but notice how his southern accent seemed to fade under duress. I'd have to analyze that thought another time, though, as he was clearly seeking an explanation.

"But I didn't," was all I could say.

He backed off a bit, shook his head, and looked down at Mary and Doris on either side of us. They were both being handcuffed and patted down while we stood there. It seems Doris' random shot had landed harmlessly in the fender of the van.

Officer Keating was still holding onto my collar when Jennifer, Mark, and Gus came around the corner. Seeing them look at the two of us with questioning eyebrows, he backed off and addressed them instead.

"Are you all ok?" he asked, still not moving away even though he was no longer holding onto my collar.

"Yeah, we're fine," Jennifer said. "What's going on here?"

"We're just trying to sort all this out," I said, saving Officer Keating from having to explain why he had pinned me against the van. I also gave Jennifer a subtle nod to let her know we were ok.

"Right. We were just sorting things out," Officer Keating said, before taking a deep breath and backing away to a normal conversational distance.

"So, you're just a consultant who came out here for a conference, huh?" He asked as he looked at me suspiciously.

I thought about declining to answer, but decided to stick to the party line.

"Yep," was a good enough answer for me.

He looked at me suspiciously again, then turned toward Jennifer, Gus and Mark.

"Young man, I understand you have been caught in the middle of this. I'm sorry you had to go through everything you've endured the last day or two. Would you like to call anyone back home to let them know you're ok?"

Gus had said nothing in a long time, but Officer Keating's question jolted him into an eager smile.

"Yes! Yes, I would love to call my mom," he said.

"Give Javi a call, too, if you don't mind," I said, nodding toward Gus.

He nodded in return as Officer Keating ushered him toward another officer standing nearby.

I turned to Jennifer and Mark. Before I could say anything, Mark spoke up.

"I'd kill her myself if all these cops weren't here. Chris was a good man, and even if she didn't pull the trigger, she killed him. And think of all the kids she put into unthinkable circumstances. She doesn't deserve to live," he said quietly, anger boiling up in his voice as he stared at Mary. She was being escorted to a waiting squad car just a few feet away.

"There's no need. She's going away for good," I said. Before I could explain anything else, a group of officers emerged from the chaos, led by a man in a suit holding out a badge.

"Good evening, I'm Lieutenant Boone. Officer Keating tells me the three of you may have some background on what has happened here today," he said.

"Yeah, I guess we do," I said, looking at Jennifer and Mark.

"We've uncovered part of it based on the recording you sent, but we need to get statements from each of you before you take off. Some of the recording needs some context. It may take a little time, as I'm sure you understand," he said, politely but firmly.

"Sure," I said, nodding.

"We'll be as quick as we can," he said, seeing our sighs at the need to give statements.

"It's no problem, really. But, before you send us to give statements, did you get the guys in Zapata who were taking all those people? We need to stop that trafficking ring and see how many of those people we can save." I wanted to make sure they knew this wasn't just a Nashville challenge.

"Oh yeah, we did. It turns out this was a pretty large operation. Details are still emerging, but we know of four different locations where people were regularly transferred from Zapata. The employees at the facility began singing as soon as they knew we were onto them. They pointed out some individuals they transported were paying to be smuggled in, and others were trafficked in for nefarious purposes.

They estimate several hundred, at least, fell into that last category, unfortunately. We may never find them all, but we'll definitely find some thanks to witnesses and some unofficial shipment logs we found. And more importantly, we'll shut down the entire operation. I may not agree with your vigilante approach to this whole thing, but it looks like we have what we need," he said.

I nodded as another officer escorted us away to spend the next couple of hours giving our statements.

I didn't get to hear much music on my last night in Nashville.

Chapter Sixty-Five

Nashville, TN. Saturday

The statements and debrief with the Nashville Metro Police Department took over two hours, with the sun setting while we all shared what we knew. I was the last one to be finished, but Jennifer and Mark stuck around and waited until I had answered the last question.

They were sitting on a curb next to the hotel parking lot drinking bottles of water when I walked up.

"You don't have to stay if you don't want to, Mark," I said as he stood. "You've certainly done more than your share here today!"

He managed a smile and thought for a second.

"Yeah, I think I'd like to get back home, if that's ok. I'm not really sure what's going to happen after all this," he said.

I hadn't thought about it, but he had just lost his livelihood with Chris' death and Mary's arrest.

Jennifer and I nodded, and I reached out my hand.

"I don't know how to thank you for all this," I said as he returned a firm handshake.

"Her arrest was all the thanks I need," Mark said, nodding toward the police cars still sitting in the parking lot.

Jennifer also shook Mark's hand and offered her thanks, adding in her assurance that Gus was grateful for his help as well. As were all the unknown others he had helped save by his efforts.

After a few somber moments, Mark went on his way toward the hotel lobby. That left Jennifer and me standing on the sidewalk, watching the flashing lights across the parking lot as the police continued to piece together the physical evidence.

"Is this what it's like to work for The Association?" she asked before she moved, looking into my eyes for an honest response.

"Occasionally it is, yes. But not every time. This one, along with Willow Creek, were two of the most intense assignments I've been on. Both, it turns out, were much bigger than The Association even knew," I said.

"That reminds me. I wonder how Paul is doing," she said as she turned to walk toward the hotel.

I had been wondering the same thing. As we walked toward the entrance around the corner, I called Paul's mobile number. He picked up immediately.

"Please tell me this thing is over," he said when he picked up.

His voice was weak, but it still made me smile. It meant he was awake and coherent.

"Yes, it's over. Mary is in custody, and we've gone through the interrogation with the locals," I said, looking at Jennifer and smiling.

She smiled back, realizing Paul must be doing ok.

"Are you still at the hotel?" I asked, realizing I had no

idea what had happened to Paul since we left him in the car in front of the lobby.

"Well, no, I'm not. Apparently, I looked pretty bad, because the guys at the hotel had an ambulance there in about thirty seconds. I'm at Nashville General already," Paul said.

"Wow, that was fast!" I said, surprised he was already at the hospital.

"I'm not booked in or anything, yet, but yeah, they got me here in a hurry," he said

"Any idea what they're going to do?" I asked.

"No, not really. I'm sure they'll have to go in and clean out this extra hole I've acquired here in my side, but I don't expect more than that," he said.

"Oh no! Alright, we'll stop by," I said, nodding toward Jennifer, who was clearly in full agreement.

Before Paul could object, which he likely would have, I ended the call and started toward the rideshare area just around the corner from where we were. I pulled up the Uber app on my phone while we walked and within five minutes we were in a silver Toyota Camry on our way to the hospital.

After a short ride, we were hustling into the Emergency Room at Nashville General hospital. The receptionist looked at me funny when I told her we were Paul's siblings, but she let us in. It was an old trick I learned when visiting my injured military buddies.

We found Paul in one of the triage rooms, pale and asleep. A nurse was by his bed tinkering with an IV.

"How's he doing?" I asked as we walked up.

"Well, we knocked him out with pain killers. I'm not sure if he'll wake up or not," the nurse said as she shook Paul's shoulder.

His eyes fluttered open, and he looked around. It was pretty clear h was feeling no pain.

"I told you guys to leave me alone," he smiled as he was Jennifer and me.

"We just couldn't stay away," I said.

"Well, I feel like I need a nap. I'm afraid I won't be great company," Paul replied as he struggled to keep his eyes open.

"That's fine. We'll just hang out while they decide what to do with you," Jennifer said.

"Oh no, you won't! You guys need to move along like normal, don't draw any more attention to our organization than you have already. You need to get home to your family, and Jennifer has had enough disruption through her introduction to The Association. I appreciate you stopping by. But please, for the love of God, go home," Paul said with sincere determination in his tired voice.

I thought for a minute about the kids back in Woodland Park, and about Judy and Oliver already giving up their week to help me out.

"Yeah, ok. But you've got to let me know as soon as you're out of there," I said reluctantly.

Jennifer leaned in and kissed Paul's forehead.

"Thanks for everything," she said.

"You got it. Just get home, both of you. Keith, say hi to Jamie and Kyle," Paul said as his eyes continued to close. It gave me comfort that he remembered the kids' names, even though he'd never actually met them.

"Ok, ok. We're going. Just, well, just thanks." It was all I could think to say at the moment.

We watched as Paul faded back to sleep, before heading back out the hospital the way we came.

"You hungry?" I asked, knowing I certainly was.

"I hadn't thought about it, but yeah," Jennifer said.

"Me too," I said as I once again pulled up the Uber app on my phone.

"There should be stuff still open at the hotel," Jennifer said.

I nodded as the blue Honda Accord pulled up to the hospital pickup area. They must have been waiting nearby because it only took one minute for the car to arrive. In another fifteen minutes, we were walking into the Grand Marquis lobby.

"I guess we'd better hurry before all the restaurants close in here," Jennifer said, picking up the pace.

"Yeah, you're right. By the way, I don't think I'm really dressed for the nicer restaurants," I said, looking down and realizing I had been running and sweating far too much this evening.

Jennifer laughed and looked down at her own clothes.

"Yeah, me neither," she said.

"Well, then it looks like it's just pizza or burgers tonight," I said.

Jennifer nodded as we scurried along the halls and walkways to the restaurant area. When we arrived, I looked around at the restaurants with lights on. It was now past 9 p.m. and some restaurants were closing.

"Yep, pizza or burgers work for me," Jennifer said as we walked across the atrium toward the lighted tables.

"Alright, pizza it is," I said as I motioned toward the closest open restaurant, The Pizza Place.

This restaurant had a cafeteria-style line to get our order, and we had to get trays and place our order before getting a table. Surprisingly, there were several people in line when we got there, so we had a few minutes to wait and talk.

"You still coming with us to Grandmother's Kitchen tomorrow?" I asked, trying to drum up some casual conversation. We had made plans to go out with the kids and their grandparents before leaving for Nashville last week.

I suppose I shouldn't have been surprised when Jennifer paused, looked down for a second, then looked at me with a sad expression.

"I don't think so, Keith. I'm going to need some time to process all this when I get home," she said with a half-smile.

I realized how foolish I had been to expect things to remain the same between us. I didn't know how to respond, so I just nodded.

"I understand," was all I could come up with.

Thankfully, we only had to endure a few moments of awkward silence before we got to the front of the line to place our order. I ordered a personal pepperoni pizza after Jennifer ordered right behind me. I was so absorbed in my thoughts I didn't even notice what she was getting.

I was still staring into space when she poked me in the ribs.

"Keith, what do you want to drink?" Jennifer asked, nodding toward the girl in the Pizza Place shirt asking the same question behind the counter.

"Uh, just a bottle of water, please," I said, forcing a smile.

We found a table and sat down with our food. After thinking about it for those few moments, I understood how drastically things had to change between me and Jennifer since Paul had brought her into The Association. The warmth was gone. The lighthearted laughter and smiling were gone. At least for now. And maybe forever.

I missed all of it already. Looking at Jennifer opening

her water, I could see she missed it, too. But we couldn't go back. I decided not to push it.

"So, we've got an early one tomorrow. 5 a.m. will be here before we know it," I said, referencing the pickup time for our ride to the airport. I had scheduled it knowing I was on the flight from Nashville to Denver, then from Denver to Colorado Springs. Paul had Jennifer moved to my same itinerary. It would have been cool to take another charter, but we knew it wasn't the time to ask Paul for a favor.

"You're not kidding," she said with a smile.

It was a different smile. Like I was her customer. Or her coworker. Or someone on the street. It wasn't really fake, but it wasn't really genuine. Her smile didn't come from the heart anymore.

That's how the rest of the night went before we walked back to our rooms.

Chapter Sixty-Six

Nashville, TN. Saturday

At 10 p.m. I was in my hotel room, packed up as much as I could be, and ready to get the last few hours of sleep before I headed home in the morning. As part of my daily ritual, I called Jamie's phone at home to see how everyone was doing.

"Hey dad, how's Nashville?" Jamie said when she picked up the phone.

"I wish I knew, hon! Too much work and not enough time to party," I said, smiling at my feeble attempt at humor. Jamie knew to expect it.

"Oh, sure! My dad, the party animal," Jamie said with a hearty laugh.

"How are you guys doing? How was hockey?" I asked, finding peace by talking to Jamie about normal things.

"Good. We won by four. They didn't know what hit 'em," she said.

"Nice! Your new skates still working out ok?" I asked again, having asked the same question every day this week.

We had bought them just before the trip, and I knew she was nervous about the change.

"They're sweet. Helped me score a goal," she added. I could picture her smiling as she said it, having waited to drop it in casually during the conversation. Jamie was a good player, but scoring wasn't her forte. This was a big deal.

"What? You didn't lead with that? Congratulations, hon, I'm really proud of you! You've got to tell me all about it," I said, sitting down and smiling as she filled me in.

After another twenty minutes, I had talked to Jamie, Kyle, and Judy. Everyone was doing well. Jamie was on cloud nine after her goal. Kyle was still trying to figure out the latest version of his favorite video game. And Judy sounded tired from keeping up with the kids all week.

It really felt good to be getting back into the groove tomorrow.

After hanging up with Judy, I decided to check in on Paul. I knew he'd be annoyed that I wasn't waiting for his call like he asked, but I wanted to find out if anything had changed since our visit.

I looked at the clock. It was 10:25 p.m., and I wondered if it might be too late to check in. I decided it wasn't and called his number.

After several rings, a female voice answered.

"Mr. Frazier's phone," she said. It wasn't the nurse from before.

Her voice took me by surprise.

"I, uh, thought I'd get Paul," I said.

"I'm afraid he's not available. He's still sleeping. Are you family?" The nurse sounded friendly but direct.

"Yes, his brother. I was with him when he was injured," I supplemented my lie with some truth.

"Oh, I see. Were you the one who shot him?" This call wasn't going as I had hoped.

"No. No, I was not the one who shot him. Can you at least tell me how he's doing?" I asked.

"I'm sorry, but I can't share his medical information without his permission. You can try back in the morning. He needs his rest, and it's well past visiting hours at this point. I'm sure you understand," she said, clearly done talking to me.

"Ok, sure. I'll try back in the morning," I said, ending the call. I shook my head at the annoyance of hospital policy, even though I knew she was just following the rules.

I resolved in my head to call Paul before the flight took off at 7 a.m., suspecting that might be before visiting hours and could generate a similar response. That thought made me shake my head.

Having completed my mental list of travel preparation steps, I sat down on the edge of the bed. I was tired, but not really ready to sleep. Looking around the room, I opted for something normal. I'd been so busy I hadn't turned the television on during my entire week here. I decided to see what was on before I went to sleep.

To my surprise, the Nashville Predators were in Denver, playing my beloved Colorado Avalanche. The Avs were having a great year, and it surprised me I hadn't remembered they were playing Nashville tonight. The third period was just starting, and I smiled as I turned out the lights, slid into bed and propped up the pillows behind my head.

The Avs were up 3-1 when I turned the game on, and had extended the lead to 5-1 within ten minutes. That must have been enough to put me at ease, because I fell asleep without turning the television off.

The 4:30 a.m. alarm on my phone seemed to arrive the second I went to sleep, even though it was nearly six hours later. That was the type of day Saturday had been! There was an infomercial on the television that I turned off immediately.

Luckily, I'm programmed to wake up with no fanfare, and this morning was no exception. I showered and packed up the last few items in the room before heading down to the lobby just before 5 a.m.

Jennifer was already near the pickup area when I got to the lobby. She was dressed casually in jeans and a light blue blouse with a brown leather jacket that matched her boots. Her suitcase and computer bag were standing next to her as she typed away on her phone.

As was always the case, seeing her made me smile. This time, however, it felt wrong. I stopped the smile before it reached my face and headed her way.

"How'd you sleep?" I asked as I parked my bag next to hers.

"Great. How 'bout you?" She said, showing the same type of smile I felt I was showing.

The rest of our morning went about that same way. We were cordial, but we were just going through the motions.

I tried to call Paul while we were in the car, but got the same treatment from the nurse as I had gotten the night before. I was calling outside visiting hours, and should try back later, they said. I suppose it was what I expected.

Jennifer and I sat next to each other in the car. We walked through the airport together, sat next to each other on two flights, and shared a table for coffee between flights in Denver.

But we lost something in Nashville. Our relationship was going to be different after that trip, and it made me sad.

I knew there was a bigger picture to consider, but it still made me sad. Yes, it had to happen, but it still made me sad. And it was the right thing, but it still made me sad.

When we finally got to the parking lot outside the Colorado Springs airport, we had reached the end of our Nashville journey.

"Thanks for everything, Keith. It was an, uh, interesting week," she said, forcing another smile.

"Yeah, it was. And I'm... I guess I'm sorry," I said, feeling my words were woefully inadequate for where our relationship had gone.

She nodded sadly, clearly understanding my lack of words for the circumstance.

"Yeah, me too," she finally said.

Jennifer stood there for a few seconds, then stepped over and put her arms up to give me a hug. It was a tight hug. And a long one. And it felt really, really good.

Then it was over.

"Goodbye, Keith," Jennifer said as she grabbed the handle of her luggage and turned away toward her Jeep.

She tried to keep me from seeing by quickly turning around, but I was certain I saw tears in her eyes before she had walked away.

I'm not sure how long I stood there, but Jennifer was long gone before I walked to my 4Runner.

Chapter Sixty-Seven

Woodland Park, CO. Sunday

The drive home Sunday morning was as uneventful as a Sunday drive should be. The weather was overcast with a slight drizzle, but that just meant even less traffic and nobody racing up the pass, like can sometimes be the case.

I made it past the invisible marker on the road where my wife had her fatal car accident without too much sadness, having been absorbed in my own thoughts before I got there. Thirty minutes after leaving the airport, I pulled into the long, evergreen-tree-lined driveway that led to my garage. I didn't have to fight to let the sadness fall away when I reached that point. This was my happy place.

After pulling the 4Runner into the garage, watching it close out of habit to make sure nobody snuck in behind me, and picking up my luggage, I headed inside to greet the family.

Judy and Oliver were sitting on the couch in the living room when I got in, and the kids were nowhere to be seen. I expected no less.

And as is always the case, the most excited greeting I got upon entering the house was from our golden doodle, Winchester. He was jumping and yipping as though he'd not seen me for years, like he always does when I come in. Even if I've just been gone for two minutes getting the mail.

"Winchester, my good friend, how are you?" I said to the dog, trying to pet him between leaps.

"Welcome home! How was the trip?" Judy said as she and Oliver walked over, appropriately less excited with their greetings.

Judy offered a hug and Oliver a handshake / hug combination as I dropped my bags and stepped inside.

"The trip was good, thanks. Flights on schedule and no disruptions, so I guess I can't complain," I responded.

"How was the conference?" Oliver asked.

The question made me stop for a second. How was the conference? From what I can recall, it was ok, but frankly I didn't really know. The week started fine, then there was that golf outing. That was supposed to be the leisurely part of the week.

From the golf outing on Wednesday until the flight on Sunday, I had seen four dead bodies. I had been to Zapata, Texas. Twice. And I'd been to a lovely place called Leiper's Fork. Twice. And to top it off, I was involved in a police standoff with a drug and human trafficker in the Grand Marquis parking lot.

But that wasn't what I said.

"Oh, it was fine. They're all the same, I suppose. Lots of sessions, lots of schmoozing, and a little fun," I said, using a fake smile to cover up the reality of my week in Nashville.

"Great, glad you had a good time," Oliver said, turning to get his own bags that were sitting by the door.

Hearing the commotion from the dog, the kids had

made their way down from their rooms for a rare greeting. I rarely get a personal greeting after returning from a one or two-day trip, but the longer ones earn me an actual physical appearance upon my return.

"Hey guys!" I said, genuinely thrilled to see the kids. Both of them appeared to have grown after only one week.

"Hey dad, welcome back," Jamie said with a bearhug.

"I missed you guys," I said, grabbing Kyle in a hug as well.

"Missed you too," he said, with as much emotion as a nine-year-old can generate.

"Do you guys have time to grab an early lunch?" I asked Judy and Oliver as they were heading out the door with their bags.

Oliver stopped and looked at Judy with a hopeful shrug. She returned a similar shrug and turned to me.

"Sure, what'd you have in mind?" she said with a smile.

"How about..." I didn't have time to get the words out before Kyle interrupted.

"Let me guess. You want to go to Grandmother's?" Kyle asked with a fake sense of exasperation.

"You know it!" I said with a broad smile. It was my favorite restaurant in town and was especially good for a Sunday brunch.

"Sounds great," Judy said. "We'll just get our bags in the car and we can go from there. You guys ready to go?"

"Kids?" I asked, looking at Kyle and Jamie.

"Yep, I'm ready," Jamie said. Kyle mumbled something that resembled a yes.

And with that, I headed to the garage with the kids to load into the 4Runner. Judy joined Oliver in their Lincoln Navigator out front.

I led the way out of the garage, closing it as I went out and watching to be sure it closed. Then we descended the gravel, then concrete road toward the highway into downtown Woodland Park. In just about five minutes, we were pulling into a packed parking lot.

"Wow! It looks like we weren't the only ones with this idea!" Judy said as we met up in the parking lot.

"No, it doesn't," I agreed.

"Must mean it's a good place," Oliver added with a smile as we walked in. I nodded. It was a good place.

We were fortunate to have to wait only about ten minutes before getting a table and launching into another fantastic meal at Grandmother's.

Everyone was eating, laughing, and enjoying their meals as I looked around the table and smiled. It was good to be submerged back into my 'normal' life once again. It felt great.

Then my phone vibrated in my pocket.

I looked at the number and didn't recognize it. I thought about it for a second, then declined the call and put the phone back in my pocket.

Then my phone vibrated again.

Deciding it must be important for someone to call me twice on a Sunday before noon, I excused myself. I stepped away from the table and went around the corner toward the restrooms before I answered.

"This is Keith," I answered.

"Mr. Morgan, this is Jordan Crawford," the voice on the other end said.

"Hi, Mr. Crawford. What can I do for you this fine Sunday morning?" I said, emphasizing the 'Sunday morning' part of my greeting.

"Mr. Morgan, I work with The Association. And more importantly, I work closely with Paul Frazier," Mr. Crawford said.

His tone made me uncomfortable.

"Uh-huh," I mumbled.

"I'm afraid I have some bad news, Mr. Morgan," Mr. Crawford said.

"Is Paul ok?" I blurted out, realizing I hadn't heard from him as he had promised.

"I'm sorry, but he passed away on the operating table this morning," Mr. Crawford said.

I felt my knees weaken as I leaned against the wall.

"What? I mean, I just saw him last night! He seemed fine." I stopped, realizing I was getting loud and someone might hear me.

"Yes, I spoke to him, too. He seemed fine to me, as well. Apparently there were complications during surgery, a blood clot formed and got to his brain, and he didn't survive," Mr. Crawford explained. His surprise seemed to match mine.

"I just can't believe this," I said, shaking my head and continuing to lean against the wall near the restroom door. It was all I could do to keep from sliding down to the floor.

"We're all still in shock over this," Mr. Crawford said.

This was going to take time to process. I didn't know how long I stood there silently, but eventually I responded.

"Well, thanks for letting me know," I said, assuming our call was about to end.

"That's not all, Mr. Morgan," he said.

"Oh, I'm sorry. I didn't mean to cut you off," I said.

"That's ok. And I hate to put this on you after hearing such horrific news, but I need to ask you something," he said.

"Sure," I replied.

"We've just had an emergency meeting with my peers," he said, then paused.

"Ok," I said, trying to push Mr. Crawford along so I could absorb what he had told me.

"Mr. Morgan, we'd like to ask you to take over as The Gatekeeper for The Association."

I stood there silently, realizing my mouth was open after several seconds. I looked around to make sure nobody was noticing my behavior during this call. They weren't.

"Mr. Morgan?" Mr. Crawford finally said, breaking the silence.

"Yes, I'm still here. This is just a lot to digest," I said.

"I know it is, sure. You don't have to tell me now, but please think about it," he said.

"I don't have to think about it," I said, surprising myself and obviously surprising Jordan Crawford.

"Ok," he said after he composed himself.

"I couldn't let Paul down by saying no," I explained.

"I understand," he replied. But I knew he didn't really understand.

"It's the least I can do for Paul Frazier. I owe him more than you know. I'd be glad to be The Gatekeeper. Whatever that means," I said, suddenly realizing I didn't know what I was signing up for.

"Great. We'll need to brief you once this all settles in. For now, go be with your family and enjoy your return to Colorado. And thank you, once again, for completing another chaotic assignment," he said.

"No problem. Talk soon," I said as I ended the call.

I stood there for another few seconds and composed myself. What had I just done?

I was now The Gatekeeper, and I was entering a mad new world. But not until I finished lunch with my family!

THE END

Follow Brent Jeffries

Watch for new adventures from Brent Jeffries and follow Keith Morgan using the links below. The next Keith Morgan adventure is scheduled for release in the fall of 2023!

Web Site (www.brentjeffries.com)
Facebook (www.facebook.com/authorbrentjeffries)
Instagram (www.instragram.com/authorbrentjeffries)
TikTok (www.tiktok.com/@brentjeffriesauthor)
Twitter (twitter.com/@AuthorJeffries)

And fine the first book in the Keith Morgan Chronicles here: Willow Creek Betrayal: Keith Morgan Chronicles #1